NIGHT OF THE OCTOPUS

Paddy King-Fretts

1·Xii·10

ryelands

First published in Great Britain in 2009

British Library Cataloguing-in-Publication Data
A CIP record for this title is available from the British Library

ISBN 978 1 906551 19 3

RYELANDS
Halsgrove House,
Ryelands Industrial Estate,
Bagley Road, Wellington, Somerset TA21 9PZ
Tel: 01823 653777   Fax: 01823 216796
email: sales@halsgrove.com

Part of the Halsgrove group of companies.
Information on all Halsgrove titles is available at: www.halsgrove.com

Printed and bound by Short Run Press Ltd, Exeter

'In September 2008, and in conjunction with the Freedom of Information Act 2000, Sections 24 and 26 (2), the UK Secretary of State for Defence instructed the Military Chiefs of Staff to de-classify the files of Operation Valhalla. *He directed that, at an agreed future date, details of the contents should be released into the public domain.'*

National News Association (UK)

This story is based on the facts contained in the Operation Valhalla files and on the recollections of the men who survived the operation.

By the same author

To France – with Love!
Staghunter
Larkbarrow
The Wild Red Dawn
Softly Cries the Curlew
Neither Hope nor Fear

KEY PLAYERS

United Kingdom
Mr Tony Blair. UK Prime Minister
Sir James Creasey KCMG, MVO. HM Ambassador, Paris
General Sir James Chateris GCB, OBE, ADC Gen. UK Chief of Defence Staff
General Sir Arthur Trant KBE, DSO, MC. Retd. ex-Director of UK Special Forces
Major General Patrick Morton CBE, MC. Retd ex-Director of UK Special Forces
Sir Alan Palmer CBE. Keeper of Egyptian Antiquities, The British Museum
Ms Amanda Gates. Special Assistant to Sir Alan Palmer
The Assault team: Captain Jed King MC together with Sgt Ned Kelly and others

France
M. Jacques Chirac. President of The Republic of France
M. Lionel Jospin. Prime Minister of France
M. Jean-Paul Debroque. Foreign Minister
M. Philippe Lespère. Interior Minister
M. Roger Trinquet. Mayor of Paris
M. Marcel Joubert. Civil Servant in the Mayor's Office, Paris City Hall
Brigadier General Le Chantou. Defence Attaché, London
M. Pierre Vignau. French DGSE agent
M. Francois Gideon. Marine Archaeologist. Head of Operation Cleopatra,
    Alexandria, Egypt
M. André Bigard. Paris based, Security Specialist

Israel
Eli Schmuel. Israeli Ambassador, Paris
Brigadier Yitzac Levi. Defence Attaché, Paris
Eddi Cohen. Member of Embassy staff, Paris
Lyla Bett. Mossad Head of station, Israeli Embassy, Valletta, Malta

Egypt
Mohamed Hosniy Mubarak. President of the Arab Republic of Egypt
Amr Moussa. Prime Minister of Egypt

Libya
Said Salim. Member of Libyan Intelligence Service (ISL), SW France
Ismail Mehmet. Head of ISL, Valletta, Malta

The Mafia

Don Vincenzo 'Enzo' Napoli 'Capo di tutti capi'

Don Mario Gambino. Cherry Hill, New Jersey, U.S.A. Head of the Gambino Family

Alfredo 'Dino' Bontate. Gambino's 'Caporegime'. Head of Mafia operations in Paris

Tommy Spadaro. Head of Mafia operations in SW France

Spain

Philippe Buxtrada. Head of ETA Freedom Fighters, Atlantic Pyrenees. Known as 'The Wolf'

PART ONE

La Piovra – The Octopus

Chapter One

SW France

Henri Lacoste stood quietly in the shadows. Dressed in a wide-striped shirt with a red cravat, a black waistcoat and dark green apron, the tall Parisian surveyed the diners carefully. The young waiter was feeling pleased with himself and smiled at his good fortune. But then he knew nothing at all about what was going on around him.

Had he even an inkling then his self assurance would have evaporated. In fact he would have been praying, like good Catholic boys sometimes do, to be elsewhere, anywhere just as long as it was as far away from the trio sitting at the corner table. Today, Thursday, the place should have been full yet, although all the tables had been booked, only three were occupied and it was getting late. He was not to know that one of the diners had booked the entire restaurant.

Unknown to him the owner had ordered his secretary to cancel all bookings for the day while, at the main gate, the security guards politely informed unexpected arrivals that an electrical fire in the main kitchens had forced the restaurant to close. As they turned away, each customer had been presented with a spray of freshly cut gardenias. And then there were the two men sitting facing the main door. They and the two by the annex door looked out of place. They were mean and hard, more like dockers from Marseille than diners at the prestigious Près d'Eugénie. Lacoste felt sure they all knew the three at the corner table by the large French windows where, despite the early spring sunshine, the curtains had been drawn tight. These, he thought, looked more interesting and so held his attention.

The large, overweight man with receding hair holding court in English gestured expansively as he talked. His features were fleshy and the rings on his fingers accentuated the softness of his pudgy hands. When he spoke his chest rose laboriously causing his eyes to bulge. Every now and then he would dab at his face with a large cream silk handkerchief, lift his chin and pull at his collar.

Next to him on his right was a short, slim man dressed more like a peasant in his Sunday best. Thrown casually across his shoulders and over a beige polo-necked sweater, was a black leather jacket with wide lapels, from which was hanging a thick, brass-buckled belt. The sky blue trousers and heavy shoes, common to the region, indicated he was indeed a countryman, probably from the wild hilly region to the south. But it was the deeply tanned face that held Lacoste's attention. Lean, almost haggard, the skin was drawn tightly across the prominent bones, forcing the hooked nose to protrude like a beak.

Even from this distance the eyes glittered beneath two huge eyebrows. His black unkempt hair, slick with oil, was swept back untidily. The man said little but stared about uneasily and the waiter watched with distaste as he stabbed angrily at his food before leaning forward to eat from his knife. Lacoste was reminded of a bird of prey crouched warily over its victim as it stripped flesh from the torso. Just watching made him uneasy.

The third man sat with his back three parts towards him. From time to time he placed his left hand under his coat and gently massaged the tip of his right shoulder. Earlier, when he had led his companions to the table, Lacoste had studied him. Unlike the other two he was dressed and groomed exquisitely. The elegant cut of the expensive light grey suit, the delicate pink of the silk shirt and the yellow rosebud in the buttonhole seemed to fit perfectly. He was taller than the others and blessed with fine, handsome features. As he passed in the foyer, he had glanced at Lacoste and smiled briefly. The face had lit up yet the eyes had remained cold, ice cold and pitiless.

The eldest of the trio – Don Vincenzo 'Enzo' Napoli – had called for the meeting and flown in from New York. Don Enzo, the Mafia *Capo di tutti capa* 'Boss of Bosses' had brought with him his heir apparent – Mario Gambino - head of the Gambino Family.

The smallest, Philippe Buxtrada, was better known as Le Loup 'The Wolf'. Currently the most wanted terrorist on both sides of the Franco-Spanish border, he ran his band of Euzkadi Ta Askatasuna –ETA – freedom fighters from their mountain lairs deep in the high Pyrenees. The three diners had known each other since the Sicilians had wrested control of the lucrative Marseille narcotic trade from the Corsicans. The successful operation became known to the world as the French Connection.

In order to move their heroin into and through Spain, the Wolf had carved open a new route then held it with gun, bomb and knife against the unwanted attention of their rivals. It had been a messy affair when leading members of the opposition had been butchered ruthlessly. It prompted the good folk of the high Basque to forget about the Wolf, and it was a wise decision. Far better, they decided, to busy themselves with their own affairs. For their part, the Sicilians were grateful and vowed one day to repay Philippe Buxtrada.

Lacoste turned briskly as the manager called him away, quietly closing the double doors behind him.

***

The Don loved his French cuisine and, Henri, the head chef, had not let them down. The 'Foie Gras cuit au bouillon de Poule Frais' had been followed by a rich rissole of wild game, the famous 'Caneton et d'Aile de Caille en Venaison.' Then had come cheeses from Roquefort and the Aveyron before the meal finished with a soufflé named after him: the 'Léger à la Pomme et au Citron Vert d'Henri.' Don Napoli belched, wiped his moist lips with the back of his hand then sat back in his chair and smiled benignly at the two younger men, as a father might regard his sons.

Among his most trusted lieutenants was Mario Gambino, son of Johnny Gambino of Cherry Hill, New Jersey. Over the years he had watched young Mario and was impressed. Even by Mafia standards he was hard, a proven killer and a natural leader – a *Mafiosi di Rispetto* 'Man of Respect'. The first man he killed, on suspicion of molesting young children, had been found crucified upside down against a barn door; somebody had then stuffed his mouth with his genitals and dollar bills.

But Mario possessed two further assets – patience and brains. Until he had been expelled from Our Lady of Grace Catholic school in Cherry Hill, he had excelled at languages, becoming fluent in Spanish and French. Soon after the great Mafia war Enzo arranged for his protégé to be installed in Paris with Don Michele Zaza. He was told to lie low but to watch carefully, to establish a network of contacts and report. The Mafia, he was told, was patient – like la piovra.

"So, Mario." Enzo spoke quietly. "Gimme the dope." He turned quickly, looked down at the small Basque and raised his voice. "Hey, Loop," he wheezed, grinning widely. "You compronay, Mario? Yeah? D'ya get all he's saying?" The Don's body heaved with laughter.

"Si, Enzo, si. Mario speaks good for me. No problem." The Wolf glanced at Gambino, nodded briefly then glared menacingly at the two guards by the main door. The men started nervously before busying themselves with the contents of the plates in front of them.

"OK." Gambino began thoughtfully, fingering the crumbs on his plate. He knew well that behind his genial façade, Enzo Napoli possessed a formidably sharp brain. Over the years many had underestimated his speed of mind and ency-clopaedic memory and had paid dearly. "Well," he said slowly, "you know the history, huh?" he paused, choosing his words with care. "It seems as though the French really are on to something big down in Alexandria. And that's *big*...real

11

big. Far bigger than we've been told."

"Who says?" Napoli asked, leaning forward and tugging at his collar.

"That little number we placed in the Foreign Ministry." Gambino glanced at Napoli, his eyes searching the Don's. "She's now in the cipher office at Quai d'Orsay where she's got access to the classified registry. Sees everything that comes and goes. She's good, knows what's important and cuts out the crap."

Napoli nodded, picking his teeth and sucking noisily. He stared at Gambino and nodded impatiently. "Yeah, OK...OK."

"She's now got the dope on that marine archaeological dive," Gambino continued. "She's seen the signals telling Paris they reckon to have found the route down to the vaults beneath the guard house. Just as the scrolls said. Remember them? The French diver, Gideon's his name, and the Gypos are certain they're on to the main treasures. And if they *are*..." He sat back, opened his arms and smiled.

"Wha' d'ya mean - if they are? So what? What do they reckon's down there?"

The Wolf studied Gambino. He noticed the thin, hard mouth and the steady gaze. It was years since he had seen the man. The young picciotti had matured and the Wolf liked what he saw. As the Sicilians would say, the man had balls.

Gambino paused and rubbed his shoulder while the other two waited. "If it *is* down there, and this guy Gideon, one of the best in the business, reckons it is, then we're talking about the whole goddam treasure house of Cleopatra and the Pharaohs. The whole goddam lot. That's what, Enzo."

"So what's that in bucks?" Enzo Napoli took the toothpick from his mouth and leant towards Gambino. "Listen kiddo." He jabbed a finger on the table. "I don't wanna be kept hanging around waiting for a coupl'a fuckin' stone statues and that kinda crap. We got better things to worry about."

Gambino held his gaze. "Difficult to know exactly," he replied, "But they're sure wired to the moon about it all. The smart money in Cairo, Paris...and now in London seems to think that what's down there could make Tutankhamun look cheap, real cheap. And it doesn't need me to tell you what *he's* worth." Gambino paused and sat back. "Believe me, Enzo," he said thoughtfully, moving his finger in circles on the tablecloth. "This could be the one we've been waiting for and we've got the buyers lined up who'll kill for just one piece of the stuff. I'm betting my life on it. And another thing too. Nobody knows we're on to this. It's a clean job...a straight run. That's why we're here now."

"What sort of time frame are we talking about?"

"Three months, maybe less. When it's ready we'll have to get in there quick before they wrap the joint up like Fort Knox." Gambino nodded towards the Basque. "That's why we need Philippe here. We gotta get it out of Egypt and back fast. Once it's lifted the whole place'll go ballistic and we need it tucked away out of sight. Lie doggo until the heat's off."

"Si." Buxtrada nodded at his plate.

"That's for sure." Napoli relaxed in his chair. He glanced down at his hands, looked up and wiped his mouth. "OK, lemme hear the facts. You sure we got a good handle on the right guys? Eh? That crowd in Paris are like a bunch of goddamned snakes, sliding around all over the shop." His small eyes flitted from one face to the other. "Know what I mean? Screwin' each others wives one minute, then fiddlin' the books or takin' back handers the next." He paused and shook his head. Then suddenly he laughed. "Holy shit, man…just plain dumb crazy."

The three remained at the table until the light began to fade. Gambino went over the plan in minute detail, the key to which was the successful coercion of outside agencies. For years he and others had planted agents within government departments, big business and the police, the gendarmerie and the security forces. Slowly these sleepers had worked their way into positions of authority or posts from which they could gather intelligence.

Enzo Napoli trusted Gambino's judgement implicitly but this patience and caution had come the hard way. Some years ago he had been sent into Marseille when the Turkish Mafia, in a fit of madness, had challenged the Sicilian operation. Mario, part of the assault team on a Turkish safe house above a brothel in the Old Port, had moved up the narrow staircase alone and ahead of the others. Finding himself cornered by two hulking Turks he had opened fire killing one but the second man had fired back. Only the quick thinking of one of the *sicarios* had saved the young Gambino. Wounded in the right shoulder, he had been dragged back as two grenades were lobbed past him to settle matters.

His rescuer had rounded on him, slapping his face viciously. "Listen, punk," Carlo Trappini had screamed. "I don't give a shit if you wanna get yourself fuckin' killed, but don't expect me and the others to come diggin' you out. You broke two golden rules – right? *One*, never move until everything's ready and, *two*, when the heat's on, keep thinking about when to cut and run. You were caught, picciotti. Next time momma might not be there to wipe your ass."

Napoli smiled benignly. It had taken him years to convince his protégé that Trappini had taught him a salutary lesson. Shoulder wound apart, the lesson had stung badly and Gambino had not forgotten. From then on he conducted operations only when he felt supremely confident and never again did he fail to leave the back door open. The old Don put his arm across the younger man's shoulder. It was a brilliant plan - difficult to put together but simplicity itself at the critical moment. And now they were ready. He was confident and he nodded slowly, hugging Gambino lovingly.

2

London

Amanda Gates leaned forward and pressed the button on her intercom. She listened and glanced at her watch. "Ten minutes?" She queried the machine. "OK, I'll be there. How long do you reckon he'll be?"

"Said he shouldn't be any longer than half an hour or so. But you know what he's like," Mary Sutton's soft Irish brogue continued. "He's got the Cultural Consul from the Egyptian Embassy in with him at the moment. Sounded very excited and was muttering something about packing his bags again. So you'd better come prepared for anything," she added with a laugh.

Amanda got up from the desk, walked over to the mirror and toyed with her hair. She thought the world of Sir Alan Palmer but he had this annoying habit of calling meetings right at the end of the day. And this evening of all evenings was not a good time to be hanging around the vast empty spaces of the British Museum. Jed King had rung earlier and she had agreed to dinner. They had met twice last week, the first time at her cousin Richard's cocktail party. At first she had thought the tall stranger with the wavy, sandy-brown hair rather chippy and out of place but it was not until she realised he was deeply immersed in the shadowy world of security that she understood why he was there. He had kept himself to himself but they had chatted briefly, and again just as people were leaving. It was then that he had asked he if she was doing anything later.

She remembered having laughed in his face at the sheer presumption of the question but he had wrong footed her completely. As he waited for her answer he just stood there watching her as she had noticed him doing earlier from across the room. His eyes, grey-green and seemingly devoid of emotion, had bored into hers, prompting her to rush her reply. She had then fluffed her words, blustering about doing something else and it had been her, *her*, who had suggested the following evening. She ran her tongue against the inside of her lips, looked at herself for a moment then cocked an eyebrow and smiled.

The dinner had been a near disaster. Whenever she tried to find out what made him tick, the man had clammed up, taking no interest in her questions. He knew nothing about most things except music which was a blessing for at least it gave them something to talk about. Culturally, though, he seemed dead and she began to find his company an embarrassment. Eventually she had snapped and told him she was finding him awkward and a bore. It was only then that he managed a smile, but it was little more than a glimmer and the wretched man appeared amused by her frustration; it had not made for the jolliest of evenings. When he called for the bill she remembered wondering what else she might have been doing with her time. He had been civil enough though, ushering her into her taxi as she supposed somebody had taught him to do and that appeared to have been that.

But the evening had irritated her. She was unable to put her finger on it and, most maddening of all, she couldn't get him out of her mind. His name and the image of him studying her with those expressionless eyes kept re-appearing. There was nothing about him she could call handsome, fine even, rather his face was hard and unforgiving. And then there was his job. Richard had told her a little about it and, rather than satisfying her curiosity, what he said had simply intrigued her. Jed King was not a dull man, most certainly not and there was something about him she found fascinating. Mary Sutton had laughed and told her that she was old enough by now to be making up her own mind. Then came his call to her office yesterday afternoon. He must have got her extension through the switchboard. She pulled a face, shrugged and went back to the desk where she began to clear the papers.

She had been appointed Sir Alan's Personal Assistant a year previously and worked directly to him through Mary his secretary. She had been lucky to get the job but then Amanda Gates had always been lucky, cruising effortlessly through life as doors opened wide. Sir Alan Palmer, Keeper of Egyptian Antiquities at the British Museum, had selected her from the short list of applicants.

Amanda's father, Sir Tristan Gates, had spent years in the Middle East, finishing his long career as UK Ambassador to Syria. It was there that Amanda and her brother had first become interested in archaeology, watching fascinated as the digs slowly revealed the ancient towns of Hama and Rueida in the desert just north of Damascus. Later, after an exclusive education at St George's, Ascot, she went up to Oxford where she took a First in Classics with Ancient History at Wadham before moving on to the Courtauld Institute where she studied Classical Art. Her education complete, she returned to the Middle East spending three hot, dusty years at the bottom of archaeological scrapes. She loved the sense of adventure, the ever-present buzz of anticipation as the dig progressed and the sheer thrill whenever a find was made and later identified.

The successful applicant, the Keeper had demanded, must be bright, very bright. Had he been totally honest, the Keeper would have admitted that the striking good looks of the tall, well spoken young woman with the husky voice and honey-coloured hair might have played some small part in her selection. He had been fascinated by her ability to describe in such detail the background to so many of the pieces they had put before her. Her command of Arabic together with her knowledge of the Middle East had swayed the panel and she had been offered the post. Mercifully Mary had warmed to her immediately, and Palmer would often hear them chattering away together in his outer office.

***

Mary Sutton looked up and smiled as Amanda walked in. "Hello, dear yourself a coffee. We might be a wee while yet. You know the others, I'm

Amanda glanced at the faces turned towards her and nodded, smiling warmly at the diminutive, bespectacled Tanya Simpson from their own Photographic Archives. Standing next to her was the formidable figure of Shirley Harcourt, Keeper of Greek and Roman Antiquities talking quietly with Connie Black her Deputy. The last, half hidden behind the door, she knew simply as 'Smelly,' a humourless, pinched-faced little creature from Admin who kept a vice-like grip on the museum's financial affairs. Getting anything out of him, a meal ticket even, was regarded as something of a coup but she returned his nod.

Suddenly the door to the inner office swung open revealing the short, neatly dressed figure of Doctor Ruhwani from the Egyptian Embassy in Park Lane. Behind him, holding the door wide, stood the taller, grey haired Sir Alan Palmer. "I wish you the best of luck," said the Cultural Counsellor in perfect English. "Now we've got both yourselves and the Louvre represented at this level, I'm much happier. Thank you so much." He held out his hand.

"Good bye Counsellor...and thank you for coming round." Sir Alan Palmer peered over his gold pinz-nez, beamed at his visitor and pumped his hand warmly. "Of course, we'll keep your staff fully up to speed as we go along. It's wonderful news...very exciting." Once the Egyptian had left, Sir Alan ushered the party into his office waving them to the chairs around the long table, then went to the office door. "Mary, I know it's rather late, my dear, but could you possibly do us some tea, and perhaps a few of those nice biscuits you keep hidden away?" Amanda caught Shirley Harcourt's eye and both smiled affectionately at the impeccable manners and old world charm.

Closing the door behind his secretary, he took off his jacket, placed it across the back of his chair and sat. Then, lifting his glasses, he lowered his head and pushed both hands through his receding hair. "Phew. Oh goodness me...well, well, well." He paused then looked up at them blinking, and replaced his glasses. "Welcome everybody," he laughed. "Sorry about that but...dear me, that really was the most marvellous piece of news. Doctor Ruhwani has just had confirmation from Cairo that Francois Gideon and his divers off Alexandria are now certain that they're on to the Ptolemeic treasures."

He paused and rubbed his hands together before looking around the table as his thin features creased into a wide grin. "There's been a complete press blackout, of course, but the divers are preparing to clear the way down to the vaults and then they're planning to lift out everything that's there. The Egyptian Supreme Council of Antiquities has asked me to go out with a French team from the Louvre. Once they start bringing up whatever's there, we've been asked to go out and help identify the finds." He paused. "So that'll mean you, Amanda...you and Mary. I'm afraid that it's going to confound your social diaries for a couple of weeks or so but it can't be helped. Best clear them now."

Amanda Gates swallowed then, suddenly and maddeningly, she felt herself blushing. She looked up and caught Tanya Simpson's smile which served only

to make it worse. Sir Alan was looking at her over his spectacles with his eyebrows raised as if awaiting her reaction. "That's no problem," she half whispered uncrossing her legs and straightening her skirt. She coughed to clear her throat. "Goodness me, no…it'll be wonderful."

For several moments the room was silent. Eventually Shirley Harcourt spoke. "You know, it's unbelievable," she murmured to no one in particular. "*If*, and it's still very much an if, but *if* the el-Gebel scrolls are right, this will be every bit as important as opening up the pyramids. And if the Ptolomeic treasures really *are* there, well…" she left the sentence unfinished and shook her head.

"I know, I know," Sir Alan replied lifting his hands in appeal. "It's simply not possible to gauge what we're going to get from all this. But both the Nathan team in Haifa and UCLA in California have given the scrolls the full burst of NASA technology. They've been using these new multi-spectral cameras and goodness knows what else on every leaf so I've heard, and once they'd found the right search wavelength the writing stood out incredibly well."

He got up and went over to the window where he looked down at the tangled mass of traffic clogging the streets far below. For a time he seemed lost in thought. Then suddenly, as if waking from a dream, he turned back to the table. "You're absolutely right, y'know, Shirley. The sheer value of what could be down there is quite inestimable, beyond comprehension. I just hope and pray they manage to keep it all under their hats and guard the stuff like the Crown Jewels." He paused, glanced at those around him and gave a little laugh. "Which they are, of course. But happily, that's not our problem. Right, come on now, it's getting late." He sat again, this time facing them. "The good Doctor Ruhwani gave me a few dates so we need to do some planning…we can't afford to miss this one."

Chapter Two

Alexandria

Francois Gideon ducked beneath the low bulkhead and climbed up into the cockpit. Although it was a calm night he could feel the gentle movement under his feet as the elderly harbour boom rose and fell against the side of the huge diving ship. It was still dark although the first hint of colour was creeping into the eastern sky, out beyond Aboukir Bay behind him.

Gideon was a wiry man, of medium height and close on fifty years old. His tousled hair and full beard all but concealed his weather-beaten face, save for his bright, alert eyes and mouthful of immaculate white teeth set in a permanent grin. His right hand reached over his left shoulder in a vain attempt to deal with the itch half way down his back. Then he shivered, clasping his arms around his chest, the tattered jersey and thin, sparse shorts failing to keep out the April pre-dawn chill that lay across the water.

He had lived like this ever since the chartered mother ship had been secured in the inner harbour six months ago. When diving, he rarely set foot on dry land preferring instead to spend his life on board either the 120′ El Rashid from which he ran his operations, or the small, nondescript harbour vessel. The latter was his bolthole into which he would disappear for his frugal meals or at the end of the day's work when he would throw himself exhausted onto his cot in the cramped and airless cabin.

But this morning he was up earlier than usual. For the last two hours he had been working at the tiny desk in the galley, his work lit by the soft glow of a smoky paraffin lamp, his thirst slaked by numerous cups of the scalding, bitter coffee so popular with the Arabs. Gideon looked out across the dawn mist lying on the water. Bending his knees slightly, he rubbed his back slowly up and down the doorframe, shook his head and smiled at the recent turn of events.

***

18

He had been diving since he was a toddler. Born at Sanary-sur-mer near the great French naval base of Toulon, the young Francois was swimming before he could walk properly and snorkelling before he began nursery school. Later, he would accompany his father on dives in the Red Sea and the Philippines where he was present at the discovery of the 'San Diego', a seventeenth century Spanish treasure galleon. From that moment he had lived for the underwater world, later pioneering new techniques to systematically search for remains of past civilisations. He refused to be rushed by his sponsors, insisting on mapping and recording the area exactly before anything of interest or value was recovered. This approach attracted divers and scientists of the highest calibre whenever word got out that Gideon was planning an expedition. It also attracted the attention of the Monroe Hanay Trust, a Liechtenstein-based Swiss foundation which sponsored his expeditions.

Three months earlier his divers had found the entrance to the strong rooms beneath what was believed to be the guardhouse of Cleopatra's Palace on the western edge of the Palace of Kings. It had been a dramatic moment. After months of painstaking search during which Gideon had forced the team to cover the predicted site again and again, they had stumbled across the first signs of buildings almost by chance. Two divers, working close to an old sewage pipe less than a hundred and fifty metres from the harbour wall, spotted what appeared to be a long pile of rubble lying in a shallow depression on the sea bed less than ten metres below the surface.

Gideon ordered the El Rashid into the harbour, moored her over the spot then got the harbour authorities to cordon off the area of surrounding dockland. Tension mounted as the clearance team removed more rubble from the harbour floor exposing large areas of collapsed building and roadways. He remembered the mounting excitement that had gripped the party as the whole area was gradually exposed. When he was satisfied that enough of the complex had been revealed, he called for a twenty-four hour break to allow the team to relax before the hard work that lay ahead. So keen were the men to get on with the dive that they had refused point blank to stop, merely pausing to party long into the night.

The following morning Gideon called a meeting where he outlined his plans before demanding total secrecy from the team: it must be absolute he stressed. Most had dived on sunken galleons or treasure ships during their careers and understood the need for such security. They worked together, diving to the maximum of their regulations then held long meetings on the El Rashid when they discussed progress and looked ahead impatiently to what the next day might reveal.

The heavy lifting gear had done its job well and his divers had been able to identify the steps leading down from the floor of the guardhouse. Piece by piece, hundreds of tons of huge masonry blocks had been removed. After each lift, suction pumps had cleared away the thick layers of silt and mud which was then sifted carefully before being sluiced into barges and towed out to sea. Gradually they worked their way across the complex towards the large pile of masonry and rubble in the western corner. During this clearing operation a number of arte-facts in superb condition had been recovered from the silt and jetsam that had settled on the Palace floor over sixteen centuries. Among the treasures already lifted was a bust of the God Serapis, a statue of the High Priest Isis and a Sphinx whose face was a portrait of Ptolemy, Cleopatra's father.

Over the years, historians and archaeologists had argued about the fate of the Royal Palaces between the time that Cleopatra had committed suicide in 30 BC and the well documented earthquake and tidal waves that destroyed the whole complex some four hundred years later. According to the many records, it was only then at around 400 AD that the area had been devastated. The land on which the major part of the city stood lay directly above two glacial plates. As the plates moved, the land had dropped over thirty feet and the sea flooded in. The mouth of the river Nile had been forced to change direction and much of the ancient city had been covered with a layer of silt several metres deep.

Until recently, modern historians believed that once Cleopatra had died, the Palace of Kings had remained at the centre of Alexandrian life – the crossroads of Europe, Africa and India – before falling into gradual decline as popularity faded. Anything of value, they reasoned, would have been removed from the Royal Palaces for safe keeping or vandalised, while the stonework would have been taken and used as building material elsewhere. Unlike the great Museum and Library on higher ground further to the east, the palace complex should have fallen gradually into disuse and neglect, until the catastrophic events hundreds of years later completed its ignominy. But not so.

In 1995 Sir Alan Palmer, by then appointed Keeper of Egyptian Antiquities at the British Museum and a world authority on the Ptolemic dynasty, had been invited to Cairo by the Director of the Supreme Council for Egyptian Antiquities. An archaeological dig at the site of a temple belonging to a noble family in the necropolis near Tuna el-Gebel in Middle Egypt, far to the south, had unearthed a number of papyrus scrolls which had been taken to Cairo for restoration and deciphering.

Later they had been sent to Israel and California where they had been subjected to the most modern techniques available. After more than two years of painstak-ing research it was apparent that the authors of the scrolls had moved from Alexandria to el-Gebel where they had recorded the story of an earlier disaster which had damaged parts of the Royal Palace. Three of the scrolls offered a possible explanation as to the fate of Cleopatra's personal treasures and told an intriguing tale.

Around 28 BC, just two years after Cleopatra's death, the region had been struck by a first earthquake. Serious but not catastrophic it had, nonetheless, done considerable structural damage to the buildings on the western edge of the city where her palace was located and in particular to the foundations. Many buildings had become uninhabitable. Two of the scrolls mentioned the treasure vaults which lay under the main guardhouse. They described how the vaults had been damaged and the strong rooms, containing the bulk of the treasures, were first buried under fallen masonry, then subsided under the sea and were finally covered by a tributary of the Nile – a fate similar to that suffered by the rest of the city many years later. All attempts to recover the artefacts from under the buildings of the Royal Guard had been abandoned while the remainder of the Palace complex, although badly damaged, lived on. The story revealed by the scrolls tallied with descriptions of the event offered by contemporary historians of the period including the Romans, Suetonius and Plutarch, who told how Emperor Octavian, Alexandria's conqueror, had to abandon his search for the treasures.

However, no sign of the buildings had ever been found and this one historical account of the treasures had been dismissed. The later and much greater earthquake, together with the resultant tidal waves, put an end to any further attempts and the site lay forgotten for more than sixteen hundred years until the Egyptians decided to excavate and identify the whole of the palace complex.

Two years before the discovery of the scrolls, the Egyptians had approached the Monroe Hanay Foundation, an acknowledged supporter of cultural and scientific projects. Francois Gideon, by then a much respected marine archaeologist, was working for the foundation and had become a personal friend of the chairman, Michel Hanay. A combined Franco-Egyptian operation was mounted to identify the location of the palace complex and recover whatever artefacts might be found.

While the site of the guardhouse had been included in the original area to be searched, no mention was made of the treasures until the writing on the scrolls had been deciphered. The ensuing conference, at which Sir Alan Palmer had been present, studied the evidence with mounting optimism. Archaeologists and historians had, for centuries, contemplated the fate of the pharaohs' treasure houses and it seemed likely that a possible site had been identified at last. The conference concluded that, as no other evidence of the treasures existed, and the writings of the Ptolemaic scribes tallied with those of the Roman historians, the site should be excavated.

***

Francois Gideon was not a man prone to gambling but he sensed that today might be a red letter day for the project. If the scribes were correct and the earlier quake had caused the guardhouse to collapse, and if this was indeed where the treasures were held, then the dream of every archaeologist might be realised. If not, then they would have to be content with clearing and exposing the remainder of the Palace complex, already well underway. The odds of anything being there, he considered, were about five to one against. It was an outside chance but sometimes the outsider won. He glanced up at the dawn sky and watched a long, straggling line of cormorants overhead, beating their way urgently out to the feeding grounds beyond the salt marshes.

"Allaaaaahua...Allaaaaahua...Akhbar!" Gideon inclined his head and listened intently as the first long, plaintive cry of the Imam called the faithful to prayer from the tall minaret on the mosque across the harbour. The world was waking. He went below, poured himself another coffee and addressed himself to the charts and drawings on his desk.

2

South Wales
Jed King had had a bad morning. He leant back in his cane chair and gazed out of the window, past the military range complex and up to the high bracken covered hills beyond. The screw would have to be tightened and it would be his job to do it. He smiled grimly. Serve the bastards right for going off on a swan like this.

He had been tasked by the Director of Operations at Venture Risk to select a training team who were scheduled to fly out to Nairobi and set up their own training camp deep in the rain forest on the slopes of Mount Kenya. There they were to run a course of bodyguard and protection drills for the Kenyan Special Forces. He had just a fortnight left but half the team were not yet fit, their shooting was dreadful and their anti-ambush drills all over the place. What hurt, though, was that he was not going to be leading them. A rest had been ordered by London. A *rest* indeed! The eight-week swansong this lot were about to embark upon was rest enough, and a nice little earner into the bargain.

Over a month earlier, seventeen men selected from the various London-based security companies had reported for training. But the quality had not been there. Jed had registered his concern but shoulders were shrugged and he had set about clearing out the very worst of the dead wood. He pushed them hard, in particular those with the soft faces and beer bellies. His efforts, together with the isolated and spartan lifestyle in the pre-war, hutted camp high on the northern slopes of the Brecon Beacons had taken their toll. Several had opted to return to their nice easy office routines but now time was against him. He smiled again.

Just eight were left of whom only two showed any promise and a further two were positively hopeless. Were it his choice he would have sacked the wet little Intelligence Corps sergeant and Mallet, the big, loud mouthed ex-Para. Unlike his days in the army however, there were no reserves to call on and he would have to make do with what there was. So perhaps it was just as well he was not going with them. He stood and stretched. And in any case, what he was going to do now wouldn't exactly put him at the top of their popularity stakes.

***

King had left the army himself three years previously. After applying for a variety of jobs all of which he found monstrously dull, he had been approached by one of the directors of Venture Risk. The security company was the best known and most widely respected in the business and had recently won a number of lucrative overseas contracts.

Requests from overseas for training assistance such as his present assignment came first to the Foreign and Commonwealth Office, where they were analysed, before being passed on to the Ministry of Defence. Under normal circumstances the Director of Military Operations would be glad to accept such tasks but since Iraq and Afghanistan the army was woefully under strength. They were fully committed worldwide to the point of overstretch and requests had been turned down. Aware that such training and advisory missions played an important part in foreign relations, the FCO persuaded the MOD to place some of the more important requests out to tender. Unthinkable a few years ago, such a decision now seemed little different to privatising the prisons, the railways or anything else. However, the one big difference to any other form of privatisation was that a number of these contracts involved the business end of soldiering – the small matter of killing or being killed.

The gentle, timorous Whitehall mandarins blanched at the very thought of British mercenaries operating at will and saw to it that any such operations were prepared with the utmost care and thereafter kept on a very tight rein. In spite of such caution, successful operations were nonetheless possible and a number of contracts had been negotiated with a few of the most highly regarded companies, among them Venture Risk.

Jed had wanted to be a soldier for as long as he could remember. Hailing from the unappealing Brown's Green district of Birmingham he had come up the hard way. Tall and strong for his age he had first learned to use his fists and boots in the school playground and had continued to do so whenever he and his friends later found themselves in a tight spot. The one person who could control the young tearaway was his mother who begged her son to remain at school and complete his education. His father had left them a year after his younger sister had died, leaving his mother to bring him up. He had become devoted to her and stayed on at school simply to be with her. Later, and to her sorrow, he threw away any chance of further education, electing instead to join the Parachute Regiment. By the time he completed his selection and basic training in Aldershot, he was just eighteen.

He was a natural soldier: big, rawboned and fearless. During his first tour of duty in Northern Ireland he saw action at Crossmaglen when, in a night-time clash with an IRA active service unit, his patrol killed two men. For his part in the contact he was mentioned in despatches. Identified as a potential officer, he completed the selection process and went to Sandhurst a year later. After two more years with his regiment he was promoted to take command of the Pathfinder platoon before volunteering for Special Force duties. He passed selection, joined one of the sabre squadrons and saw action in Bosnia and Kosovo where he was awarded the Military Cross, before returning to Hereford and leading part of the Counter Revolutionary Warfare team. Time passed quickly and he was selected for staff training but the very idea of leaving his soldiers and spending years behind a desk appalled him. He refused to countenance it and, after a year's extension at Hereford and an inconclusive argument with his regiment, he left the army with no idea at all of what he might do.

***

After lunch he called the team together in the rusty and leaking Nissen hut which they used as a communal dining hall and bar. A number of things were irritating him and he did not mince his words. The two remaining weeks were, he told them, going to be hard, as hard as necessary to get what was left of them up to the required standard. "We might be out of the army but I still call the shots around here. Right?" He looked at the eight men in front of him. "Don't get the idea that it's all even-Stevens cos it's not. They're paying me to produce the goods and that's what I'm going to do. From now on in it's pressure all the way. And if anyone can't hack it, you know where the door is." He held up a mobile phone. "A quick call to your boss or whoever and that's it…away you go. But don't expect any more offers in this line of business." King stared back at the faces. "Right then, we go back out on the range until we can hit the sodding targets double tap every time. The shooting's crap and the drills are weak…you're staggering around out there like a bunch of old women, all of you. So…fingers out or you'll be there all night." He paused. "Right, get outside and on the transport."

Later that evening, Mallet the ex-Para went for him. The metal chair ground loudly as the big Geordie climbed to his feet, and he swaggered across to where Jed was talking with two others. "I'd like a word, Mister King," he called loudly. "An' outside'd be best…just you an' me." The room fell silent.

Jed glanced up as one of the others rose to his feet but the face looked worried not angry. No problem there. Mallet, he sensed, was on his own and he turned to face him. "Yeah, sure. No sweat, but let's talk inside, right here…no need to be shy," he said softly. "So, what's your problem?"

Mallet stepped forward jabbing his finger. "You, mate. You're the problem round here. Way out of touch, you are. Know what I mean? Think we're still in the army, you do. Typical bloody officer mouthing off an' shouting the odds. All this bollocking an' criticism an' that. Fancy yerself as a hard case, an all." Mallet's chest was heaving. "Don't make me laugh for fuck's sake. Nowt but a load o'old shite, man." He laughed, turning briefly to glance at the others.

The room was now very quiet. Mallet had been drinking. Jed stood facing him, studying his man closely, their faces little more than a foot apart. Mallet moved forward almost stumbling into the man he was confronting. A dark, powerfully built figure appeared at King's shoulder. 'Horse' Ligioni, a Fijian and one of the team's instructors, muttered something. Without taking his eyes off the man, Jed inclined his head to listen then nodded and motioned Horse to one side. Mallet moved again, menacingly this time.

Suddenly and without warning King stamped down hard with his boot, driving the heel down on to the arch of the other man's foot. The can of beer in Mallet's hand crashed noisily to the floor but his shout of pain was cut short as King chopped him sharply on the side of the neck then drove his knee upwards to meet Mallet's face as he fell. The figure jerked backwards, collapsed, and lay still.

King bent down and prodded the body with his boot before straightening himself. "He'll live," he said to no one in particular. "OK lads, that's it for tonight." He nodded to those around him. "Get him cleaned up and off to his bunk, then away and get your heads down. On your way then." He left the room and walked briskly across the drive to his tiny cabin at the end of the Nissen hut.

Chapter Three

Corleone, Sicily

The two men sat side by side in high-backed chairs. Only their heads could move. Ankles, knees, thighs, waist, chest and arms had been bound tightly with leather straps. Their breathing came in short gasps. One sat with his head slumped forward. His eyes were screwed tightly shut and his hands grasped the wooden arms of his chair. The other sat staring at the ceiling. His eyes were wide with terror and his mouth opened and closed silently.

The short, squat albino in the white coat turned slowly. His pale face was round, the smooth contours broken only by a pair of thick, oval-shaped and rimless spectacles and a thin blond-white moustache. His white hair, short and badly cut, stood up straight from the top of his head, giving him an air of permanent surprise. As he moved towards them so he limped. They started, transfixed by the pink eyes beneath the white eyebrows, but they were unable to move. They could do nothing except stare back, utterly petrified.

"We will begin now," the albino whispered. "I will be as slow as I can but I have my orders. A pity, such a pity." One hand, pale and blue-veined, yet heavily bloodstained, wiped across his mouth. Suddenly he giggled. "But we will see what I can do." He muttered something to himself then turned and limped back towards the metal table where a man lay naked, strapped down with his head clamped brutally in a vice.

Sensing the return of his tormentor the man spluttered frantically to clear his throat. "No, no. In God's name no. *No more*. Please, God, no more." The words came out in a harsh croak. His toes wriggled desperately in a pathetic attempt to move while his hands clenched and unclenched.

"Don't worry, my dear. Keep your feet and hands still. I will see to them later but first I must show my friends your *eye*." The small figure went to the head of the table, scratched savagely at the back of his neck then selected a curved knife

26

from a metal kidney bowl. He then bent over his victim. Seeing the blade above his face the man's voice rose to a shout, followed by a loud scream as the white-coated figure, pulling the lids of the left eye tightly together, cut swiftly into the soft flesh.

A thin trickle of excreta and urine slid down the table leg, filling the room with its sharp, bitter stench. The two in the chairs stared wildly, their eyes wide while their hands clutched desperately at the sides of their chairs. They watched horrified as the albino rummaged through his box of tools beside the table, smiling to himself. Eventually he found what he wanted and held up a large three-pronged fork in one hand and a small scoop in the other.

"Dear Christ alive, he's going to take out the eye," gasped the smaller of the two captives.

"I know, I know." His companion, eyes tight shut, shook his head. "I can't stand it, so help me God."

The torturer swung round towards them, his coat now spattered with blood where he had leant against his victim. "Come now, my friends. I show you how. You can see how me, Enrico, does it." He pointed at them, giggled once more and wrinkled his nose. "Maybe next time it will be you." As soon as he turned back to the table the captive began screaming hysterically calling out to his mother. "They all call for their mama now," the little albino cried, shaking his head from side to side as he bent over the trapped head. "All of them, just like little children...the tiny ones."

Forcing the remains of the eyelids apart he pushed the fork down between the eyeball and socket. A long, high-pitched howl filled the room as the eyeball was forced upwards and out of the socket with the fork. The hunched figure then cut the nerves and blood vessels free before scraping the eye into a small bowl. The tormented soul on the table screamed again and again while his muscles pulsated as though an electric current was coursing through the body. But gradually, while the room watched in silence, the cries subsided into a series of low whimpers.

Holding the bowl carefully in front of him, he lifted it high to show them. Both men stared in horror. One of them heaved and retched violently before vomiting. "That is but the start," the albino whispered, grinning widely. "Now Enrico really begins to play. Now you will hear real screams." Spitting to clear bile from their mouths, they watched as the slim figure rummaged through his toolbox once more before lighting a brass blowtorch and pumping it into life. "Now, my dear friend, you will let everybody know how this feels. Everybody...eh?"

With surprising speed, he hobbled to the far end of the table where he stopped by the tightly strapped feet and began to wave the hissing torch slowly back and forth across the underside of the toes. Again the victim shrieked desperately.

One of the witnesses began to sob while his companion sat slumped forward with his eyes tight shut. The creature in front of them moved up the table until he reached his victim's genitals where he stood grinning at his audience. Muttering to himself, he reached out and caressed the man between his legs then turned back to the men in the chairs. "Come now, my friends," he called. "Enrico will show you something. Look at me," he commanded.

Instinctively the men glanced up and watched horrified as the torch was turned up to full power. Chuckling to himself the tormentor began to play the flame slowly back and forth over the man's crotch. The agonised screams rose to a series of wild, hysterical shrieks, joined this time by hoarse shouts from the two witnesses. The room filled with the acrid smell of burning flesh and hair. A thick, oily smoke rose from the victim while globules of pink, sizzling fat slid down his thighs.

One of the men in the chairs again retched violently, spitting out the half digested food. The other remained motionless. The slight figure hopped nimbly towards the chairs but stopped suddenly; his white head inclined like a dog listening. Apart from the hiss of the blowtorch and the victim's low moans, the room was silent. With head inclined, the white-coated figure listened intently to the loud banging on the heavy studded door accompanied by muffled shouts. "Come on, open up. Open up, it's us," cried the voice. "We've come for the visitors. Open the door and get them out of the chairs."

Now limping badly, he hobbled towards the door then pulled away the tightly padded cloth around the edges before drawing back the three bolts. As he struggled to open the door light streamed into the room revealing several figures in the doorway. The first two into the room stopped, recoiling in horror at the stench before clasping their hands to their mouths. One spun round and threw up. A heavily built third man pushed his way past them, his face contorted with revulsion. Catching the squat figure by his bloodstained coat, he struck him sharply across the face with the back of his hand.

"Come on," he snapped at those behind him. "Move yourself. Get these two jokers out of this god dammed horror show."

Others followed them into the room, blinking in the unaccustomed darkness after the bright afternoon sunlight. They moved swiftly across to the two chairs and unfastened the straps. The first man rose unsteadily but his knees buckled and he collapsed to the ground. The other sat trembling violently, unable to move. "*Hey,* come on! Pietro, you and Philippe take this one. *Ernesto,* grab the other with Manuel. Watch out for all the puke and shite. Wrap them in the blankets and get them into the cars...and go carefully. Then back to La Strada and start cleaning up. I'll be up in a minute."

The leader rounded on the figure in his grasp. "All right, you. Signor Gambino says finish this now. So get on with it...you've had your fun. Get him into the acid. Ernesto'll be back in the morning to collect whatever's left, so make sure it's all ready for him. I don't want any hanging around. Get it? Any problems and I'll shove that horrible, fucking blowtorch right up you arse. *Go on!* Get that rotten little body of yours moving."

"OK, Carlos. OK, OK. But just a few minutes more with him," the albino pleaded, shrinking away from the sunlight.

"*No way.* Playtime's over. Get it over and done with now. *Right now.*" The voice rose to a shout. "And I mean now." With that he grimaced and spat, then turned and ran up the flight of stairs. He paused at the top waiting for the door to shut behind him. As the bolts slid quietly into place, he heard the pitiful cries coming once more from the room behind him. "Christ," he muttered, shuddering violently. "And I thought I'd seen it all."

The two captives were helped into the back room of the humble, cheerless Hotel La Strada. As she led the way to the washroom, the old concierge raised her eyes. She, too, had seen it all many times before but the money was good and she asked no questions. Once there they found their suitcases open and waiting for them. Fresh clothes, towels and soap lay on the bench by the showers. A few minutes later Carlos joined them and took command. "Right, get yourselves cleaned up and changed. We've got ten minutes to get sorted and that's it. Signor Gambino wants to have a quiet word in your ears. And just remember this." The large shaven head rounded on the other two. "Any more little tricks like that and we'll hand you over to Enrico. An' I'll tell you something for nothing - it would make his day. That little nightmare'd just *love* to get his claws into you two. When Signor Gambino tells you to stay put – you do just that. Right?"

✳✳✳

The three cars wound their way out of Palermo, moving slowly through the late afternoon traffic, before picking up speed along the A29. They passed the provincial airport at Punta Raisi and sped along the narrow coastal road towards Terrasini. Jean-Pierre Renee and Anton Blosch sat together in the back seat of the second much larger Mercedes, the interior darkened by tightly drawn blinds and tinted windows. Behind them a third car followed and behind that again a powerful motorcycle prevented other vehicles from getting too close. Both men looked distraught and haggard. Renee stared out of the window, his red-rimmed eyes and drawn features were that of a broken man. Next to him, the younger Anton Blosch sat with head bowed. He was breathing heavily and still shivering. Neither spoke but both started when the dividing window was pushed back.

"See here, my friends. Springtime in Sicily. Is not the coastline beautiful in the evening sunshine?" The heavy, dark jowled features broke into a broad grin. "You will like it here. Signor Gambino will make you welcome. Soon you will be happy again. Yes?" With that the glass divide slid shut, the figure turning back to face the road ahead. He spoke briefly to the driver and jerked his head towards the men behind him. Both laughed, the driver turning briefly to glance at his charges. But for the two in the back, the last twenty-four hours had not been fun.

2

Five years previously Jean-Pierre Renee and Anton Blosch had been part of the international team working for the French government on Bikini Atoll, part of the Pacific Marshall Islands. It was here that France had elected to conduct her highly controversial final series of underground tests, at the conclusion of which she had hurriedly signed up to the Nuclear Test Ban treaty. Renee and Blosch's particular expertise had been in the field of the miniaturisation of nuclear weapons, a subject which had been baffling scientists for years.

Prior to this, the two men had conducted most of their work at Nantes on the French Atlantic coast, home to the secret atomic research and development centre. And it was here, while the post-report analysis was being completed, that they had been arrested on charges of espionage and taken in for questioning. Such was the nature of the evidence that the trial had been brief yet had caused intense and prolonged interest in the French and international media. Years before both men had been blackmailed by foreign intelligence services then forced to work for the North Korean and Iranian intelligence services, two countries desperate to obtain nuclear weapons.

Both had been found guilty of passing nuclear secrets and both were given long sentences, Renee fifteen years and Blosch eighteen. The media furore resulted in the French Ambassador being recalled from Tehran and the military training team withdrawn. The North Koreans had insisted in closing the French Diplomatic Mission in Pyong-yang. The scientists had been committed to serve out their sentences at Frèsnes Prison in Paris, close to Orly international airport. It was from here, six weeks earlier, that they had been sprung by the Mafia and abducted to Sicily where they had been held. Just two days ago they had made an abortive attempt to leave the island, had been recaptured and were now on their way to explain themselves.

❊❊❊

Prison life in Frèsnes had been the usual melange of dull routine and the hideous, suffocating existence of life in undignified conditions from which there was apparently no escape. They were held in cells along with others whose company they were forced to accept but from whom they distanced themselves as much as possible. Quiet, obedient and totally compliant with the prison regime they were soon regarded as model prisoners. After a year they were allowed to receive visitors but, deserted or forgotten by their families, these precious moments of contact with the outside world were denied them.

Their predicament was brought to the attention of the Board of Visitors who, in conjunction with the resident priest, arranged for them to meet a number of volunteer visitors. Gradually a relationship developed between the two scientists and a retired Italian bank official now domiciled in Paris. Leonardo Guecci, an elderly and kindly disposed man had been working at Frèsnes since the death of his wife. The governor, delighted that at last they had found someone to work amongst those without family visitors, gave him every encouragement and free access to those in his care. However, whenever his modest pension permitted, Leonardo Guecci would spend as much time as he could with his large and well-connected family at San Ciprello, a remote village in Sicily, between Palermo and Corleone.

The Mafia chose to strike on Bastille Day. Two media helicopters veered away from the swarm of light aircraft covering the great parade in the Champs Elysées and turned south-east. They descended to rooftop level and raced across Paris towards Frèsnes. The first headed straight for the main building complex where it hovered noisily behind the high walls before lowering two ropes.

Two men abseiled down skilfully with grappling hooks attached to strong wire hawsers. Their task was to attach the hooks to the wire netting above the exercise yard. The second helicopter hung back, lowered two rope ladders then waited to replace the first aircraft. Most of the prisoners, together with the majority of the prison staff, were watching the July 14th celebrations on the large TV screens in the main dining hall. Another large group of inmates, watched by a few bored warders, were exercising in the main yard.

The assault was quick and professional. Within seconds the first helicopter, rocking perilously with effort, dragged several square metres of heavy netting from above the exercise yard. The second moved swiftly over the gap and lowered the ladders. As it hovered, two men in the helicopter's wide open side-door blasted the watchtowers with a Kalashnikov assault rifle and a Remington pump action shotgun. Scuffles broke out in the yard as inmates, on the orders of the prison barons, surrounded and overpowered the warders. Others blocked doorways and access points to the yard. Renee and Blosch fought their way through the melee and sprinted hard for the ladders. In less than a minute they were clear of the prison – Leonardo Guecci's planning and coordination had been thorough.

The first helicopter flew north, skirted west around the peripherique before heading north-west across the wide bend of the Seine at Colombes. Minutes later it landed near the minor airfield near Cormeilles en Vexin where it was abandoned. The crew escaped by car. The second turned south-east, dropped to ground level then flew directly across the end of the runway at Orly airport. Several hours later, a still shaken Captain of Air France Flight Number 632 filed his Mandatory Occurrence Report. Inbound, on short finals and immediately prior to touch down, the fully laden 747 had been forced to take violent evasive action when he and his co-pilot spotted the rogue helicopter. So close had been the miss, that the stunned First Officer swore blind the two men he had spotted sitting in the open doorway were carrying weapons. The helicopter turned south again and made for Bretigny where it landed briefly at a disused commercial airfield.

Two cars collected the four men and drove hard to Melun where vehicles were switched. The fresh cars moved off at once, easing themselves one at a time into the heavy holiday traffic on the A5 autoroute. Less than half an hour later they crossed to the Autoroute du Soleil and began the long drive south through Lyon to Marseille. The whole operation had taken less than an hour. Prison guards, gendarmes and the media had been wrong footed by the national events taking place in the capital. Twenty-four hours later Renee and Blosch were with their hosts deep in the wild Sicilian countryside.

Jean-Pierre Renee and Anton Blosch looked out of place amongst the short, swarthy vineyard workers of Roccamena. Guests of the Don, however, were not uncommon. The villagers accepted their presence with little more than a casual glance and murmured greetings as they passed in the street. Blosch, a tall, thin, bespectacled scholar from Vienna retained his family's Jewish looks. Renee was of Flemish extraction. Fair skinned and blue eyed he wore the ruddy complexion typical of the Low Country farming stock. To those who knew such people, Blosch looked as though he might be the brilliant nuclear physicist that he was; Renee did not. Both might well have passed for benign, middle aged tourists except that such folk rarely ventured so deep into the Sicilian mountains at this time of the year. Neither, however, resembled the sort of person at whom the French legal system had just recently thrown a very large book. Since their arrival on the island they had been treated well, living comfortably in a modest first floor apartment at the edge of the attractive village, their guards and caretakers housed above and below them. But the sudden change to their environment and enforced lifestyle did not come easily. They were not in control of their destiny; they were a long way from anyone they knew and they could not converse with those around them. They were lost. Their guardian had explained that they would be staying there for some time, perhaps several months. Later, they were told, they would be sent to Libya where they were to be employed in Colonel Gaddafi's nuclear research centre at Misratah, a large rambling modern town of high-rise apartments on the coast, a hundred miles east of Tripoli.

The Libyans had promised to look after them well. They would be housed comfortably and paid well for their work on the miniaturisation programme, at the completion of which they would be rewarded handsomely. Soon after their arrival at Roccamena, they had been handed three large briefcases containing copies of much of the technical evidence produced in court and large quantities of microfilm taken from the laboratory library in Nantes. They were to relax, they were told. They should enjoy their time on the island and do their homework. They could move around freely but were warned that it would be unwise to entertain any thoughts of leaving.

Blosch had not taken kindly to these plans. He had no idea when the last Jew managed to escape from Gaddafi's clutches but suspected it must have been very soon after the dictator had seized power more than thirty years earlier. The prospect of an enforced life amongst those who vowed to tear every last member of the Jewish faith limb from limb did not appeal to the tall, sallow Austrian. The mere thought of it terrified him and he wanted none of it.

The two discussed their predicament whenever they could, huddling together and speaking furtively in whispers. From the moment he knew their fate Blosch became determined. Their guards, such as they were, appeared casual and indifferent to their presence. The warning that they should not leave the premises seemed no more than an idle threat. Blosch urged the older and easygoing Renee to join him in a bid for freedom. He had a cousin in Rome and they decided to seek him out. Escape, it seemed, would be little more than a formality. But they were in Gambino territory where Mario's family ruled supreme and, from the start, their attempt was doomed. No sooner had they begun to make enquiries than the young Don was alerted. Their every move was observed and, while waiting to board the Messina express, they were unobtrusively picked up. Gambino had them brought to his office.

He spoke to them quietly, almost in a whisper. They had disregarded his advice and disobeyed his word he reminded them. But they were not to worry, he soothed. He understood their anxieties and would let it pass. "*But only this time,*" he yelled suddenly, sending his chair crashing behind him as he jumped to his feet and slammed his hand down on the table in front of him. The two scientists leapt back in fright. Blosch stared down at the finger jabbing into his chest. "So I'm going to teach you a lesson you'll never forget," he snarled. "You'll come to no harm but only because I still need you. Cross me again and you die."

What followed was to be fixed in their minds for the rest of their lives. They had been forced to witness the barbaric and slow torture of some wretched soul whose screams continued to haunt them long after they left the scene. Their nerves shattered, their confidence destroyed, the two scientists had meekly succumbed to anything that was asked of them. Scared out of their wits and too terrified to think for themselves, they were now being taken to face Gambino once more. It was unlikely to be a convivial reunion.

3

Just past the picturesque fishing port of Balestrate, the two cars swung off the main road and began the long ascent into the hills. Save for the odd cluster of stone houses amongst the vineyards, the countryside appeared deserted.

Looking more closely, they were able to see the occasional group of workers labouring in the vineyards, half hidden by the tall vines now dressed in their early pale-green leaves. The road became narrower and rose ever more steeply, leaving the coastal plain far behind. They reached the isolated mountain village of Giardinachio and wound their way carefully through the narrow streets before climbing once more into the open countryside, making their way deeper into the range of high, barren hills.

Suddenly they were there. The cars slowed and closed up into a cage set between a pair of ornamental wrought-iron gates. As the second pair of gates closed noisily behind the third car, a short, heavily built man, accompanied by a large mastiff, emerged from the gatehouse talking into his mobile phone. He spoke briefly to the leading driver, moved to the second car and ordered the men out where he frisked them expertly. Once satisfied, he opened the front gates and nodded them through.

After a further gentle climb the land levelled and the cars turned onto a wide gravelled sweep to the rear of an extensive house where a butler, dressed formally in white jacket and black tie, was waiting for them. He opened the heavy oak door and led the visitors down a tiled hallway to a sumptuously furnished reception area, at the far side of which were two imposing glass doors. Moving ahead, he ushered them on to an expansive area of terrace.

The view was breathtaking but the two men stood in dejected silence. They looked out across the rugged Sicilian landscape towards the Tyrrhenian Sea in the far distance which shimmered in the evening sunlight. The valley floors, already in deep shadow, were hidden from the setting sun by the high hills around them. Smoke curled up from the chimneys of the stone cottages clustered together in tiny hamlets. Far below they could hear the cries of children as they played. Occasionally a dog barked. Somewhere behind and above them a herd of goats was on the move and they could hear the call of the shepherd and the sound of goat bells. But that was all. The vast expanse of the panorama and sense of tranquillity were startling. Renee and Blosch moved cautiously to the balustrade at the far side of the terrace and stood looking around nervously.

At the sound of footsteps hurrying down the marble stairway, both turned anxiously and saw the tall figure of Mario Gambino standing in the hall. With him were two women in evening dress. The taller and elder of the two, dressed in a full-length red gown, had her long, grey hair set elegantly to reveal the diamond pendant earrings and her necklace. Bending forward slightly, he took her hand and raised it to his lips. Laughing lightly, he lowered her hand and turned to the younger woman. Leaning forward, he lifted her face towards him then kissed her gently on both cheeks.

The two scientists looked on in silence as he turned back to the older, more gracefully dressed woman. "Pray forgive me, Mimi, but I have visitors. They've been waiting for me and I have to see them but I'll not be long. Wait for me by the fountains on the lower terrace. Vincenzo will see to you." Taking her arm he lead her towards the double doors at the end of the reception room. Moments later he appeared on the terrace, walking briskly. He, too, was dressed for the evening. The scarlet lining of his white jacket matched the broad silk cumberbund around his waist. His dark, perfectly cut hair, was swept back to finish just above his winged dress collar. Apart from one yellow rosebud in his buttonhole his clothes and person were devoid of any adornment or garish jewellery. The impression was one of elegance and authority.

As he approached them he smiled warmly, holding his arms out in greeting. "My friends, my friends. I'm so sorry I wasn't here to welcome you earlier. *Thank* you for coming. It's so good to see you again." Gambino beckoned to the waiting manservant who was ordered to serve drinks. "But come…sit here by the wall. The view is magnificent, is it not? Now then, tell me. You've had an interesting time, no?" The voice was soft. "Carlos took you to see something. A little show."

The two men stared. How was it that a man could behave in such a fashion when, just a few hours earlier, he had ordered such revolting and unspeakable horror? Anton Blosch cleared his throat. "We met or rather watched your man Enrico, Signor Gambino," he said hesitantly. "We saw what he did. We had no choice."

"Ah yes, poor Enrico. I have to keep him happy." Gambino looked at them, a soulful expression on his face. "Enrico, he's something of a simpleton…a little sick in his head. But he's useful. I need him."

"What do you need him for and who was that poor wretch he was torturing?" Renee half whispered.

"Him? Oh, he was nothing." Gambino waved his hand dismissively. "An illegal immigrant from Marseille or from Napoli maybe. There are countless creatures like that. Whenever we need someone, whenever Enrico needs to be satisfied, Carlos arranges for their collection." Gambino paused, seemingly puzzled by the question. "But it's never a problem," he continued, his voice raised in surprise. "Anyway, nobody knows them. They've no identity and the police couldn't care less."

The two men sat motionless, ashen faced. Their eyes never left Gambino, their drinks remained untouched. "You see my business is very complicated," he continued. "It is difficult. I sprung you from Frèsnes for a very good reason and you have no option but to do as I ask. When people disobey me I give them to Enrico to play with. Or I make them sit in the chairs, like you did, and watch while he enjoys himself with their families. But you can relax." He wagged a finger in admonishment, looking from one to the other with his face devoid of any emotion. "Your womenfolk are quite safe…it is against our code to harm women or young children. They are safe, you have my word."

He paused, noticing their blank looks. Slipping his left hand under his jacket he rubbed his right shoulder slowly, then glanced down at his watch. "Look, my friends, I'm afraid I must leave you now. As you can see I have an engagement this evening. Please help yourself to more drinks. Don't hurry away. And when you have finished they'll take you back to your apartment. Supper will be there. Yes?" He paused, arms on the sides of his chair, ready to stand.

"But please remember to do as I ask. You must understand that we know a great deal about you both. See here, we have several photographs of your beautiful families. Your two fine teenage boys, Monsieur Renee. They're not children any more and that is a very different matter for us. And you, Monsieur Blosch, there is your brother and his son, another good-looking young man. We must hope that it will not be necessary for them to meet Enrico."

Gambino pushed two buff envelopes across the table, smiled and rose from his seat before holding out his hand. Meekly and without rising the two men took his hand in turn. The hand, like the eyes, was cold. As his footsteps rang on the marble floor behind them Jean Pierre Renee and Anton Blosch turned and stared at the envelopes in front of them. For some time neither moved.

Chapter Four

Peter Harrington looked across his desk at Jed King. The tall, urbane Director of Personnel could see that the man was tired and, most likely, as bored as he claimed. He had known him since he joined Venture Risk when he, Harrington, had been the newly appointed Assistant Director of Operations. Although never close friends, Harrington admired him: every time he looked through his record of service he found something new. Twice, in the last year alone, King had narrowly escaped with his life, the ambush in Kabul had been closer than healthy and they had decided to rest him. In spite of the fact that there was always work for him, the Board decision had been unanimous. The trouble with Jed King was that whenever he was back in the UK he started to behave like a caged animal.

"Look Jed. Be sensible for Heaven's sake." Harrington sat back. "Courage or endurance…whatever you like to call it, is expendable and you've been through the hoop."

"Oh, come on, Peter." King shrugged disconsolately. "Cut out the Sandhurst stuff. Afghanistan was months ago. I've had more than enough leave now, and I'm as fit as ever I'll be. I've not taken to the bottle, y'know, not yet anyway." He frowned at the very thought of it. "Honestly, I'm fine…just hacked off with all this fiddling about in Brecon…Christ I was running ranges ten years ago as a bloody subaltern."

"But it's not the present I'm thinking about, it's in six months or a year's time. OK, you're feeling fine now but you do need a good break…*and* you know it. If you crack and we've got to come digging you out…then what? A fine old mess that'd be."

"So there's no chance of Kenya, then?" The two men looked at each other. "Come on, man," Jed muttered. "It's an absolute doddle and it's what…eight weeks?"

Harrington smiled thinly and shook his head. "Sorry chum. Look, get this little training number finished and it's three months away with the fairies...*and* it's the full whack of pay and allowances as well." He closed the file and caught Jed's eye. "Honestly, Jed, that's it. And it's from over there." Peter Harrington jerked his head towards the office behind him across the passage. "Orders're orders, my friend, so lie back and enjoy it."

The two rose. King reached for his jacket on the back of the chair, hitched a finger through the collar tab and swung it over his shoulder. "Oh well...can't say I didn't try but don't let me catch sight of the lucky bastard who's picked up this Kenya job." He wagged a finger at his handler. "Especially as I've done all his dirty work for him...jammy sod."

Harrington grinned and grabbed his coat. "How about a bite of lunch?" he quizzed. "On me this time."

Jed shook his head. "Thanks but no. I'm on my way." He glanced at his watch. "Late already."

"Somebody special?"

"*Me?*" Jed queried. "Hmm, hardly...it's just that if I hang around here I might get wrapped up in bloody cotton wool."

"Well, enjoy it while it lasts, my friend." Peter Harrington held out his hand. "But you never know...you're still on the standby list remember."

"Yeah, I know. And the moon might drop out." Jed took the other's hand and grinned. "Keep me briefed, Peter. I need it and it's not just the money either."

✳✳✳

Amanda watched him squat down in front of the music centre and begin to flick through the CDs. The afternoon in Richmond Park had been fun and she smiled to herself. They had walked as far as the track between the two Pen Ponds where she watched him work his way towards a herd of deer. He had moved quickly and easily between the trees, keeping the animals upwind until he had seen what he wanted. The hinds were heavily in calf and he sat watching carefully as they approached grazing quietly until one caught wind of him. She remembered laughing in delight as the hind coughed and stamped her foot defiantly before trotting off with her head high.

The ducks in the smaller pond, fat and replete, had definitely been full of the joys of spring, until he had picked her up and threatened to throw her in like a crust of stale bread. She had squealed in protest and kicked her feet causing a flurry of activity on the water. But then had come the drizzle and they had run back to the car, her hand in his. His kiss, with her back against the car door, had been rough and his face wet but he had laughed as he pushed her hair back. It was the first time she had seen him like this and she had reached up and pulled his face down. The second kiss was longer.

"Well, come on…Chinese or Indian?" she queried.

He half turned and overbalanced, putting out a hand to steady himself. "Curry?" He glanced back at her. "Yes? There's a good one on the corner of Cato Road. I'll give 'em a call." He rose just as the first strains of The Pastoral floated across the room. "There you are, see…listen to that. Quite the classical groupie you've found for yourself."

Amanda got up to meet him and put her arms around his neck. "Listen you," she half whispered. "You're not going to leave me here in the middle of the night again, are you?" She frowned at the look on his face. "You're not are you? Meanie. No, Jed…please."

"Six," he replied. "Well, six-thirty…but no later. Wales's bloody miles away, y'know."

"Good." Amanda stood on tiptoe and kissed him. "What's it now? Nine…Heaven's! Come on, let your chums in the curry shop know we're on our way.

⁕⁕⁕

Jed glanced through the curtains. The view from his dark and pokey second floor flat was as grim as ever, worse perhaps because the earlier drizzle had turned to steady rain. Everywhere he looked it was slanting down obliquely past the fluorescent orange streetlights. Acres of glistening wet tiled roofs stretched away as far as he could see. The traffic crossing Clapham Common and disappearing into Cavendish Road was making a meal of it, even the taxis were crawling in the downpour. The thought of three months of enforced idleness in this did not appeal and for a moment he wished himself back in the Brecons. There at least the air was clean and sweet and the springs ran straight from the hillside. He looked again and wrinkled his nose.

"What're you looking at?" Amanda, one arm propping up her head, had been watching him. The sheets on his bed which she had demanded to be changed before she got in last night were still cool against her skin. He had come in from the bathroom with a towel around his waist, so small that it looked ridiculous, like a mini-skirt split way up above the thigh.

"Just checking for bogey men." He wiped at the condensation on the window and bent forward to peer more closely before turning away and letting his towel fall. "None there. Ran away as soon as they saw me."

"Don't blame them." She glanced approvingly at the lean, freshly showered body and wriggled away to make room for him beside her.

"Your hair smells of the rain," Jed muttered. He had tight hold of her where he had pulled her back across the bed towards him. She had made a half-hearted effort to elbow him away but he had held her close and now she lay back against him with the contours of their two bodies curled snugly against each other. For a moment they were silent. "Hey, but listen. It's *you* who's going to be doing the runner, isn't it." Jed's mind went back to the curry supper on the Formica kitchen table when she told him of the likelihood of her going to Egypt. "All those grotty little Aye-rabs and randy Frenchmen. They'll be trying to put salt on your tail, y'know. "

"It's only for a week or so," she protested, forcing herself away then turning to face him. "Anyway nothing's for certain yet, we've got to hear what they've found first."

"Bet the harbour there's piled high with junk…full of old tyres and pipes…and Sainsbury's trolleys." Jed laughed to himself.

"Oh, I don't know," she said slowly. "They're long past all that sort of stuff. It's looking good…quite exciting really."

"Like you." He pushed her shoulders flat then rose above her and looked down. He could feel the warmth of her body and moved himself so her legs could part. "Just you get your wee self back home in one piece. Mmm? And no nasty thumb prints on that pretty little bum of yours." He leant forward slowly. As her mouth opened in response he felt her moist tongue flickering urgently.

2

Paris
Nina Joubert sat at the dressing table, her clothes for the evening laid out on the ornate double bed behind her. Her long blonde hair was hidden by the white towel wrapped, turban-like, round her head. Pursing her lips, she stared intently into the mirror with eyebrows raised, concentrating on her make-up as droplets of the still warm water ran from the nape of her neck onto the thick towelling robe.

The door of the bathroom opened and her husband appeared, silhouetted against the steam from the shower where he had been luxuriating. As usual he had turned down the hot water for the last thirty seconds and Nina had listened to his gasps and cries as he forced himself to withstand the icy jet. He stood in the doorway wiping the side of his head with a small hand towel before walking slowly across the room and standing behind his wife. She glanced up at him in the mirror, smiled briefly, then returned to the serious business of her face.

Half an hour later, Nina had dressed. Bending forward to pull the brush through her hair she turned towards her husband. Joubert, smoothing his white evening jacket, sensed she was watching and looked up. He bent down and kissed her neck. "Why the hell can't we be like this all the time?" he complained. "Life's so much easier and more fun without all the hassle."

"Oh, come on," she glanced into the mirror and caught his eyes. "You men are all the same…you know perfectly well that nobody's like this all the time. In any case," she pouted, "I reckon we do pretty well." Nina Joubert turned her back to the mirror and checked her dress. "Anyway," she said with a shrug, remembering his accusations earlier. "I can't help it if I've got my admirers. And, come to think of it, you don't do so badly yourself. Quite a lad, so I'm told. In any case, *you're* the one who's always saying that life out there's for living. Come on or we'll be late."

Marcel Joubert looked across at his wife and smiled proudly. She was dressed to kill. The simple, well fitting, black cocktail dress complimented her full figure perfectly. With her long mane of blonde hair swept back and her head inclined as she fixed her earrings, she was a stunning sight. Her hazel eyes and fair complexion belied her South American background although the full mouth and high cheekbones gave lie to a hint of native blood. Joubert could see that his last remark had touched a raw nerve. "OK, OK. Sorry I spoke. Just don't get them all fighting over you tonight. I'm the one that gets the flack from the jealous wives."

Nina tossed her head. "Oh rubbish. Don't give me that. You *love* it," she replied with a smile. "I've seen you sitting there waiting to pick up the bits." Joubert laughed and watched as his wife filled her evening bag. As soon as she had arrived from Brazil the intelligent, beautiful and fabulously rich nineteen year old had quickly gravitated towards the most influential and best-connected circles in which she began to socialize freely.

***

In 1970, her mother, Maria Christina Almeida had met and fallen madly in love with Tomasso Buscetta. Buscetta, then a leading Sicilian Mafia supremo, was living in luxurious circumstances amidst the Sao Paulo high society. Also, and unknown to her, he was directing the huge narcotics trade between South America and western Europe via Brazil. Life for the young Nina had been pampered and exotic but she soon tired of the juvenile society that surrounded her.

One of Maria's cousins, Edouardo Conte, was attached to the Brazilian Embassy in Paris and Nina was packed off to the care of distant relatives, as far removed as possible from the sources of temptation. The idea was for *'la petite'* to cool her heels in a more refined environment. It was a disaster: Paris took one look at the exotic young Brazilian, opened its arms and beckoned. Nina Almeida needed no second bidding. The Paris embassy circuit offered countless opportunities to the young, full-blooded beauty from Sao Paulo. Shrewd and ambitious, Nina moved quickly towards the rich, the famous and those in power. Then, a year later, she met Marcel Joubert.

Barely noticing him at first, she had gradually been attracted by the solitary figure standing alone by the door at the reception. Eventually she caught his eye, smiled and he had responded shyly. She found herself drawn towards the boyish, almost effeminate good looks, the large dark eyes and his steady gaze. A week later they met again when they were introduced formally. The bright young graduate from the exclusive École Nationale d'Administration had recently begun an appointment in the Paris City Hall where he had been selected to work as a *'Conseiller Special''* or aide in the private office of the Mayor. Nina found him different to the other more pushy, brash members of the society around her.

Not until much later did she learn that Joubert had suffered a hard, lonely childhood. As a boy he was tall for his age, so tall that he had outgrown his strength, did not play games at school and was bullied mercilessly. Later, although frequently bereft of male company, he began to notice that girls were drawn to him. He found their company safe, amusing and, before long, exciting. And he was clever. He learned to think quickly and to choose his words carefully. The suffering taught him to be streetwise and he learned to anticipate trouble. Guile and cunning became his weapons.

Convinced that she was in love with the tall, quiet young bureaucrat, Nina accepted his hand to the delight of her family and amid fervent hopes that the *enfant terrible* would now settle quietly into married life. She did not. Cravenly ambitious, she set about cultivating whatever contacts she thought might further her husband's career and her own position in society. Surprised at first, Joubert soon realised that through Nina's connections doors opened. Among those who courted her attention was Roger Trinquet, the massively powerful and influential Mayor of Paris – Joubert's boss. In addition she decided to develop her discreet and supposedly clandestine affair with Alain Déschampes, the French Minister of Culture. Life was fun, until Pietro Conte arrived from Corleone, a small hilltop town in Sicily.

Over dinner at the Villa Vinci Italian restaurant Conte talked at length about the growing Corleone business interests in Paris and Marseille. Gradually and subtly he steered the conversation towards the need to extend their network of contacts with those in positions of influence and authority. He impressed upon them that he and a number of other Sicilians were major shareholders in Commerz Deutsch, the international construction company that was heavily involved across the city. The company, already well established, was looking to extend its contracts. He was well aware, also, of Joubert's position in the City Hall and of Nina's personal connections.

Some time previously, Joubert had decided to distance himself as far as possible from those who were acquainted with his father-in-law. Their business interests were nothing to do with him and could never be so. Since taking up his appointment he had noticed how his position, so close to the seat of power, had been recognised by those seeking access to the Mayor. Usually it began with the unimportant or innocuous invitations - to dinner, a box at Longchamps, the Opera and so forth. He had become wary, doing his best to refuse the more obvious approaches, but Nina revelled in the introductions, a situation that soon led to heated arguments.

"What the hell's the matter with you?" she would cry. "They're good friends of Papa" or "Everyone else does it. What's so special about us that we have to pick and choose like this? You're being so silly. Well, *I'm* going. You can stay and look after the kids." The words would ring in Marcel's ears and he became increasingly torn between supporting his wife and embarking upon practices he knew to be dangerous. He tried to strike a diplomatic balance, accepting the invitations Nina liked most but, inevitably, those were the ones offered by her father's friends or others who were seeking favours. As the invitations became ever more difficult to decline, so the arguments became more tempestuous. Yet, in spite of her ways, her indiscretions and her affairs, he was proud of her high profile and the attention she drew.

***

"Oh come on, Marcel. Don't you ever listen," Nina chided as they settled into the back of the waiting car. "It's time you learned who's who with Papa's friends. Honestly, it's getting embarrassing. The Salvatores are giving the party – *you* accepted the invitation for heaven's sake. *You* told *me* that he's the banker behind Pietro's Commerz Deutsch. They've got some folk over from Sicily – the Torrinis. She's fun but he's a ghastly little creep."

Joubert knew only too well who was hosting the evening's engagement. Enrico Salvatore had already approached him about the impending contracts for the city development. Initially he had warmed to the man's friendly and persuasive manner but soon detected another side beyond the bonhomie. Salvatore, thickset and swarthy, exuded power. He was used to getting his own way, often publicly bullying into submission those who challenged him. Joubert sensed that if he was to help Salvatore on this occasion then the banker would be back for more. Once he had access to the Mayor's office, Salvatore would never let go. It was as if a long arm was reaching out, trying to curl round him and draw him in. But, if he were to ignore the requests he knew were coming, what would be the reaction of Nina and her family?

A year or so ago, Nina had talked about the Sicilian Families. They were, she explained, not necessarily blood relations as such but more like a clan or tribe. Although based on the lineage of one family tree, outsiders were occasionally invited to join. Selected with meticulous care, they were made to swear solemnly the oath of allegiance. After that their loyalty to the Family would be total, absolute and forever. Some Families were relatively small, numbering less than a hundred, others were vast organisations. Through her father Nina was connected to the Corleonese, one of the largest, and it was they who were behind Commerz Deutsch, using Salvatore as their banker.

"But don't go mentioning anything about all that tonight for God's sake," she warned. "Just remember that what dear old Enrico Salvatore has to say counts for a lot in this part of the world. I wonder if the Trinquets will be there," she mused. "I wouldn't put it past Enrico to have them along too."

Nina smiled at the thought of Roger Trinquet, now firmly installed as the Mayor of Paris. It was more than four years since they had first met when she had at once been attracted by the vitality and power of the man. Before long he had made a pass at her but she had kept him at bay until Marcel had applied for and been appointed to his post in the City Hall. A year later Trinquet had become Mayor and had selected Joubert to be one of his Principal Aides, working directly to him. It was then that Nina allowed him his way and the affair had continued ever since.

3

The party at Palais de Chaillot was a success. Angelica Salvatore had seated fourteen around the long antique dining table in the penthouse apartment just off Avenue Mandel. After a sumptuous meal prepared by an Italian chef, they gathered in the elegant drawing room and sat enraptured as a young Italian violinist from the Orchestre Nationale played for more than an hour. Soon afterwards, as the first guests began to leave, Salvatore caught Joubert's eye, signalling subtly for them to remain behind. When finally they were on their own, he took Marcel into the booklined study across the hall.

Apprehensive and on his guard, Joubert took the chair Salvatore offered as he shut the door with a flourish and crossed briskly to a beautifully preserved miniature cabinet. Moments later he turned, holding out a bottle of vintage Remy Martin and a box of Havanas. Joubert's smile and nod of appreciation hid his revulsion at the theatricals of the sweating, corpulent figure in front of him. Drawing up a chair with his foot, Salvatore pushed the brandy and cigars across the table and sat heavily. "OK, Marcel," he growled. Leaning forward, he placed his elbows on the table and scratched at his bulbous nose. "Let's talk, huh?"

Joubert knew what was coming but waited patiently. "It's these contracts, my friend. We've gotta consider them and there's not much time left." Salvatore paused as if in thought. "Commerz Deutsch needs the big one, the job on the peripherique around the city. You're well placed to see it comes our way. Huh?" He lifted his head, exhaled the thick smoke then stabbed a finger at Joubert. "We need that one badly. It would get us into the city and we could move on from there. What d'ya reckon? Of course, I could always ask Roger Trinquet direct," Salvatore continued. He pulled a thoughtful face as he looked at the piece of tobacco he had picked off his tongue. "He owes me a favour or two and I know he wants to push things our way. But that's not the point." Joubert watched in disgust as Salvatore slid a large hairy finger into his mouth in pursuit of trapped food. "You see, it's *you* that should be seeing this one through. It wouldn't be lost on Trinquet, you know. He'd stand to gain and you'd look smart, real smart." Salvatore threw his head back, drained the last of his brandy and reached clumsily for the bottle.

Joubert moved uneasily. "Look, Enrico," he began hesitantly. "I'd love to help, but it's all far too late now." He gave Salvatore a plaintive look and opened his hands. "It'd be devilishly hard to swing something like that." He paused, shaking his head slowly. "But why don't you hang on a bit? There're plenty more coming along, you know. Some very good ones too. We'll be putting out tenders for the new barriers around Ile St Louis…down on the river, across from Notre Dame." Sipping from his glass, Joubert continued. "Then there's Le Bourget. We're going to be enlarging the whole complex and there'll be some excellent contracts out there – a new runway and a complete overhaul of the servicing facilities. That's big stuff, Enrico, not to be sneezed at."

"*Poof,*" Salvatore waved his arm dismissively. "Chicken feed. And in any case, the peripherique contract's bound to lead to other things. Whoever gets this one'll be in for the duration. Come on, man, let's cut out the crap. Fix it."

"Well." Joubert looked down. He felt the Italian's eyes on him and was thinking fast. "I'll see what can be done, but it's not going to be easy and I can't make any promises." He paused once more. "All these things have to go before the committee, y'know, and I'm not even a member." Then he shrugged. "And once the decisions've been, the Mayor himself puts his signature behind it."

"Yes, yes," Salvatore waved his hand, a note of impatience creeping into his voice. "Roger and I have already had a word. But let me tell you, he's going to watch you playing this one." Enrico smiled and leaned forward "Listen, Marcel, you're not stupid. Huh? We're all in this and I need that contract. What's more, you'll be doing your career no harm at all. And as for rewarding your efforts, well…" Salvatore drained his glass and wiped his mouth. "Roger and I thought you might like to move apartments. He's got something in mind that's much more your scene. I think Nina's been shown it already." Salvatore smiled lecherously, staring at Joubert. "Come on, Marcel. You're not plain dumb. You know what I'm talking about?"

The two studied each other across the table. Joubert's heart was racing. If Salvatore knew about Nina and Trinquet, and if the Mayor knew of Salvatore's request for Commerz Deutsch then it could be done. It would be difficult but it could be done. "All right, Enrico," he said hesitantly, thinking how best to reply. "I see what you're getting at. It seems to make sense and I'll see…see what can be done."

✳✳✳

All in all it had been a profitable evening. On the way home Nina had snuggled up to him in the taxi. Once home they had a quick drink before going upstairs. Now he, too, was feeling good.

Momentarily, before dropping his gaze to where the lower half of her silk night-dress had fallen open exposing two long, well tanned thighs, he had caught her look. Her eyes were alive. Placing his hands on her slender shoulders, he pressed gently, kneading the soft flesh between his fingers and thumbs. She stopped and closed her eyes before leaning forward and resting her head between the folds of his towelling robe.

"No, Marcel. Not now, cherie" she murmured slowly. "Please, not. I'm so tired…and it's late." Feeling her body respond to his touch, he continued, gradually increasing the pressure. "Mmmm. My God, that's lovely, though. Oh…yes," she whispered, lifting her arms lazily. Marcel leaned forward, slipped his hands under the silk and cupped a full, soft breast in each hand. His fingers teased the hard nipples as his lips closed on her shoulder before parting to let his tongue feather lightly up the side of the neck. When he reached her ear he flickered delicately as he drew in his breath. She gasped then moved her head against his before rolling away.

"You're a beast, Monsieur Joubert. Nothing more, nothing less. D'you know that? Half the time you drive me mad, but now this. Sometimes I could kill you," she paused to kiss him on the mouth. "But then, sometimes I could eat you, too…what's more you're making me beg for it. Loving every minute, aren't you?" She laughed lightly, brushing the hair back from his forehead. He held her gaze and pulled her gently towards him, lifting her nightdress until she raised her arms to help him ease it over her head.

As he sank to his knees, he felt her hands in his hair guiding him towards her. Brushing his lips across her soft blonde hairs, he moved his hands over her thighs then behind her, pulling her fragrant body towards his face and caressing her taut buttocks. He glanced at her then bent forward again his mouth moving slowly. Gently and slowly he kissed the soft moist lips before looking up once more. "What was all that about, mm?" he asked quietly, rising to his feet. His fingers trailed lightly down her cheek to her mouth. "Some kind of a state-ment…or just an invitation, perhaps?"

"There's no difference," she shrugged, picking her clothes from the bed and draping them over the chaise longue. They fell together and lay back, their mouths now locked. Nina half turned to lie on her back, parted her legs and reached out for her husband. Opening her legs further, she lifted them high and crossed them behind his back, drawing him down urgently.

✳✳✳

By noon the following day Joubert's mind was made up. He knew what was required of him and how he had to set about it. If it was in Trinquet's own interest for Commerz Deutsch to win the major contract then he would see to it. If he succeeded then everyone, and that included Nina and himself, would stand to gain. It would mean testing the water with a number of committee members but that was the name of the game.

Chapter Five

Paris

The evening before the committee met was bitterly cold. Although now mid-March, an icy north-east wind straight from the Ardennes blew flurries of snow along the pavements and into doorways. Heads were bowed, scarves and collars were drawn tight as people struggled along, slipping on the pathways as they hurried towards the warmth of their homes.

Joubert climbed the last few steps of the escalator and headed towards the Exit of the Metro at Avenue Martin. Outside it was dark. He stopped briefly at the main entrance to pick up an evening paper, dropping the change into the hat of an elderly man playing an accordion. As he did up his coat, he paused for a few seconds, listening to the plaintive music. He was about to move on when he felt a hand on his arm. Turning quickly he saw a shortish, bespectacled figure in a dark overcoat at his side. "Excuse me, Monsieur. Are you, by any chance Monsieur Joubert, Monsieur Marcel Joubert?"

Joubert glanced around suspiciously, then peered more closely at the nonde-script character in front of him. "Well, yes, that's my name," he replied warily. "Who're you and what do you want?"

"Perhaps we could step inside the café for a minute, Monsieur. It won't take more than a few moments. I have a message for you and you will want to hear what I have to say." Suddenly they were buffeted by a powerful gust of wind, causing the figure in front of him to sway unsteadily and grab at his hat.

"Look," Joubert called above the noise of the traffic. "If you've got something for me, tell me here and now. I haven't got time to waste in cafes. It's getting late and I want to get home."

"All right, Monsieur. But I don't like talking out here in the cold. However, if you insist." He beckoned Joubert closer. "Now, Monsieur, I believe you work in the

City Hall, for the Mayor himself? Yes?" Without waiting for a reply, he continued. "And I believe they are due to award some big construction contracts tomorrow." He looked up at Joubert questioningly, blew on his fingers and stamped his feet.

"Look, who the *hell* are you? It's none of your bloody business who I am or what I do for a living." Joubert glanced nervously at the young woman who had turned surprised at his raised voice. He lowered his tone to an angry hiss and tried to push his way past. "Now then, if you'll excuse me..."

"Just a moment, Monsieur. Don't get angry." The stranger grabbed Joubert's arm with surprising strength. "I'm just the messenger and, I can assure you, it's all very much to do with you. Perhaps it would be wise for you to hear me out and then think carefully about what I have to say, Monsieur Joubert."

Joubert stopped, alarmed at hearing his name spoken so formally. He had detected a note of steel in the voice and his pulse quickened. Little red warning lights were beginning to flash. He turned back to the man. "OK. Let's hear what you've got to say, then let me get on."

"Well, Monsieur, it's probably nothing at all. I don't know what it means but they told me you would want to hear. Does the name Corleone mean anything, Monsieur?" Joubert felt himself staring at the face in front of him. "You see I was given this name and told to tell you that they, the Corleones...Monsieur Salvatore, that is, are after the city contracts. I was told to tell you that they should *not* be considered. Not the Corleones, not at all. You would do well to reject their tender, Monsieur." The stranger sniffed, wiped the end of his nose and shivered convulsively before continuing. "I was told to tell you that if they are awarded the contracts then there will be much trouble, Monsieur. Those concerned could pay dearly, and your name was mentioned. That's all, Monsieur. I'll bid you a very good evening." The little man touched his hat, turned and disappeared into the Metro crowds.

Joubert stood motionless. He had never received a threat like that before and his heart was pounding. It had been as clear and direct as if it had been from the muzzle of a gun. He was being warned about awarding the big peripherique contract to Enrico Salvatore's Commerz Deutsch. If he chose to ignore them there would be trouble, but from whom? Rapidly he went through the names of the other contenders. One name kept re-occurring – Zagossi Internationale. There was something about that name. He had heard of the man behind the bid, an Italian called Maletto. Tony Maletto, yes, that was him. He remembered Nina talking about them. Something about being involved with another Italian – Gambino, a Mario Gambino. He shivered in the cold, threw his scarf around his neck and hurried onwards, determined to find out what he could in the few hours remaining.

※※※

The big apartment was bright and warm. Joubert took off his coat and scarf, wiped the tears of cold from his eyes and swept up the two children. Lucille, now almost twelve, had the blonde good looks of her mother while Pietro, just five, promised to retain his father's dark hair and swarthy complexion. They grabbed the sleeves of his jacket excitedly and led him to the large sofa where the three of them sat chatting about the day's activities.

Pietro, soon tired of the conversation, wandered off leaving Lucille pressed against her father, both arms wrapped around his. A short while later he reluctantly moved her arms then smoothed her hair. "Come, come, ma petite, I've got to get on." He bent down and kissed the top of her head. "I've a busy day tomorrow and lots of homework to do. And I must have some time with your mother as well. Later on, when you're in bed, you can tell me about your plans for the morning."

Joubert wandered into the kitchen where Nina, dressed casually in jeans and checked shirt, was preparing supper. She looked up, smiled and pouted her lips in a kiss. He decided to tell her about the meeting at the entrance to the Metro and the message that had been passed. As soon as he mentioned Maletto, Nina stiffened, scowling. "Don't touch that lot," she cried, waving the short vegetable knife at him. "Honestly, Marcel, don't go near them. Those Gambinos are a dreadful crowd. Don't you remember I told you that Enrico's younger brother asked one of the Gambino girls, Maria, I think she's called, to marry him and she turned him down. Turned him *down*, for God's sake. Can you believe it? Mind you, he must have been mad." Nina's voice rose and she shivered with disgust. "How *dare* she, the little slut? How dare any Gambino female reject an offer like that from a Corleone. Who the hell does she think she is?" She tossed her head angrily. "Probably from Corso Tukory up one of those back alleys behind the railway station. Still there waggling her arse, I'll bet. Little bitch."

"So you reckon they're pretty harmless, these Gambinos?"

"Absolutely. They're a spent force. Honestly, no one has anything to do with them. Forget about the little weirdo who stopped you. Don't know how he had the nerve to even mention Corleone. Cheeky little shit." Marcel smiled. Mention the big Sicilian Families and Nina would be away. Out it would come, pure undiluted Sicilian invective. Blonde or not there was a whole lot of Latin there. He poured himself a drink, went into the study and picked up the phone. An hour later he emerged when Nina called him to say good night to the children.

2

Two days later the contracts were announced. Salvatore's Commerz Deutsch was awarded the peripherique flyovers, two other companies picked up three more contracts between them but there was nothing for Zagossi Internationale. Paris was in the grip of a cold spell followed by days of driving rain and most outside construction work came to a halt. The children were unable to play any form of organised sport, so the school staff took them for afternoon walks instead.

Each day Lucille Joubert was taken to Trois Soeurs, an exclusive private school at the Musée Cernhuishi near Parc Monceau. Regularly, after lunch, a long croc- odile of closely escorted young girls would enter the park under the fussy super- vision of the nuns. There they would walk in procession along the metalled paths around the edge of the lake, laughing and joking before breaking up near some large cedars where they would feed the waterfowl.

The long line of children had just reached the trees and split into groups when three powerful motorbikes drove into the park and raced towards the girls. A large group of frightened youngsters became isolated by the bikes that roared around them in small circles, packing them tightly together. Three men in helmets and black leathers leaped from the pillions and ran into the middle of the tightly packed mass of screaming children, caught hold of Lucille Joubert and dragged her to one side. One held her roughly by the arms, while the others tore off her coat before stripping her half naked.

The tallest then drew a heavy riding whip from one of his boots and began to thrash the wriggling child, the vicious blows biting deep into the delicate flesh. Another lashed out at the nearest of the children. One of the nuns rushed forward but was knocked to the ground, the others remained huddled protec- tively around the children. The pitiful screams of Lucille Joubert were drowned by the powerful bikes which continued to circle the terrified group with their engines revving loudly.

The assault was over in seconds. The men leapt on board the waiting bikes which roared off in the direction of the Bois de Boulogne leaving the hysterical group of nuns and young girls. The prostrate figure of Lucille lay still, her body a mass of livid weals.

✳✳✳

Three hours later the Jouberts sat together on the sofa in their drawing room staring blankly at the doctor in front of them. Marcel, looking white and shocked, sat with his arm around his wife. Nina had stopped crying but remained trembling with a handkerchief to her mouth. The young doctor, not long out of medical school, had been called to the house and had spent over an hour with Lucille and her distraught parents. Upstairs a nurse was settling the heavily sedated and bandaged child.

"Well, Monsieur, Madame," the doctor said quietly. "This is a most terrible business but I do implore you to talk to the police. They will be here soon, that's for sure. If you really have no idea who was behind this then you must tell them just that, even negative information helps. Next time somebody might be killed. You must understand that."

Nina shook her head and began to cry. "Oh, my God. I can't believe it. How could anyone do this?" She looked up the doctor. "Yes...of course. I mean...we will, but I need to think first. I need a bit of time." She buried her head in her hands and began to sob loudly.

The doctor looked at Joubert glumly, raised his eyebrows and sighed. "Perhaps you should get on with this as soon as we have gone, Monsieur. The authorities need whatever help you might be able to give them. They will need to take statements from everyone and the sooner the better. There is little more that we can do for the moment." He rose to his feet and picked up his bag, waiting for his companion to join them.

"She's asleep now and looks much more comfortable," the nurse reported, smiling reassuringly as she came down the stairs. "I'll be back tomorrow to change the dressings. Please call if you are worried about anything."

Joubert showed them to the door then turned to his wife. "Nina, cherie, listen. The police will be here any minute...we have to talk to them; tell them everything. Look, I'll give them a call right now." He turned towards the phone in the hall.

"For God's sake," Nina screamed. "Are you mad? Have you no idea what all this is about." Joubert stopped, aghast. "It's those bloody contracts of yours," she yelled. "I thought you knew how this Paris of yours worked. The whole goddam place is stiff with filthy corruption and now we've been dragged into it." She got out of the chair, her hair dishevelled and mascara smudged with tears. "The police won't do a sodding thing. They'll just stamp around all over the place trying to look important. I can tell you who was behind this afternoon without the Chief of Police holding my hand. Zagossi Internationale, that's who. They reckon you've given them two fingers and they don't like it. That's what it's all about. Simple as that."

Joubert stood ashen faced shaking his head slowly. "I can't see them ever doing anything like that. I mean, they're a well-known, bona fide company for Heaven's sake. They deal with us at the office. They're a proper organisation, highly regarded and quoted on the Bourse." He waved his arms in despair. "They'd never behave like that."

"Oh, can't they just," Nina cried. "Then what the hell happened to Lucille? Who do you think picked her out of the crowd and did that? Someone had a damn good reason and, my God, they've made their point."

"Well, if that's the case, let's make a clean break of it," Joubert replied, his voice rising. "Let's tell them everything we know. Put a stop to all this shitty business before it goes any further. What about all the witnesses for Heaven's sake...the nuns, all the kids and whoever else was there? We can't just sit here doing nothing. Come on."

"Oh, for fuck's sake, Marcel. Get with it for crying out loud!" Nina came across the room and stood in front of him. Her eyes were blazing. "Listen, will you. These people don't run scared, you know. We've got ourselves caught between two rival Sicilian Families. That's what. And what's more they're using bloody sadists against *kids*. They've gone mad; they're power crazy and couldn't give a shit for you, me, or anyone. What they did to Lucille was just a warning. Say one word to the police and you up the stakes. If you do that I'm off, I promise you." Nina's voice rose to a shout. "If you think I'm staying here caught up in all this madness, you can think again. Any more bright ideas like that and I'll be on the next plane with the children…so don't push me," she screamed, storming out of the room.

Joubert walked slowly across to the bay windows and stared morosely at the grey landscape. He felt sickened, deflated and, now, the cold chill of fear. It was Nina who told him that the Gambinos behind Zagossi were a spent force. She was the one who pushed him to dinner with the Salvatores and had urged him to help with the contracts. And now this. But what else could he have done? Had he used his head and followed his instincts he would have resisted Salvatore's pestering. But then what? A word from the Sicilian, Enrico Salvatore, to Trinquet that his young aide was being uncooperative and he would be out on his ear. And who was going to touch a reject from the Mayor's office? Either way the outlook was beginning to look bleak. He stood with his head bowed and hands thrust deep into his trouser pockets.

The family remained housebound for three days until Lucille recovered her composure and the wounds began to heal. It was a further week before she returned to school. Three times the police called but each time they were sent on their way, the last time after an angry scene. Nina and Marcel discussed the event endlessly. Undoubtedly it was something to do with his job but they were unable to decide if the attack was an act of revenge or a warning for Joubert to show more consideration. The confrontation at the Metro should have put them on their guard yet they had chosen to ignore the signal.

It was, so Joubert knew, a classic Mafia warning, just one finger raised but a warning nonetheless. Nina would have none of it. "There's no such thing," she insisted. "All this Mafia stuff's just one great myth. Sicilian Families, yes. Big business, yes. Crooked business, maybe, but that's the sum of it. Who and where are your Mafia? And don't tell me that's the only thing that's crooked in Paris. The whole stinking rotten place is *stiff* with corruption. They're *all* at it for whatever they can get away with."

✳✳✳

Joubert, determined to brazen it out and buy himself more time, went back to the office. Nina pulled her life together and went back to her social round. Some months ago she had started to take piano lessons. Now, twice every week she would drive out to the Boulevard Maurice Barres at the edge of the Bois de Boulogne for a lesson with the renowned Signor Torelli.

Despite warnings from her husband to vary the time of her lessons and her routes to and fro, she never listened and a pattern emerged. Three weeks later, late as usual, she was driving fast towards the Palais des Congres and had begun to navigate the Porte Maillot where the road works forced the traffic into two lanes. Approaching the interface between Avenues Charles de Gaulle and de Neuilly she was forced to slow right down, hemmed in by the traffic.

She failed to see the heavy cement lorry coming alongside until it was too late. A loud blast on his horn made her swerve towards the wall on her right but the huge front wheel of the lorry was already grating noisily along the left hand side of her Fiat, forcing the small car against the side of the underpass and into the concrete wall. The car scraped along the wall before the truck's two sets of rear wheels slammed it heavily against a concrete pillar. Nina screamed and clutched desperately at the steering wheel as the small car spun back into the traffic lane before coming to a halt. Neither she nor the other drivers noticed the lorry as it moved away into the heavy morning traffic. She slumped back in her seat staring at the blood trickling down her face and on to her cream blouse from the deep gash just above her hair line. When she tried to move a sharp pain shot down her left arm from the point where her collarbone had snapped. She was unable to move her fingers. Vaguely she heard distant voices calling and sounds of the door being wrenched open before she lost consciousness.

***

Marcel Joubert was now a worried man. It was obvious that those behind the Zagossi Internationale enterprise had been infuriated at losing the contracts and were now driving their message home. Nina, sensing they were now becoming dangerously entangled in the murky jungle of the city business, begged him to ask for a change.

"Look," she pleaded, "You've done more than your bit for Trinquet and now you're exposed to this lot. Enrico and Roger Trinquet are both riding high on what you've done and owe you one hell of a vote of thanks. Honestly, Marcel, ask for a change *now* while the going's good. Roger will be able to fix something, for God's sake. First it was poor little Lucille. Christ, that was a nightmare," she muttered. "Then somebody tried to murder me in the underpass. Look at this," she cried pointing at her arm in a sling. "What next? You? Pietro? Get out of this before one of us is killed." Nina put a hand to her face and shook her head. "I can't take any more. You *must* go and see them about a change." As his arms closed around her, she leaned against him and began to weep.

His mind was racing, calculating the odds. He had shown favour to a friend of Trinquet's but the plan had backfired while those he had chosen to ignore had declared their hand. They were unlikely to forgive him. It was time to move. "Yes, all right," he said. "Enough's enough. I'll try to get in to see Trinquet tomorrow." He paused. "You're right. I've done him and the others well enough and he knows it." He felt her breath on the nape of his neck. "I'm due a move anyway, so I'll ask for it now."

3

Early the following morning Joubert hurriedly arranged two meetings. Looking through the contract tenders he found Zagossi Internationale's number and called them first. After a number of wrong connections, he was put through to the manager's secretary. He heard a click followed by muffled voices before he spoke to a man who announced himself as the manager. Joubert recognised the voice immediately. It was Maletto, the man who had dealt with the contractor's office several weeks ago. He introduced himself curtly then asked for a meeting with Signor Gambino as soon as it could be arranged.

The sudden request took Maletto by surprise. He replied deferentially that Signor Gambino was out of the country at present but was due back shortly. Promising to arrange a meeting he suggested lunch. If he was agreeable then he, Maletto, would confirm the plan and get back to him within the hour. Joubert replaced the receiver and rubbed his chin.

Now was the time: it had to be done right now and he lifted the receiver again. His call to Trinquet's outer office was taken by Marie, his Personal Assistant, and he persuaded her to book him in for a meeting at the end of the day. After he had done so, he sat back, thinking hard. Could it be that Trinquet knew he, Joubert, was aware of the situation between him and his wife? The very idea intrigued him and, to his surprise, the more he thought about it the more it excited him. He collapsed into his chair and gazed into space. What would be the scene, he wondered, when he and Nina met? Would Trinquet flirt amorously with his wife and she with him? What would he do with her, with his hands and his mouth and how would she react? How would they lie together making love – slowly and languorously taking their time, or urgently and passionately? And what if Trinquet realised that he was aware? How would the Mayor face his aide and what would he have to say to his request later that afternoon?

✳✳✳

As soon as Joubert entered the spacious office, Roger Trinquet rose from behind his desk, smiled warmly and waved the younger man to a seat. "My goodness, Marcel, you Jouberts have been in the wars recently. I've been expecting you to come and have a chat. How are things and how's the family?" Trinquet ran a hand through his grey, receding hair and took his seat. Tall and distinguished, the Mayor of Paris, dressed elegantly as always, seemed very much his calm, unruffled self. Although in his early sixties, Trinquet retained a youthful and vigorous appearance. Blessed with a keen wit and phenomenal memory he drove his staff hard yet retained a ready smile. As he welcomed his aide, his eyes twinkled merrily.

Joubert glanced down at his hands and paused. "Thank you, Monsieur. You're very kind to spare me the time and I daresay you already know about my request." He took a deep breath. " I've come to ask you to release me from my appointment, to give me a change. Perhaps a move to Quai d'Orsay or something like that." He was surprised at the steadiness of his own voice. "As you know, life's been difficult these last few weeks. There's been a lot of pressure just now and things seem to have gone mad. For some strange reason, somebody out there doesn't like us Jouberts." He caught his breath. "I can't imagine who or why but Nina and I have had enough."

Trinquet crossed his legs and gently drummed the ends of his fingers against each other. "I thought you might be coming to see me about this and I understand exactly. In fact I discussed you with Alain Déschampes, the Minister of Culture, when we met a couple of days back." He saw Joubert frowning. "You know Déschampes of course?" he queried.

Joubert leaned forward and nodded. "Yes, naturally, but not in person you understand."

"No, of course not. But I rather agree that you could do with a break." He raised a hand. "Alain is an old friend and we spoke at some length about your predicament. He appears to have heard quite a bit about you on the grapevine and would like to see you." Roger Trinquet smiled reassuringly. "He mentioned one or two things but I will leave all that to him. Mind you, I told him I wanted you back," he laughed. "Ask Marie to call his bureau and fix an appointment."

Later Joubert told Nina about the meeting and the appointment with Déschampes but omitted to say anything about his lunch date with Gambino. She was overjoyed. "Oh, that's brilliant," she cried. "Just think of it, away from it all somewhere. I know Alain will do what he can. He's fun and he quite likes us, you know," she added as an afterthought.

"Yes, I know."

That evening they dined at one of their favourite bistros – Beaujolais d'Auteuil – tucked away down a narrow, badly lit side street off Rue de Passy. Nina was ecstatic. Her laughter and chatter had returned at last and Marcel noticed how men at other tables would look across at her before glancing enviously at him. They pondered over the future, what it might bring and where it might take them. They remained at the table long after the meal was over, whispering to each other and laughing happily as their fingers touched over the coffee cups.

Later, back in their apartment, Marcel found some old cassettes. Shoes off they danced slowly to the music of their courtship days, like a couple of teenagers. A while later they rolled slowly onto the bed, giggling childishly.

***

Joubert was ushered into Déschampes' sumptuously decorated office. Again he experienced the strange sensation that he was coming face to face with a man who knew far too much about his wife. Was this really the price he was going to have to pay for having such a beautiful and ambitious partner. Was this really what politics in Paris was all about? He shrugged. High stakes needed good cards and he was now in the game.

As he entered the room, he saw a neat, balding man standing by the window that looked out onto the large gardens. Déschampes turned and walked briskly towards him holding out both hands in greeting, and motioning him to a chair. For someone so diminutive, Déschampes had a surprisingly deep, soft voice. He spoke slowly, never once pausing to check or falter over his words. He had heard about Joubert from the Mayor and had read his folder, he advised, waving casually towards a green file on the desk.

He would be delighted to help. "I have something coming up that might just suit you. It's out of the way and might give you a chance to catch your breath." He went on to ask Joubert if he knew anything about diving or marine archaeology, or if he had heard about the Franco-Egyptian dive taking place at Alexandria on the northern coast of Egypt.

Joubert felt himself tense and he stared back at the large, clever eyes set deeply into the thin, almost skeletal face then shook his head. Déschampes took off his half moon spectacles and dangled them between his fingers. "None of that matters, really" he continued. "The reason for us sending someone out there is to take the pressure off the divers. They're a civilian organisation albeit a very high powered one, funded by a massive Swiss trust. The leader, a French national called Gideon, Francois Gideon, has pulled together a top team and a few weeks ago they got on to the lost city of the Pharaohs." Joubert nodded. Déschampes glanced at him and paused.

"You may have read about the dive, it's been going on for sometime but you won't have heard that they've just found what they reckon to be the treasures.

The Louvre and British Museum have warned us that the find could be vast. They've known for years what the palaces were supposed to contain but everyone's believed that it all vanished centuries ago. Plundered like the tombs out in the desert." He pulled a wry face. "It's all very exciting but requires careful handling, and that's where I thought you might come in."

He went on to explain that for sometime the find had been kept secret, but eventually, rumours had begun to circulate. The team had been under constant pressure from the media. They were being pestered by museums also, by their sponsors and by an increasing numbers of tourists. The whole project was in danger of falling behind schedule and they had requested help in the shape of an experienced government *fonctionaire* to relieve the pressure. The Egyptians, while doing their best, were finding it difficult to deal with the interest shown by Europe and America. "The request came in last week, via our Embassy in Cairo," he continued. "Having seen your name at the bottom of the list I thought I would ask you first." He paused and looked up, laughing quietly.

Joubert stared at Déschampes. He could imagine the expression on Nina's face when he told her. "How long before you want a firm answer?" he queried.

"Talk it over with the family and let me know in a couple of days. But if you don't want it there'll be an ugly rush, that's for sure." Déschampes went into some detail of what would be expected of him. "You would be my man on the ground and would have the title of Deputy Director," he continued. "Gideon would be responsible for everything to do with the dive and you would look after everything else. We would let you select a few staff assistants and you would report back to me through our people at the embassy. How does that sound?"

"It sounds absolutely marvellous," he replied, grinning widely. "We'll talk it over tonight and I'll let you know in the morning." Joubert left the office and made his way slowly home trying to clear his mind. His emotions were mixed. It sounded amazing and he was certain that Nina would love the idea but there were a number of questions he needed to answer. What would be the reaction of Enrico Salvatore and the Corleones who had been pressing him so hard? Would they continue to breath down his neck when he was out there? They would expect him to return to Paris and to continue producing the goods, that was for sure. And what about the other lot – the Gambinos? They had forced him out of his last job and wouldn't want to let him slip from their grasp.

4

Joubert reached across from the filing cabinet, picked up the phone and listened to a female voice asking him to hold the line. A moment later he heard Maletto's voice and grimaced. "Aha, Monsieur Joubert. It's Maletto here, Tony Maletto." Maletto coughed heavily and Joubert could hear his breath wheezing with exertion. "Remember me? Yes? We spoke the other day about meeting up with Signor Mario Gambino. Well, he's back in town and would be delighted to meet you. He's agreed that lunch would be best. He says perhaps you know Il Guildo Rebellato, close by to Maison de Balzac in Rue Raynouard. Yes? Oh, that's good. *Superb* Italian cuisine, m'sieur. Maybe he can meet you there tomorrow. How about midday?"

✳✳✳

Joubert arrived early and bought a copy of Le Monde. He selected a table in the corner and sat facing the main entrance with his back to the wall. It was an attractive restaurant, bright lights, tall mirrors, apple green décor and expensive cane furniture. He glanced around casually studying the diners for any sign of his host. As he showed his customers to their seats, Vito the headwaiter chatted and fussed around the salon.

Just after midday two heavily built men strode in and beckoned to the headwaiter. Joubert watched uneasily as the shorter of the two, still a good head taller than Vito, called him aside. The headwaiter listened intently and gestured towards the stairs. One of the men ran swiftly up the ornate staircase while the second undid his jacket and moved purposefully through the bar to the kitchens and back area.

A moment later a tall man dressed in an exquisitely cut pale grey suit entered the restaurant. Without pausing to look round he walked up to Joubert. "Marcel Joubert?" He held out his hand. "Mario Gambino. I'm sorry to have kept you so long." Joubert rose and took the hand which was cold.

"Very good to see you," Joubert lied, then added hastily, "I've only been here a few minutes, hardly had time to glance at the paper." Gambino ignored the remark and beckoned to Vito who immediately excused himself from the table he was serving and hurried across. For a few moments they spoke rapidly in Italian before Gambino turned back to Joubert. He pulled out a chair and sat down.

"*So.* Maletto says you have something to tell me?" Gambino enquired casually.

Joubert cleared his throat. "Well, I'm sure you know why I'm here," he began. Gambino stroked his chin slowly and continued to stare then raised one eyebrow enquiringly. It was an order for Joubert to continue. "I've decided to quit my job," he went on. "And I've reason to believe you know that my life was becoming very difficult. I need a break and I need to get away for a while."

"Ah yes. I heard you had some bad luck. So sad about the little girl." Gambino shook his head slowly. "Who could ever have done that to a young child?" Two days earlier he had ordered the execution of the leader of the motorcycle party for breaking the Mafia code of honour which explicitly forbade violence against women and children. Three others had been held down while their fingers were broken by a man with an adjustable spanner.

"And as for your poor wife. I heard about that also. Not too bad I hope." Gambino paused and looked down at his hands. In the silence that followed, Joubert felt his heart beginning to pump. The Sicilian looked up again. "But now you have decided to leave the City Hall? Is that really necessary?" he queried. "There are ways and means by which your luck might improve, you know. We all have these little setbacks now and then. It's not always easy...oh no." Gambino paused and Joubert watched as he rubbed his right shoulder. "Maybe if you stayed for a while things might change." Gambino leaned forward lowering his voice. "We might be able to help you there. Do you understand me? Things could get much better for you and the family."

Joubert sat back and looked at the man across the table. He was reminded of a well-known television wildlife documentary where the camera closed on the eye of a rattlesnake as the reptile paused before pouncing on the rodent crouched in the grass. "No," he replied, surprised at his own confidence. "We've thought long and hard about it and it's really too late now. Our minds are made up. I've told them at the office and they're hoping to fix me up with a complete change."

For a while Gambino said nothing. He sat quite still studying the backs of his hands then looked up. "Yes," he said, nodding slowly. "I understand. Egypt is very beautiful in the Spring."

"How on *earth* do you know about that?" asked Joubert his voice raised in surprise.

"Because, my friend, it's my business to know these things. And while we speak of business I must remind you that we still have a little matter that needs attention. Losing out on every one of those contracts like that a few weeks ago was a pity. I'm afraid we regarded it as something of an insult."

Gambino paused as the first course arrived. He glanced briefly at the bottle of Chateau Lafite-Rothschild '55 that was offered for his acceptance and nodded. "We made a very good offer, you know, and now it's time we squared the books. It would be sensible for you to start co-operating with me now, rather than continuing to ignore my presence. I *do* exist, you understand, and I'm here to stay. Right now I'm interested in what's going on in Alexandria, and I need your help."

Gambino explained that his earlier questions about Joubert remaining in Paris had been simply to confirm the situation. He pressed him to accept Déschampes' offer, then quizzed him at length about his knowledge of the archaeological dive. "They're just a shallow dive away from untold riches. You realise that, of course," he emphasised, tapping the table lightly with his finger. "So now you know. In fact you know too much and that could be dangerous...very dangerous. You'll be going out there shortly but, before that you'll be selecting your team," Gambino reminded him. "You will, of course, be looking for an assistant: somebody who knows Egypt and the Egyptians. Somebody who can converse in Arabic as well with government officials as he can with street traders and taxi drivers."

Without waiting for a reply, Gambino turned and rose to greet two diners who had come across to their table. One clasped his hand affectionately, speaking rapidly in Italian then turned to introduce his companion. The second man bowed, took the Sicilian's hand deferentially and raised it to his lips. It was obvious to Joubert that they were plying his host with compliments, flattering him effusively to the point of fawning at his feet. He watched fascinated as Gambino listened attentively before nodding appreciatively and dismissing them.

Joubert regarded his host. Who was this man who commanded such respect? How could he, how could anyone, know so much about what lay in store for him? He picked up his napkin and dabbed at his mouth.

"I've just the man for you," Gambino continued now back in his chair. "He has all the qualifications you need. He's worked with me for many years and I trust him. We will ensure he goes with you. His name is Alfredo Bontate, we call him Dino. He's a very good man. I've also found an excellent secretary for him and a driver for you. You'll feel secure with them working for us. Maletto will introduce you and you can see them when you are ready. Interview them of course, that looks good. But then take them. Right?"

Joubert stared. "What the hell do you want from me, Gambino?" he blurted. "Why don't you just get on with all this and leave me out of it? You seem to know exactly what's wanted. I've had enough of it all, OK? I just want you and your nasty friends to stay out of my life and away from my family."

"Aha." Gambino sat back. "Well said, Marcel. That's well said and straight from the heart. But you must listen to me." Joubert noticed the look. "Do your job out there, my friend, and do what I say when I tell you. No more, no less." He spoke softly, scarcely above a whisper but Joubert caught every word. "You do that and life will be all right. OK? You'll have your fun. But you've crossed me once and that's it. From now on you play things my way."

He threw one arm over the back of his chair and smiled suddenly. "But, hey, come on. It needn't get like that. Let's drink to a successful enterprise...to Alexandria and all that's there." He turned to the two men sitting at the table by the door then tapped his watch and raised five fingers.

Chapter Six

Alexandria

"Well, it looks as though we have found it all right." Francois Gideon turned to the four men in the command room of the El Rashid. "Problem now is to get it all up...anyone got any bright ideas?" He eased his way past the chart table and over to the large-scale model of the palace complex, now covered with architect's drawings and photographs of the vaults underneath the guardhouse which the divers had located earlier. Initially the search had been a nightmare. With nothing more than the evidence thrown up by the scrolls and Gideon's dedication, they had been working blind.

The first positive indications were found one morning during a dawn dive. Gideon had gone down early with three others in the hope that some of the sediment in the water would have settled during the night, enabling them to see more clearly. The large pile of masonry lay across a depression in what appeared to be a floor or courtyard from which they could see the stumps of a long balustrade protruding. It was as though some invisible force had pulled the blocks towards this point, just as dead leaves in the water might be drawn towards a drain. The divers circled the area carefully, filming the scene and taking photographs from several points.

Gideon ordered the suction pumps to clear the layer of mud and fine silt then sent the sensors down to the location. Watching the evidence appear before them on the screen in the operations room, the crew stared spellbound as first a short walkway was revealed followed by a wide, open stairway that disappeared under the foundations of a large building. For three weeks cranes and lifting equipment had struggled to remove the masonry one block at a time. As each was recovered it was numbered and placed carefully in a nearby car park that the Egyptians had commandeered and secured. Gradually the full extent of the stairway was revealed and entry into the vaults themselves became possible. A day later a diver called over the radio, his voice breaking with excitement, that they had came across what appeared to be a huge sarcophagus.

Slowly the true size of the find became apparent. At first they were unable to tell whether it was solid or some form of container. Measuring some eighteen feet long by six feet wide and almost five feet in height, the sarcophagus lay on a stone plinth. It had been carved from a single block of pink granite taken from the quarries near Luxor and closer inspection revealed a series of holes along the sides of the stone, each one about six inches in diameter and some twelve inches deep. On further inspection the divers found evidence of a joint in the block indicating that the top half was some form of lid. Whoever had carved the sarcophagus had done a magnificent job, the two parts of stone fitted together exactly. Three days later they came across a second. The tension was now unbearable. As the days went by and the vault was cleared, no less the fifteen were found arranged neatly in lines with evidence of some wooden walkways between them.

✳✳✳

Progress had been slow. They had been working on the site for weeks before Gideon decided to arrange a further meeting with the Supreme Council of Antiquities. Sir Alan Palmer had again been present and, after conferring all day, they decided that the sarcophagi should be lifted. A large warehouse on the old quayside had been taken over by the Supreme Council and preparations to receive the sarcophagi had already begun. It was here that whatever lay inside would see the light of day for the first time in over two thousand years.

Henri Kriessler, Gideon's chief engineer, eased back in his chair. "As I see it there are only three ways we can get 'em up. Either we can try to somehow manoeuvre them across the floor, get them back up the old stairway, and then lift them that way. Or we can go in through the floor and foundations directly above and do a vertical lift." He paused and looked at those round the desk. "That would be easier but I don't like it," he continued. "If we got at them that way we'd have to do one hell of a lot of damage. In any case I should think the Egyptians would put a stop to anything like that,"

"And the third choice?"

" The third option would be to remove the staircase. We'd have to take it out bit by bit but once we'd cleared enough room we'd move the blocks across the floor and get them straight out with a vertical lift."

Gideon scratched the stubble on his chin thoughtfully. "What would be the problems if we go for that option?" he queried.

"Time really," replied Kriessler. "It will be a long and fiddly job getting at the stairway and we might have to clear away quite a bit of the rock behind and underneath the steps. The actual steps themselves were manufactured elsewhere, brought to the site and set into whatever it is down there. My guess is that it's sandstone which shouldn't be too difficult."

"Yep, I agree." Yannis de Beer, a big Dutch salvage diver from Rotterdam, looked up. "We can't go breaking the place apart from up top and the stone down there's real soft, man. We should go for that. I agree with Henri." De Beer scowled at his gnarled hands and returned to the business of chewing the ends of his nails.

Throughout the day they debated the pros and cons of each option. Twice they broke off, donned diving gear and went down to check on their theories. Eventually they settled for the third option and made plans to take up the stairway piece by piece. "It must have been one hell of a job getting those sarcophagi into place all those years ago," commented Yves Didier, one of Gideon's principal divers.

"Yes, but clever," countered Gideon. The others looked up at him. "Well, it meant that whatever they kept in them was pretty secure. Assuming that whatever we find inside's of value, then who could steal it?" He looked around the room, his arms raised in question. "Eh?"

"Try lifting one of those lids when we get them up. They must be a couple of tons at least. I reckon that they used to keep the main palace treasures there and whenever they wanted to get the stuff out they would put long rods into those holes with half a dozen or so slaves on each one. Then heave, and off it comes. No nasty little klefti wallah could get his fingers into those containers, that's for sure." He shrugged expansively. "Hardly even need for a guard on the door, come to think of it. Cleopatra would have had her day to day jewellery with her, guarded by whoever it was that was allowed near her...the lucky devils." Everyone laughed. "But I reckon they kept the big stuff in these containers. Take your Buckingham Palace, Alan. Your Queen'll have her bits and pieces with her, but the heavy gear, what they need for the state occasions and that kind of thing is locked away safe and sound. Eh?" Gideon looked round at the silent faces. "But that's all theory...for the moment anyway."

"Anyone got any ideas of what's down there might be worth?" Kreissler asked quietly.

"God knows," Gideon replied. "What about you, Alan? Is it possible to make a guess?"

" Not really," replied Sir Alan Palmer, shaking his head and frowning. "I never like making forecasts. But what I *can* say is that if you care to go through all the records, the treasures of Ptolomy could bulk out at anything between thirty or forty times Tutankhamun's. And it would all be just as beautiful and much of it up to fifteen hundred years older." The team of seasoned, professional divers looked at each other. One of them blew heavily. "Bloody hell," someone muttered.

"Right, that's enough day dreaming," Gideon cried, clapping his hands. "Let's get back to business. Remember Ramadan's coming up soon. The weather's getting hotter and the Arabs won't be doing much work after midday. "Now, Jacques." Gideon turned towards his work's manager. "This means that you'll have to look at the work schedule. There'll be few enough spare labourers about and we'll have to get on with it as best we can." As he spoke those around him took notes.

"Timewise, I'd like to get the steps out of the way in the next week or so...all the lifting gear's in position and ready now. After that it'll be question of moving the blocks across to where we can get at them...that's your baby, Yves." The diver nodded. " Now then, once we get the stuff to the surface we've got to get it under cover and out of the way before news gets out. It's the usual game. Our security's been good up to now, very good in fact but far too many people seem to know something's in the wind." Gideon reached for the back of his neck. "I've asked our embassy to get someone out here to handle security, the press and everything else."

"Thank goodness for that," Sir Alan Palmer interjected. "Quite honestly, Francois, I don't know how on earth you've coped."

"Neither do I," Gideon laughed. "Anyway, it's our job is to get it all up and under cover. Then that's it, 'Finis'!" he cried, sweeping his hands together. "Apparently Paris are sending somebody out in the next few days," he went on. Fellow by the name of Joubert...Marcel Joubert. Supposed to be a bright young spark from the Culture Ministry. He's bringing his own crew and I can't wait." Gideon ran a hand through his tousled hair. "Once we start taking the lids off, he'll really have his work cut out. But that's his problem."

2

Paris
Joubert glanced out of the window behind the desk in his small temporary office. It was at the back of the third floor and he looked down into the pit of the central courtyard: a dark, soulless place, the preserve of overgrown weeds and litter. Since moving across from the Mayor's office, life had been different – and hectic. He had spent his time wandering through the maze of corridors at the Ministry of Culture, meeting new faces and trying to establish how they wanted him to operate in Alexandria. Now he felt ready. The backlog of administration had been cleared, and the long hours with the department's financiers behind him. Mercifully the Hanay Foundation had agreed to underwrite the costs, including the team's pay and allowances, thus sparing him from the clutches of the Shylocks in the accounts department.

The intercom buzzed. He leaned forward, pressed the switch and listened. The voice of Marie-Clare, the secretary he shared with two others, told him that a Monsieur Maletto had rung to confirm today's meeting. He acknowledged the call, asking her to arrange their security passes at the main desk and for them to be escorted up to his office.

***

Joubert pulled out the file on Alfredo Bontate and began to read the details again. All being well, his deputy would be flying out to Alexandria in a week's time followed by himself a few days later. The remainder of his newly formed team would be moving out some days after that. Hooking one leg over the arm of his chair, he began to study the curriculum vitae and references of the man Gambino had imposed upon him.

He had to admit that Bontate fitted the bill admirably. Alfredo Bontate "Dino" was born in Bierut to an Italian (Sicilian) father and Lebanese Christian mother. He lived there until he was twelve when his father, a civil engineer, took up an appointment in Marseille, renting an apartment in the Quartier du Panier district just north of the Vieux Port. His first job had been as assistant to the operations manager of a large construction firm carrying out improvements to installations in Marseille harbour. Three years later he had joined Marine Inc, an international marine engineering consortium, working in Oran harbour where he had been responsible for media relations and site security. That was four years ago and, as his contract had now expired. Bontate was back in Paris looking for further employment.

Flicking back to the covering letter, Joubert glanced at the last paragraph again. Bontate had to be a strong candidate for the job, the writer stressed, due to his fluent Arabic and close working relationship with Arabs at all levels. His extensive knowledge of PR and proven security track record made him a natural choice for work in major port complexes. It was an excellent CV but 'Dino' Bontate was Gambino's man and that, thought Joubert, he could have done without.

Everything he had discovered about Gambino confirmed his worst fears. The man was sinister; far more powerful than Nina or Salvatore could have known. He should have gone to the police immediately after Lucille's beating but the moment had passed and Gambino was now coercing him into work. Joubert looked through Bontate's details again. Perhaps he could work with this man. Perhaps he would find an ally in Gambino's lieutenant. He would wait and see.

***

An hour later Marie-Clare knocked on the door. Ushering the two men into the room she announced that she was going out for her lunch. Joubert nodded, crossed the room and held out his hand. Maletto revolted him. The short, oily man with the soft, clammy handshake was making an obsequious fuss as he made his introductions. One glance at Bontate told Joubert that the man had seen it himself.

Bontate, almost a head taller than his escort, was well built. As he took Joubert's hand, his eyes stared back unflinchingly. Joubert noticed the well-cut suit and neatly groomed appearance of the man sent by Gambino. His carefully chosen words came across slowly, in a measured tone without faltering. As he spoke, Bontate looked directly at the person he was addressing, holding the attention and exuding a quiet authority. With Maletto sitting discretely to one side, the two men talked across the desk. Joubert quizzed Bontate closely about his previous experiences on his CV and how he thought he might be most gainfully employed. In reply, the Italian explained that whoever ran the forthcoming operation would find it essential to have somebody who understood the mechanisms of a major seaport.

"Take all the different facilities for instance," he explained. "We'll need to have direct access to all the various departments there – water, electricity, accommodation, the labour and transport offices, dockyard security and so on. There'll be a whole mass of minor departments, working independently of each other and we'll need to get at them. Not only that, we'll have to tell them what to do, and all in quick-fire street Arabic too. Forget the Port Authorities, they're a nightmare. The whole place is asleep – has been for centuries," he said, pulling a face. "You see, I know where to look," he continued. "I know exactly where to go, who to talk to and I speak the language like a native. I've spent the last seven years ferreting around large Mediterranean ports and no two-bit minor official's going to pull a fast one on me." Bontate nodded defiantly. "And, if that's not enough, I know what makes the Arabs tick and how to make them jump. It's the Arab in me," he added with a laugh. "I think you'd be hard pressed to get hold of someone better qualified than me." He paused, looking closely at Joubert. "There'll be problems, that's for sure, but nothing that can't be fixed."

Joubert looked up from Bontate's file. The man opposite him could be an indispensable ally; on the other hand he could very quickly become a dangerous and implacable adversary. "Yes, I know. I wouldn't have a clue where to begin. And as for the language," he threw his hands in the air.

Before he had time to reply, Bontate turned to Maletto. "Right, you can go," he said curtly. "I have a little more business here with Monsieur Joubert." He looked at his watch. "I'll be half an hour or so. Get the car sorted and wait by the main entrance." Joubert looked on in surprise as Maletto got to his feet hurriedly, excused himself and left the room. Turning back to Joubert, Bontate smiled and said, "Now Monsieur, we need to talk for a few minutes. Is there somewhere we can go?"

"What's wrong with this office, for Heaven's sake?" Joubert asked in surprise.

"Monsieur, I'm naturally cautious and have learned to be very careful. Sometimes walls have ears." Bontate rose, doing up his jacket. "Perhaps we can find another office or conference room somewhere? It's lunch now and most should be free. I'd rather we were not disturbed." As he lead Bontate down the dark corridor to a sparsely furnished conference room next to the secretary's office, Joubert felt his pulse quicken. He glanced around anxiously before opening the door and ushering Bontate into the room. Once inside he locked the door, hurried across to one of the covered tables and pulled up two chairs. Ignoring the gesture Bontate sauntered casually across to the window, checked carefully then leant against a table with the sun streaming past him into the room.

"Monsieur Joubert, I think you and I should understand the position between us." Joubert leant forward, raising his hand to shield his eyes from the bright light. "You should know that my father's family hails from Sicily, from Palermo, the Porta Nuova area. We're very well connected there, and include the Gambinos amongst our most dear acquaintances. Don Mario, an old friend of mine, now comes from New Jersey, of course, but has retained many close links with the island. "I have been working for Signor Gambino since leaving Montpelier. He first engaged me when I was working in Marseille and I continued to work for him when I moved to Oran. Assisting him with his operations in the two ports, you understand. And now he has brought me to France. I am his *Caporegime,* his Captain. In business terms you would say I was his Chief of Staff." He paused, looking down from the window at the office workers taking their midday break on the spacious Ministry lawns. "There are others also, the Spadaros and Inzerillos for instance. All our Families work closely together in a number of areas. That's my first point and you should not forget that."

Bontate stopped abruptly and held up his hand, listening intently. Moving silently to the door he listened again, quietly turning the key then suddenly wrenched open the door. Joubert watched in amazement as the Italian surveyed the corridor from the shadows of the doorway before closing the door quietly. "Thought I heard something," he said returning to the window. "Must have been downstairs. Now, where was I? Oh yes, Marine Inc. That's my next point. I used to work with them in Oran. I had two jobs." He laughed briefly. "They're a satellite of Zagossi Internationale. You'll remember, of course, that Zagossi put in very reasonable tenders for some work coming up here. When you were working at the City Hall. Remember? We failed to secure a single contract out of all that and became something of a laughing stock as a result. All very unfortunate. We wouldn't want anything like that to happen again."

"That was hardly my responsibility."

"All that's history now," Bontate waved his hand dismissively. "But you should know where I fit into things. When we're out in Alexandria, we'll be working together. I'll do my job to the letter and you'll want for nothing. From time to time I may ask you for some assistance, a small favour perhaps." Bontate paused and inclined his head. "I trust I can count on your co-operation?" Joubert nodded glumly.

"Now then, the diving; both Paris and the embassy are concerned about outside interference," Bontate continued. "You'll be running the show. They'll all be looking to you to keep the heat off them. But, Monsieur, it's only right to point out that you are, in effect, working for Mario Gambino. And I, Dino Bontate, am his eyes, his ears and his mouthpiece. OK? You see, your position's a difficult one," he went on. "Your beautiful wife, Nina, she's a Corleonese. We know them well, of course, but it's fair to say that we approach things rather differently. We know she's got many good friends in Paris, friends from Sicily like the Salvatores. The ones you helped with the contracts."

"Now, hang on," Joubert remonstrated but Bontate held up a hand.

"I haven't finished yet," he said quietly. "We know also that your wife likes the boys. She's very close to the Mayor and we all know that our Monsieur Trinquet has an eye for a pretty girl. Your wife's certainly that and very ambitious for you as well. A potent combination. And so what?" he shrugged. "It's right that she's generous with her favours on your behalf." Joubert half rose and began to speak.

"Sit *down*," said Bontate in a commanding voice. "We know also that she sees your man here...Déschampes. We've evidence of that too. You might be committed to the Corleonese cause but now, how shall we say...now we've borrowed you." Bontate paused, and brought out an ivory handled flick knife which he clicked open. Studying his nails carefully he applied the knife delicately and expertly. "Think very carefully about this, m'sieur. Don't say a word to anyone, no one at all. Just get on with your job in Alexandria." Bontate clicked the knife shut and looked up at Joubert. "And don't underestimate my advice."

Joubert stared at the man in disbelief. "You can't do this," he whispered. "It's sheer, bloody blackmail for God's sake."

Bontate saw the startled look. "Well," he said slowly, "Make a run for it if you want, but where? Trinquet? I don't think so. Déschampes? Hardly. The police?" He paused again. "Run if you like, but we'll find you. Then what?" Bontate pushed himself away from the table. "Wake up, Joubert," he said icily. "It's far too late for all that now."

3

Paris

Slowly, a hand emerged from under the duvet and felt its way clumsily along the bedside table. An empty mug and a sheaf of loose papers crashed to the floor but the alarm persisted until it was found by the groping fingers. André Bigard cursed softly, scratched his head and yawned before hauling himself out of bed. As he did so he reached automatically for the packet of Gitanes, swaying slightly while he selected a crumpled cigarette. Unable to find a match he grumbled to himself, coughed and shuffled towards the door adjusting his pyjamas as he went. Behind him and from the depths of the duvet the other side of the bed came a grunt. Annie, Bigard's Belgian wife, acknowledged her husband's presence but no more.

André went to the front door, collected the post and wandered through to the kitchen. Eyes squinting through the tobacco smoke, he studied the headlines of Le Figaro as coffee and cigarettes began to work their mysterious ways, forcing life back into the spare frame. Muttering to himself, he climbed back up the narrow flight of stairs to his cluttered dressing room, emerging a few minutes later wearing an old rugby shirt, a pair of faded blue shorts and his battered but faithful trainers.

***

When pressed, Bigard would smile shyly and admit that, in his younger days, he had boxed a little. That was his description but to all those in Les Paras, Bigard had been an uncompromising street fighter, first and last. Unskilled, inelegant yet brutally successful, his huge reservoirs of raw courage had more than compensated for his lack of the basic skills. If the many hundreds of soldiers who had been ordered into the gymnasium had lost a free evening they wanted blood in return and looked to Bigard. He never failed them and they loved it.

Eventually, he was banned. After a two hour operation where they attempted to reassemble his features, the surgeons announced that they had done what they could, but his face would for ever remain one of character. And so it had. Bigard's battered and lugubrious features, never pretty and now sleep befuddled and unshaven, were living testimony to the doctors' verdict.

Outside, the early morning air was crisp. He paused briefly to flex his muscles then set out on his morning run. In spite of his forty-five years he remained surprisingly fit and jogged briskly into the nearby park where, for almost an hour, he mixed some hard bursts of running with a series of demanding physical exercises. An hour later, showered and breakfasted, the old trouper felt ready for the day. André Bigard was a rare bird in that he had served in both the French and British armies. His French father, Philippe, had served during the war with the British clandestine force Special Operations Executive – known simply as SOE - where he had developed a great admiration for the way the British Army conducted its affairs, in particular the way it selected and trained its officers.

A good British regiment was, to Bigard's father, the last bastion of order and civilisation in an increasingly chaotic world. Shortly before D-day he met Angela, a solicitor's daughter then working as a cipher clerk at Bletchley Park. Their courtship continued throughout the remainder of the war and they were married in 1946, settling near East Grinstead before moving to Paris where he took up work with a shipping company. Bigard arrived sometime after his three sisters and spent his early years grimly defending his corner against the supposedly fair and gentle sex. After completing his early education in Paris, André was sent to Downside, the Catholic, rugby playing public school in Somerset before returning to France and joining the elite Parachute Regiment - 1er RCP - then based at Bayonne in the south west.

He joined as a lowly paratrooper, saw active service in Kolwesi and Djibouti where he rose to the rank of Corporal, played rugby and paid his dues in the boxing ring. Two years later he returned to England. After completing officer selection at Westbury, he entered the Royal Military Academy, Sandhurst before joining the regiment of one of his father's friends. Bigard loved the life and three gloriously happy years followed, after which he decided it was time to put into good use some of which he had learned during his brief military career.

***

The 1970s and '80s had seen the western world bedevilled by successive waves of terrorism that stretched the armed services and nerves of several governments to breaking point. One by one, nations found they were both the targets and safe havens of this new invisible enemy. A niche in the market appeared and a number of entrepreneurial ex-British Special Force officers created their own security companies, offering advice and protection to those who considered themselves vulnerable. Later the offer was extended to governments of friendly nations who began to employ such expertise quite unashamedly when their own resources were found to be wanting.

Across Africa the colonial empires had all but disappeared, the old order often replaced by hopelessly inept dictatorships that used power and terror to suit their own needs. Many regimes clung to office by sheer brute force occasionally employing white mercenaries to do the dirty work for them. Sometimes these freebooters were successful, sometimes they were wiped out but, more often than not, they found themselves involved in hideous and indiscriminate blood-baths. The largest and by far the most sinister influence sweeping the western world was the effect of drugs. Seemingly innocuous at first, even dismissed in the early days as some harmless fetish, drugs rapidly took a stranglehold on all strata of society. Suddenly, at some point in the early '90s, the world woke up to the fact that they were staring a monster in the face, a monster which was growing rapidly even as they watched.

The civilised world was becoming an ever nastier and more dangerous place in which these conflicts swallowed up increasing numbers of manpower and greater resources. Yet it was a time when military assets were diminishing at an unprecedented rate. One by one European governments made savage cuts to their military budgets – in particular to their manpower – in the popular belief that the money could be spent better elsewhere. More and more peripheral aspects of military life were either contracted out to civilian organisations, priva-tised or simply disbanded.

For those who were able to provide resources and fill these gaps, opportunities arose. With the help of his father, Bigard set up his own consultancy service in which he moved freely between countries identifying what one government might need and what another might have to offer. Specialist weapons, ammunition and pyrotechnics, items of clothing and equipment: he would go shopping for them, arrange demonstrations and supervise the transactions. The most valuable commodity of all was manpower. Bigard knew only too well that ex-servicemen possessed the experience he sought and the best of them were men of exceptional quality. If their skills and knowledge were of a specialist nature they became highly prized and readily marketable.

And so he began to recruit and form specialist teams for operations around the world. Similar in many ways to the big London security companies yet Bigard worked alone. First he limited his search to those who had already left the police and armed forces but, as demand grew, he turned to those still in uniform. Bigard judged astutely that a man in his prime could be headhunted from the armed forces just as easily as he could from any other occupation.

Slowly but surely he built up a network of contacts from which he organised his teams. There was a huge demand for top quality and he forged close links with those countries well versed in the art of special force operations – in particular the Dutch and South Africans, but above all the British who were widely regarded as the best. It was a tough and ruthless business but Bigard had few scruples and made his way, supplying men or equipment here, organising a team for an operation there; his eyes and ears ever open for the next opportunity.

***

Today he was to have lunch with one of his most productive contacts. The fact that Eddi Cohen was an old and trusted friend made the meeting that much more enjoyable. Every time he thought of Eddi he grinned. They had first met at Sandhurst where some clerk with a warped sense of humour had posted them to the same platoon. The huge and bewhiskered Company Sergeant Major Murphy of the Irish Guards had been charged with developing the character of the thirty or so 'young gentlemen' in his care. Twenty-five years ago, the first few months at the Royal Military Academy came as a culture shock to even the most alert of the new entrants. Should the unfortunate soul hail from the other side of the world, the other side of the Channel even, this new lifestyle presented a number of additional challenges. Officer Cadet Cohen was five feet five, rotund and smoked heavily. Officer Cadet Bigard, although taller, seemed incapable of co-ordinating his limbs when on parade. Mister Murphy did not like what he saw: it made him angry and for a year Mr 'Bee-Gar' and Mr 'Cor-wen' received a good deal of his undivided attention, but they survived and a close friendship developed. One that stood the test of time.

Since Sandhurst they had twice found themselves working together, once in Cyprus and later in the Lebanon. Now Eddi was here in Paris working at the Israeli Embassy. After serving briefly in the armoured corps he had moved across to military intelligence before leaving the army. They met frequently for lunch or coffee to discuss the ways of the world and to consider snippets of information.

Today it was to be at the Moulin a Vent 'Chez Pierre'. Bigard arrived to find Eddi already at the table. Banter and greetings over, the two men listened to what each other had to say while the meal was prepared. Bigard knew that whatever he said would be passed back to the embassy but that he, the source, would be protected. Eddi was aware of France's close relationship with the Arab world where, due to her lack of oil, she was prepared to go further than her allies in fostering the necessary good relations.

In particular, France's approach to the fledgling regimes of Syria and Jordan concerned him, as did her recent arms deal with Egypt and her involvement with the development of Gadaffi's new Libya. Bigard was always keen to hear Eddi's views on counter terrorism throughout the middle east, where an opening might be found to establish a training mission or set up a network of bodyguards. Today they sat chatting long after the other diners had left.

Chapter Seven

Paris

Nina Joubert noticed that the agent's board outside the terraced house across the street had been removed and wondered idly who might be moving in. Rue de Longchamp was in a quiet area of the Sixteenth Arrondissement and popular with diplomats and politicians. The tiny second floor apartment at No 143 had only been on offer for a week or so and she asked herself if the new arrivals would be kindred spirits, with children perhaps. She did not see the furniture van arriving. If she had she would have thought it strange that the removal team themselves appeared to have taken up occupancy. From the salon window of No 143, the new arrivals had a clear view of the houses across the street, in particular the central block. Here the tall plane trees along the boulevard had been cleared to make way for the ornamental flowerbeds near the junction with Rue de la Pompe.

The three men did not take long to unload the van which left as soon as it had been emptied. They had been given instructions to set themselves up in the apartment. Their target was No 86 and they had been told to prepare the photographic and recording equipment. Their orders were to monitor everyone who came to the house and, in particular, to record the activities that took place in the extensive apartment on the first and second floors. This last task was to be done with the miniature cameras and surveillance devices they were to install inside the accommodation.

***

Two days later, after Joubert had left for the office and Nina had returned to No 86 from taking the children to school, she was talking to Anita, the Puerto Rican nanny when the doorbell rang. Outside it was raining. A neatly dressed young man introduced himself and produced his credentials, shielding them from the

74

rain. He confirmed with Nina that this was No 86 and that she was the occupant. He went on to explain that he had been sent round on behalf of the landlord's agency to arrange for some work to be done at the front of the house. They had been contracted to replace a number of the old window frames and he warned that it would be a fiddly job taking several days.

"What I'd like you to do, M'dam, is to call up the office and check first," he suggested in a friendly manner. "You never know who we might be. You should call up your agency as well, just to make sure everything's in order. I've got all the numbers here, look." He handed Nina a sheaf of papers, pointing out the numbers on the letterhead. "Once you're satisfied, I'd like to get the foreman in to measure up."

"Look, come on in out of the wet while I make the calls," Nina said smiling at the pleasant looking young man. "It sounds fine but we'll have to work out what to do with the keys. We're out quite a bit during the day and the maid comes and goes as well." Nina took the clipboard and picked up the phone in the hall.

She did not ring Marcel but simply called the number of the works' office who confirmed the contract. She then rang the number on the letter attached to the foreman's work sheet. Again the contract was confirmed. Both numbers she called belonged to a dingy, ground floor apartment on a run-down housing estate in the St Maur district to the east of the city. Two middle-aged women, sitting smoking in the back kitchen, took it in turn to answer the telephones and confirm the contract.

The workmen made good progress. After three days the front windows had been removed and the frames prepared. The following day, after Joubert had left, Nina busied herself about the house before leaving for one of her weekly music lessons. The nanny was on her own but, half an hour later, she announced to the foreman that she was going out to do some shopping which would take her about an hour and a half. The surveillance team moved quickly. Within minutes a man and woman left No 143 carrying two small holdalls. They hurried across the street, into No 86 where they joined the remainder of the team. Two alabaster jars in the bedroom were replaced with exact replicas, the apertures for the minute camera lenses concealed cunningly in the bright flowery pattern. A third camera was hidden in a small hatbox that had been taken from the top of the wardrobe. Moving to the bathroom, further cameras were installed in the grilled cover for the overhead fan and behind the grill to the air duct on the outside wall.

Microphones were placed under the bed, in the wardrobe and behind the bathroom towel rail. The team then moved to the salon, attaching a microphone to the underside of the telephone, another behind the armchair covers and underneath the electric clock on the mantelpiece.

"OK, you two love birds," called the leader. "Let's get on with the show." One of the team pulled out a pocket sized two-way radio, moved to the open window and spoke rapidly to the monitoring team across the street.

Turning back he grinned and called out "Right then…and let's have a perform-ance and a half. We'll let you keep your clothes on but don't forget plenty of whispering and sweet talk." For fifteen minutes Jean-Pierre and Michelle played out the part of a seduction scene moving from the salon to the bedroom, then to the bathroom and back again to the bedroom where they writhed realistically on the large double bed. Several times the leader called a halt to allow a camera or microphone to be adjusted. Across the street in No 143, the two men crouched over the consoles manipulating numerous illuminated switches and dials, their eyes concentrating on the master screen in front of them until they were satisfied their recording equipment could capture anything in the target area.

In less than half an hour the apartment had been prepared. By the time Anita, the nanny, reappeared the rooms had been checked for evidence, tidied carefully and the contractors returned to the business of the windows. There, two thin wire antennae that ran up the join between the window frame and wall had been cleverly disguised. "Right, Madame, let's be seeing the colour of your knickers then," muttered one of the surveillance team in No 143. The other looked up and grinned. "Well, if it's true what they say she's certainly a goer and we're in for a busy time. Ringside seats as well."

***

The day before Bontate left for Egypt, Joubert had his final meeting with Déschampes. They conferred for half an hour. After giving an update on the prepa-rations Joubert answered questions about the team and their responsibilities. The meeting over, he rose, bade farewell and turned to leave the room. Déschampes called across to him. "Marcel, just a moment. You all right? Just don't seem your-self today. Something on your mind? Something you'd like to discuss, perhaps?"

Joubert hesitated at the door then turned back. He hugged the slim file to his chest and avoided Déschampes' gaze, his eyes on the floor. Suddenly he looked up. Their eyes met and he started forward towards Déschampes. "Look, M'sieur," he began, the words tumbling out. "There's something going on that I don't like." He paused. " I don't like it at all and, if I may, I would like to speak quite frankly."

The smile left Déschampes' face. His eyes narrowed warily. "Well, if it's that important, Marcel." Déschampes motioned towards the chair by his desk.

Joubert stopped. For what seemed an eternity the two men looked at each other, then Joubert held up his hand. "No," he said quietly. It's all right. It's nothing to do with…no, it's quite all right, M'sieur. You wouldn't understand." He wiped his mouth. "Really, it's nothing at all. I'm sorry."

Déschampes rose, his composure returned. He walked round the desk and put a reassuring hand on Joubert's shoulder. His smile had reappeared. "You're quite sure, are you…that everything's all right, I mean? If there's something worrying you, now's the time to talk."

"No, Monsieur. Honestly, I'm fine. It was just a thought and it really doesn't matter." Joubert shut the door behind him, took two steps and stopped. He half turned, and reached back for the door. Then he stopped again. A second later his hand dropped and his shoulders slumped. For several seconds he stood alone in the corridor before continuing on his way to the meeting with Bontate.

The Italian had returned from a brief visit to Alexandria. He was in high spirits and the meeting was convivial, no mention being made of Gambino or other members of the new team. Bontate explained that nothing they had asked to be prepared had been done. "It's exactly as I expected and it's always the same," he said, shrugging his shoulders. "All a load of hot air and big promises but absolutely *zilch* progress." He cut the air with his hand. "When you're dealing with Arabs it's no good yelling and screaming at those at the bottom of the pile.

"You've got to go in right at the top and make a big fuss there," he nodded belligerently. "At least three levels above the one you're dealing with. As soon as I get back, I'll put a bomb underneath the so called Port Authority then go straight to the Supreme Council. Oh yes, I'll wind them right up then turn them loose. That's the way to get the show on the road." He looked at Joubert grimly. "It's the only way to treat those bums. When you come out next week," he continued, "I'll more or less have the place organised. I've booked myself into a convenient place near the harbour but I'll get you all well established in the El Pasha. Remember, out there we make it like you're the boss." He caught Joubert's eye. "And that's what you are…sort of."

2

Alexandria
The six men pushed against the heavy metal doors of the old warehouse. Slowly and with the metal wheels complaining noisily, they rolled back allowing the afternoon sun to flood into the dark interior. Those inside moved, shielding their eyes against the light. Then the mobile crane inched gently towards them with another sarcophagus suspended in the large cradle. Eight more men in yellow safety helmets, two on each rope, were holding the cradle steady while, in front, an engineer walked backwards, signalling directions to the driver high in his cab.

Hours before, the sarcophagus had been teased from its resting place where, like all the others, it had lain under thick layers of silt and rubble on the western side of the old harbour. The last remnants of dirt had been hosed carefully away and the pinky grey-white hues of the Aswan granite glistened in the sunlight.

The cool, cavernous interior of the warehouse was empty save for the eight sarcophagi that lay waiting on plinths like a line of giant coffins in some huge public morgue. A high canvas screen had been erected on the far side to partition off the area where they were to be opened. The area had been surrounded with wire and, at the entrance, a security guard sat slumped in his chair, his guard dog asleep at his feet. Behind him workmen were putting the finishing touches to a number of cloth-covered shelves while, high above, electricians were fixing extra lighting, suspended from the roof girders.

Francois Gideon and Dino Bontate emerged from one of the three portakabins in the far corner of the warehouse. They were talking earnestly about the programme they had arranged for Sir Alan Palmer of the British Museum and the team from the Louvre. Engaged by the Egyptian Supreme Council for Antiquities, this was to be Palmer's final visit and the culmination of several years' research.

Gideon was delighted with the way that the new arrival had breathed life into the lethargic and half hearted approach of the port authorities. "Honestly, Dino, it's as though they've had the wrath of God or Allah behind them," he joked, turning towards the taller man and clapping him on the shoulder. "Whatever you did has done the trick but we've got to keep them at it," he added. "Ramadan's in a few days now and, unless I'm wrong, we'll lose half the work force and the rest'll be in bottom gear." He stopped and looked across the harbour towards the cranes next to the El Rashid. "We've just about got the knack of the lifting operations. Hopefully they'll all be up in a couple of days and then it's over to you and this Joubert fellow. So keep the whip out."

"Yes, I know all about Ramadan," replied Bontate. "But look, I want to get the offices sorted out first. I'm putting your shore office and Palmer's cabins in here but I'll keep mine outside. I can keep an eye on things better out there and head off any trouble." The two strolled across the warehouse to the line of sarcophagi where Bontate listened intently as Gideon explained how the caskets had been lifted.

Bontate looked at the Frenchman. "You know, if your crowd brings up just a small fraction of what they say's down there, all hell's going to break out. When word gets out to the press, as it will, they'll be here in hordes and it'll be out on the internet in a flash. We'll have the whole world breathing down our necks."

"Down your neck, you mean," Gideon replied. "The first whiff of the press and I'm off to the El Rashid. They're your babies, mon ami, so keep them away from me for Christ's sake." He grinned mischievously, patted the Italian on the shoulder and walked briskly over to the main door where he watched the new arrival being trundled gingerly across the warehouse towards its companions. Bontate glanced at the notes in his hand, then looked across at the guard sitting by the entrance gate. He frowned, cupped his hands to his mouth and yelled in Arabic, before gesticulating angrily. The man shuffled to his feet, adjusted his cap and kicked out at his dog.

Bontate worked swiftly to secure his position among those around him and to gain the confidence of the few who really mattered. He established contact with the Cultural Attaché at the French Embassy, and, in a carefully orchestrated demonstration that gave him enormous pleasure, he managed to ruffle the feathers of those sitting at the top of the Port and Harbour Authority. They had been humiliated and now could not do enough for him. The old trick had worked perfectly. To begin with he had gone cap in hand, speaking respectfully in broken French and poor Arabic. He had waited patiently in dusty corridors until he had been summoned by a minor official. He approached the man with deference, nodding and smiling obsequiously. Those in the office ignored him or discussed openly how best to deal with this tiresome foreigner. Sometimes they made crude jokes about the French; on other occasions he was treated dismissively or left standing on his own. Throughout the long day he returned their looks of scorn with a pleasantly submissive smile.

Eventually he had been granted an interview with Ali Mehmet, the short, fat deputy chief of operations, who made no effort to disguise his irritation at being disturbed at this late hour. He made Bontate stand as he shouted importantly into the telephone, bellowed for his subordinates and shuffled papers on his desk. Again Bontate listened to the officials as they chatted away, gesticulating or nodding in his direction. At six Mehmet rose to leave. He summoned his clerk, telling him to dismiss the foreigner. It was Bontate's cue.

In the classical Arabic of the Levant he rounded on the astonished officials. They stood dumbfounded, eyes wide and mouths open, as Bontate addressed them as only a highborn Arab might speak to inferior beings. Throughout the day, he told them, he had understood every word that had been spoken. He, a senior official working on behalf of a friendly government, one who had been sent here to help the government of Egypt, had been deeply offended and insulted. The room froze. Every eye was on him. Mehmet sat rigidly in his chair, eyes popping and bald head shining. Bontate moved to the front of his desk, leant forward and stared down. The Hanay Foundation, he explained quietly, was here to help Egypt free of any charge. In return, those working for Hanay had been treated with contempt by their hosts, had received virtually no help and were now at the end of their tether. The Foundation was on the point of pulling out and he invited them to consider the impact this would have on the Egyptian Government. Mehmet remained motionless.

The President of France himself, Jacques Chirac would be visiting the site in the near future with their own President Mohamed Hosniy Mubarak. What then, he queried. Prior to this the French Ambassador was planning a visit with Amr Moussa, the Egyptian Prime Minister soon after the first of the sarcophagi had been opened. The Foundation had decided, for the moment anyway, to remain and see the project through. Right now the whole place was a filthy mess, unfit even for the stray dogs and beggars that littered the area. Bontate banged the table and raised his voice. The little man jumped. They were a disgrace to their country, to the proud name of Egypt and an insult to France. Unless the operation was given their highest priority, the very highest, he would see to it that heads would roll. Bontate glared at the face in front of him, pushed himself back from the desk and stalked from the room.

For a few moments there was silence. Seconds later, as he paused briefly in the corridor, the office behind him erupted. Walking swiftly down the stairs, Bontate heard the sounds of raised voices, one rising shrilly above the rest. Feet ran along the corridor above him, doors opened and slammed shut. As he walked briskly across the lawn to his car, Bontate threw back his head and laughed.

***

Later that evening Sir Alan Palmer arrived at the El Pasha hotel accompanied by Mary Sutton and Amanda Gates. They had flown in to Cairo earlier and then up to Alexandria that afternoon. Bontate met them at the airport and, together with an official from the British Embassy, they spent an hour going over the arrangements before driving across to the warehouse where they were greeted by two guards at a side door.

A few minutes later a car from the French Embassy in Cairo pulled up. Three men climbed out and stood in the glare of the security lights. Palmer knew two of the men well, including Professor Didier Charante from the Louvre, and there was much banter as introductions were made. The new arrivals, sweating uncomfortably in the unaccustomed heat, could barely contain their excitement as Bontate ordered the guards to open the side door. The two parties were led in together, their footsteps echoing eerily inside the huge warehouse. Now silent and peering around them, they followed Bontate across the floor to where the fifteen sarcophagi lay in a long line. The whole group gathered around the nearest sarcophagus, standing in almost reverend silence and gazing at the extraordinary sight before them. Palmer took off his hat. Professor Charante and another of the French party crossed themselves. It was impossible not to be moved.

The granite caskets, gleaming under the powerful security lights, lay quietly, almost serenely, waiting to yield up their secrets. Sir Alan Palmer and Professor Charante walked slowly around the line of caskets together, the others behind them. Everyone had their own thoughts. Who, they could not help wondering, had ordered these great sarcophagi to be built? Ptolemy? Cleopatra? What craftsmen had designed the exquisite shape of the caskets with only the eye and hand to fashion the lines? And, above all, *what*, if anything, lay inside?

Palmer moved forward slowly and touched the side of the nearest sarcophagus, running his hand gently over the smooth pink stone. He shook his head and turned to Charante. "It's just incredible," he muttered, "It's really all quite, quite incredible."

"Incroyable," Charante whispered to himself. "Mais oui, oui. Bien sur."

✳✳✳

Early next morning the Anglo-French party met with a number of senior officials from the Supreme Council. The day was spent examining the sarcophagi and deciding on how best to open them. Water had been detected seeping from some while others bore no sign that they had been submerged for so long. If whatever there was inside had survived intact it would no longer be held securely in place. The padding and fabrics would have disintegrated centuries ago and further movement would undoubtedly endanger any artefacts. They decided to open the sarcophagi in the warehouse, one at a time, and under the authority of the Egyptian Supreme Council who would use their own technicians for the operation. The contents would be stored on site temporarily, under heavy guard, while an initial examination was conducted, photographs taken and an inventory compiled.

The caskets were to be opened just as they had been in the past. Poles, this time metal bound with cloth, would be inserted into the holes and a crane would be used take up the pressure before lifting the lid. The seal around the joints appeared to be a concoction of bee's wax and resin, a sealant often used by the ancient Egyptians and common throughout the Ptolomeic era. Although the seeping water suggested that some of the seals might not have survived intact, nobody was able to say how effective the carefully crafted bevelled edges might themselves have acted as seals. Most important of all it was impossible to tell how quickly the sarcophagi had been enveloped by the waters of the Nile which had then thrown a protective mantle of silt around them.

In less than a week the warehouse had been transformed. The heavy mobile crane had been installed, the port authorities had connected the necessary facilities and Bontate had begun to improve the security arrangements. Early the following Sunday evening a large group gathered around the first sarcophagus.

The mobile crane inched towards the plinth on which the casket lay. Underneath the lifting arm an extensive metal cradle, to which sixteen metal hooks had been attached, swung gently. A thick piece of hemp rope was attached to each hook. Once the metal frame had been positioned directly above the sarcophagus, the ropes were placed over the metal bars protruding from the casket lid. Heat had been applied to the seals on the joints and the base of the casket had been secured by well-padded metal clamps.

Sir Alan Palmer looked across to Wasim Machtoum – the Director of the Supreme Council – standing with Didier Charante. He smiled and nodded. Wasim glanced up at the operator in the cab and raised his hands, palms upwards. Slowly, inch by inch, the strain was taken by the crane until the sixteen ropes were taut. An Arab worker jumped onto the lid of the great casket and tested the ropes for tension. Satisfied that the pressure was even, Machtoum nodded again. Palmer glanced around at the circle of expectant faces, waxen under the powerful lights. The hemp creaked, the engine of the crane took the strain then, suddenly, the lid was off and swinging above the body of the sarcophagus. For a moment there was silence, then gasps and cries of surprise followed by shouts and loud applause. The crane lifted the lid clear and Sir Alan Palmer stepped forward with his hands raised.

The warehouse fell silent as everyone craned forward, staring at the open casket and what lay inside. For some time nobody spoke then Palmer cleared his throat. "I am unable to be sure but I believe we have just discovered some ornamental miniatures of the statues of the great tombs." He paused, staring into the casket. "What you see here appears to be miniature replicas of the statues that were placed in and around the Royal tombs of ancient Egypt." He glanced at Professor Charante expectantly. "What do you think, Didier?"

The Frenchman moved forward, peering into the well of the casket. For several seconds he stood quite still, gazing at the artefacts, gleaming amid the dust and remains of wrappings, long-since disintegrated. "Yes, Alan, I agree," he gasped. "Nothing like this has ever been seen by modern man. Nothing at all. We have no record of anything like this ever being found." He continued to stare. "And just look at the jewels and the exquisite workmanship" he whispered. "These artefacts could only possibly have graced the most noble palaces of the era. Without doubt we are looking at some of the Royal treasures of ancient Egypt."

"What age?" a voice cried out. "Tutankhamun?"

"No, no. *Much* earlier, much, much earlier," Palmer replied, his voice rising with excitement. "I'll have to check my facts, of course, but we can see here the face of Khaskhemwy. So tiny, like a doll but look at the incredible detail. He lived almost two thousand years before the boy king. Just look at the lapis lazuli and turquoise stones set in the gold plating." He hesitated briefly then pointed to a diminutive ebony statuette with gold edgings, no more than a few inches in size. "And there is King Den, known as the Killer King, for reasons you can well imagine. They found his tomb in 1936. And look there." His voice rose again to an excited shout and crackled as he pointed to a larger statuette, the sheet-gold gleaming in the glare of the lights. "There's a face mask of Senworset III. Would you believe it? The conqueror of Nubia. We have a stone sphinx of him in the British Museum, but just look at this – ebony and ivory, carved so beautifully and interlaced with gold. And look at these stones. It's unbelievable."

He paused for a moment, blinking in the light, before going on. "And over there, look, is King Sneferu, whose pyramid is at Dahsur." Palmer looked up smiling. "He was reputed to go boating on the Nile with the most beautiful women in the land dressed in nothing but fishing-nets. Quite a character!"

"A true Frenchman, of course." Charante interjected. Everyone laughed and from behind somebody clapped. For a moment the tension was broken.

" And look there, over there – Queen Hatshepsut," Palmer continued. "Next to her is one of her vases of Kharu, and there is a statuette of Ramesses II. That gold will be from the Wawat mines in northern Nubia. Gentlemen we are privileged to be looking at some of the most beautiful sculptures spread over some three thousand years of Egyptian history."

The party remained hushed, each one trying to take in Palmer's descriptions. He spoke again. "Gentlemen, really, I cannot tell you the importance of this find. These treasures are quite priceless…quite, quite priceless." He choked, removed his glasses and wiped his eyes. "I do beg your pardon. For me this is an incredible moment. Very moving. Never in my life have I seen anything to match this. Unless I'm mistaken, Francois, you and your team of divers have indeed come across treasures that only the ruling family would have owned." He nodded towards the diver. "You have done the most remarkable job bringing them up here to see the light of day once more. I'm of the belief that what we are now looking at was last seen by the house staff of the last of the Ptolemys. The last eyes to gaze on these treasures were probably those of Cleopatra herself and Mark Anthony more than two thousand years ago." He turned back to the Director of The Supreme Council and held out his arms. "Wasim Machtoub, I commend to you these wonderful treasures of your country. They're unique, *peer*-less and *quite, quite* priceless."

Outside the warehouse Alfredo Bontate walked rapidly to the harbour wall. Out of earshot he made a short call with his mobile phone. As he finished his report he was told that Marcel Joubert was on his way.

Chapter Eight

Paris

In the front room of No 143, the red warning light on the command console began to flicker brightly. Immediately he saw it, the operator adjusted his headphones and crouched by the machine. "In-coming call by the looks of it, Pierre," he called quietly. "Popular girl this morning."

Nina had been at a loose end, unable to decide whether to drive out to the Boulevard Maurice Barres for her lesson with Signor Torelli or to remain where she was in the hope the phone would ring. Angry with herself for behaving like a child, she vowed to wait no more than an hour and began to fiddle aimlessly with the magazines on the salon table.

Two days ago Anita had taken the children and gone ahead to stay with Nina's cousin. They had planned to spend the whole of the Easter break together at her rambling holiday home near Cap Ferret, close to Bassin d'Arcachon on the Atlantic coast. At the last minute Nina had decided to remain in Paris. Now, with Marcel in Egypt, she was on her own.

The third call was the one she had been waiting for. She recognised the voice immediately and smiled. "Are we still on for our meeting today?" It was Roger Trinquet. Across the road, the two operators began to record the conversation. He explained that he would be able to escape for a couple of hours around noon. "I've managed to rearrange my schedule and it would be lovely to see you again, cherie." Nina felt her breathing quicken. "I'll get Anton to bring the car right up to the door, so make sure it's on the latch," he advised. "But after that there'll be nothing to worry about," he chuckled. "After all, we're on our own. Oui?"

Nina glanced hurriedly at her watch calculating rapidly what she would have to do in the time left. She hurried out to the line of shops in Rue Provence bought some lunch from the delicatessen and charcuterie then returned to prepare the meal. Once the table had been laid she luxuriated in the bath, humming quietly to herself, wondering how events might unfold.

***

An hour later Trinquet stepped inside. Four or five inches taller than Nina he looked down and smiled. Stretching out his left arm he hooked the bottle of chilled champagne gently round her neck and pulled her towards him. She squealed and shivered at the cold touch then kissed him tenderly. Reaching up she kissed him again and slipped the jacket from his shoulders. "Come here," she said seductively. "I've waited long enough, so lunch can wait a bit, too." He nodded, stroking her hair then allowed her to take him by the hand and lead him into the bedroom where she drew the curtains. She turned back to him, undid his tie then lifted his shirt from his trousers and ran both hands slowly up the inside of his thighs before clasping him tightly. His hands moved to the top of her dress behind her back. Only their breathing and the rustle of clothes broke the silence.

Nina threw back the duvet, took his hand again and drew him onto the bed where they lay together, their legs entwined. It did not take long. They had both waited impatiently for this moment and their mouths locked together. The love-making was urgent and passionate. Nina heard herself cry out as he forced himself down upon her, thrusting powerfully. For a while they lay exhausted before moving into the bathroom where they showered together. Over lunch they chatted about the future. Trinquet assured her that the omens were good. "Marcel's ringing all the right bells," he said. "You see, not only is he sharp, but there're good connections as well. In a funny way, I'm very fond of your boy. And then there're your own strong contacts in the business world."

"With Corleone?" she queried, wrinkling her nose. "We could do without that. I would like Marcel to get up the ladder without being pulled and pushed all the way."

"Of course, and so he shall. But in this game you need other things apart from just ability – you need luck, timing *and* connections, in equal proportions. Here, in Paris, the last is the most important. The whole system's run like that for years. Call it patronage, favouritism or just plain common sense backing the devil you know. Your family's got fabulous connections, and not too much in the way of competition either."

"Only that Gambino lot," Nina tossed her head. "They're parasites. One minute they're grovelling at your feet, next they're at your throat. Give them an inch and that's it. I can't *stand* them and don't intend to let them get in my way." She failed to say anything about the threats over the contracts or that Gambino was behind the violence against the family. She wondered what hold they might have over the man now in her house? Were they closing in? On him, the most powerful man in Paris? She looked across, smiled and squeezed his hand. "Thanks for coming round." She said, suddenly quiet again. "I'll be back from Cap Ferret in a couple of weeks before flying out. Perhaps we can fix something then?"

"Yes please, my love, can't wait for the next round," muttered the operator shaking his head as he took off the headphones and switched off the equipment. "Cor, stone the bleedin'crows. Who's next on 'er shoppin' list, for Christ's sake?" Later he and his companion edited the film, made copies of the most explicit shots and selected anything of interest from the voice recordings.

2

Alexandria

Amanda adjusted her silk gloves, leant forward again and checked the range of the powerful magnifying glass. Her tweezers picked out the tiny acacia seeds of gold, feldspar and cornelian one at a time. Holding her breath she turned the minute adornments, searching carefully for marks and blemishes, before recording her findings. Sir Alan Palmer and the Supreme Council had collated an initial catalogue of the Queen's Jewellery and he had given her the task of checking them before they were sent to the Californian Institute for electronic analysis. She looked at the label on the artefact and read his spidery handwriting. 'Girdle, akin to those found at Dahshur.Tomb of Sithathor. c.1850 B.C.'

Moving the glass to one side she studied the exquisite gold cowries surrounding the central brooch where the two minute falcons wore their own jewelled crowns above collars of gold and turquoise. Inscribed underneath in hieroglyphs were the words 'The Gods are content'. She picked up the cartouche, no larger than a small postage stamp, and gazed at the remarkable craftsmanship of the jewellers, whose eyes and fingers had created such perfection almost four thousand years ago.

Behind her the door opened and she listened to Mary's voice. "My goodness the guards are on their toes today," she grumbled. "It was all I could do to get past the gate. And I can see why."

"You can thank Sir Alan and Dino for that," Amanda replied. "Come and look at this, Mary. You've never seen anything like it." She looked up and smiled. "Dino insisted that the guards should be doubled whenever we're handling the jewels. It's an awful bore but better that way I suppose."

The two women looked at the contents of the three boxes in front of them. Sir Alan considered that, of all the finds to date, these were the ones most likely to be the personal treasures of Cleopatra VII, the last of the Ptolemaic dynasty. When they opened the sarcophagus they found the jewels laid out in complete sets. It was as if the owner had decided to match for herself what she would wear and had ordered the sets to remain as such. As a result the team of archaeologists and Egyptologists from the Supreme Council had agreed to keep the sets together, exactly as they had been found, pending a final decision on their display.

Amanda groaned as she lifted the next package from the box. "I know what this is," she muttered, blowing with exertion. "Over six thousand grams – almost fourteen pounds of solid gold. They think it's from the tomb of Psusnnes the first. Around one thousand B.C…quite modern really," she laughed. After Amanda had laid out the fifteen gold cords hanging from the main collar the two women stood gazing at the beauty of the goldsmith's work. The five concentric bands of the main collar were made up of thousands of coils of gold wire held together by a central brooch, itself of solid gold. The cords would have hung down the back of the neck like long thick tassels of interwoven gold chain, reaching below the centre of the back. Each cord chain was decorated with solid gold beads and knots.

For over an hour the two women checked the contents of the three boxes. After examining each item under the magnifying glass, Amanda attached notes of her findings to Palmer's labels, wrapped the items individually and returned them to their temporary home. The boxes checked that afternoon were just a small portion from one sarcophagus. Others contained further personal jewellery, tableware, table ornaments, drinking vessels, lamps, footwear and personal effects from the bedchambers and royal baths. Still more contained items of male jewellery, knives, daggers, swords and other weapons. It would take weeks to check and annotate all the artefacts before they were despatched for scientific analysis.

✳✳✳

Bontate had not wasted time. As soon as Joubert arrived he had taken him to the contacts he had established, interpreting patiently for him. They met several Egyptian officials but at a level below those Bontate had approached earlier. He was at pains to explain that the French government official had been sent from Paris to deal with the Press and French Embassy matters only and that they should continue to deal with him, Bontate. He was running the operation.

When alone, Bontate quickly developed his own contacts. He noted that the head of the transport division, Said Musalim, bore a deep grudge against the westerners who had moved in, taken over the port and were now unearthing Egypt's past glory. Bontate befriended the man, playing hard on his own Arab background and speaking to him in the dockworkers' rolling slang. Ramadan, the great Muslim religious festival had begun, during which the Islamic faithful fasted throughout the day allowing no food or water to pass their lips. In the evening the fast was broken, whole groups of families often feasting together and Bontate frequently ate with Musalim and his family. He brought them gifts – a little pocket money, some sweets for the children and, always, some food for the house. On one special occasion he brought Musalim's wife some coins and a tiny ornate bracelet that had been recovered from the seabed.

Bontate's greatest concern was security. Not because it was lax – that was perfect – but, when the moment came, they planned to breach the security silently. It would be out of the question for them to get caught in the act and have to battle their way out, and just as impractical to conduct an armed raid. The security would have to be adjusted to suit their needs.

Earlier he had come up against a lieutenant from the Harbour Police. The man had tried to retain control and had, in Mafia parlance, become tedious. Bontate insisted on handling security matters himself and complained about the man's behaviour. The Port Authority, fearful of another confrontation, had the officer replaced. Bontate studied the security of the warehouse carefully, then approached Gideon and Palmer pointing out the lack of awareness. He went on to show that, once past the perimeter security and the warehouse guards, the artefacts lay virtually unprotected while work went on around them. "Once somebody's inside the place, there're practically no further checks. People can pick up almost anything they want," he complained. "We must see that everything is secured, under cover and out of sight."

The two men, experts in their own fields, had neither the knowledge nor inclination to become involved in such matters. They were delighted that Bontate had taken it upon himself to tighten security and were impressed by his knowledge. He suggested that individual reinforced cardboard packing boxes, such as a removal firm might use. "Everything would then at least be out of sight, away from preying eyes. It would also offer some sort of protection against accidents and keep out the worst of the dust. Furthermore," he continued, "Once an inventory's been made, the items will be far easier to move around." They agreed and Bontate arranged for a large quantity of boxes to be bought from a packing factory. Nobody queried him when he ordered some port workers to make up a second set of boxes.

Palmer, in particular, went out of his way to help, pointing out the items which, in his opinion, were the most valuable. "They should be kept in the middle of the secure area," Bontate explained. "If ever a snatch is attempted the items nearest the doors would go first." He could have added that if anyone wanted to make a security check on the contents, those nearest the doors would be checked first. Once satisfied they were secure, those checking would assume that everything else was safe also. Come the day, that might buy a little more time.

He then turned his attention to the physical security and the guard force. He found the guards better accommodation, a little further from the warehouse. "Those few extra hundred metres don't matter," he stressed. "The key, in an emergency, is speed of reaction. I could have them living right here in the warehouse but it wouldn't be much good if they couldn't get out of bed when the moment came. He flattered the guard commanders. "I can see you're professionals all right," he flannelled. "So why not live like professionals. Any fool can be uncomfortable."

He taught them to rely more and more on electronic equipment – alarms, lights and CCTV – testing their reaction time over and over again. Gradually he weaned them away from the concept of a close physical presence. Nobody saw any need to stop and check the credentials of Ahmed, the new electrician, as he rearranged the electrical alarm system and tampered with the close circuit cameras and command console. The system, he ensured, would never work.

After a lengthy discussion he persuaded the officials that the guards should carry weapons but should not be issued with live ammunition. He caused consternation among the commanders about the consequences of a negligent discharge of a gun on such a high profile project. For sure, he warned, heads would roll. "Look," he said. "Nobody who's bent on mischief will know one way or the other if the men are carrying live ammunition or not. We'll do a bit of range work off the beach and word will soon get around that they're trained and prepared to shoot. But one accident, and who's to take the blame, eh? The man in charge, of course." Bontate noted their startled looks.

And it was the same with the dogs. "They're not much use at night," Bontate decreed. "It's the sight of a dog that puts people off but who can see them at night? And, in any case, with all the strays around they aren't going to be much use after dark. Far better to have a show of force when it can be seen." The dog programme was switched to daylight hours. His next concern was to get the guards used to late night activity at the warehouse. Sir Alan Palmer, he pointed out, would often work late and so too would his team as they began to prepare for the forthcoming visits. The guards should thus stay clear of the warehouse itself. "You're far better out on the perimeter after dark. You won't hear or see a thing with all this coming and going. And, in any case, there'll be too many people in the warehouse, everyone will be tripping over one another."

The lorries from the transport division became accepted around the warehouse. The drivers went happily about their business, sometimes during working hours, sometimes late at night. The guards became used to the sight of vehicles noisily loading and unloading boxes, building materials and diving equipment. Bontate controlled the work schedules himself and nobody queried the vehicle movements. Occasionally they were parked up in the warehouse over night, sometimes next to the compound where the treasures were stored.

It had taken him almost two weeks but, in the end, he had severely degraded the physical security. He had installed a system for the rapid handling of the treasure and his own equipment was in position. Finally he turned his attention to the Abdul Gamel Nasser airport. Gambino had already decided that the haul would leave by air. Although only a provincial airport and staging facility, it was nonetheless busy and handled a considerable amount of commercial and freight traffic. Somehow he had to get the airport authorities to accept the lorries late at night and get the airport police used to their presence at the gate and freight loading terminal. He decided to play his trump card and solicited the help of the Supreme Council. Still smarting over Bontate's report on the Port Authority, they ordered the airport to offer him every assistance.

Armed with this directive he demanded that an area close to one of the freight sheds be set aside for the operation. He arranged for the lorries to meet the scheduled flights from Paris and Geneva. Time and again he ordered the lorries into the airport to meet night flights, noting with satisfaction that their movement became accepted by the guards who merely waved them through. The drivers memorised the airport's internal driving circuit and, once at the freight terminal, the vehicles were left well alone by the airport security.

***

Gambino arrived as he promised. Having flown to Cairo, he flew up to Alexandria and booked into the El Pasha hotel. It was here that Bontate, worried about Joubert's nerve, suggested they should take him to task. "He's the weak link," Bontate explained. " I like to think we've got him pinned but he's clever. All it needs is for him to flip...to run to the Embassy or Palmer. *Anyone*...even the Supreme Council. We wouldn't know he'd gone, until it was too late...then what?"

"So why hasn't he done it already?" asked Gambino.

"My guess is that he's hanging on to his Paris scene. He's an ambitious little shit and's got his eye on the future. Sees all sorts of ways up. He's already got both the Mayor and Deschampes on side."

"On top of his wife, too," Gambino interrupted grimly.

"Yes, all of that," Bontate replied. "And that's how I reckon we deal with him. He's the sort that would sell his mother for a leg up the ladder. Dammit, he's passing his wife around as it is. He knows exactly what's going on here but if we can convince him he's got a clear road after this then he'll play along. That's the way he's made."

"And if not?"

"Then his lights go out, and fast. If he gets in the way, that's it. What's more you can let him know that's part of the deal as well. There's a big yellow streak there. You watch."

Later Gambino phoned Joubert. He had a number of ideas he wanted to discuss and asked him to join him for drinks in his suite. When he entered the lounge Joubert found Bontate sitting with Gambino by the window overlooking the harbour. The three of them talked for a while before turning their attention to press matters. Under their questioning, Joubert admitted that he was finding the language a barrier. Pressed by Gambino, he assured them he was using all the contacts Bontate had given him and was happy that things were under control.

"But what happens if things are *not* under this control of yours?" Gambino was staring coldly. "You know the media. Suppose things are not as you claim? We haven't come all the way out here for you to preside over some gathering of the international press corps."

Joubert shrugged helplessly. It was an impossible situation. Once word was out, and it was only a matter of time, there would be no hope of imposing a news blackout. He was helpless and knew it. Before he could reply Gambino continued. "Monsieur Hanay has not paid for you to come out here on a holiday, you know. Your job is to keep the press off the backs of everyone until you're told otherwise. I don't wanna see sight nor sound of any press heading my way."

Gambino rose, crossed the room and stood in front of him. "Perhaps you still don't get me." His voice was soft. "I was hoping to hear, point by point, that everything's absolutely buttoned up, water tight. When I ask for something to be done, you'd better treat it with respect. D'you read me?" Gambino let the question hang on the air. "Dino's, told you that we know all about your performance in Paris." Gambino produced a slim folder from his jacket pocket and drew out a set of photos showing Nina and Roger Trinquet as the cameras had caught them. "Here you are, hot off the press and you haven't been away five minutes," he mocked sarcastically. "You're using your wife to climb the ladder, aren't you? And she's doing a bloody good job for you. *Look!* Look at this! And *this!*" One by one the photographs were tossed on to the table, some fell to the floor. "What sort of man is it that can countenance such behaviour?" he sneered.

The colour had drained from Joubert's face. He slumped forward devastated before covering his face with his hands. When Gambino spoke again his voice was hard and unsympathetic. "OK Joubert, let's talk. We know what you want out of life and we know how you're going about it. That's fine. If you like that sort of game we can help you along." Marcel Joubert looked up in surprise.

"Sure we can. We've got some clout in Paris, too, you know. We can push things along for you. But and this is the but." He paused. "You know what we're here for and that makes me uneasy." Gambino despised the man in front of him. Anyone who could sell their own womenfolk for personal gain was, to a Mafioso *Capo*, the lowest form of life, something to be loathed, wiped from the bottom of the shoe. Furthermore the man, here, was playing the options, sitting on the fence and that was bad. Worse still, it was dangerous. He would have to go.

"Well, OK. What can I do about that?" Joubert asked.

Gambino leaned forward. "By keeping on your feet and by keeping smart. You play along with us and we'll see you fine once this one's over. That's a deal. But one tiny slip, my friend, and you get blown away…very quickly and very surely."

Joubert looked across at Bontate then back at Gambino. He nodded and tried to smile. "OK, that's a deal," he whispered. "You have my word." Then louder. "Now for Christ's sake get off my fucking back."

"Hey, now, that's what I like to hear," Gambino said quietly, sitting back in his chair. "See here…you're in with us and there's no hiding place, nowhere to go. If you changed your mind you'd be arrested and there'd be a show trial. You'd be forced to confess everything…and that would mean a long sentence." Gambino saw the other man's eyes. "It'd be no good remaining silent either," he went on. "France would wash her hands of you and life in an Egyptian jail's not to be recommended, so I'm informed. Take a look at the one here in Alexandria. You can smell the place half a mile away. And then we would be waiting for you."

Gambino strode across to the balcony, hands in pockets. "OK, that's it. We're on…no going back." Suddenly he turned. "When the heat's off we'll take good care of you. Right now, get back out there and make sure no goddam reporter or news hack gets within ten kilometres of this place."

3

Paris
Eddi Cohen hurried along the corridor of No 3 Rue Rabelais and went into the ambassador's outer office. Two days earlier he had been alerted by his opposite number in Rome and warned that the two nuclear scientists – Renee and Blosch – had been moved from their hiding place in Sicily. The contact in Marsala had not been able to confirm their destination but was certain they had left the country. Eddi had been unable to cross check the information until this morning when he had heard from the American Consulate in Casablanca.

Two Frenchmen, answering to their description, were among a party of Italian holidaymakers that had flown in from Rome. They had moved on to Marrakech and were due to remain there for a week's holiday sightseeing and walking in the Haut Atlas. At some point on the drive between the airport and their hotel, the car carrying the two men had become separated from the main party and they had not yet booked in.

As Cohen entered the main office of the Israeli Embassy, Eli Schmuel the Ambassador, rose, smiled briefly and offered him a seat. Squeezing around the edge of the table, Cohen nodded to the First Secretary and Charge d'Affaires who had also been called to the meeting. Ever since the trial in Paris two years ago, Eddi had been monitoring the events surrounding the two scientists. Israel had long appreciated the enormous potential for disaster were the two scientists ever to get out of Frèsnes maximum security prison. This threat would remain for as long as their knowledge and understanding of nuclear physics was current. Right now, they remained way ahead of the field.

Once they heard of their whereabouts the Israelis had considered whether or not to eliminate the pair. In their opinion it would not have been difficult. The debate had been heated but, in the end, it had been agreed to let them run. Mossad was monitoring the Libyan nuclear programme closely. The Americans had given Israel first class satellite photography of the Libyan nuclear and chemical weapon production centres and, after meticulous target analysis, the Israeli Air Force was confident of destroying the facilities in a single strike. Israeli intelligence wanted the men to run in order to identify their handlers. Slowly but surely they were building a picture of espionage rings throughout the Mediterranean and Renee and Blosch were an integral part of that programme. And finally France, with an eye on relations with Iraq, had requested the recapture of the scientists rather than their elimination.

"Good morning, Eddi," said the Ambassador. "Perhaps you would be kind enough to bring us up to date on Renee and Blosch. We must keep our finger on this one…if we can, that is."

Eddi went back over the ground from the time the men had been sprung from Frèsnes on Bastille Day last year. The French, indeed the whole of the west, had been caught napping. The Israelis had soon suspected the hand of the Mafia – very few other organisations had the ability to mount such an operation.

For years Israeli intelligence services had been infiltrating the leading New York and Sicilian families. A highly placed but sensitive source had passed information about those behind the escape and where the fugitives were being held. Quite understandably, they had kept this information to themselves and had painstakingly reactivated their small but effective network of informants in Sicily. Israel, and Mossad in particular, were under no illusions as to the power and capabilities of the great Mafia families.

What they had been unable to establish was the purpose behind the escape and their subsequent confinement. Initially Israel believed they had been sprung for their knowledge of the miniaturising of nuclear warheads. Now, it appeared, this was not the case. If they had been moved from Sicily to the North African mainland, the Israelis would look for some other motive. But what and where? And by whom?

The Ambassador turned to Cohen. "So what do you make of it? A bit worrying, don't you think?"

Cohen looked down, laughed and shook his head. "It's a devil of a question to answer but, for what it's worth, I reckon somebody out there's trailing the coat. Either trying to attract attention or gauge reaction from somewhere. Nothing else makes sense and they're far too smart to have made a nonsense of it."

The room was silent, nothing seemed to quite add up. "And where does that get us?" Schmuel asked.

"Well, and again it's only a guess," Cohen replied, "But I reckon there's more to come. They're going to give out an ultimatum, make demands like the release of some of their guys. Something like that." He looked at the Ambassador and shook his head. "It's certainly not over yet, that's for sure."

The discussion ran long over time and eventually the Ambassador had to call a halt. The problem, as he saw it, was that they had no direct eyes or ears in Morocco. "It's not so easy when you don't control the sources, when there's somebody else between you and the raw intelligence. One never really knows how watered down or corrupt the feedback has become. And usually they all want something in return."

It was not going to be easy and the four men in the room felt distinctly uncomfortable at the idea of two embittered scientists, full of nuclear secrets, at large and unaccounted for in the Arab world. Furthermore one of them was a Jew, a traitor caught red handed. Orders or not, those sitting round the table would rather not have been tasked with taking them alive.

4

Alexandria

The two French officers got out of the car and made their way towards Joubert's office next to the large warehouse. Dressed in the tropical service dress of the French armoured corps, they picked their way cautiously over the usual pile of ropes, boxes and stacked palettes that litter any busy harbour front. Joubert had been expecting them and stood waiting by his office door.

Planning arrangements for the Franco-Egyptian arms deal ceremony had been in progress for some time. Both Presidents had expressed a strong desire to visit Alexandria after the ceremony in the desert. The more senior of the two visitors, a two star General de Division, suggested that an evening visit, as late as possible when the worst heat of the day had gone, would be the preferred option. The acceptance trials had gone well and he explained proudly that the Leclerc MarkV main battle tank together with the new Panhard armoured troop carrying vehicles had more than surpassed the Egyptian requirements. "We've come a long way since the Gulf War where we learned one hell of a lot," he confessed. A point not lost on the Arab world. "It's been the same in the air," he went on. "We've always been pretty confident with what we've had to offer but the two new aircraft – the Dassault Rafale Multi Role and the Mirage FIC - have proved far superior to anything else they were prepared to consider. It's all gone well and there appear to be no last minute hitches."

The signing ceremony had been arranged to take place at ten in the morning in the shadow of the Giza Pyramids. Immediately afterwards the two Presidents had been scheduled to visit the troops, spend some time with them and inspect the weapon systems purchased by Egypt. This would be followed by an official lunch at the Presidential Palace. Then, after a short break, the Presidents were to be flown north to visit the site of the dive.

"They would like to see something of the dive itself, talk to the men involved and then see the exhibits," the general continued. "So why don't we put a circle around six o'clock for them to arrive at the airport, come straight here and have a good hour or so on site? Until it's dark, later if necessary. Incidentally, I hear you've found some pretty fantastic stuff." Joubert nodded but regretted, much to the visitors' disappointment, that he would be unable to show them around. He bit his lip and looked away in embarrassment, realising that he was now helplessly trapped by Gambino. Anything he said or intended to do was governed by the necessity of keeping his part of the deal. It made him angry and his hatred for the man grew.

***

The following evening Gambino asked Bontate and Joubert to join him for dinner at a fashionable beach restaurant a few miles up the coast, overlooking Aboukir Bay, the site of another marine archaeological dive. Joubert had no desire to go. His fear of Gambino was such that he tried to distance himself from the man but it was difficult and, here, he had no choice.

They ate outside on the terrace under the high date palms, the sea only a hundred metres or so from their table. Gambino came straight to the point and announced that the raid would take place on Saturday night, in four days time and shortly before the presidential visit. The artefacts would still be in their containers and Bontate's carefully orchestrated preparations and plans would be complete. It would still be Ramadan but it would be the weekend and everybody would be suitably relaxed.

They went over the plan in outline where Gambino took them through each phase in minute detail, turning either to Bontate or Joubert for clarification wherever he thought he might have spotted a flaw. Of particular concern was the selection and identification of what they were going to take. Bontate described what he had arranged after discussing the value of the items with Palmer.

Gambino took the lead once again. "In that case we go for the smaller ones and the jewelled items first…OK? I don't want the guys staggering about with great lumps of granite. And we've got to get the routine on the trucks down to a fine art." He turned to Bontate. "Just half a load each, OK. That means you bring in a half load of dummy boxes to change with those you've selected. Any more than that and there'll be a shambles…there won't be the room. Ever tried loading and unloading a full truck at the same time?"

He paused, leant back in his chair, put his arms behind his head and looked at

Joubert. "I expect you're wondering why we're making such a fuss, yes?" He paused again. "You simply cannot imagine the value of what you've been looking at these last few days. Man is a greedy animal. The richer and more powerful he becomes the greedier and hungrier he gets." He paused then waved his arm. "Just look at the money some people spend on paintings - twenty million, thirty million, more maybe. And that's for a piece of canvas perhaps a hundred years old. Very beautiful, to be sure, but still just some paint on a strip of canvas that's nailed to a wooden frame. And many of those who have bought such things, or who have had such things acquired for them, simply have them locked away at home. Nobody else sees them, just the owner and a few close friends who sit there drooling. These people pay fortunes for the stuff, and there're plenty more of them out there.

"So what do you suppose they would pay for some of the jewellery and treasures we've found? That coronation necklace of Cleopatra's, the gold one with those stones. The one that would have laid on the soft, white breast of the Egyptian queen. Can you imagine what someone would pay for that? My friends, these treasures make all the Van Goghs and the Monets that are hidden away around the place seem like kids' stuff. And we've people out there who've got the sort of money I am talking about."

"Where do you find that sort of money?" Joubert asked suddenly, unable to contain himself. Gambino's eyes shone. The operation had fired his imagination and he leant forward, looking from one man to the other "Well, they're not queuing up outside the auction houses, that's for sure," he replied. "They're waiting for me to call them. Colombia, Russia, Japan and right here in the Arab kingdoms. That's where the real money is today and that's what we're here for.

"Now, here's an important point. We won't be able to do the complete move in one night; that is do the lift here, get to France, land and sort ourselves out. There're simply not enough hours of darkness, so we'll have to make a stop over in Palermo." Gambino pursed his lips. "So, let's go firm on the routine. We want to catch the weekend. As I said earlier, we'll do the job on Saturday night. Sunday will be pretty quiet here." He turned to Bontate. "Dino, after Palermo you'll see the stuff on to France. I'll be leaving you in Sicily."

Bontate nodded. He had gone over the plans with Gambino time and again. Now, like the good *caporegime* he was, he stepped back, allowing his master to take the stage. His task now would be to listen carefully, pointing out any oversights. His time would come later once the operation got underway.

Gambino turned to Joubert. "And you'll remain here holding the show together on Sunday then leave for Paris late Sunday night. Someone's got to keep the place looking normal, so just keep the lid on things. Right? People might start wondering where everybody's got to but they shouldn't start to go crazy before Monday midday at the earliest.

"Now for the timings. I reckon we should get on with the show at eleven thirty. Nobody's yet stayed working anything like as late. Allow thirty minutes to take what we want and another thirty minutes to get to the airport. Say we get there just after midnight, then another thirty minutes to load. We should be in the air soon after one. It's a good three hours to Punta Raisi and I want the whole thing put to bed by daylight. I've fixed everything there. Then France, Dino. The crew knows the little airfield at Mazamet in the Black Mountains. Jean-Michel and his people are going to meet you with a couple of trucks. The pilot has instructions to get there just after midnight. Remember the time change. It gets light early in France but that should give you time to get up to La Trampa.

"I'm leaving the handling of the stuff entirely to you. Make sure your crazy gang know the plan backwards. The last thing we want is for some jerk to panic and lose the plot." He paused. "Well, here's to it…it's taken long enough."

"And what happens if we're bounced in the middle of it all?" Bontate asked.

"Depends who it is," Gambino replied. "If it's a guard then we blow 'im away. Simple," he shrugged. "You've got the silenced weapons." He saw the startled look on Joubert's face. "This is for real, my friend. Anyone important then we'll have to sweep them up and drop them off once we're clear. If they're well known players we can't just leave them or they'll start screaming before we're out of the door. And we can't start knocking them off either. Not nice."

***

Sir Alan Palmer threw down his pen and leant back. It was hot and airless in the cramped office cabin. For the last three hours he and Mary Sutton had been checking the inventory against the numerous historical records they had brought out with them. In spite of the air conditioning, working through the afternoon had been hard going but now, just before six, the temperature outside was beginning to drop.

"Mary," he called out. "I've had just about enough…I really have." He sauntered over to the door of her office, hitching up his trousers. "Come on, down tools. Let's get a breath of fresh air out on the harbour wall then go for a drink. Leave everything here. We can finish later."

The two walked slowly along the harbour front before turning on to the long jetty that stretched around the old port and out to the lighthouse. Alone, save for some wheeling gulls, they took their time. After two hundred yards they climbed a set of stone steps on to the outer jetty. Beyond was the open sea. They paused to watch a group of naked urchins playing noisily and laughed as the boys threw stones into the water and dived after them.

"You know, Mary, I haven't done this for years," Palmer said slowly.

"What's that?" Mary queried. Moving to his side she half turned her foot on a cobble and fell against him. He caught her hand to steady her and they laughed. "What's that you haven't done?" she asked.

"Well, it's not really a holiday, but I haven't enjoyed a walk so much for simply ages." He checked himself momentarily. "I mean, I walk miles on my own but I haven't been *with* someone like this. Not since Emma died. It's lovely to be able to share an evening. So different to when you're on your own."

"You still miss her dreadfully, don't you." Mary had started work for Palmer a few months after his wife died and often looked at the photograph he kept on his desk. Unknown to him, she cleaned the small silver frame every week. Only once had he spoken of her.

Resting his arms on the buttress he looked out to sea. "Yes, I suppose I do," he sighed, screwing up his eyes. "After Jack, she was all I had."

Mary looked at the man beside her. All of a sudden he was no longer the great, international figure of the archaeological world, knight of the realm, Cambridge scholar and acclaimed author. Standing there, instead, she saw a sad, elderly man, drawn and stooped. A father and husband bereft of the two people in the world he had loved and lost. "You've never spoken to me about Jack," she said quietly. "Would you like to tell me? He must have been a wonderful boy."

"Yes, he was. A lovely young man, so full of life and promise." Palmer raised his hand to shield his eyes from the sun. "He was only twenty three when he was killed. It was during the Falklands, you know." He turned to face Mary. "He'd just finished at Durham and joined his Regiment. Nineteen-eighty-two it was. A long time ago now but it seems like yesterday. The Scots Guards had been ordered to capture Mount Tumbledown. They chose to do it at night. The fighting was heavy, very heavy. It went on all night and must have been a terrible business." He paused for a moment then continued quietly. "You see, they didn't find Jack and the others until dawn next morning."

Mary turned towards Palmer, slipping her hand under his arm. She wanted desperately to brush the wisps of long, grey hair from his face, to put her arm round the tall, spare figure and pull him towards her. He took off his glasses and gazed out to sea, blinking in the light of the setting sun. "The Regiment was marvellous about it. Made a huge fuss of us but what could they do?" He shrugged despondently. "We went up to the Memorial Service and met the other relatives. There were so many questions still in our mind. You know, the details every parent dreads but has to know. Just to be sure.

"Then one day, out of the blue, the phone rang. It was Jack's Platoon Sergeant. Asked if he could come down and see us. A wonderful man." He paused, trying hard to recollect. "Sergeant Campbell, that was him. A great big highlander from Perth." He paused again, thinking back. "He came because he knew that we still wanted to know. How Jack had died and all that." Palmer dropped his head and rubbed his hand across his mouth. "Emma wanted to leave us on our own but he begged her to stay then told us gently, in that lovely soft highland voice. He told us that Jack had been killed instantly by a machine gun. He was out in front on his own, he said. Leading his men, all on his own." Palmer's voice rose sharply, the last few words tumbling out.

As Mary slipped her hand from behind his elbow, she felt his body shaking. Gently she turned him towards her. Lifting her hand to his face she wiped a tear from his cheek. "Oh, my poor dear. My poor, dear man," she whispered. "I can imagine how it must have hurt." Taking one of his hands in hers she raised it to her lips. "Come on, now," she said softly, shaking the hand gently. "You know there's something else as well. In it's own strange way, for all the horror, it's a wonderful story about a very brave young man. You must have been so proud of the boy." She stood quietly, holding his hand in hers. "Come on, let's walk back. You'll feel better." As they walked she took his arm in hers.

✳✳✳

The following morning Gambino asked Gideon if he could have a look around the El Rashid and perhaps hear a bit about how they set about the diving. He walked into the hanger and made his way across to where the sarcophagi lay. The door of the office opened and Palmer's assistant, Amanda Gates, came out and walked towards him. Mario Gambino looked at the tall, blonde girl and liked what he saw.

Her long hair was tied back untidily, but a stray lock had fallen across her bronzed face. As she looked towards him, she smiled and tried to push her hair back, lifting her face as she did so. He noticed, too, how the light, cotton laboratory coat fitted snugly over her generous curves with the bottom three buttons undone seductively.

"Oh, hello," she said smiling. "I'm Amanda Gates, Sir Alan Palmer's assistant. Excuse me asking but are you sure you're allowed in here?" She felt herself blushing deeply at the futility of what she had just said to this devastatingly handsome man standing in front of her.

"Well," Gambino replied, making a wry smile and extending his hand. "Sir Alan is a lucky man. Where I come from they don't make assistants anything like *this*," he opened his arms expansively. "And the answer to your question is no. I'm ashamed to say that I've no business in here whatsoever." He caught the surprised look on her face. "So you'd better pick me up, hold me tight so I can't run away and then carry me gently outside." The two of them burst out laughing.

"Oh, I'm sorry. I didn't mean to be rude," Amanda replied. "You are a friend of Dino's aren't you?"

"Indeed I am. Gambino, Mario Gambino's my name and I would be delighted if you could tell me how to get hold of our tame Neptune out there. I've arranged to meet Francois Gideon. He's promised to show me around. Any chance of your company?"

"I'm afraid not." She shook her head. "We've got an awful lot to do and we're taking it in turns to finish the catalogue entries. It's maddening but I've completely run out of superlatives trying to describe these incredible things. What's more exquisite than exquisite?"

"Er...what did you say your name was again?" he quipped and they laughed again spontaneously. There followed a short silence before Gambino continued. "Look, you're going to have to stop sooner or later. How about joining me for dinner this evening? Or is that against the rules as well? There's a lovely little fish restaurant just up the coast. We could meet in the hotel lobby at about eight?" He looked at her with his head on one side as his eyes searched her face. "Unless, of course, you've already got something planned?"

She frowned. "Well...I'll have to see. No, no," she joked, suddenly grinning happily. "Only teasing. No, I've nothing else in mind. And thanks. Yes, I'd love to."

***

After the meal they walked down to the beach, took off their shoes and ambled through the still warm sand. Gambino felt his whole body yearning for the girl yet forced himself to be patient. Over dinner she had teased him mercilessly about being a typical Latin lover boy, all dark, handsome looks and promises. She asked him about his private life, his family and sat enthralled as he told her about life as a boy in the Sicilian mountains.

It was after they had turned back, while strolling along the water's edge that she caught part of a shell between her toes. They stopped and leant momentarily against each other while she wiped her foot. Once back at the car it was his turn to tease her. All that promiscuous behaviour on the beach, hanging on to the arm that was steadying her like it was. What did she think she was up to, out there with a strange man at this time of night?

"I'm not a child you know, Mario," she retorted. "I'm a big girl now, nearly thirty, and am quite capable of looking after myself, strange men or not."

"Yes, I can see that," he murmured. "But you're more than that. You're a very beautiful young woman and to prove I'm not your naughty little Italian boy, I'm going to take you straight home, but only if you promise to come out again tomorrow night."

"And if I refuse?" she asked.

"You'll regret it for the rest of your life and never forgive yourself." As he looked at her, he stroked a loose strand of hair from her forehead. "And anyway it's our last chance. I'm on my way in a couple of days."

"Well," she said slowly, looking down. "I'm afraid, dear man, that it's just too bad. I can't...I'll be working. Sir Alan's got behind and we're trying to catch up." She looked at him. "I'm sorry, Mario, dreadfully sorry. It would have been lovely," she whispered, leaning forward and kissing him briefly. "But thank you all the same."

He looked at her, smiled and shrugged ruefully. "Yes, it would have been lovely...that's for sure."

On the drive back he asked her if she thought she'd ever be likely to see him again. She watched his face as he drove. It was a beautiful face with fine dark features yet there was something just beneath the surface, something cold and calculating. She couldn't put a finger on it. It was nothing he had said or done just something strange tucked away as if the owner of the face was waiting to pounce. Suddenly, and for no apparent reason, he asked her if she had ever been to France. "Years ago," she replied. "I used to go over quite a bit when I was studying. Paris mainly, places like the Tuileries Palace, Chambon and Chateau d'Anet. Later on my father took me over a couple of times when he was looking for his favourite wines. But that's about it." She looked at him. "But why do you ask?"

"Would you like to go back again?" He slowed the car and turned briefly to look at her. She stared back then leant towards him and asked where they would go and what they would do.

"It would be down in the south," he replied. "Right down in the south where you can see the Pyrenees and there's miles and miles of vineyards, sunflowers and lavender fields. Maybe one day we might meet there."

"Well, maybe," she sighed. "Yes...that'd be nice."

5

The warehouse
Joubert had not slept well; hardly at all. Bontate had left to prepare things and he was alone on duty in the warehouse. He looked around nervously. The combination of Ramadan and the weekend had left the harbour empty and strangely silent. Amanda was working in the office and came out to tell him that

Palmer would be joining her and that they would both be working late again. Joubert felt himself gasp. As soon as Amanda left, he hurried to the hotel in an attempt to find Gambino and warn him, but he had checked out. All he could do now was to wait and the day dragged interminably.

He did not want to disturb Amanda and spent the time meaninglessly working on his plans for the following day, trying to decide how he was going to get away after the others had gone. It was impossible to concentrate and twice he found himself wandering aimlessly, barely noticing the activities around him. What, he wondered, would he say to Palmer and Amanda in the morning? Who would be the first to raise the alarm and what would the reaction be? He prayed hard that by the time the bells were ringing, he would be many hundreds of miles away. But then, most important of all, what the hell was he going to do in Paris?

✳✳✳

Sir Alan Palmer came into the warehouse at eight o'clock and began to work in the office. Every now and then he would emerge, walk across to the compound to examine the contents of one or other of the boxes. Joubert was now certain that there was going to be a clash. Nobody had foreseen that people would be working so late. He raced back to the hotel again and searched frantically for Bontate but found no sign. Just after eleven a second lorry came into the warehouse. Joubert hurried over to the vehicle but stopped when he saw the two men had lifted the bonnet and were tinkering with the engine.

Suddenly, just before eleven thirty Bontate was there, standing in the doorway talking to the guard. He waved the man away and Joubert could see him looking at his watch. He wanted desperately to warn him about Palmer but he stayed talking to the drivers and Joubert could not get close. He tried to attract his attention but Bontate seemed to ignore him.

A minute later the two lorries started up and reversed down the length of the hanger and up to the entrance of the compound. Their tailgates were lowered and, at Bontate's word, the six men set to work. They moved quickly to a well-rehearsed drill, knowing exactly which boxes to take. To his horror Joubert watched as the door to Palmer's office opened. Sir Alan Palmer stood in the doorway watching the activity in front of him. Joubert saw him cup his hands to his mouth and heard him shout. "Hey, Dino. What on earth's going on? What are those men doing with all those boxes? Who told you to do this?"

Bontate moved fast. He told the men to continue then walked quickly across to Palmer. "Look, I'm terribly sorry, Sir Alan. I'd hoped that you wouldn't be working so late. I'm afraid you're going to have to come along with us." Palmer was about to speak when he looked at Bontate again. In his right hand a lightly oiled, silenced automatic gleamed in the light.

"I'm sorry, really sorry," Bontate said again. " Will you please come quietly now. Both you and your secretary. Come on Miss Gates, just leave everything like it is. I'd hate to have to use this, they make such a mess. This way please and into the back of the lorry. Come on now, hurry up."

Amanda stopped and looked at Sir Alan Palmer who was standing quite still with a hand to his head. "My God," she whispered. "Oh, dear God alive...why didn't I see it...I might have guessed. Now I see it...yes, yes everything." She glanced at the gun in Bontate's hand and then up at his face. For a moment she held his gaze then she turned and hurried across to Sir Alan Palmer. She took his arm gently and helped him into the back of the lorry before climbing in after him.

Keeping close to the wall, Joubert made his way to the main doors and out into the night. Once clear of the warehouse he began to run.

PART TWO
A Very Long Week Indeed

Chapter Nine

Alexandria

Joubert returned to the El Pasha an hour later. Hot, tired and confused at what he had witnessed, he showered, lay back on his bed and tried to think coherently. The next twenty-four hours were going to be difficult. The omens were not good and, even now, he was tempted to ring the French Embassy and make a clean breast of it all. But today was Sunday and the switchboard would put him through to the Duty Officer who would simply log his call and tell him to call back in the morning. And what was there to say anyway?

Sooner or later the finger of suspicion would be pointed at him; at the very least he would be held partially responsible. And there, in the back of his mind, was Gambino's warning that France would simply turn her back on him, offering him up as a sacrificial lamb. His heart sank. Once it was all over they might negotiate his release from wherever the Egyptians chose to put him, but what after that? And finally, lurking all the while, was the constant spectre of Gambino himself.

The most obvious course was for him to play out the next day as best he could and get back to Paris where Gambino had promised to look after him. However, once word was out, the head of the Foreign Ministry's Security Department would come looking for him as well; a full and satisfactory explanation being the first of his many demands. If Gambino made contact first he would hear what he had to offer. If Déschampes came before him then he would go down that route.

So, home had to be his starting point. It was the only option. He glanced at the clock on the bedside table and saw the time – three o'clock. Cursing, he reset the alarm for five, vowing to rise early, get back to the warehouse office and clean up any evidence that might indicate Palmer and Amanda Gates had been disturbed and abducted. After that he would come back to the hotel and tidy their rooms, rearranging their belongings so the casual observer would believe they had left deliberately rather than suddenly gone missing. That should buy a bit more time. Then there was the Sutton woman to consider, and Francois Gideon. He would try to hold them until Monday morning but by then things would be very different. The place would erupt, but that would no longer be his problem.

Unable to sleep, Joubert rose before the alarm went off and packed most of his belongings before going down to the warehouse. He recognised the guard at the main door but was surprised at the way the man looked at him. Eventually he waved him past and Joubert let himself in. The office was easy. He simply removed any evidence that showed Palmer and Gates had been working there. Palmer, he knew, was a tidy and precise man who carried his personal effects around in the brief case he always brought to work. Joubert cleared his desk, returning what papers he assumed had come out of the case, and took Palmer's white jacket from behind the door.

Amanda Gates, ever the meticulous personal assistant, had few belongings at her place of work. He tidied her desk then closed down the computer and word processor, noticing the scent of her perfume on the back of her office chair. The line he would take with anyone asking for them would be that they had not worked late the previous evening, in fact he had heard them discussing about doing some research in Cairo.

He returned to the El Pasha as the place was beginning to stir. Before he confronted the receptionist Joubert took the back stairs to his room, stripped off and forced himself to lie on his bed until he had stopped sweating. He then showered again, changed his clothes and returned to the foyer where he asked the girl at reception to call the two rooms. Anticipating the reply, he explained that he expected them to be away but needed to go up and to collect some material. As she handed him the keys she glanced at him inquisitively. The wild, unshaven face that looked back at Joubert from the dimly lit mirror in the elevator gave him a shock. He had clean forgotten to shave and found himself gazing into the eyes of a hunted man, someone he had never seen before. For a moment, the panic returned.

Once inside their rooms, he smoothed down the beds, collected their overnight things into a small holdall and tidied the remainder of their clothes. Satisfied that the rooms would look temporarily vacated, he hid the holdall in his own room and went down for breakfast. After seemingly endless cups of coffee, he set out on a long detour to his office thereby killing another hour. Once inside, he switched on the air conditioning and sat disconsolately, aimlessly shuffling through the papers on his desk.

At around ten Mary Sutton came in to the complex and began to work in the small inner office. After typing a number of short articles for the inventory she stopped and went over to where Joubert was working. "Morning, Marcel," she called. "How's everything today?" Then, without waiting for an answer, "Look, where is everyone? It's almost eleven and there's nobody about. Dino should be here by now and it looks as though Sir Alan and Amanda hardly touched the place last night. I know it's Ramadan and Sunday," she continued, "But we've got a dreadful amount to do and I can't understand why nobody's in."

Joubert rose, forcing himself to smile. "Good morning, m'dam," he replied. "Now, now…give them all a chance. For a start, you won't find Dino here, he's off for the weekend. I think he's gone to Cairo with Mario and his friends. As for the others, well…let them have a bit of a lie in. We're pretty much up to schedule and it is Sunday." He walked over to the coffee percolator, thinking hard how best to deal with the woman's concern. "They'll be here in a while," he urged. "How about a coffee? Come on, I fancy one myself. Let's take them outside."

They moved away from the buildings and took in the morning sun but suddenly, after a few minutes silence, Mary Sutton got to her feet and stood facing him, hands on hips. "*No*, Marcel. It's no good…I don't like it," she announced. "Something's wrong, I don't care what you say. It's just not like them to be away like this. They always let me know when plans have changed. I think we should do something."

Joubert felt his pulse quicken. "Look, calm down, for Heaven's sake." He got to his feet, placing his cup on a nearby bollard then caught hold of her arm. "Listen. If anything *was* up, the hotel staff would have been on to us by now. Sir Alan did talk about going into Cairo yesterday afternoon, to do a bit of work in one of the museums. Wouldn't surprise me if he if they're staying with the Carvers – the Cultural Attaché at your Embassy."

"Then why on earth didn't they let me know?" Mary Sutton looked at him closely. "It's all very odd."

"Well, they were due to go down there sooner or later, so why not now?" he replied as casually as he could, cursing himself for having to deceive this friendly, trusting woman. "Honestly, my advice would be to get on with whatever has to be done while there's peace and quiet. If they're still not back in the morning then it's a very different story. But there's no need to get into a spin…really."

An hour later the two lorries drove into the warehouse. Now that she could see and hear the usual bustle of activity, Mary felt easier. But after that, the long afternoon dragged, minute by minute. Eventually Joubert went over to see her, telling her that he was going to finish for the day and suggested she should not bother to work late. He could barely refrain from bidding her farewell but it was time for him to leave. He went back to the hotel for the last time and packed the remainder of his belongings, taking care to leave just enough behind to make the room look occupied. He wanted to create the impression that he, too, had left only temporarily. He moved his bags out of the hotel side entrance, hailed a taxi and left for Masr station in time to catch the late afternoon Cairo express. At the station he stuffed the holdall containing Palmer's and Sutton's belongings onto a pile of smouldering rubbish. A little over five hours remained until his Air France flight was due to depart from Cairo International Airport and he began to relax.

Mary Sutton worked on for another hour then closed the office. She tried to find Joubert but he too had disappeared. It was then that her nerve broke. She rang the British Embassy and tried to explain her concern. The Duty Officer's attempts to placate her served only to make her angry and she found herself shouting into the telephone telling him that he had missed the point. Eventually she calmed herself, apologised and listened dejectedly as he told her that unless she had concrete evidence that something had gone seriously wrong, he could not disturb the embassy staff at this hour. The best course for her would be to call Mr Carver in the morning. He would leave a note on his desk advising him that he should expect a call from her.

2

Flight No JA 306
Several hours earlier the turn around and departure of Flight No JA 306 from Alexandria had gone according to plan. As soon as it was loaded the turbojet eased out of the cargo terminal and waited patiently on the pan until it was called forward. It then taxied out to the main runway and turned ready for take off.

Inside, the large pile of cardboard boxes had been stacked neatly in the central freight bay and were held secure by cargo nets. The passengers and freight crew sat facing each other in uncomfortable net seats suspended along either side of the aircraft. Suddenly, the engines increased to a howl. Amanda grabbed Palmer's arm and closed her eyes. The aircraft shuddered violently then surged forward down the runway forcing the passengers back into their seats. Once airborne, the engines were throttled back and the undercarriage clattered into the wing frames. The pilot continued to climb steadily, heading first north then north west before settling on the long journey across the Mediterranean.

The flight to Punta Raisi airport took three and a half hours; conditions in the freight bay were spartan. One of the crew offered the passengers coffee and blankets to protect themselves from the cold, but that was all. Some dozed fitfully, others read. Bontate checked his watch, loosened his tie and lay back against the supporting net. Palmer stared at the man. To him it was violent, criminal skulduggery, the very idea of which revolted him. He had never come across such people before, in fact he had no idea they even existed.

Eventually, after sweeping around Palermo in a wide arc, the Super Nor Lander dipped sharply before levelling out. The pilot cut back the engine and allowed the aircraft to feather down gently before it touched with a slight bump. Obeying the instructions from the control tower he taxied away from the passenger terminal to the cargo sheds at the far side of the airfield where he turned and came to a halt.

Earlier that evening, Gambino had arrived on a scheduled flight from Cairo. Although momentarily thrown by the news that Palmer and Miss Gates were

107

caught up in the raid, he remained calm, even intrigued. Dino Bontate's decision had been the right one: there was no alternative other than to bring them along. As soon as he heard the news he moved swiftly, arranging for the two hostages to be held in an apartment on the outskirts of Palermo until they were called forward for the second leg.

***

Once the party had assembled in the deserted foyer of the cargo terminal Gambino had Palmer and Amanda Gates brought to him. He offered them seats in the cramped waiting area but they chose to stand. As he spoke, Gambino noticed the pale, drawn look on Palmer's face. The archaeologist looked shocked and held on to the arm of his assistant.

Amanda glared defiantly. "Well, well, well...*Mi*-ster lover boy Gambino," she sneered. "If you dare to call yourself a gentleman, might we ask what the hell you think you're playing at?" She paused, catching the faint smile on Gambino's face. "And don't start grinning at me like that, damn you. What's it all about for Heaven's sake? Oh, come on, man, you had all the patter and soft talk the other night...dreaming of France and all that. So what's all this?"

Palmer coughed, squared his shoulders and tugged at his collar. "God alone knows what you're trying to achieve Gambino," he said. "You'll never get away with this...you'll have the full might of several countries on to you as soon as word is out." He looked at the thickset man standing next to him. "And I would ask your friends to keep those wretched guns out of sight. I've given you my word...and mine's a word that still counts, you understand. What on *earth* d'you suppose we're going to do, for God's sake?"

Gambino motioned them to sit. "Listen. Had we left you back there we would have created a problem for ourselves. However, we don't want you here with us, and that's for sure." He smoothed back his hair. "You're not required and, to put it politely, you're entirely surplus to our requirements. If you do exactly as I say you'll come to no harm." He raised a finger in warning. "But I warn you, this is no game. We are serious people and have much to do."

"Don't you *dare* threaten me." Amanda's eyes were blazing. "Just a couple of nights ago you were begging me...weren't you now, begging for it so you were. You're no better than the rest of them, Mario Gambino...just a nasty, oily little spiv...and stop smirking like that for God's sake."

"All right, Amanda, that's enough." Sir Alan Palmer lifted his chin and straightened his tie. "Now look, Gambino. I've already given you my word that we're not going to do anything untoward and I'm fed up with all these melodramatic threats." He took off his glasses and wiped them. "I've no idea what your plans

108

are but I trust you'll have the good grace to explain yourself in due course. Right now we'd be obliged if you would find us somewhere where we can wash and tidy ourselves up and then find something to eat."

For a few seconds the two men stared at each other before Palmer turned away, choosing to ignore the presence of the Italian. "Yes indeed, I understand your difficulties." Gambino inclined his head. He went on to say that they would be the guests of one of his friends for the day and would be continuing the journey with them that night. He appreciated that they had no change of clothes or hand luggage but they knew of a new supermarket where they would be happy to buy the essentials for them. "And that's *my* word," he concluded.

"Well just keep to it for once." Amanda turned her back on her captor. The Italian saw that his hostages remained quite unmoved by his presence. Their attitude irritated him yet he found them a fascinating couple. Nobody reacted to a Mafia supremo, a senior Family Boss with such indifference, nobody at all…ever. He smiled and shook his head, warming momentarily to their courage.

***

Flight No JA 306 took off from Punta Raisi soon after ten that evening. Maintaining his north westerly course, the pilot skirted around the south of Sardinia, thus avoiding the Italian air traffic control. Then, an hour later, and in an attempt to duck beneath the radars at Nice and Marseille, he descended to sea level. Racing across the calm, moonlit water they crossed the coast of France between Montpelier and Beziers.

Immediately the pilot increased power and climbed steeply to clear the mountains of the Haut Languedoc. Once above the crest line he altered course to the west and followed the ridge for several minutes before picking out the lights of Castres beneath the starboard wing. He had made the same run on a number of occasions before and brought the aircraft down in a low arc over the town before heading back towards the mountain town of Mazamet. It was a difficult approach into a steep valley with mountains on three sides and the runway was short. There was no homing beacon and no control tower, not even a friendly voice on the radio. As the black outline of the mountains rose either side of him, the pilot prayed that those on the ground would do their stuff.

Below on the deserted military air strip at Labruguiére an aldis lamp winked at the approaching aircraft. JA 306 replied by flashing its landing lights momentarily then banked steeply before circling for a final run in. Two lightweight Peugeot scooters left the reception party and sped down the runway. Driving fast and fifty metres apart, the drivers slowed every hundred metres so that the pillion riders could lean over to light a long line of firelighters placed in small tins along the sides of the strip. Moments later the flickering flight path and circular turning area at the end were visible from the cockpit of the aircraft. As soon as the wheels touched, the pilot threw the engines into reverse thrust, slowed and turned before taxiing back along the line of lights. Before the aircraft came to a stop, the crew were out of their seats, had uncovered the freight and lowered the rear loading ramp. It took barely twenty minutes to transfer the cargo from the aircraft to the waiting lorries. As soon as the plane had been emptied, the scooters repeated their run, relit the flight path and the Nor Lander was on its way, climbing hard to clear the four thousand foot peaks of the Black Mountains.

In less than half an hour, the convoy of four cars and the three lorries left the airstrip, skirted around the sleeping town of Castres and headed for their destination deep in the vine covered hills some two hours away. It was early Monday morning.

3

Alexandria

Now frantic with worry, Mary Sutton had been ringing the British Embassy since seven-thirty in the hope that the Cultural Attaché might have come in early. When finally they spoke, his first reaction, after calming her, was to ask if the artefacts were secure and if the diving programme was continuing. She admitted, somewhat sheepishly, that everything appeared to be in order and listened in despair as he asked her to call him later when he would make arrangements to come out to the site if she was still concerned. Still worried, she called Gideon and was relieved to see he, at least, shared her fears. He agreed that the situation was unusual and suggested that she went back to the hotel to check with reception and to search their rooms. The receptionist confirmed that Gambino had checked out early the previous afternoon, followed by Bontate several hours later. On the other hand Joubert, Palmer and Miss Gates were still booked in.

She explained her concern to the manager who sent staff with her to help check the rooms. Finding the clothes and personal effects of Palmer and Amanda Gates folded up and hidden away raised her suspicions. But it was when they searched Joubert's room and found he had left with everything except a few personal possessions, that Mary Sutton knew for certain that something was horribly wrong.

"Right, come on. Let's go and check the place." Gideon cried before shouting across the water to Yves Didier. He then turned and ran after Mary Sutton who was on her way to the warehouse. The search did not take long.

"Oh my God. Francois, *quick*, over here." Mary stood aghast, a fragment of paving stone in her hand. "I can't believe it," she muttered opening another box and pulling out another stone. She spun round. "Francois, *look*," she gasped. "They've gone. I just can't believe it. The jewels…they've been stolen. Look. Here, and here. This one too." She went from box to box.

"OK, stay right there," Didier called. "I'll get the team in from the boat and fetch the guard commander. We'll have to check everything. Where're all the others for God's sake? Where's Dino, Alan Palmer, Marcel and the others?"

Mary Sutton slumped against the portakabin door. She stared bleakly at the sight of the divers running towards her, closed her eyes and turned away with her head in her hands. It took an hour to discover that over one hundred of the very best artefacts had gone and the finger of suspicion pointed at some or all of those now missing. Both Francois Gideon and Mary Sutton rang their embassies then the Supreme Council of Antiquities. Gideon suspended all diving activities and organised the divers to secure the warehouse, asking the guard commander to increase security around the perimeter. His cameramen checked the CCTV only to find that the critical cameras were either broken or had been set incorrectly.

It was almost two hours before the officials and diplomats began to arrive. Their presence, each with their own national interests at heart, served only to confuse further. But slowly and inexorably throughout the morning the initial, half-hearted flurry of diplomatic activity gathered pace. By noon, not only were those in Alexandria caught up in the drama but the staffs of several embassies and numerous political luminaries in Cairo, Paris, London and Berlin had been made aware of the situation.

***

In Paris, the Duty Officer at the Foreign Ministry received the initial call from the French Embassy in Cairo. He asked Cairo to keep him informed and penned a note to the Ministry's Chef de Cabinet. A few minutes later he decided to try to call Alexandria in an attempt to reach Joubert's office in the warehouse complex. It was a tenuous link but he realised the seriousness of the initial report and was determined to try for more information. "Come on, come on," he muttered impatiently into the phone. "Somebody answer the bloody thing, for God's sake." He was lucky. Francois Gideon had just finished speaking to the French Embassy in Cairo when the phone rang. He picked up the receiver and Paris came on the line.

Frustrated at the slow reaction from Cairo, Gideon spoke slowly and clearly. He replied that almost all of the very best treasures had vanished. The Culture Ministry's man, Joubert, was missing with most of his team and his absence was being regarded with suspicion. Thirdly, the British professor, Sir Alan Palmer, and his assistant were unaccounted for. And finally, the only lead thus far from the airport was that the destination of those involved might be France. "You guys back there had better start moving," Francois Gideon gesticulated as he spoke. "There's an earthquake on its way and, in case you didn't know it, France is slap back in the middle of the epicentre. So get your arse out of that comfy chair and start ringing every bell you can lay your hands on."

In Cairo, the British Embassy attempted to distance itself from the melee, regarding the affair strictly as a matter between Egypt and France. The rustle of diplomatic umbrellas was clearly audible. The French Embassy, now seriously rattled, wrapped a protective cloak around their own man, then challenged the British assessment, reminding them cynically that London's own British Museum was seriously implicated.

The reaction of the Egyptians was instant and positive. Without further delay, the Ambassadors of France and the United Kingdom were summoned to the Foreign Ministry but without the usual diplomatic niceties. Even as the messages were being passed, Egyptian government limousines were on their way to collect their charges. Passports of all foreign nationals working on the project were seized. The Supreme Council ordered the immediate arrest and interrogation of every Egyptian national involved. "We need the facts and we need them fast," the Head of the Secret Police was told. "Get on with it," the voice barked. "Do whatever's necessary, and don't stand on ceremony." Then the line went dead.

Ever since they could remember, the Secret Police had prayed fervently to be given a chance to get at the vast port complexes of northern Egypt. Narcotics, drugs, prostitution and petty crime raged out of control, subject only to the law of the underworld. Now was their chance and they took it. When the call came, Commander Barak el Farouk was not at prayer, rather he was settled comfortably in his deep, well padded leather chair. His door was locked. Above him, the old ceiling fan battled slowly and ineffectually against the stifling heat. For the last half hour he had been sifting through some choice items of literature picked up in a warehouse raid earlier that day. The magazine photographer had done well, catching every last detail of the entangled young men and the woman performing miracles with a rampant Doberman. His coffee had gone cold. But, as he listened to the call his eyes swept upwards and closed. Even before the phone was back on its hook, the shouting began.

✳✳✳

The British Ambassador in Cairo warned the Foreign and Commonwealth Office that the situation was looking grim and would, in his opinion, deteriorate further. The Egyptians took little time in reminding the French that it was their men, Bontate and Joubert, who had been in charge. They would be pleased if the Ambassador would furnish them with a full and satisfactory explanation. Unfortunately for him, the Ambassador had yet to be briefed.

Simultaneously, the Egyptians pressed the British Ambassador for the immediate presence of Sir Alan Palmer. The Supreme Council had a number of urgent questions they wished to put to him. Sir Geoffrey Gladstone, Her Majesty's Ambassador, stared bleakly at the Egyptian Minister who could barely conceal his rage. "My dear Minister," Sir Geoffrey replied coolly. "Could you please explain yourself. I'm afraid I haven't the faintest idea what you're talking about."

After an uncomfortable morning, the French Ambassador spoke to Paris. He had little to offer other than the news that the Egyptians had already briefed their own Prime Minister. He concluded by advising Quay d'Orsay that their own Prime Minister, Lionel Jospin, should be informed without delay. Paris took a deep breath and replied that this could take some time. Prime Minister Jospin, along with the UK Prime Minister, Tony Blair, was currently in Berlin attending the EC summit. Furthermore the Prime Minister was accompanying his Foreign Minister, Jean-Paul Debroque. In Berlin it was ten o'clock and the EC summit was about to begin. It had two full days to run.

In Cairo where it was midday the tension was rising. In Paris it was eleven o'clock and ten o'clock in London. For a variety of individuals, many still blissfully unaware, Monday was about to become a very busy day.

4

Paris

Gambino had been up before dawn. Although anxious to get down to the southwest he had much to consider. The room was almost bare but he found himself a chair and worked at the table, jacket off, the papers in front of him lit by a solitary lamp. He looked at his empty cup, grimaced and wandered into the kitchen. A member of the surveillance team had left behind a portable music centre and, as he waited for the water to boil, he looked through the pile of cassettes. The man had taste and Gambino was impressed. He ducked over the sink to look out of the window at the dawn light as the strains of *'Il Trouvatore'* began to fill the room.

It was a very old recording of Gigli singing *"Ah si, ben mio"* and the great voice seemed hard pressed in its battle against the background crackle and hiss. But Gambino heard none of the interference, only the voice of the maestro. He closed his eyes and found himself taken back once more to the Sicilian hills, to the village of his childhood. He had returned to the dusty, cobbled square and was sitting next to his mother. There, as she gossiped to her friends in the shade of the tall cypress trees, they could hear the music coming from the old gramophone belonging to the café owner. He remembered how he and his friends would gather wide-eyed around the old lady as she proudly wound the handle of the ancient machine. Then, scolding loudly, she would blow the dust from the chipped record before triumphantly placing the needle on the whirring disc.

As he hummed the aria, Gambino smiled to himself, swaying gently before a knock at the door made him start. He called quietly and three men entered. One, the leader and a brute of a man, strode across to Gambino and took his hand. The man mumbled his greetings, bowed deferentially before turning to introduce his companions waiting nervously by the door. Gambino took the leader aside, spoke rapidly in Sicilian then listened as the team were given their tasks.

He watched with satisfaction as the leader checked the rooms meticulously and noticed the hard, muscular frames of the three as they prepared themselves. Bontate had assured him they were good. As soon as they were ready, Gambino ordered them to wait in the kitchen then closed the door behind them and returned to the paperwork on the table.

Across the city, Joubert waited anxiously at Baggage Arrival. Though barely five in the morning the giant airport was already busy and he could see short queues at Passport Control and Customs. Throughout the long flight from Cairo, he had been considering his best course of action. He was nervous of what the next few hours might bring but satisfied he was doing the right thing. He had weighed the options carefully and felt comfortable. He would indeed head for home – Rue de Longchamp. Number 86 would be empty. Nina and the children were still away at Cap Ferret and not due back until the end of the following week. There, at least, he would be able to tuck himself away and have a little more time to collect his thoughts.

✱✱✱

He put the key in the lock of No 86, opened the door with his shoulder and stepped inside. Suddenly he stopped and turned. Behind him, standing in the doorway he saw a middle aged woman who introduced herself bashfully, explaining that she was one of the new occupants from across the street. She had seen him return and decided to come over straight away. A couple of nights earlier, she explained, her husband and a friend had caught two youths coming out of No 86 with a television set. When challenged they had run off but had left their van with a number of household items in the back that had most likely been taken from houses in the street. Rather than call the gendarmes, who would have simply shrugged off the incident, they had decided to take the contents into their house for safe keeping then ask those in the neighbourhood to come and identify anything that was missing.

He glanced into the drawing room noticing immediately that the television set and sideboard clock had disappeared. "God dammit," he muttered. "Yes, for certain. It's gone, look…and my clock. Better come and see what you've got."

As they walked across the street the woman turned to him and asked in a pleasant voice if he had been away long. "Just a couple of weeks," he replied cheerfully. "Pleasant enough trip, but it's always good to be back," he added, rubbing his hands together. Joubert followed her into the house where she let him pass, motioning him to go up the stairs. He did…then stopped. There, sitting in the chair on the other side of the front room was Mario Gambino.

Looking past Joubert, Gambino nodded and the door was shut firmly. Turning, Joubert saw the three men, now stripped to the waist. His body went cold. As he turned back to face Gambino his mouth opened. "What's all this, Mario?" he gasped, his face suddenly haggard with terror. "I've only just got in and I hear there's been a burglary. How come you're here? What's going on?"

Gambino stood. "Monsieur Joubert," he said with a sigh. "Your time has come. Everything has gone to plan except that you know too much. We had to tell you a great deal to keep you on side but now you are, quite simply, *too* great a risk. One that we can no longer afford." He nodded again. Joubert felt himself grabbed. A muscled forearm snapped around his neck. Before he had time to kick out, his feet were held and bound tightly. As he struggled to free his arms he felt his hands forced together and the metal claws of handcuffs bit painfully into his flesh. A terrible fear gripped him and he tried to call out, begging for mercy, but the arm around his throat tightened, preventing any sound.

The massive pressure around his neck increased until, suddenly, he felt a snap. His collarbone was broken and a searing pain shot along his shoulder. His scream of agony came as nothing more than a gasp and he felt himself being moved bodily towards the door. As soon as he realised they were heading for the bathroom, a mad, wild, panic swept over him. He struggled desperately to wrestle himself free. His lungs gasped for air as the pain in his shoulder surged through his body, but he was helpless and the men knew their business.

Joubert could feel himself blacking out. Desperately he fought for air but could not breathe. His lungs were bursting as he was forced sideways through the door into the bathroom. Suddenly the grip around his neck was released. He gulped at the very moment a fist slammed into his stomach, causing him to collapse, his gasp turning into a wheeze. He felt himself lifted up and tipped forward. As the ice cold bath water closed over him, he felt his hair floating and saw the first air bubbles escaping from his mouth.

Desperately, frantically he kicked, twisted and lunged but to no avail. Inadvertently his lungs, now bursting for air, forced his muscles to contract in an attempt to breathe. Water poured in. He coughed, then breathed again. More water. A hand grabbed his hair and forced his head further and further down. He breathed again and again. His struggles grew weaker. Gradually his consciousness blurred and faded. As life ebbed away so his body twitched feebly.

Ten minutes later the bath was empty. Joubert's limp body, having been wrapped in towels and a sheet of polythene, was bent double and forced into a household packing case. A cleaning lady had been arranged for the morning to tidy the apartment again in readiness for the new occupants. "See to it there's no sign of anything. Nothing at all," Gambino commanded. "Go over the place with a magnifying glass. No marks, no hairs, no fingerprints, nothing. The men nodded and stood in respect as he left the room. His car took him to Charles de Gaulle airport where he boarded the Airbus shuttle for Toulouse.

✳✳✳

Outside it was raining steadily. The street was empty when the removal van returned. Had anyone been watching they would hardly have noticed the extra packing case brought out of No143. As soon as it was loaded, the van started up and headed south out of Paris on to the N20. After half an hour it swung off the Route Nationale and drove east before slowing near the small village of Bouville. Turning off the road it made its way slowly down a pitted track, stopping finally at a large complex of buildings. They had arrived at a primitive processing plant where animal remains were converted into fertilizer. The van turned and backed up to a pair of large doors. As the men struggled with the packing case, the doors opened. The stench of burnt offal and rotten flesh was overpowering. It was dusk and still raining.

An elderly woman limped towards them, dressed in a grubby hat and a blood-spattered apron over her short dress and wellington boots. Pointing towards the dark interior with a large knife she motioned them to follow her. "Bring it in, then wait outside," she commanded. When she reappeared, she gave the driver a bundle of Joubert's clothing. Behind her a number of dogs were quarrelling over something near the empty packing case.

5

Alexandria
The paucity of communications at Alexandria and the distance from Cairo meant the passage of information to and fro was a tortuous affair, one nationality often putting a different interpretation on whatever information there was. It was difficult, if not impossible, to differentiate between fact, allegation and supposition. Initially each nation attempted to absolve itself, many fingers being pointed accusingly. Problems with language served only to confuse the situation further.

In London and Paris matters were made worse by the absence of both Prime Ministers and their Foreign Secretaries. In Paris, the Chief of Staff at the Foreign Ministry appreciated that a major diplomatic row was in the offing. He called in his own Deputy and ordered him to set up a Crisis Committee, pulling in senior representatives of the government departments most likely to be involved. Next he called the French Embassy in Berlin to ensure that Foreign Secretary Debroque was briefed and kept up to date.

Michel Clemençeau had been Chief of Staff at Quai d'Orsay for three years during which time he had witnessed a number of crises. He knew the drills well for the most likely emergencies and had overseen the practice and rehearsals for many of the less likely contingencies. What he saw here was something quite different, something new and Clemençeau sensed trouble. France, so it seemed, was at the centre of what appeared to be the early stages of a serious international row yet they had no control over the situation and could do none other than cater for the most likely developments.

As soon as his Deputy had begun to organise the Crisis Committee, Clemençeau, using the secure telephone, rang Palais de Matignon, the Office of the Prime Minister at 57 Rue de Varenne, and spoke to his opposite number Laurent Seguin. Seguin, Jospin's own Chief of Staff, at once appreciated the severity of the problem. "If we are involved," he commented grimly. "If we *are* then we should deal with it through our normal criminal procedures, but that's only relevant to certain situations. It's the political fallout that worries me. This could escalate."

"In that case we've got to keep the PM up to speed," Clemençeau replied. "We've no control over what the Egyptians may or may not say and we can't afford to let them get ahead of us by speaking directly to Berlin. He'd wonder what the hell's going on. All we can do at this stage is to get the Crisis Committee underway, feed them with the stuff as it comes in and see what their own agencies come up with."

"Exactly," Seguin replied thoughtfully. "Jesus…this looks a right bastard." He paused. "Y'know I can't recall anything like this before, ever. We need a much broader based committee than usual. I mean we've got the Culture Ministry involved – up to their bloody eyes by the looks of it – probably the Interior Ministry and all the usual home agencies as well.

"Then we've got the Defence Ministry involved with that big arms deal going through." Seguin grimaced. "And they've got to know what's happening. That said, we've *got* to slam the lid tight. I'll speak to Maurice Carnet, the head of the PM's Press Office right now. We can't afford to let this one get out. Christ, can you imagine if it breaks? Security is paramount…has to be."

✳✳✳

In Cairo, the British Ambassador rang Whitehall and spoke to the Deputy Foreign Secretary – the Minister of State for Foreign Affairs – warning him again about the developing crisis. It was likely to become Prime Ministerial and he advised London to brief the British Embassy in Berlin so that Prime Minister Blair could be warned.

Meanwhile, in Paris, the French Deputy PM attempted to placate the Egyptians but to little avail. The Egyptian Prime Minister – Amr Moussa - wished to speak to Prime Minister Jospin at the earliest opportunity. "You cannot possibly expect us to wait until Mr Jospin has finished in Berlin," he said forcefully. "This is the most terrible business. We need all the help we can get and if you remain determined to distance yourself from the situation, we'll go elsewhere, and soon. I must insist on speaking to Monsieur Jospin right away. And I mean *now*." Amr Moussa glared at the telephone in his hand.

**

The French Embassy in Berlin, at the insistence of the Egyptians, warned Quai d'Orsay that Prime Minister Jospin was about to become involved personally. In their opinion the situation could no longer be kept at Departmental level and the Chief of Staff, Seguin, should consider assembling the full Council of Ministers - the French Cabinet – under the chairmanship of the Deputy Prime Minister. Initially Seguin disregarded the advice. He argued that not enough was known about the situation and if the cabinet were to be assembled then the political press would pick it up immediately, something they were seeking to avoid. As he was speaking to Berlin, he received news from the Cairo embassy that the Egyptians felt obliged to take strong action against those responsible and had decided that the arms deal was the stick with which they would beat France. Furthermore they were considering aborting the dive and were preparing a suitable press release.

Eventually Seguin asked to speak to Prime Minister Jospin who was called from the conference hall and briefed. He was warned that he would have to deal directly with Amr Moussa, the Egyptian Prime Minister for they would accept nothing less. He advised Jospin that the best place to do this would be from Paris where they had all the necessary communications and infrastructure to deal with the situation as it developed.

**

Soon after one o'clock Prime Minister Jospin decided to cut short the Berlin summit and return home. He directed his Chief of Staff to keep the Crisis Committee in session at Quai d'Orsay but to consider all other possible contingencies. "It's a very long shot," Jospin said. "But if whoever carried out the raid comes anywhere near French soil we need to be ready. Indeed, we must be fully prepared to offer our assistance wherever they go to ground. Don't take any steps just now," he ordered, "Just think it all through. However, if push comes to shove, we might just need the full CILAT committee established and we had better think about the activation of RAID and GIGN. We want to be right on top of all our options."

CILAT – the Interministerial Liaison Committee Against Terrorism – an offshoot of the French Cabinet, was staffed not only by a number of senior ministers but by police and service chiefs as the situation demanded. It was in many ways similar to the UK Cabinet Office Briefing Room team, code named COBRA, which is assembled at times of national crisis, in particular when military action against terrorists is under consideration. The principal function of COBRA is to take the necessary executive decisions against the threat and, in order to do this successfully, it is essential for first class, real time intelligence to be readily available. In France this intelligence is made available through a specialist intelligence committee. The Unite de Coordination de la Lutte Anti-Terroriste – was set up in the 1980s to coordinate and centralize information coming from numerous different agencies including the DGSE (MI 6), DST (MI 5), the Security and Intelligence services and the national police forces.

Jospin directed Seguin to make preparations but gave specific instructions that no contingency plans were to be set in motion without his personal authorisation. Seguin took no further action himself other than to speak to those in command of the various departments and organisations. However, on learning of these decisions, both the Director General of the Gendarmerie and the National Police Chief of Staff decided to tip off the strike force and headquarters of their anti-terrorist units. Contrary to orders from the Palais de Matignon, the two men issued instructions for their units to be brought to a higher state of readiness in preparation for possible operations.

The special police unit known as RAID – Research, Assistance, Intervention and Deterrence – was based near Villacoublay, the military airport to the south of Paris. The Military strike force came from the Gendarmerie Nationale. Known as the GIGN – Groupement d'Intervention de la Gendarmerie Nationale – and had its base at Satory near Verseilles. RAID was organised to deal with urban terrorism while the GIGN was trained to conduct more wide-ranging operations. Inevitably there was an overlap and an intense rivalry had developed between the two forces.

As a result of the tip off both units reduced the notice of their Alpha standby teams from six hours to three. The message was sent in code and immediately triggered several events in both camps. Quietly and unseen by the outside world the tempo of life inside Villacoublay and Satory increased as numerous well rehearsed drills were activated. Both units, highly motivated and at a constant state of readiness, reacted instantly.

Command Party vehicles and helicopters were checked, key personnel assembled at the Operations Centres, while the teams themselves moved to predetermined tasks throughout their camps. The Intelligence cells, armouries and equipment halls were opened. Equipment was checked and the numerous weapon systems tested in the indoor ranges. In addition to the two leading teams, the reserve Bravo standby teams were brought to six hours notice from their previous twenty-four hours and were ordered to assemble in the camps' holding areas. Once everything was in place the teams relaxed and waited. Most events went according to the well-rehearsed contingency plans – but there was something else.

Amidst all the increased activity, and unnoticed by the staff in the headquarters, one of the cipher clerks from the police RAID HQ met another clerk from the Operations Cell. Across Paris in the GIGN barracks at Satory, an NCO from the Intelligence cell walked across to the main equipment hall where he met one of the armourers. Before joining the armed forces the four men had been well trained. Years ago they had been placed with care in these key appointments after which their masters had ordered them to go to sleep – until the right moment. Now they knew exactly what had to be done and how to set about it. Quietly and unobtrusively several pieces of information were collated and several short telephone calls made. Soon afterwards, a number of faxed messages and e-mails were sent. As soon as the transmissions had been made the four took pains to ensure that all evidence of the relevant messages were destroyed and they returned to their places of work. Their masters had been alerted.

It was three o'clock on Monday afternoon. At Flughafen Tempelhof on the outskirts of Berlin, the plane carrying the French Prime Minister taxied out to the main runway.

Chapter Ten
Monday Night

The Tarn

Humphrey and Patricia Stamford-Barton had settled in France more than ten years ago. After a long search involving numerous lengthy visits they had finally decided on the Tarn, a beautiful and in those days little known Department, north of Toulouse. Eventually they found La Trampa a huge old manoir and farm complex more like a small hamlet, complete with its own pigeonniers and chapel.

It had been love at first sight and they paid the French owners what the locals considered to be an amazing fortune. A well-known local architect had been engaged and an English landscape gardener flown in from Horsham. They were given instructions to take the place apart and put it together again. They were to restore the property to its former glory, ensuring the best of the original features were retained while incorporating all the most modern amenities. During the two years taken for the restoration, Patricia spent a great deal of her time, and Humphrey's money, in the art galleries and antique shops of Paris, London and south-west France collecting paintings, antique furniture, carpets and *objets d'art* with which to furnish La Trampa. Outside, the enormous gardens had been stripped of surplus trees, scrub and undergrowth before being planted with a colourful balance of British and Mediterranean flowers and shrubs.

Hundreds of lorry loads of soil had been brought in to create sweeping lawns around the Italian water features. Pergolas, rose gardens and herbaceous borders had been planted cleverly to break up the area, creating a magnificent year round spectacle and hiding the large pool and floodlit tennis court. La Trampa had become an elegant residence, sumptuously furnished and surrounded by more than two hundred acres of its own vineyards and farmland.

Humphrey, or SB as he was known, was regarded with a mixture of affection and awe by the local French and the British expatriate community alike. Debonair, elegant and beautifully mannered, he would tell his friends with a smile that he had sort of retired from the city, but not quite. "Daren't stop, old boy," he would say. "If I did, I'd never get going again. As long as there's a buzz, I'll muddle along somehow."

Their one problem in life was SB's younger half brother, Antonio Barcellini. SB's father had died when he was still a boy and his mother had later married Count Enrico Barcellini, heir to a well known Italian dynasty with estates near Florence and in the Tivoli hills outside Rome. The Count's son, SB would recall remorsefully, had set out to enjoy himself in the fast lane. Humphrey grew fond of his half-brother but became increasingly alarmed by his outrageous behaviour and the company he kept, culminating in a bitter family row after Antonio had been interviewed by the police. Among Antonio's closest associates were a number of Italians and Sicilians, whose parents had been befriended by Antonio's father including the Torinis from Palermo, and the Gambinos.

✳✳✳

Mario Gambino had stayed twice at La Trampa. Always immaculately behaved and exquisitely turned out he would make a great fuss of Patricia, would shower the household with gifts and, during the spring Verdi festival in Toulouse, he would arrange excursions to the opera. Afterwards there would be a lavish dinner party at the famous Hotel Les Jardins de l'Opera in the Place du Capitole or he would take a barge for the evening on the Canal du Midi. Over the years he had become involved with several of the fledgling high-tec companies that were proliferating around the Aerospatiale and Marconi Matra business parks near Blagnac airport to the west of the city.

A month earlier Antonio had asked SB if he could have the use of La Trampa for the three months that he and Patricia were scheduled to be in South America. There was business to deal with in Toulouse and the thought of renting an apartment in the city during the suffocating heat of the summer appalled him. "I really do need a good base, Humphrey," Antonio explained. "I've good contacts in and around the city, especially with Deutsches Airbus and British Aerospace. Airbus is now forging ahead and I've got myself established. This is an ideal place to do the entertaining."

Whenever Antonio used his family name, SB was on guard. He agreed but took his brother aside. "Now look, old thing." He paused, choosing his words with care. "If I do let you have the keys, I don't want the place taken apart...no more of what we had a couple of years ago." Antonio tried to protest but SB held up his hand. "You know exactly what I mean. Entertain, by all means, but *none* of that other business...none at all."

✳✳✳

The moment his brother had left, Antonio moved into La Trampa. Three days later he was joined by Gambino who explained that he would be moving a small consignment of art through France and was looking for a place such as La Trampa for a holding area. Antonio, as willing to please as ever, agreed at once. "Stacks of space," he offered. "And there's only us," he laughed.

"No problem," Gambino replied. "It'll be nothing much…a few antiques…some house ornaments and that sort of thing."

"Off the back of a lorry, I suppose," Antonio joked.

"No, *no*. Nothing like that," came the reply. "And anyway they won't be here long. A week, two at the most. And I'll pay as usual. How about a quarter of a million…UK sterling, that is?"

"Oh, for Heaven's sake." Antonio stopped and looked at Gambino in amazement. "You *mad*, Mario? That's one hell of a lot. What have you got, for God's sake?" Gambino laughed silently. La Trampa was now his for the next few weeks. Antonio was going to play and preparations began. He would need a substantial and secure storage area and they selected the spacious vaults next to Humphrey's wine cellars under the two cottages next to the main house. In times gone by the vaults had been used for carts and carriages, but now the great open archways had heavily studded doors.

Mario announced that, once the goods had arrived, there would be upwards of twenty people on the place including his security team and household staff. "I've got my own people so I'm planning to pay off the house staff for three weeks or so, generously, mind you." Finally they went through the calendar. "They'll be coming in over the next few days," he explained. "I've left all that to another old friend from Paris, Tommaso Spadaro. Everyone knows him as Tommy. He's a fine man, great sense of humour and a great bon viveur. You want to get him to show you around your Toulouse." Gambino then talked about the merchandise. "It'll be arriving by night, late. Usual nonsense with the flight times. The guy in charge of all that's the one who'll be my man here…Alfredo Bontate…Dino. He's sharp. Once you've shown him what's where just stand back and relax. Let him get on with it. He knows his stuff."

It had taken Gambino just three days to secure his base in France. Initially Sicily had seemed the obvious choice: it was, but it was far *too* obvious. La Trampa met all his requirements and, above all, it was secure. He flew back to Alexandria. The convoy arrived as Gambino had ordained, grinding its way painfully through the hills and reaching the gates of La Trampa just before four o'clock that Monday morning.

2

Paris

The Prime Minister's flight from Berlin had taken a little over two hours. Rather than taxiing up to the entrance of the VIP suite at Le Bourget, the aircraft was directed across the airfield to a side gate where two unmarked black Renaults were waiting. The Deputy Chief of Staff met Jospin at the bottom of the aircraft steps and followed him into the second car. The two vehicles, accompanied by a lone police motorcyclist, moved out on to the busy N17 where they were picked up by a heavier escort which forced its way through the dense afternoon traffic, across Porte de la Villette and into the city. On their way to Palais de Matignon in Rue de Varenne, the Deputy Chief of Staff briefed his Prime Minister.

Seguin, Jospin's Chief of Staff, was at that moment preparing a report for him at his office. He had assembled a number of key government figures including the Defence, Culture and Interior Ministers plus Michel Clemençeau the Foreign Minister's Chief of Staff. The Crisis Committee had been assembled at Quai d'Orsay but Seguin felt that such a committee might not be able to handle matters should the situation escalate.

"What's he got in mind?" Jospin asked glancing at the heavy traffic on the Quai des Tuileries. "Place Beauvau, I suppose?"

"That's certainly one option going through his mind, M'sieur," the Deputy replied. "He doesn't want to initiate anything until he's spoken with you and you've had a chance to discuss it with the others."

"Ye-es." Jospin rubbed his chin slowly. "Right...go on."

"The other thing is PR. Messieurs Seguin and Clemençeau have ordered a news blackout and your Press Office is dealing with that now."

"Yes, we don't want any leaks here, that's for sure." The Prime Minister shook his head slowly. "And to think that things were going so well with the Egyptians... with the whole Arab world in fact. Doesn't look very good, I'm afraid."

Seguin spoke to the Prime Minister for ten minutes in his private office then arranged for the call to Cairo. Jospin listened patiently to Amr Moussa, his Egyptian opposite number. "We will, of course, do everything possible to recover your treasures, Prime Minister," Jospin assured his counterpart. "No stones will be left unturned," he promised. "We will deal with this matter regardless of cost. And if, when they're found, they're not on French soil then we'll give whoever's responsible every assistance. We're preparing to do that right now," Prime Minister Jospin continued. "However, in the meantime, and as a measure of our sincere goodwill, we would like to reinforce our team and to continue with our good work. And we will be more than happy, of course, to place all those involved under the control of the Supreme Council."

The Egyptian Prime Minister was sympathetic but warned that President Mubarak remained deeply concerned and suggested that President Chirac should speak with him. He went on to say that Egypt could afford to give France a week to recover her national treasures after which she would be forced to release details to the media. Jospin concluded the conversation by assuring Amr Moussa that he understood Egypt's deep concern, that he would inform President Chirac as soon as he himself had been appraised of the situation, and that he should expect a call from the Élysée Palace later that evening.

*✻✻

Prime Minister Jospin made his way across the hall and into the main briefing room where Seguin had gathered all those he wished to be present. Before the meeting commenced, he told those assembled that he had spoken to Prime Minister Moussa who was sympathetic to France's position but had given them just the one week to deal with the problem.

Chief of Staff Seguin began from the well-lit podium in front of a huge map of France. He briefed the assembly that the Crisis Committee, now assembled in the Foreign Ministry, would coordinate activities. They had been ordered to conduct an immediate and wide ranging inquiry into the whereabouts of the aircraft. The French airport authorities and air traffic control staff would carry out their own investigation including a search through all air traffic and radar records.

The police, through the Crisis Committee, would check with all local authorities controlling internal airfields including military air bases. Monsieur Clemençeau, currently chairing the committee, would take any other action he saw fit, including incorporating the information network of the postal services together with the agricultural and public service unions. Covert surveillance was to be stepped up at all airports, seaports and border crossings, and preparations to close them were to be put in hand. "The Schengen agreement would be smartly side stepped," Seguin commented drily.

But then, just as the Prime Minister was turning to the Defence Minister, the door opened.

A senior aide from the Interior Ministry at Place Beauvau came into the room and handed a sheaf of papers to Seguin. He pointed to the top two pages, whispered something urgently to the Chief of Staff who nodded, and then stood back. Seguin read the covering letter, looked up quickly, brushed a hand through his hair and made as if to speak. Instead he motioned to the Prime Minister and walked across to him.

Lionel Jospin adjusted his glasses and read quickly. He leaned forward studying the paper intently, turned the page, then flicked quickly through the attached papers. He turned back to the front page and read it a second time. Putting down the papers, he took off his glasses, blinked then held his head in his hands. All eyes were on him. When he looked up he shook his head and raised his eyebrows. "Dear God alive," he said to no one in particular. "Can all this *really* be true? Now we have a problem…and I mean one hell of a problem."

In his hand was a letter that had been handed to the security guard at the front gates of the Interior Ministry less than two hours previously. The courier, a motorcyclist, had said nothing. Instead he had sped off down Rue du Faubourg St Honoré and into the Paris traffic before he could be questioned. Jospin looked at the document, adjusted his glasses and began to read aloud.

***

"Cher Monsieur,
By now, you will be fully aware of the events in Alexandria. We appreciate that you will be doing everything in your power to identify the location of the artefacts and will be making plans for their recovery. However, you are to take no further action, either unilaterally or in conjunction with others, be those actions covert or overt, be they on French soil or within the wider international community. Should we receive any indication that this letter has been ignored, we will, without further communication, carry out the following:

1. Release to the international media all activities at Alexandria including the involvement of Minister Joubert and his links with the Paris underworld.

2. Release evidence of the full extent of corruption within both your government and in the Office of the Mayor of Paris. Names, documents and personal details will be released to the international press corps and onto the Internet.

3. The UK Professor, Sir Alan Palmer, and his assistant, Madamoiselle Gates will be beheaded. The execution will be filmed and released to the media, their bodies to the International Committee of the Red Cross.

4. Jean Pierre Renee and Anton Blosch, released from Frèsnes last year, will be moved to Libya and commence work on the Libyan nuclear weapon programme. Gaddafi will have nuclear capability within eighteen months.

Should you have any doubt as to the sincerity and authenticity of this statement, you will find attached numerous details concerning the Gendarmes, Police and military units you might consider deploying against us. We can confirm that, around 1500 hrs this afternoon, the standby notices of your GIGN and RAID special forces were reduced from six to three hours. Nominal roles of both teams together with the reserve teams are attached.

We recommend you study with care the attached copies of movement details from these camps together with examples of classified radio and signal traffic sent to and from these units. Enclosed also are similar copies from the Gendarme and Police Headquarters. We hope you agree that it will not be possible for you to order military action without our knowledge, the consequences of which you are now aware.

***

The Prime Minister put down the letter and looked at the faces around the table staring back at him. There was a long silence before Jospin cleared his throat. "Right, let's just confirm one or two things first." He turned to the aide from Place Beauvau. "Have we had all this information checked out by anyone?" he asked, waving the papers. "Is all this stuff true or just a load of old bluff?" He looked across to Philippe Lespère, the Interior Minister. "Well, Philippe, what do your boys make of it all?"

The aide took a deep breath and spoke first. "Sadly, Prime Minister, everything there appears to be accurate…to the letter. It was received at the main entrance a couple of hours ago and we have been crawling all over it ever since, together with the police and gendarmes. We decided not to tell you earlier as we wanted to make quite sure it was all authentic.

Lespère broke in. "We have done a lot of cross checking, Prime Minister, and I'm afraid it looks to be genuine. Whoever drafted the letter has got a number of close insiders. And they appear to have a very good line on what we've got up our sleeves."

"And what about these?" asked Jospin picking up a number of photos.

"Again, they're genuine. Two are Palmer's and Gates's passports. We've checked the numbers with London and MI5 have confirmed them. The other two are of Renee and Blosch. Taken a couple of days ago…you can see the dates on the newspapers they've been made to hold up. We've had the photos positively identified against the prison mug shots. It's them, all right."

"And who the hell *are* these people, for God's sake?" Jospin asked holding up the letter.

"At the moment we can't be sure," replied the Minister. "When you look at what's happened in Alexandria, the sheer professionalism of it all and the manner with which they got away and covered their tracks, only a very few organisations in the world could do something like this." He pointed at the papers in front of Jospin. "And look at the research and effort behind all that. Way, way beyond the capabilities of most criminal outfits. How the hell did they get inside like this and how long has this been going on?"

"Well, come on," Jospin snapped. "I'm asking the questions around here. You and your team must have some idea. I suppose you're going to tell me that the Mafia or some other outfit are behind it all?" he replied sarcastically to nervous titters.

"Actually, Prime Minister, that's exactly who we do have at the top of the list." The room exploded into a chorus of angry shouts.

"Oh, come on, man. Pull the other one." Jean Charbonne, the portly, right wing RPR junior minister from the Foreign Ministry slammed his hand down on the table and looked around incredulously. "Why not tell us we're playing cowboys and Indians. For God's sake, what next? I've never heard of such nonsense," he guffawed.

Jospin held up his hand. "And what makes you believe that The Republic of France has been held to ransom by a bunch of Sicilian gangsters...might I ask?" Philippe Lespère detected the hard edge to the Prime Minister's voice. The Interior Minister leaned forward and looked around the table at those who had just derided his suggestion. Some looked back scornfully, others were still talking amongst themselves. He raised his hand and called for silence. "Well Messieurs, perhaps I can explain."

"It had better be convincing," came a call from the end of the table.

"Well, at least, permit me to try," Lespère scowled. "In the first case it's a simple process of elimination and we're hoping to cross check with positive identification from FBI photographs. The Mafia, as we would be happy to show you, are hardly small beer. Has anybody in this room any idea of the size and extent of their drug empire? Mmm?" He paused, sensing he now had the attention of the room.

"Did you know that the annual turnover of their business, and I'm *only* talking about narcotics, has been estimated at more than $175 billion, *billion*? A fact agreed by the USA, Israel and the UK only a couple of years ago. That puts them on a par with the world's richest nations. Last year they actually laundered more money than the GDP of Denmark." Lespère paused. "Just think of the sheer size of it all. It's a global enterprise from Moscow to Madrid, from Sydney to Alaska." He looked at Jospin. "And the Americans, Monsieur, have just thrown a billion dollars at the problem and are pouring in a whole army and air force worth of equipment against them. But it will come to nothing. And narcotics...they're but one of their interests." He shrugged his shoulders.

The room listened intently as Lespère continued. "And I must advise everybody never to underestimate the resilience of the Mafia. Time and again the United States and Italy have declared war on the Families, eight times in all so I'm told. They're resilient all right. They keep coming back. In the great Mafia war of the eighties, three times as many were killed as we lost at the battle of Dien Bien Phu in Indo China. Compared with the complexity of some of their operations this business in Egypt must have been like taking sweets from a kid. They could *not* have believed their luck."

He leaned across and picked up the papers. "They had our man Joubert wrapped around their little finger and he virtually opened the door for them. If you multiply the value of Tutankhamun's treasures by a factor of even fifty or so you will be getting close to the size of this haul. And, as we all know from what we've had stolen from our own art galleries, there's always a ready market for such stuff. Just ask the Director of the Louvre or Musée d'Orsay." He paused, gathering his thoughts. "I'm sorry to go on like this but when you look at what's just happened…then go back to the springing of Renee and Blosch from Frèsnes. And that was another highly proficient operation, as we found to our cost," he added hurriedly. "No, mes amis, we're up against the best in the business. The very best and I really mean that." Lespère tapped the table with his fingers. "At least we now know who sprung the scientists and why. What worries me is that we don't have time on our side. Thank you Prime Minister."

"OK, Philippe. Now then, unless anyone has got any immediate questions about what has happened or who might have done it I suggest we have a short break and sort ourselves out." Jospin got to his feet and put on his jacket. "We'll get some food and coffee brought up and we'll just keep at it. I don't want any of you to pass word of this to your departments. And no more unofficial instructions down the line." Jospin banged the table. "I've yet to come to that little matter. So, no briefings, no tip offs, warning orders or anything else. If what we've been told is true the stakes are high." He glanced at his watch. "Look, I'm going to try to get across and speak with President Chirac. We've got to brief him fully before he talks to Egypt. Let's say an hour, yes? We'll reassemble back here in an hour."

***

The car carrying Jospin to the Élysée Palace swept across Pont Alexandre III, crossed Les Champs Elysées at Place Clemençeau then crept slowly up Avenue de Marigny. A hundred metres short of Place Beauvau the driver pulled into the side of the road, hard against the high wall and railings of the Palace. Jospin and an aide got out and were let into a small gate on the sidewall.

The two men conferred for half an hour, balancing carefully the likely outcome for France. They considered not only the arms contract with the Egyptians but two further deals under negotiation with Iraq and Syria. "We must accept that the Arabs will close ranks with Egypt, making things damned awkward for us around the place." Jacques Chirac watched his Prime Minister carefully as he spoke. "I know we buy oil from the United States and the UK, but the vast majority comes right through the Straits of Hormuz from Saudi Arabia and Qatar. It's our very life-blood. The Arabs know that and we may have to make a number of concessions."

The two French leaders decided to ask for more time. In return, they would offer to financially repackage several components of the arms deal and guarantee more comprehensive after sales support. President Chirac then spoke to his Egyptian counterpart.

The discussion between the two Heads of State went well. Having listened to the French President, President Mubarak declared that he would be happy to see the French team in Alexandria reinforced on the condition that all aspects of the operation would be placed under the direct authority of the Supreme Council of Antiquities. They agreed that the key witness – Madame Mary Sutton – would be flown to France for a debriefing by the French intelligence services while enquiries in Alexandria would continue. The news blackout would be maintained and the reputation of France would be upheld. Then came the sting in the tail. President Mubarak concluded by confirming that Egypt was prepared to give France one week to deal with the matter, and one week only. If, by early the following Monday, the treasures of the Pharaohs were still unaccounted for, Egypt would have no option other than to break the news to the world for which France would take full responsibility.

"For God's sake," Chirac exploded after he had replaced the handset. "*One* week. One *bloody* week. Who the hell does he think we are? And where in God's name do we start?"

✻✻✻

Before the committee reassembled at Palais de Matignon, Seguin had had a number of meetings with individual ministers. The arrival of the ultimatum and the tough stance taken by Egypt had put a different complexion on the situation. Initially the problem had been regarded as one of a purely criminal nature, a matter that could be handled by one Ministry – usually the Interior Ministry at Place Beauvau.

It was now very different, involving a growing number of nations, a direct threat to foreign nationals and the possibility of further escalation to international dimensions. The Ministers agreed that the Prime Minister should be urged to form the CILAT committee at Place Beauvau. Here both national and international communications were available as were the facilities for the majority of France's principal intelligence agencies.

The start of the meeting was delayed while Jospin discussed the situation with his Chief of Staff and several ministers over a hastily arranged dinner. He agreed to the request and directed that CILAT should be run in the usual fashion. It should come under the chairmanship of the Interior Minister, would be located on the third floor of Place Beauvau and be staffed, in the main, by deputies. The intelligence committee would be constituted also and would operate alongside CILAT. The first meeting there, Jospin decreed, would be at noon the following day. "And what about the media?" he added. "They'll be on to this in a flash. No? Probably there already."

"No, not yet anyway," Seguin replied cautiously. I've got Maurice Carnet on to it right now. He thinks we've got a little time. In a funny sort of way, being given

130

just a week helps the PR boys. They can plan back from Armageddon and work out how much leeway we've got. Maurice and his team are doing just that."

***

The conference reassembled immediately after dinner and began with an intelligence update. Snippets of information had been coming in during the evening through a variety of sources and a picture was beginning to emerge.

An unidentified aircraft had appeared for a short time on the Marseille air traffic radar before going off the screen. A medium sized aircraft had approached the French coast on a north westerly bearing of 315 degrees soon after midnight on Sunday. A low flying aircraft was seen crossing the French coast by the harbour master of Sète at about the same time. The Parachute Regiment and police at Castres had received complaints about low flying activities near Mazamet but the military confirmed there had been no night flying over that period.

Mary Sutton had been flown to Paris where she was being questioned at the British Embassy by the Direction de la Surveillance du Territoire. She had already given valuable information on some of the personalities involved and, in particular, had been able to make a number of positive identifications from FBI photographic records. It was looking more and more likely that the group was somewhere in France, possibly somewhere south of a line from Bordeaux to Marseille. Although only a relatively small corner of France it was, nonetheless, a vast area of more than thirty thousand square miles, equivalent to almost one third of the United Kingdom. The team would have gone to ground and no one was in any doubt about how difficult the task of locating them would be in the time available, unless they got a break. And if they did, the next problem was how to deal with them and with whom. It was agreed that if the target was pinpointed they would have to be taken by force. Protracted negotiations would simply give them time to get Renee and Blosch into Libya.

"If we do manage to get hold of them, we're going to have to go for them hard and fast," the Defence Minister said grimly. "If we don't then we can be sure of a very nasty blood bath." For over two hours the meeting debated, with growing frustration, the problem of getting the highly trained French teams out of their camps and into holding areas from where they could be deployed. That, so they saw, was the key to the whole business. If the artefacts had to be snatched or fought for, then only the best trained teams would do.

Again the Defence Minister spoke. "It's got to be done by a team that's not only superbly trained but correctly motivated as well. The civil police are just not equipped for such a task. And, with all due respect, the average French policeman is the wrong kind of animal for this sort of work. I have to say, the same goes for the Gendarmes and the CRS," he added. "They do a great job out there with batons and water cannon but this is a whole different game." Somebody suggested calling for outside help and the room erupted again. If the operation was to be on French soil then the operation had to be conducted by French troops.

"For Heaven's sake," Charbonne and Yves Saulot cried together. "Monsieur Prime Minister, I ask you. Can you imagine how we'd look sitting here, held to ransom by a bunch of hoodlums and all we can do is bleat for help?" Saulot held out his arms in despair. "France has the men and the means. She can do the job herself. Using anybody else would be the final insult."

Again Jospin called for order. "Messieurs, messieurs. Listen. It's simply no good blustering on about national pride. Of course we should do it ourselves. But how, and with what? That was Russia's problem when the nuclear submarine – the Kursk – went down. For almost a week they tried to do the job themselves, too proud to go for help. Then, when at last they held up their hand, it was all too late. Their humiliation was total, but…had they asked before, then?" The Prime Minister left the question unanswered and raised his hands.

"Who is there out there who could do the job?" the Minister for Home Affairs asked the DG of the Gendarmes.

"Only three, possibly four countries. The Brits are very good and lead the field. Remember we went to them after the London sieges - Balcombe Street and Prince's Gate. They gave us a lot of help. Ran our training, too. Their teams are taken from the armed services and they're kept up to the mark in Ireland, and the Balkans…and more recently Sierra Leone. I would go to them first." He paused, scratching his nose. "Then there's the Dutch. They know what they're doing. Their teams did well in the Moluccan sieges in Holland. Remember the Chapel in Amsterdam and the train siege? We rate them pretty highly. Then, of course, there are the Israelis. Can be brilliant but are inclined to go in with the big guns blazing. Where the Brits would use a man with a pistol, they tend to fire a missile – or use a tank. Look what they're doing around Gaza right now."

"But they're good. Nonetheless," Jospin interjected.

"Yes, for sure, Prime Minister," the Director General continued. "However their employment here could be tricky politically, seeing we've got the Arab's so closely involved. Then, after that and some way behind, there're the Germans. Their GSG 9 aren't too bad." He paused again. "Possibly the South Africans, but they're far too far away." He looked around the table. "That's about it. I wouldn't give something like this to anyone else – we could do better with a team of Gendarme Reserves," he concluded cynically.

Jospin held up his hand. "Look, I understand how everyone feels about this but, as far as I can tell, we're all in agreement that it's just too great a risk to use GIGN or RAID. We might be able to ease them out gradually over a period of time - but that's the one element we haven't got." He glanced up at the clock on the wall, checked his watch and pulled a wry face. "D'you realise, we're nearly at the end of our first day already? I suggest I get onto the British PM right away. Tony Blair's still in Berlin and I can get him there. My own feeling is that he'll want to help but it'll be too difficult for him. Just one slip in getting their team up and away and that's it. We'll have two scientists in Libya and two Brits in flag-draped coffins. I'll see what he has to say but I'm very doubtful." He detected the mood of the room was behind him and that everyone was struggling to find a way of using their own men and keeping it within house.

"The bastards've got their hands right inside our trousers and grabbed us by the balls," growled the commander of the GIGN. He and a number of other military, police and intelligence officers had been called into the meeting and were sitting behind the table following the discussions and giving their expert opinions when asked. The meeting dragged on, jackets and ties were off, voices were raised and tempers were becoming frayed.

***

It was around midnight. Jospin had returned empty-handed from his call to Prime Minister Blair. Amid the sense of helplessness and frustration, a hand was raised. A tall, young DGSE officer in the back row got to his feet shyly "Excuse me, Monsieur. May I be permitted to make a suggestion." The Prime Minister frowned, called for silence and asked the man to speak. All eyes turned towards the figure of Pierre Vignau.

"Thank you, Monsieur," Vignau looked around uncertainly. "It's only an idea, Messieurs, and I'll be brief. As I see things, we're hopelessly stuck. We've been in here for almost five hours now and the best minds of the government, the police and the military can find no way out of the impasse. What I'm going to suggest is a very long shot but I believe it's worth considering.

"I've a contact here in Paris. He's half French, half British and will, I'm sure, be known to certain people in this room." He looked across at the Service Chiefs. "He's served in both the French and British armies then retired to set up his own business. He's involved in the world of defence. In actual fact he's an accredited arms dealer operating from here quite legally with an international licence. He deals with arms and equipment but, in addition, he deals with *men*." He paused, looking down at the notes he had made. The room was hushed. Jospin waved him on. "When I say he deals with men I mean he organises teams of ex-military men into operational groups for missions around the world."

"You mean mercenaries," someone called out. One or two others laughed. "Strictly speaking that's exactly what they are, but any similarity between these men and your dogs of war ends right there." Vignau held up his hand, moved forward and began to speak more confidently. "Some of their work is purely advisory – dealing with government agencies and business corporations on matters of risk analysis and security. Others are sent abroad as training teams where many governments are desperate for high quality trainers for such people as bodyguards, security personnel and so forth."

"How's he got into this business?" a voice asked.

"These jobs used to be done by special force and police teams from countries like the UK," Vignau explained. "However, recent cuts in police and the armed services have meant that much of this has had to be given up. But the demand is still there...now probably more than ever. And this is what I'm coming to. Now then." He paused, wiping the beads of sweat from his top lip. "In conjunction with the British security companies, he coordinates and masterminds a number of highly dangerous combat operations. These are happening right now and the two most obvious examples are in Colombia where they've had huge success against the narcotic warlords...the Colombians *and* the Mafia would you believe, and in Bosnia and Kosovo." Vignau glanced at the faces looking at him. He could see that he now had their full attention.

"Over there they've accomplished some of the best hits and the very best snatches of war criminals. Operations that any of our special forces operating there would be proud of. And how does he do it? The secret of his success is that he selects only the very best men, and sometimes women, that come out of the police and armed services. He pays them handsomely, supplies them with state of the art weapons and equipment and always guarantees the operations with a first class back up service. Messieurs, I can assure you that his top teams are of the very highest quality. I've seen the British SF at work as well as watching our own teams in action, and the Germans too. His men are right up there along side them. *If*, and it is a big if, *if* we can get him interested we could begin immediately. There would be none of this business of being held back in barracks by threats. And he's right here in Paris." He paused. "Thank you, Monsieur."

After a long silence Jospin looked around the table. "Well, gentlemen, there you have another option. What are the disadvantages? If these men are as successful as we hear, perhaps that is our way ahead."

"The bloody rosbifs again," muttered a voice from the back to a ripple of laughter.

"Yes, I know," replied Vignau with a smile. "But, if it's any consolation, Messieurs, my man is at least half French, lives here and has served with Les Paras in Djibouti - almost a Frenchman. His team would be mostly Brits but they would have all worked alongside our blokes in the Balkans. You can't get much closer than that. And there's a great deal of respect for each other...is that not so, Monsieur?" Vignau turned to the Defence Minister who shrugged his shoulders then nodded his head.

"Yes, yes. I have to admit they are very professional men."

Another silence then Jospin tapped the table. "Right, that's it. My mind's made up. We'll see what this man can do to help. We need to know that for a start." He turned to Vignau. "Thank you for that. Look, Monsieur...er...er"

"Vignau, Monsieur. Pierre Vignau."

"Ah, yes. Of course. I want you to get across to see him this instant. Is that possible?" Jospin turned to Seguin. "Get him a car and driver." He turned back to Vignau. "Put the facts to him, straight. Tell him about our predicament and see what he has to say. How long will this take – one hour?"

"Two maybe, M'sieur. And that's if I can get to him" replied Vignau looking at his watch. "But there's something else too. He's a professional and I'll have to go prepared to make an offer. And it's not just him." Vignau went on to explain. "The best of these men command very large salaries and bonuses. Many will be deployed already and he'll have to get them back fast from wherever they are. If he does agree to help, he'll have to break lucrative contracts, and pay handsomely. It's all possible but there'll be huge financial penalties. However, they'll be written into the contracts, so we'll have to go in with an extremely good offer to cover all that." Vignau paused, offering his Prime Minister an apologetic smile. "I suggest, Monsieur, we offer him a budget of five million Euros and that's just to begin with."

Jospin looked long and hard at Vignau. "All right, young man. I hope to God you know what you're doing. That's a lot of money in anybody's language. Just remember that while you're off talking to your chum, you've got your Prime Minister sitting waiting in his office with half his emergency cabinet...more or less the whole the French first fifteen...all sitting here and biting their nails. Well, OK. Off you go and be back in two hours. Oh, and one more thing. "Bon Chance!" Jospin smiled at the young secret serviceman and nodded. "We could all do with a bit of that right now."

Chapter Eleven
Tuesday Morning

Paris

Pierre Vignau hurried out of the room and down the main stairs of Palais de Matignon. Almost immediately he was followed by one of the Prime Minister's aides who caught up with him in the entrance foyer. "Monsieur Vignau. One moment, m'sieur. I've been told to get a car for you. It's just outside and the driver knows Paris like the back of his hand. Come on, this way." Vignau followed him outside then stopped.

"Whoa…hang on." He pulled out his mobile phone and punched in Bigard's number. "Better make sure my man's at home…we'd look bloody daft back there if we end up chasing ghosts." The phone rang for some time before he heard it being picked up and the sound of André's voice. Obviously the man had been asleep.

"Oui, 'ello." The voice was breathing heavily.

"André. It's Vignau, Pierre Vignau. I've got something urgent and I need to come over right away."

"Oh, for God's sake man, have a heart. D'you realise what the time is. Call me in the morning." The phone went dead.

Vignau called again. "André, it's me. Don't hang up…*wait*. I've got to get to you *now*. This is serious. I know exactly what the time is…I've been sitting in Place Beauvau for the last five hours."

"Bollocks."

"No, seriously, André. Over here every light's burning and the place is heaving. I've been sent to get hold of you by the Prime Minister."

"Not taking the piss are you, Vignau? Too late for all that kind of shit."

"Honestly, André, listen. This is straight, dead straight. I wouldn't muck you around like this. Look, they've given me a Ministry car and driver. Get yourself up and ready. Go and have a cold shower and get the coffee on. Get that grey matter going. This is a big one, my boy. I'm on my way and I'll be with you in twenty minutes or so."

"OK, I'll be ready. But if you're pulling my plonker, Vignau, I'll have your guts." Once more the line went dead.

Vignau was introduced to the driver and explained where he wanted to go. "Twenty-two Avenue Michel Bizot, General Bizot. Just off the Porte Dorée before you come to the Bois de Vincennes. Know it?" The driver grunted and gunned the powerful Renault into life. "Look," Vignau continued, leaning forward in his seat. "Don't bust a gut but the quicker you can get me there the better. They've got me against the clock." The big car shot forward, throwing him into the back of his seat.

As he swung into Place du Palais Bourbon and headed towards Pont de la Concorde, the driver changed down and accelerated hard. Weaving his way through the traffic on the bridge he then turned right and sped down the Quai des Tuileries. Horn blaring, he jumped the next set of lights and swung left with tyres screaming before swerving hard to avoid a refuse truck just as a diminutive blue Honda appeared in their lights. Vignau saw quite clearly the terrified looks on the faces of the two occupants and watched fascinated as the little car turned sharp right and shot straight across the road before disappearing through the hedge and into the emptiness of Le Jardin du Carrousel. Eyes shut once more, he preferred to concentrate on the coming meeting with Bigard. Ministerial drivers, he assured himself, knew their stuff.

Twenty minutes later he was on the doorstep of No 22. André Bigard threw open the door and waved him in. "Hey, Pierre. Good to see you. What's this load of bull about these late night sessions then? Eh?" He led the way into the kitchen, pulled back two chairs from the pine table and began to pour the coffee. "OK my friend, I took the chance you weren't bluffing," he continued. "And I'm all ears, so tell me the score…the *whole* score too, and listen pal." He rounded on his visitor, wagging a finger. "If you want me to play, I need to know every goddam snippet. None of your DGSE nonsense of leaking just enough to get me hooked." He drew out a cigarette and pushed the pack over to Vignau. Then he coughed. "Right. Shoot."

For ten minutes Vignau spoke without interruption. Covering the story from the time that Joubert's family had been roughed up in Paris, he took Bigard through the whole drama finishing by describing the sense of anger and powerlessness at the meeting he had just left. "So there you are. That's it and I've put it all on the table. Everything." For a long time Bigard said nothing. Then he sniffed, stubbed out another cigarette and sat back in his chair.

"One question before I start." Bigard pulled on his nose. "Why haven't they gone for French ex-servicemen? There are some pretty good blokes around, you know...Ginneste and Cappa for instance."

"They looked at them," Vignau replied. "However they thought it might be a bit close to home, security and all that. And another thing: if I'm not treading on your corns, we both know that the security companies over here are a good way behind the Brits. We looked at the mercenaries, too, Rodruigez and Schnieder, but everyone's terrified of them running amok."

"Yeah, OK, point taken. I don't know of any crowd over here that could hack something like this. But now, listen." He jabbed a finger at Vignau. "If they seriously think I'm going to come in just like this they must be crazy. It's pie in the sky stuff." Bigard flipped another cigarette from the packet of Gitanes and coughed harshly. "Do they honestly think that in five days I can rustle up a bunch of guys from wherever they are, get them together, turn them into a high grade team and take on what looks to be an ace Mafia hit squad? War party, more like." Vignau's mouth dropped.

"Has anyone thought about the legal aspects of this?" Bigard continued. "Say I do get a team together and we manage to run this lot to ground. What about the rules of engagement? Who's going to give the orders to open fire? And what about the consequences of innocent bystanders getting caught up in it all?" Bigard held out his hands. "And who's going to carry the can when the fur starts flying? Anyone thought about *that* sort of thing?" He paused, drew deeply on the cigarette and exhaled slowly. "Listen pal. I'll tell you something else for nothing...I wouldn't put my head on this particular block until all that was absolutely water tight."

"Are you saying it can't be done?"

"No, I'm not. What I *am* saying though is that it's got to be thought through pretty damn carefully. Remember the dramas the Brits had, and the Dutch with their train siege? You can't just let a bunch of foreigners loose on French soil and give them carte blanche to blast off. The media will go *ape*. We're not shooting pheasants you know." Bigard got up and walked across to the coffee percolator. "And another thing. This five million euros of theirs won't get very far in today's real world. If I do take this on I'm going to be asking my contacts to break contracts all over the place. You can't just remove a team of bodyguards from some poor sod in Bogota or Caracas and say sorry mate. He'll crap himself then get bloody angry, and I don't blame him." He put Vignau's cup on the table and leant towards him. "Some of these contracts are government sponsored, you know, and that's going to take one hell of a lot of unscrambling. And the penalty clauses will be big bucks...very big bucks indeed."

Vignau sat disconsolately. "And even when we've paid off all the hundred and one overheads, we'll have to pay the firms who employ the blokes we want.

Then we have to pay the guys themselves. That won't come cheap either, my friend."

"Sure." Vignau pulled a face.

"They're not being asked to do a bit of Saturday night bouncing, you know. They'll be operating on behalf of the French government, for God's sake. I mean, when a ruddy footballer can command over a hundred thousand euros a week for belting a ball around the park and we're asking these guys to put their lives on the line, we've got to think big. What do you think that's worth? Then there's the business of command. Who's going to run the show? From where and how? Eh?"

"Well, from here it's...."

"Oh, no it's not." Bigard held up his hand. "It's no damn good some minister sitting on his fat arse calling the shots from here, in Paris, some three or four hundred miles from the action. He won't have a bloody clue and there'd be a right old fuck up on the ground. And while we are on about command and control, I see a great opportunity for some wonderful Anglo-French squabbles breaking out about who does what and when." Bigard paused, rubbing his chin thoughtfully. The room was quiet. "If I do take this on I'll only do it if my guys run the show from the top down. I'll come back to that in a minute."

Vignau looked down and rubbed the back of his neck. "Well," he said finally. "That's it then. Where do we go from here? It strikes me you reckon it's all too complicated in the short time we've got. D'you want me to go back to them and tell them that? You're our only hope, André," he said, looking at Bigard plaintively. "The bastards have got us and nobody can see a way out of it."

André lit yet another cigarette, drew deeply and looked at the ceiling. "No," he said slowly. "No, don't let's go under to this crowd, not yet anyway. If I can get my hands on the right team and if I get the full cooperation and support from your lot then there's just a chance. It's a mighty slim one mind you and we need to get everything we can going for us. And it's going to take guts too," he added, laughing suddenly. "Not from my guys. If I get the right ones it'll be bread and butter to them. But it's your pals back there who're going to be shitting themselves while making some damn tough decisions."

Bigard reached for a pen and piece of paper. "OK, Lets just think about it. It's now just gone one thirty here. If I can see a way ahead I'll need to make my calls to England before everyone wakes up and disappears for the day. If I miss them that's another twenty four hours gone, so I need to get the green light soon." He scribbled rapidly. "Say I'm prepared to give it a go. And that's if, and only if, my demands are met in full. Firstly I need one hell of a lot more money. I've told you why and unless I get it these guys'll just laugh in my face." He continued to write quickly, head on one side, eyes screwed against the smoke. "Right. I'll need fifty million euros, and I'll need it up front. That means before I get down to business.

Added to that I'll need a further fifty million as a bonus on a successful completion. And you can tell them that that's a pittance in return for the treasures, the
scientists and the safe return of the Brits...let alone their own reputations.
Christ," he shrugged. "Some of these guys out there are getting damn near ten
thousand a week on the streets of Kabul so it's peanuts I'm after."

He thought for a moment. "Come to think of it, that's a bloody good deal and
well they know it," he looked at Vignau. "And that means they've got to dig
some smart arse banker out of his pit at the crack of dawn this morning and get
the money order into my business account sharpish. You can tell them that until
I hear all that's fixed I'll do nothing more than make a few phone calls. Why
should I? Eh? So, now we come to the legal aspects. This is an absolute minefield.
Whenever anything goes wrong on these sort of capers everyone tries to fuck off
out of it and leave good old Bigard, here, to carry the can." He jabbed his thumb
towards his chest. "It's happened to me before and that's why I won't touch a
number of places."

He reached into his briefcase. "If I get involved then I want my lawyers to be
happy that everything's buttoned up and that the government's held responsible. Not me, OK?" He laughed and shook his head. "Hopefully we'll pull it off
and they can all run around slapping each other on the back, basking in the lime-
light. But if it turns to rat shit I don't want any sloping off or passing the buck. I
know that lot." He paused. "My lawyers are Schmitt, Hanscom and Nobel – just
about the best. I don't intend to go far until they give me the nod that everything's sewn up. You know, all the dodgy little bits like carriage of weapons,
rules of engagement, opening fire and *killing* people. Politicians are a squeamish
lot and don't like getting blood on their hands. They always wriggle like hell
trying to get off the hook, bleating about a public inquiry and all that crap. But
they're not going to get off *this* particular hook, so that's the second of my
demands. As soon as I can get my very expensive friend, Mr Jacob Schmitt, away
from the synagogue, I'll get him to draw up a contract and he won't let me move
until your lot's signed on all his dotted lines."

Vignau was writing and talking into a throat microphone. "OK," he said. "Got
that, what's next?"

"Back to command and control." Bigard went on. "If I know that Place Beauvau
crowd, they'll all want to be in on the act. Until the shit hits the fan, that is," he
added ruefully. "Well, no dice. My top man will be right there, in CILAT alongside the Minister, the PM even, or whoever's running their side of things. None
of this being tucked away down the corridor without a telephone in some gungy
side office. Then, once the executive command's been given to my man, he'll
pass it down *his* line...bingo. No dithering or farting about. So there's a point.
The Defence Ministry are going to have to get us the right sort of communications. And make sure the bloody things work this time," he added.

"Also, seeing it's my baby I want to have access to whoever I need to talk to. I won't take kindly to being fobbed off by some dough bag in the outer office. Unless I have a complete overview, things'll get into a buggers' muddle and we'll lose precious time sorting out the mess." He got up and refilled both cups of coffee.

"So, let's recap. I'm prepared to give it my very best shot. My aim will be to recover the treasures…intact, to prevent Messers Renee and Blosch from legging it to Libya and to get this guy Palmer and his side kick out in one piece. I'll go for that on the following conditions: One. I'm paid the fifty million up front, before I begin *and*," his hand slapped the table, "a further fifty on a successful completion. Two. My lawyers tie up every single dot and comma with the government in a watertight contract, and we don't make a move against the opposition until I get the nod from them. And three. My commanders and I run the show from wherever the Prime Minister or Interior Minister makes the key decisions. I'm given direct access to whoever's in charge and I want to be able to call on whatever government or military communication systems I see fit."

The room was silent as both men made notes. "Right, I've got all that." Vignau paused and looked up. "My God," he shook his head. "They're going to just love this little package of goodies. I can see their faces now. The blood's going to freeze."

"*Good*. But if they can agree to all this then we can get started," Bigard continued. "However, point out that these men are scattered all over the place, not only the members of the team but the people I want to run the show as well. Tell them I shall be after at least one, if not two, Brit ex-SF generals. I need people in there right at the top who can handle this sort of thing. Now then." Bigard looked at his watch and double checked with the kitchen clock. "I'm going to need every minute we've got." He looked at Vignau. "I need to know where we stand by four thirty this morning, at the latest. OK? That's three thirty UK time and I've got to make the calls one at a time. Any later and some of the early birds will have flown. We'll have lost a whole day and if we do, to be frank, I'll lose interest. I know I'm asking a lot," he said. "But tell them to consider what they're asking of me."

✳✳✳

Shortly before two thirty, Vignau began the journey back to the Prime Minister's office. He was starving, having eaten nothing all day, and asked the driver to pull in at an all night café. Treating him to a large coffee, the two men sat together at a metal table near the door while Vignau wolfed down a hot crois-sant jambon and a large baguette stuffed with egg salad. As he sat writing between mouthfuls, Vignau sensed the man eyeing his notepad.

Whichever way he looked at the figures in front of him, Bigard was driving a very hard bargain, he thought. But, then, he held all the aces so good luck to him. The government could afford it. Vignau glanced at his watch, wiped his mouth and got to his feet, dropping an extra coin into the saucer for the pretty waitress in the tight blouse. Returning her coquettish smile, he wondered casually what she would be doing with herself later that night. Some lucky sod with nothing else to worry about, he thought, fitting the earpiece of his recorder into place.

In the car, he tried to think how best to put across what many in the room would deem to be totally unacceptable. The amount of money, for a start, would raise the roof. The legal aspects seemed to be straightforward and he could sell them to all concerned as a sensible mind-clearing exercise. Command was different and he could imagine the reaction of the Defence Minister and military Chiefs of Staff once they heard of the proposal to cut them out of the chain. He decided that he would have to brazen out any interruptions and appeal to Jospin himself if the going got too tough.

An aide met him at the top of the stairs and directed him to Jospin's private office where he found the Prime Minister waiting alone with his Interior Minister. "Well," asked Jospin, waving Vignau to a chair. "How did it go?"

"Very difficult, Prime Minister. Very difficult I'm afraid." Vignau put his brief-case on the desk. "My man's happy to give it his best shot but he's highlighted a number of very tough hurdles we're going to have to accept. Basically, he's prepared to have a stab at it on the condition we meet his demands and we've only got a couple of hours." He saw the look on the two men's faces. "If we do give the go ahead he wants to make contact with his people before they leave for work this morning. He knows our time limit and reckons that if we lose another day it'll be too late. Simple as that. It'd put it beyond his reach and he wouldn't be able to do it."

Vignau ran through the list of demands emphasising why Bigard had made them. The Prime Minister whistled and took off his glasses. "Mon dieu, that's tough, very tough indeed but...when you think about it, we have no choice. Do we?" He looked up at the other two and blinked.

"I'm afraid not, Monsieur," Lespère replied. "Unless someone has had a brain-wave, it looks as though this is it. All we can ask of everyone in the conference room is to put Bigard's demands on one side of the scales and what we stand to lose or gain on the other. His demands are steep but there're good reasons for them. I think it's a fair deal." The Interior Minister paused. "Now, Monsieur, we ought to get on. Would you like Vignau to address the meeting, or would you prefer to lead, yourself?"

"Oh, I think Monsieur Vignau can deal with this one." Jospin looked at Vignau and laughed. "Don't worry, I'm not throwing you to the wolves," he joked. "In fact, the way you've put it all, I'm happy to let your man, Bigard, go ahead. What about you Philippe?" The Interior Minister gave a large shrug, shook his head slowly, then nodded his assent. "I'll keep my powder dry in there, for the moment," Jospin said. "I want to see how they react – I think I can guess most of it. Right, my boy, you've got my backing, so let's get on with it."

The room stood as the Prime Minister lead the way, followed by Vignau and the Interior Minister. Prime Minister Jospin spoke briefly then concluded by saying that there appeared to be a faint glimmer of hope. "I think it's better for you to hear from the messenger himself," he said waving to Vignau. The DGSE officer had prepared himself carefully. After outlining the problems raised by Bigard, he reminded them what was at stake and what success or failure might mean before he tackled his list of demands. When he came to the amount of money demanded by Bigard a number of voices were raised loudly in protest, but it was when he reached the final point, command and control of the operation, that the Defence Minister, the DG of the Gendarmerie and Army Chief of Staff interrupted. Only when the Prime Minister banged on the table and demanded their attention did the room fall silent. Eventually he finished, turned to the Prime Minister, and sat.

Jospin took the lead. He ordered the Interior Minister to deal with Bigard's lawyers telling him to get things under way without delay. Next he turned to Vignau and asked him to justify the enormous sum demanded by Bigard. Vignau went through the figures one at a time, highlighting the financial implications of valuable contracts being broken. Clients left high and dry like this would expect hefty compensation. "The plain fact is, Messieurs," he concluded, "The world today is dominated by obscene amounts of money. For instance, the value of the French football squad, world champions or not, is more than three times the figure my man's asking."

The final problem of command and control was the most difficult. The Defence Minister fought hard to retain control of the operation. He stood and addressed the table. "Messieurs," he began. "We have perfectly good and well rehearsed standard procedures already in place for such an eventuality. They are based on sound advice and we have witnessed similar systems working time and again around the world", he continued. "Why is it now necessary to throw all this away and hand the whole thing over to a group of foreigners? Nobody has even seen them and they could not possibly understand the way things should work here? If we have to use these people then they should be brought into our existing chain of command."

Jospin could see the military chiefs behind the Defence Minister nodding their heads approvingly and realised that he would have to make a hard decision over their heads. Eventually he brought the discussion to an end. "All right, Messieurs, thank you very much," Jospin called. "I hear exactly what you have to say and I understand how you must feel. However, what we have here is not a standard in-house operation. This is something that we could not possibly have foreseen or prepared for. It's unique. We are having to rewrite the rule books as we go along" He paused, noticing the military chiefs shaking their heads in dissent. "Have any of you stopped to consider that neither our gendarmes, the police nor the French army would be involved at all if we proceed with this option. There is thus no point whatsoever in tying these people to a chain of command they neither know nor require. They will have enough to do without having to worry about all that, for Heaven's sake. Quite apart from that, we would have language problems. And then, at some point command will have to pass from us to them. No one's yet told me how we're proposing to do *that*. Personally, I think if we tried to control the tactical handling of things we would get into a most dreadful mess. Once we get going things are going to move very quickly.

"The simplest solution by far seems to be that we get UCLAT set up at Place Beauvau first thing in the morning then collate every scrap of intelligence, as normal. After that, and when we're ready, we make the executive decision at the appropriate moment and pass command straight across." He paused, as if to be certain. "Nobody wants to clear up this wretched business more than me. Unless someone can produce a convincing argument to the contrary I have decided that we give them the go ahead and get ourselves right behind them."

The room fell silent. Jospin asked each minister in turn if he had any further comments or suggestions. One by one they shook their heads. The mood in the room had changed to one of resignation. Everyone appreciated that the chances of success were slight. It appeared to be hopeless and, as they saw it, the honour of France now lay in the hands of a group of mercenaries – and British ones at that.

*****

Bigard worked fast. As soon as Vignau left he went into his study and began to consider how he might put his team together. First he tried to make clear in his mind the type of operation he would be asked to undertake. If what they knew about the opposition was true, he would be up against a party of between a dozen or twenty. If given half a chance they would opt to fight their way out of a corner, most likely killing the hostages on the way. They would be armed, for sure. That would mean automatics and silenced weapons in addition to the usual handguns.

He assessed the task clinically and dispassionately. His principal mission would be to secure the artefacts. Palmer and the woman would have to take their chance. But what about the scientists? Where the hell were they and what could he do about them? The simple answer was that he could do nothing. He shrugged instinctively. If they were with this lot then they, too, would have to take their chance. Serve the bastards right if they stopped one. Vignau would have to make the French government aware of this.

His team would need to be around sixteen strong. Twelve would be very tight, twenty unwieldy. He would look for an ex-officer to lead the assault. A first class Warrant Officer might do but nothing less than that. He would need three or four ex-NCOs to command the various elements of the team and the rest could be junior ranks but they had to be good, very good. This meant that he would have to cast the net far and wide, offer enormous incentives and then have a quick selection of whatever came up. Somehow he had to get his hands on the very best that were available on his first trawl, there was simply no time for recruiting campaigns. Christ it was going to be tight. He would have to get his message across as soon as possible – the very second he was given the green light.

Next he looked at command and control. The key to the whole thing would be to get a very able man alongside the PM. He would have to have an outstanding track record and be a well known figure who the French would respect and with whom they could identify. He would have to speak good French and keep his head when the shooting started. In addition he would need a link man between the top and the team on the ground, a cool head who could take the pressure off the team commander, allowing him to get on with the job in hand.

Here he would be looking for an ex-SF squadron commander or commanding officer. Again someone with a good record, who understood what was happening at the sharp end and who could be relied on when the going got tough. If ever there was a time to keep things simple, this was it. Then there was the small point of warning the British government about what was afoot and keeping them fully up to date with events. Once it was set up, the CILAT operations centre would, no doubt, be dealing with London through the British Embassy just down the road in Rue Faubourg Saint Honoré. Vignau would have to ensure they were informed and fully prepared.

The UK MOD in Whitehall would need to know what was taking place, and he would need their cooperation. The Home Office, too, would have to be brought in – weapon permits and all that. Then, once they knew that it was to be France, the Foreign and Commonwealth Office would start breathing heavily. The UK Defence Attaché here in Paris would have to make quick decisions. Bigard had met the present incumbent at the Armistice Day reception. Very smart, very bright and from all the right military academies, he and his French wife perfectly matched the diplomatic bill. But Bigard doubted if the man had ever heard a shot fired in anger or had ever been near real soldiers. They would have to get someone in there who knew the ropes and wouldn't start flapping when the moment came.

MOD (UK) was going to be responsible for finding him an assembly point somewhere in southern England where the team could collect, get themselves sorted out and do a bit of individual and team training, especially weapon handling, while waiting for things over here to develop. A range complex with some accommodation, not too far from an airfield would be ideal. It was imperative for the team to use equipment they knew and understood. There would be no time to fiddle around wondering how safety catches worked or how the radio frequencies were changed. He would need access to British weapons, equipment, dress and communications.

Finally, he turned to his most important files – the ones that held the information on all his contacts. He had all the principal UK Private Security Companies arranged in alphabetical order, the name of the Director or Chief Executive alongside followed by the number of employees and the number of teams they could deploy at any one time:

Company	Director	Manpower	Teams
1. Brake Force	Fred Danaby	40	3
2. Centre Point	Henry Llewellyn	50	3
3. Crisis Trap	Sir Jock Sligo	50	4
4. Guard Watch	Alan Michael	40	4
5. Electron	Bill Davis	30	5
6. Holdfast	Jeremy Lyons	50	4
7. Saracen	Tom Cable	30	3
8. Venture Risk	Peter Harrington	50-75	3

Each firm had its own set of files which showed the type of services they offered and their specialist roles. He held lists of all the key personnel together with a comprehensive CV. In addition he had information on their preferred area of operations, reports on their most recent accomplishments and full details about their contracts, including the financial packages.

He knew most of the Directors as old friends, others less well although there had been numerous contacts with all the firms on his list. Three years ago they had met at the Army and Navy Club in St James's. The aim had been to coordinate their methods of operating and eliminating, wherever possible, any overlap or likely areas of conflict. It had been a useful exercise. An element of trust had been born and it was agreed that they should be able to call on one another for information, equipment and, most importantly, manpower.

Bigard recalled how they had attempted to draw up a code of conduct but it had come to naught. A number of firms conducted operations in Africa and south east Asia that went far beyond the ethical code and operating procedures of the others. Finally, they had considered joint ventures with Bigard and had discussed how they might react if ever a major operation erupted. Everybody agreed that security and speed of reaction were of the essence. Contact between the firms would be initiated by a codeword and a meeting arranged between those concerned. If the operation involved only a few the codeword was to be 'Vitesse'. Bigard knew that this had happened on several occasions, two of which had involved him. If a major operation was on offer then the code would be 'La Grande Vitesse'.

He had it in mind to call up every one of his contacts and to meet them as soon as he could get across to London. All were security conscious and used secure telephones which they changed frequently. He knew three serving British generals and decided to tip them off as well. Once the MOD had absorbed what was at stake and had delegated responsibilities, it would be useful to have a few friends in court.

Finally he turned to the commander and the second in command. Three men came to mind. All had commanded regular Special Force regiments before moving on to become Director of the British SF. They had all been involved in major anti-terrorist operations and had been decorated for gallantry. Each one had made General rank and all were now out of the army. They had been given telecommunications provided by HMG for their personal security, and they knew his code words. He would call them all.

His first choice, Sir Arthur Trant, was now writing and lecturing from his home in Wales. James Decourcy was a close second. Recently retired, he was now farming in Somerset and had told Bigard, whom he had known since they were young officers, that he wanted to get well away from anything to do with the army. Patrick Morton, his third choice, had just as good a track record but was a bit older. He had been out of the game for several years and would be out of touch, but was still good nonetheless. All three were clever, decisive men and were, in Bigard's opinion, strong contenders. He would be happy to have any one of them there and reckoned that the French would be well satisfied also.

***

Bigard looked at his watch. It had just gone four and Vignau should be back at any time. He got up, stretched and rummaged in the fridge for a cool drink before wandering through to the drawing room. What more could he be doing at this stage? Every minute was vital and he couldn't afford to lose any time. Was there anything else that had to be thought through? He sat on the sofa, going over his plans again and again. Everything seemed to be in hand but somewhere, deep in the back of his mind, he felt a tiny niggle. Thus far things had gone well, a little too well perhaps. Whenever things went too well, too soon, Bigard became nervous.

2

The Tarn
Sir Alan Palmer blinked as the light filtered through the shutters. He looked at the ceiling before glancing across to the other mattress. Amanda Gates lay on her back, the tattered blanket pulled up to her chin in a subconscious attempt to ward off the dawn chill. He tried to lift his head but a searing pain forced him back on to the damp horsehair pillow. He gasped at the discomfort. Lying there, staring at the wide cracks in the ceiling plaster, he tried to focus his mind on the last twenty-four hours.

In spite of Gambino's promises their journey through the night had become increasingly uncomfortable. After the long drive from the airstrip, in the back of a closed down lorry, they had been bound and a hood placed over their heads. He recalled that three men had then pushed them roughly into the back of an empty van and locked the door. As he lay on the floor he could hear Amanda moving beside him. A little while later he heard her crying and had done his best to comfort her. Palmer closed his eyes and winced at the pain. Then, as far as he could recall, when the van eventually stopped, they had been taken from the back and manhandled aggressively until they reached a building. Here, their hoods and bonds had been removed and they had been propelled roughly up a flight of stairs into a loft space.

The room had not been used for years. The shutters were closed but there was enough light for them to see the small piles of leaves in the corners, the mass of ancient, dusty cobwebs and the several broken window panes. The damp plaster on the ceiling had started to collapse exposing lines of slats where creatures of some sort had built their nests. In a corner lay a pile of old clothes and some remnants of books and newspapers now yellowed with age. The whole place smelt of thick dust and old apples. As they went out of the room the guards had locked the door behind them.

✳✳✳

Later, much later it seemed, when two of the guards appeared with a tray of food, Amanda had complained about the state of the room. The two men simply grinned and shrugged dismissively. She was furious. "How dare they," she cursed. "How dare these dreadful people, these…these peasants treat us like this." When they reappeared with two old mattresses, and some soiled bedding her composure snapped. He smiled at the memory.

"What the hell d'you call this?" she had cried waving an old blanket. "How on earth are we supposed to keep ourselves clean in this place? And where's the washroom?" she shouted, gesticulating angrily. One of the guards smirked, made some obscene gesture with his trousers and pointed to a door at the back of the room. She had glared at the man, spun on her heels and strode angrily across the room to the door which she threw open. Inside she found an ancient washroom with a basin, a single tap and an old wrought iron toilet. He remembered hearing her checking the system. Mercifully everything had functioned and he watched as she came back into the room and nodded imperiously at the guard who had insulted her a few moments earlier. Later they had laughed at the startled look on the man's face.

Throughout the latter part of the day they discussed their predicament. He had kept feeling tired and they had stopped so he could nap. Below them they could hear Italian voices talking loudly and laughing. Eventually, they discovered that they were in the loft of an old pigeonnier. Beneath them, in what was now an elegant summer house, a number of the guards were housed.

***

The pain at the back of his head where a guard had pushed him roughly was still there. He had stumbled, helpless under his hood, and knocked his head before falling awkwardly. Inconvenient rather than serious, it nonetheless hurt whenever he moved. An hour later Amanda woke. He watched as she banged on the locked door, calling out in her excellent French for the guards. Two men, different ones this time, opened the door and faced her wrath. "Just look at this will you now," she cried, pointing to the mess around them.

She turned towards Palmer. "God," she muttered. "I can't stand this filth. Then she looked more closely at the figure lying on the mattress. "Are you all right, Sir Alan? You don't seem yourself. Here, wait a minute." She knelt beside him. "There's blood behind your head. Listen, I'll have to get you cleaned up." She felt his forehead. "And there's a temperature there too, that's for sure." Palmer tried to rise but fell back.

Chapter Twelve
Tuesday – Later

Paris

Vignau sat in Bigard's kitchen, a cup in his hands. "Mon Dieu," he sighed. "What a night." It was late and he was tired, very tired. "And what's next, for crying out loud?"

"Not much." Bigard cocked an eyebrow and grinned. "Only six more days and it's all over. But if it's any consolation, I reckon I've got a day and a half ahead of me so as soon as we've finished the coffee, I'm going to show you the door."

"Fine by me," Vignau shrugged.

"A few points before you go then." Bigard considered the list in front of him. "Now look, for the next few days I'm going to be all over the place, and moving like hell just to keep up with it all. And if I'm going to be doing *that*, I'll need transport, good transport – wheels and wings. So get your notebook out, laddie."

"Fire away." Vignau checked the ink in his biro and rolled his shoulders

"Right. Now I've got to have a car and a driver here, full time, and that's your problem. They can't expect me to do this while queuing for cabs and the Metro. What's more, I'm going to have to get across to London and I'll need the same there. The place is a nightmare." Bigard scratched his chin. "Furthermore I'm planning to hit all these guys with this charming snippet of news in the next hour or so, then get myself over to London later today." He paused. "And for that I must have wings. Get them to fix me up with one of those little government jet runabouts, but it's got to be entirely at my disposal...and stress that. OK? Again, I can't waste half the day hanging around Charles de Gaulle or the whole goddam thing'll be over before I've started. I'll need to fly out of Le Bourget and into RAF Northolt. That's where the UK VIPs come in. It's quick and easy to get to the centre of town from there. When I've landed I'll need to be

150

met by the Embassy. The Foreign Ministry boys had better get on to our chaps in London and get the path cleared or I'll be stuck out at Northolt."

"Don't worry, they're used to it…they'll bring in the Met."

"OK, but before all that starts I've got to get across to Place Beauvau, check the new set up and meet as many of the faces there as I can. I know most already but I reckon I'll be none too popular with a number of them, but there we are." Bigard chewed on his lip, nodding to himself as he thought. "And you'll have to give me a call if you reckon Philippe Lespère wants to have a word. He might want to pick my brains." He looked at Vignau. "If nothing else he'll want to satisfy himself that he's not strapping himself to a loose cannon." Vignau's body jerked as he laughed suddenly.

Bigard glanced at his watch and took out a cigarette. "So, I'll spend the next few hours here alerting everyone who needs to know. Then I'll come over to the Ministry around midday and spend an hour or so there." Thinking about what he had just said, Bigard nodded his head from side to side. "After that I'll have to get away so let me know when the plane's fixed." He saw the look on Vignau's face. "Sorry, old lad, but your bed's got to wait a bit longer."

"Ah well." Vignau shut his note book, slipped it into his jacket pocket and stood. "Looks as though you're going to be earning that truck load of lolly you've demanded." He yawned loudly and stretched. "I'll see you the other end." Bigard got himself a bowl of mueseli, made some toast then sat at his desk. Glancing down the list of calls he had to make, he assembled them into an order of priority and took a deep breath. It was just after four in the morning UK time when he dialled the first numbers.

✳✳✳

The further he went down the list the more he began to enjoy himself, grimly satisfied that if he was up and about at this godforsaken hour, then they could damn well suffer too. As he dialled each number he would pause and chuckle, imagining the scene at the other end. For a moment there would be nothing. Then *bang*, pandemonium as the news sank in.

Only once, when he called Sir Jock Sligo, Chief Executive of Crisis Trap, was the importance of his message grasped immediately. "Got it," he said at the end of the short call. "I'll be there." In spite of the codeword, no one else appreciated the true extent of *La Grande Vitesse*. It was the trigger to which they should have reacted. He needed an immediate and clear-headed reaction, something that would galvanise them instantly, forcing them to drop whatever they had planned for the next couple of days and to re-arrange their diaries. Time was of the essence and he wanted to meet them at six that evening in the Army and

Navy Club at the corner of Pall Mall and St James's Square, just as they had done three years ago. He had to hit them hard but could say little on the phone, even with the technically advanced systems they were using, other than to say that it was a crisis of international magnitude, the target was somewhere in Europe and it had to be resolved within a week.

The fact that three Prime Ministers – including their own - and two Presidents were already involved did the trick, and he sensed that the impact of his call was getting through. Four of the eight he wanted were at home and all agreed to meet him. He failed to contact the others and called their deputies, managing to run two of them to ground but drew a blank with the last two – Brake Force and Hold Fast – making a note to try them later. Before he began to make his round of calls he decided not to mention the size of the contracts, other than to reassure them that they would find the exercise financially rewarding. Far better, he thought, to start on a low key and let them declare their hands rather than put a large pot of gold on the table.

Next on the list were the three commanders. He decided to start at the top and made a call to an isolated hamlet on the outskirts of Brecon in South Wales. After a short pause he heard a woman's voice. "Good morning," he replied. "I'm terribly sorry to call you at this hour but would it be possible to speak to Sir Arthur Trant?"

"No, I'm sorry, he's not here. Is everything all right?" the voice asked anxiously. "Might I ask whose calling? It's terribly early you know."

"Yes, I'm afraid I do know what the time is and I apologise for having to disturb you like this," Bigard soothed. "I can assure you, madam, that everything's fine and no one's come to any harm. I'm calling you from Paris and I'm an old colleague of Sir Arthur's. We need to speak to him rather urgently."

"Well, I'm afraid you won't be able to. He is in New York and he's due to speak to the United Nations this evening."

Bigard cursed silently. "Yes, I understand. I don't know how to explain this over the phone but it's vital we speak to him. I'm calling on behalf of the French government and I can let you have a number so you can call back and check my credentials if you like. Would it be possible for you to tell me where he's staying so we can call him there later?"

"Yes, the British Embassy in Washington booked him into The Waldorf Astoria – they'll be able to find him for you. Oh…that's in New York of course. But don't disturb him yet, they are three hours behind us, or is it four."

"No, I promise I won't do anything like that. But thank you so much and, once again, I'm sorry to have disturbed you. Good night."

Bigard thought quickly. He had a little time before the lights came on in New

York, but how the hell was he going to get Trant to cancel this lecture tour? It was high profile stuff. There was only one thing for it – he would have to get at him right from the top. This was one for the UK Prime Minister via the UK Ambassador at the UN. If he was going to get that under way, Jospin would have to go cap in hand to Blair – and Blair was still in Berlin, for God's sake.

He dialled Vignau's mobile and caught him in the car approaching Place de la Concorde. Explaining the situation he told Vignau that he would email through a copy of Trant's CV. In that way the French Premier would understand that he was after the best man available. Bigard got out Trant's file, took out the CV and read it quickly. This was the man he wanted: it was one hell of a track record. Trant was tailor made for the job – or any other for that matter.

Educated at Marlborough and Worcester College, Oxford where he read Political Science and Modern Languages, Trant had then taken a sabbatical in Paris. There he studied at the Sorbonne and lectured on the history of British politics before joining the Welsh Guards. He had moved rapidly up through the right jobs before joining Special Forces in the late 60s.

He served with them in Oman where he won a brilliant MC and the Falklands before commanding in The Gulf War when he had been awarded the DSO. He had been instrumental in setting up the original French anti-terrorist force with 1er Regiment Chasseurs Parachutiste – the elite 1er RCP - based on his own experiences in London, Ulster and Colombia. His last operational command had been to oversee the British effort in Kosovo and he had retired after attaining the rank of full General.

Bigard smiled at the mention of his old regiment then added a note of his own to Vignau, urging him to get the message passed on to Berlin as soon as he could. Trant was the best in the business and the French should pull out all stops to get hold of him.

His second call to James Decoury was a busted flush. Decoury had no intention of coming back to have another go for anybody – not even his old friend André. When he left the army he had never even glanced back over his shoulder. Not then and he wasn't interested now. "Listen, Bigard, you old rogue. I've hung my boots up, OK? I'm too old for that sort of stuff now," Decoury had told him.

"OK James, I hear you. But listen, do me a favour, will you? I'll try to get Arthur Trant and Patrick but, if I'm out of luck, let me come back. Can I do that?" Decoury agreed but sounded none too keen.

His third call was to Patrick Morton. Morton was a bit older than the others and Bigard remembered him as a very tall, austere and somewhat forbidding figure in his old regiment. Lurid tales of his SF exploits preceded his return to the Officers' Mess after his tour at Hereford and the subalterns had given this mysterious, rather awesome captain a wide berth. Later Morton, like Decoucy and

Trant, had moved up through the SF ranks finishing up at The Duke of York's Headquarters as Director. He left the army a few years later and had become involved in a number of charities in the south west of England. Morton took the bait immediately. He happened to be free at the moment and would be delighted to help Bigard in any capacity he thought suitable. He knew Trant well and would be more than happy to work with him. He was available as of now.

It was Bigard's first lucky break and he grabbed it, taking a chance to brief Morton in some detail. He asked him to call the French Embassy in London, speak to the Defence Attaché, a Brigadier General Xavier Le Chantou, and check on a number of points that he had set in motion earlier. He assured Morton that he would call the Embassy well in advance and warn them to expect his calls. He then discussed a number of additional points that Morton could tackle and finished by suggesting they should meet in the VIP arrival lounge at Northolt before travelling into London together in the Embassy car.

Patrick Morton would be an excellent man to accompany him once he got to London. Bigard would have to lean heavily on the UK Ministry of Defence over the next couple of days and Morton would know his way around, and probably knew most of those in the key appointments. Furthermore they would be able to discuss the size and composition of the assault team they were going to put together. Here, Morton's experience would be invaluable. Finally, if they could get Trant back, Morton would be an ideal middleman for the operation.

✱✱✱

Place Beauvau was already a busy place by the time Bigard arrived. One of the Minister's aides met him and took him straight into the re-activated CILAT operations room. Although a number of the key personnel had stood down for a few hours he was able to meet many of those who had fought against his involvement a few hours earlier.

Luckily Vignau had already circulated Trant's CV. The Army Chief of Staff, General Robert Briançon Noire, remembered him well having served with him in the Balkans. The Deputy Chief of the National Police recalled the lecture on counter terrorism Trant had given at the École National d'Administration. Both men spoke highly of him thus spiking the guns of others, some of whom were sceptical if not openly hostile to the very idea of any outside interference – especially from the British.

At the invitation of the Interior Minister, Bigard spoke to key members of the freshly assembled command group who had foregathered in a side office. He explained what he had done and how he hoped things might progress, warning them that the crucial meeting was going to take place that evening and by tomorrow morning he hoped to have the first members of his team assembled. He had it in mind for Morton to secure the loan of a military training area somewhere in southern England where they could put the team together. Selection would take place over the following twenty-four hours and the team should be ready and equipped by Thursday midday.

"That, Messieurs, is as far as I have gone. In fact it's as far as I can go at this stage. Please don't forget that I was dug out of bed less than twelve hours ago and, like you, I've been running about the place ever since. Once we've got the team together in the UK we'll hold them there, conduct whatever training we have time to do – and wait for you." He caught their look of surprise.

"Yes, I'm afraid it's then up to you. We'll be waiting to hear from you that everything's rolling this end. "*And,*" he emphasised, "in particular, we'll be waiting for the answer as to where the hell these people are. After that it'll rest with the gods."

***

Two and a half hours later Bigard stood in the VIP lounge at Northolt waiting for his luggage to be brought through Baggage Check. As Patrick Morton came across the room with two cups of tea, the door opened and the French military attaché walked in. Lieutenant Colonel Michel de Puylaurens wearing the full dress uniform of Les Chasseurs apologised for being dressed to kill. "I didn't think it would be the best time to get held up at the main gate with formalities and car checks so we came along with all flags flying. Worked a treat," he said with a smile. "Now, gentlemen, I've two pieces of news. The first is that we have managed to get hold of Trant."

"That's excellent," Bigard exclaimed, his face breaking into a wide grin. "Through Tony Blair in Berlin, was it?"

"No, it didn't have to go that far. The British Ambassador in Berlin spoke to his opposite number at the UN. Sir Peter Oldfield, the UK's Permanent Rep in New York, immediately saw the size and shape of the whole business and pounced on Trant when he was still in his room...having breakfast and working on his UN speech would you believe?" All three laughed loudly. "Apparently he was a little miffed at first but didn't take long to realise what's at stake." De Puylaurens lifted his hat and rubbed his forehead. "They tell me he's a great Francophile and can't wait to get back. Anyway he's now caught a mysterious diplomatic illness and will be coming in to Charles de Gaulle this evening. A bit later than we would have wished but as you know, the Concorde fleet's still grounded so we'll have to get him across by Airbus. Some of the airmen wanted to shove him into a Super Étendarde, in-flight refuelling and all that but we knocked that on the head. We don't want him here half scrambled." De Puylaurens thought for a moment. "The plan will then be for your Embassy in Paris to take him under their wing. We'll give him free access to CILAT and whoever else he wants, so he can read himself in...then he just get's on with it.

No doubt the PM will want a chat with him and I daresay President Chirac will want to see who we've come up with. Anyway, with his record he should be OK."

"Great, yes great news," Bigard remarked. "Then Patrick...look, would you be able to take on the middle job for me? It's absolutely imperative I have someone there with the team who knows the score and can steady things. Also a cut off between the team on the ground and the rest of the world is vital."

"No problem," Morton nodded. "I agree it's essential and we can discuss the detail later." Suddenly he laughed. "During the Falklands, Maggie used to love rabbiting on to the blokes on the ground while the flack was still flying. OK once in a while but after a bit she drove them mad." Morton, like most military commanders, had a deep distrust of meddling outsiders.

✳✳✳

As the Embassy staff car pulled out of the airport on to the A40 and headed towards London, the three men continued their discussion. De Puylaurens explained that his boss, the Defence Attaché, had arranged a meeting for them at the French Embassy – No 58 Knightsbridge. What Mr Blair had managed to achieve from Berlin was to alert the UK government to the crisis and had directed them to offer every assistance. The Chief of the Defence Staff had arranged for a senior member of the Defence Central Staffs to be at the Embassy meeting. He would have the authority to secure whatever resources were necessary.

The Home Office was to be represented also and they were sending along a junior minister to arrange for the clearance of any paperwork or legal matters, in particular the issue of special weapons and explosive permits and diplomatic immunity for the team. The UK authorities had an ongoing phobia about the carriage of firearms, air rifles even, and the sight of sniper rifles, grenades and belt fed machine guns appearing on their security screens would be unlikely to amuse HM Customs and Excise.

The meeting in the Defence Attaché's office had gone well but it had not been without its problems. The UK Assistant Chief of Defence Staff for Operations (ACDS) had seen the requirement for speed and that many of the usual corners were going to have to be cut. He and Morton quickly prepared a list of their requirements. They agreed that the best assembly and holding area for the team would be the range complex at the Cinque Ports training area near Hythe on the Kent coast. All the facilities they needed were there, Lydd airport was close to hand and could take a C130 Hercules aircraft which the RAF would position there ready to take the team and their equipment over to France. Furthermore, the range authorities were well prepared for the unusual. Thirty years of trouble in Northern Ireland and elsewhere had spawned a variety of special force and intelligence units, many of whom sought peculiar and unusual facilities at short notice.

The ACDS left the meeting with Morton and made a call to the UK military headquarters at Wilton near Salisbury. He spoke to the Chief of Staff, a Major General, who replied crisply that he and the Commander in Chief had been warned by London already and he had ordered preparations to be put in hand. His next call was further down the line to the Headquarters of 2 Infantry Brigade at Dover, the formation responsible for the ranges.

***

Brigadier Rupert Galworthy, a civilised, genteel officer of the old school, was fifty-four and a half years old. In six months time he would be quietly pensioned off. His career had been steady rather than spectacular, a fact underlined by his ample girth. Earlier that day, he had enjoyed an excellent lunch with the range inspection team in his Officers' Mess. The inspection had gone well – it always did. He had returned briefly to the office, had taken his usual cup of tea with the Adjutant, then slipped home quietly to watch the racing at Haydock Park. Jacket undone, a glass of good port in his hand and his comfortably slippered feet on the coffee table, Galworthy was a contented man. Then the telephone rang.

The ACDS did not speak - he barked. The senior General, currently in ruthless competition for the Ministry's top job, possessed many fine personal qualities but neither patience nor tolerance featured with much prominence. Several years ago he had savaged Galworthy publicly and unpleasantly over his men's lack of aggression at bayonet drill. The ACDS did not like idle or unfit soldiers and had not forgotten the incident. Neither had Galworthy and he left the sofa at speed.

For all his apparent limitations, Galworthy was no fool. Neither was he quite the liability the ACDS perceived him to be. In fact, many years before he had won his spurs in the Radfan mountains and knew well how to cope with fast balls and tiresome Generals. He suggested politely to the unattractive voice at the other end of the line that Morton should come straight to the range complex where he would have his staff prepared, including the quartermaster who would have the necessary weapons and equipment ready. The range officer would be instructed to handle their requirements for weapon training including the use of Close Quarter Battle and vehicle anti-ambush areas. In addition, the brigadier continued, he would arrange for them to be housed in the Number 2 Mess Annex. Here, there was ample accommodation and excellent training facilities. His staff, he reminded this irritating man, were well used to such requests at short notice. He paused: the voice at the far end grunted and the line went dead.

After the meeting Morton and Bigard sat together and discussed André's forthcoming conference with the security company executives. Morton knew several of them. Sir Jock Sligo was an ex-Navy man. Morton had known him a number of years ago and held him in high regard. Sharp and with excellent judgement, he was one who could be relied upon. Morton pointed at the list in Bigard's hand. "I know Peter Harrington of Venture Risk and Harry Llewellyn of Centre Point, too. They both served with us years ago. Peter commanded a squadron in Oman and did very well in one of the last battles out there. Harry I met in Kuching, in Borneo. He was a good jungle operator and was in Aden before that. You've got another two first rate men there." Then he paused.

"I wouldn't touch that guy Parsons though. He came to us from some Jock outfit. Left after a short time to set up his own security firm. Nothing less than a front for old fashioned mercenaries. A pretty useless crowd at the best of times. Characters like Macateer and Callan, just after blood and a wad of cash. The press had a field day following them into Angola and Ruwanda. Later on they cropped up again in Sierra Leone. Always a blood bath, diamonds being the big attraction there. Might just be one or two good operators there but watch them like a hawk."

Davis of Electron had been a very clever signaller in his service days, commanding the technical branch of Number 14 Intelligence Company in Ulster before leaving the army and working for the Security Services. Electron was one of the smaller companies but his men were good and sometimes worked with the other organisations. Their specialisation was eaves dropping and bugging, often working in operations dealing with industrial espionage or, occasionally, for wealthy individual clients. "A very useful outfit," Morton remarked thoughtfully. "We could use them and should get them to bring along some of their surveillance gear. We might be glad of it."

Tom Cable of Saracen was, they both knew, heavily involved in mine clearance in Angola and currently had a team operating in Eritrea. Unless one of the other teams had an acknowledged explosive's expert, Cable should be able to provide a man with the right skills. Lastly, Alan Michael of Guard Watch. Until recently he had been involved with the anti-drug operations in Colombia and his teams were likely to have had the most recent combat experience. A year ago he had turned his attention to Bosnia and Kosovo where his men had participated in the identification, tailing and then the snatching of suspected war criminals. The British and French SF had been hard pressed to cover the ground and Michael had filled the gap with two notable success stories – Zibck Sadic number two to General Mladic and, a short time ago, Andrei Kozevic deputy chief of Radovan Karadzic's security police. The only problem here was that Alan Michael might have most of his men deployed in the Balkans.

❋❋❋

Shortly before they left 58 Knightsbridge they had another brief meeting with the French Defence Attaché. Brigadier Le Chantou told them that all the efforts in Paris were now concentrating on locating the whereabouts of the gang and their haul. The British Embassy there was looking after one of the key witnesses from

Alexandria. Apparently when the gang had taken Sir Alan Palmer and his assistant captive, the third member of the team from the British Museum had not been picked up. She was now in Paris and was being debriefed by the Renseignements Généraux (RG) and the Direction de la Surveillance du Territoire (DST) the departments responsible for counter terrorist intelligence. "That lot'll make her remember everything she saw, what she heard and what she did out there," said Le Chantou with a grin. "And the naughty bits too, if she was that way inclined."

"As soon as we get over there, they should release her to us," Morton said firmly. "We'll be the ones needing the intelligence then. It's no good the spooks keeping her in Paris writing reports on whatever she's got to say. We'll want it first hand and in real time."

Intelligence was beginning to build up some sort of picture, Le Chantou advised. They had enough evidence to focus their attention on the south-west. The debate now was whether or not they could risk asking the influential public service sector and agricultural unions to help them. In France the powerful unions spent most of their time standing toe to toe with the French government arguing about their members' pay and conditions of work. On matters of national importance, however, the dispute was forgotten and the adversaries would close ranks.

"If they can manage to do that it would be an enormous help," Le Chantou explained. "Imagine every postman in France having a careful look at every one of his houses as he walks his beat, every dustmen doing the same and every farmer scouring his land. That's over a million and a half extra pairs of eyes and ears covering the ground and looking for anything unusual. It's a fantastic, all embracing net but it takes *time*. It's a huge effort to get under way and difficult to implement without making a lot of fuss. So if this gang really have got their ears to the ground Paris might decide it's too much of a risk."

At four o'clock they parted company. Le Chantou agreed to send a courier to Lydd the following morning with whatever Bigard may have collected from the meeting. An MOD driver was waiting for Morton and, after phoning and telling his wife to pack some clothes and his old operational kit which was still in his bergen rucksack, they set out for Dover and the south coast.

Bigard, meanwhile, sat quietly alone collecting his thoughts about the forthcoming meeting at The Army and Navy Club. Why, he kept asking himself, was that irritating little niggle still at the back of his mind?

2

The Army and Navy Club, London
The Embassy car swung into St James's Square from Pall Mall and pulled into the kerb outside The Rag. Bigard could remember first coming here with his

father when he was still at Downside. He would look on fascinated and proudly as his father met up again with those he had served alongside during the war, marvelling at such strong bonds of friendship. He remembered also some of the stories and the laughter at the bar in the members' lounge and dining room.

Bigard had become a member as soon as he was at Sandhurst. It was an oasis of peace and calm, a haven of civility and decorum, far removed from those terrible Sergeant Majors. He and Eddi would come up once a month and eke out their meagre pay on a good dinner before disappearing into the maze of dingy streets behind Piccadilly which offered a different kind of hospitality.

✳✳✳

But today it was business. He pushed his way through the swing-doors and walked quickly across the hall to the reception desk, his footsteps ringing loudly on the marble tiles. "'Ullo, Mr Bigard, sir. Very good to see you again." Thompson, the bald ex-artilleryman and now the hall porter grinned widely. He was renowned for making a fuss of those members he liked – *his* officers. "We 'eard you was on your way in, sir. Good to see you again, stoppin' long, are you?"

"Thanks, Bob. Good to see you, too. No, 'fraid not. Just a quick meeting. Hope they've booked the Nelson Room for me at six. Do you know if the duty manager's managed to fix us up with some grub?"

"Yes sir, that's all been arranged." Thompson collected up the papers on his desk. "General Morton looked in earlier and said that's what you wanted. Got a light buffet laid on for about a dozen or so. Drinks will be done on the chits, sir." He grinned at Bigard. "Picking up the tab yourself sir?"

"Yes…best make sure everything goes on my Mess bill. Tell the manager, if he does us well I'll pay him in euros," he quipped.

"Now, now sir. None of that talk in 'ere. None of that continental stuff. Pounds an' pence so it is. Always bin that way, sir, an' we don't see no reason for changing nuthin. They can keep all that other lot." Bigard laughed and waved him away then walked across to leave his coat in the cloakroom. The Rag was an incredible place. Just about the last place on earth where one could leave things in complete safety and forget about them. He checked his tie in the mirror, gave his hair a quick comb and turned to allow the steward to brush down the back of his jacket. Wandering back into the main hall, he stopped to glance at the news coming through on the telex then went on up the stairs.

He felt his progress followed every inch of the way by the unforgiving gaze of past luminaries, who stared down from their huge portraits on the wall above him. At the top of the second flight he turned and entered the elegantly furnished Nelson Room, set aside by the management for meetings and seminars. He looked around at some of the artefacts and memorabilia of the great Sea Lord then sat checking through his papers, waiting for the meeting to assemble. He did not have long to wait.

***

Before explaining the reasons behind his untimely call earlier, he apologised for asking them to gather with such unusual urgency. He asked them to accept that what he was about to divulge was highly sensitive. The slightest leak could result in the most catastrophic consequences for his country. "None of us is bound by The UK Official Secrets Act or anything like that," he reminded them. "All I can do is to ask all of you to respect what I'm going to say and keep it very much to yourselves."

For the next ten minutes he lead them through the story. When he reached the meeting chaired by the Prime Minister, in which they had struggled for so long to find a way out of the impasse, he had their undivided attention. He spoke at some length about his dealings with Vignau, how he had given a number of conditions to the emergency committee and how they had agreed to meet his demands. "In fact, we've achieved one hell of a lot in a very short time," he went on. "I've already got Patrick Morton up and away and Sir Arthur Trant's on his way to Paris from New York. But what we need now is *manpower*. A properly structured team of the best guys available." He paused, lit a cigarette and looked around the table.

"This, in case I have to remind you, is exactly in keeping with the spirit of our previous meetings. It's worked before to *Vitesse* and now it's the big one, *La Grande Vitesse*. But this is fraught with difficulties and there's a tremendous amount at stake. And if that's not enough, my friends, we haven't got time on our side." The room remained very quiet. Without pausing, Bigard got straight down to business and began by asking them to nominate a team leader. Only two names were put forward – one by Sir Jock Sligo from Crisis Trap, the other by Jeremy Lyons of Holdfast. Four senior ranks were nominated and less than a dozen others. Bigard rubbed the bridge of his nose thoughtfully and looked round the table in silence. Very few eyes met his.

He thought an impasse such as this might develop. They were all holding on to their best operators, not all of those on their books could possibly be away on operations. He knew for a fact that at least three teams were getting themselves ready for assignments and that two others had recently returned from abroad. The men in front of him were acting cautiously. That was their nature, that was how they survived out there. But it was not good enough for tonight and he decided to regain the initiative from what had now become an awkward stalemate. He would send the ball back over the net with a fast top-spin. One whereby he would force each one of them to declare his hand in front of the others. They wouldn't like it but that was too bad. "OK everyone. Thanks very much. I've listened to all that you have got to say about how difficult it is to produce the right sort of chaps and you have my sympathies. But perhaps I should put a few of my cards on the table." He put both hands flat on the table in front of him, then turned them over, palms upwards.

"First, this is a one off. None of us have ever had to deal with anything like this before and I would ask you to reflect quietly on the sheer magnitude of what's at stake. Secondly, between you all, you can muster some 350 men and a handful of women. Of those, around fifty are ex-officers. I know exactly how many teams you have deployed at the moment – not very many as it so happens." He waved a file in the air. "I've got it all here…and it was your offices, my friends, that told me so. And from all this you have given me a paltry list of just two officers and about fifteen blokes. To be frank with you all, it's pretty bloody piss poor and I've found it most interesting to see who's offered what." He nodded at those who had produced names.

"Therefore, perhaps you will permit me to up the ante a notch or two then leave you for a few moments to reconsider your offers, such as they were. Let's face it everybody, in spite of whatever we like to call ourselves, all of us in here are nothing more or less than mercenaries, or people who deal with mercenaries – "a hired soldier in foreign service" as the Oxford English dictionary likes to call us. Well, if that's the case, how does this sound?" Bigard paused to light another cigarette. After exhaling he pulled a single sheet of crested paper from his file.

"*The Government of France is willing to pay each firm that produces men for this oper-ation two million pounds sterling per man.*" He glanced up. "*Each officer or NCO selected will receive two hundred and fifty thousand pounds, every other man one hundred and fifty thousand. All expenses will be covered and, on a successful outcome, there will be a one hundred percent bonus for all concerned.*" He paused and looked up. "Sadly we're not quite in the realms of footballers or pop stars but this is not bad for one week's work." Those round the table sat motionless; the only sound being carriage clock on the mantelpiece as it leisurely chimed the hour. "Now, if you'll excuse me, I've got to pop downstairs for a couple of minutes. Perhaps you might like to reflect on this offer and see if it might somehow help to jog your memories…help you to come up with a few names perhaps." Every eye followed him to the door.

✵✵✵

Ten minutes after his return Bigard had a list of fifty-one names including seven officers and eight senior ranks. Several of the names were well known, resulting in a fair amount of horse-trading and some fierce lobbying. He noted with satis-faction that every firm was well represented.

Bigard had the initiative and now he held it. He told them they had just forty-eight hours to produce the men at Lydd ranges, after that selection would be completed and training begin. Too bad if somebody had strong contenders who were away on the other side of the world. No matter how good they were, they had to be in on time. The MOD had warned the Army commander in Kosovo that any such operations involving these men might have to be aborted at short notice. Men could get back from the Middle East, southern Europe and North Africa by using the daily schedule flights into Heathrow and Gatwick, but that was about the limit.

They drew up a short list together. In the end three possible team leaders were identified and four deputies. Thirty-five team members would report for selection, from which they would keep fourteen and two communication experts to go with Morton. Among the team there had to be two explosive experts, a medic, two signallers, two climbers and one diver. Weapons expertise had to include two gun teams and two snipers. All of them would have to be conversant with the latest SF weapon systems including night visibility equipment. Bigard asked them to nominate some of their women. They should be able to drive and, if possible, speak a little French. He told them he wanted to have all their CVs and records of service emailed through to the French embassy in Knightsbridge that evening and no later. They would be sent down to Lydd first thing in the morning. They should bring their own clothing and equipment, reporting to the guardroom at Lydd Camp as soon as possible.

At the end of the meeting Bigard summarized what he intended to do. "I'll leave the selection and training of the team to Patrick Morton and whichever leader he selects. I'm sure that between them they'll pick a damn good crew from the list you've given me. Morton will live and work with the team," he continued. "Until they deploy for the operation, that is. I'm going on to 58 Knightsbridge from here, make sure that all's well at the Embassy and then return to Paris. I shall probably go to the Interior Ministry…Place Beauvau…then home to bed. I'm absolutely knackered. And if anyone has the neck to return my early call they've lost their contract." Everyone laughed and the tension was broken. Bigard looked at his watch.

"Right now we are thirty-six hours into our one week of grace. I've told them we need forty-eight hours after they've pin-pointed the target. So, if my maths is correct, Paris has just three and a half days to come up with the goods…that's just eighty-four hours. Anyone prepared to place bets?"

Chapter Thirteen
Wednesday Morning

SW France - La Trampa

Mario Gambino woke early. Since flying into Toulouse on Monday evening, more than thirty-six hours ago, he had been working non-stop. Several things about being at La Trampa worried him but now he was committed and it was too late to change. He lay back on the large double bed and put his hands behind his head. After dealing with Joubert, he had listened intently as his electronic surveillance team reported back to him. Orders emanating from the Defence and Interior Ministries had caused mayhem. The commanders of both units had immediately turned their camps upside down in desperate attempts to find the sources from which so much highly sensitive information had been leaked. The Special Force anti-terrorist units were not enjoying their enforced incarceration one bit. Life at Villacoublay and Satory had become mighty uncomfortable.

All uniformed personnel and civilian staff had been confined to camp, his sleepers had managed to report. Logs and records of all recent communication traffic had been checked, as had the transmission equipment, recording machines, tapes, and spools. Even the classified waste had been collected by the Military Police. Mobile telephones and personal computers had been confiscated and staff working in the communication centres and cipher rooms were no longer permitted to work on their own. Roll calls, head counts and room checks had gone on incessantly. Although struggling desperately to find a way out of the dilemma, nobody could guarantee there would be no further breaches of security. As far as the French government was concerned, the deployment of the GIGN and RAID teams remained an unacceptable risk. The units were shackled.

✳✳✳

So where did this lead him? At this stage a raid by Special Forces, he guessed, was unlikely. A raid by armed police, gendarmes or the military themselves, even less

164

so. Such an assault would entail a great deal of preparation and take time to mount, far more than the quick, surgical strike by Special Forces. The heavy signature of such an operation would be picked up by his own agencies – and the media.

The Mafia families in France were well aware that the media had an uncanny knack of spoiling the script by arriving at the scene before the action. They were forever jumping the gun, as during the anti-terrorist sweeps in the early '90s and the more recent drug-busting operations in Marseille. Under these circumstances, any major operation was likely to be blown wide. In spite of this, Gambino remained unhappy with the close security around La Trampa. There was no electronic surveillance, it was too isolated and there were too many covered approaches. All the opposition had to do was to contain him and call in the heavy cavalry. Dino Botante, who had charge of the overall security, had done well with the numbers at his disposal but he was unable to secure the complex with so many different options open to a strike force.

For the moment he would have to lie low, wait for his buyers to be organised, then slip away. Until then he must rely on concealment and stealth, something for which he needed a surveillance force. Time and again they had debated how best to deploy their meagre resources and the conclusion was always the same – more men were needed and that, both he and Botante had agreed, was impossible.

He would get the Nor Lander brought into the airfield at Albi, just fifteen kilometres away, and hold it there. That would give him two choices. First he could backtrack to Palermo. There were plenty of places on the island where they could go to ground temporarily, but it would mean running the gauntlet of the French and Italian air traffic control systems again. His second option would be to head for the isolated mountain airstrip at Orreaga in the Pyrenees, just across the Spanish border. Philippe Buxtrada had suggested the strip which could be approached through the mountains between Pau and Biarritz. His contacts in nearby Roncesvalles had been alerted and had assured him that he would be safe.

Two days ago, and before he had flown in from Paris, Dino Bontate had removed the house and ground staff. It had not been easy. "I couldn't get it into their heads that it was for a short time only," Bontate had complained. "Jesus, they were stupid. No matter what I told them, they were convinced they had been given the push." He went on to explain that he had retained the services of one of the Arab gardeners. "Sort of had a feel for the guy. Something about him," he replied to Gambino's questions. "Just had this gut feeling that the guy's a useful connection with the Arabs around here. There're thousands of them and he could come in handy."

"What's on your mind? Figure we could turn him…use him?"

"Reckon so." Bontate nodded. "Seems to hate the white eyes. Could be a mean bastard, too. I'll put it to him quietly." Said Salim was indeed an interesting man, coming from the large immigrant community in Graulhet, an industrial town beyond Albi. The French had brought labour into the area from Algeria, Tunisia and

Morocco soon after their North African campaign had ended in 1963. Salim hated the French but his family had elected to come over for the better quality of life, the economy around Algiers having been devastated by the years of hostilities.

During the war his father, together with an uncle and several others had been rounded up in the casbah by the 10th Colonial Parachute Regiment. The interrogators had used car batteries and the contents of a carpenter's tool box. They had taken three days and he had never seen his father again. But the Algerian campaign, brutal and unforgiving, had not been all one sided. It had developed into a hideous game of tit for tat, the rebels taking revenge on individual soldiers or small isolated groups. The fellahin would try to capture them alive then incapacitate them before handing them on to the womenfolk. They would be taken by night to within earshot of some lonely military outpost when the women would set to work with their long bladed knives – the khunjas. The ghastly screams would carry for miles in the still desert night, sometimes lasting until dawn. Later, the French patrols would come across the bodies, hideously mutilated, disembowelled and sometimes skinned completely, with their uniforms folded neatly nearby.

Gambino agreed that Botante should approach Salim, speaking in Arabic, leaving himself free to gauge the man's reactions. The Arab would be far happier with just the one point of contact but it would be a delicate business. Should he decline and spread the word, their position at La Trampa would be compromised.

Sensing he was a man who could be bought, Bontante talked at length with Salim. The three men sat around a gnarled walnut tree in the courtyard at the front of the house. Bontate invited Salim to 'taffadal', to sit with him on the ground, cross legged as Arabs, chatting in the north African dialect. They prodded the ground in front of them with sticks and gesticulated as they spoke, like traders in the souk. Bontate had arranged for coffee to simmer on a charcoal fire at their feet and offered a plate of tiny sweet-cakes and fresh dates. Sitting apart, Gambino studied the man carefully. Unable to understand a word, he watched Salim's body language noting his mannerisms and could see the Arab was warming to their proposals.

"Better than I thought," Bontate said eventually, looking up. "He's a pretty hard nut and has sure got it in for the people round here. He says there's constant racial tension. Probably no better or worse than anywhere else," he shrugged. "But they reckon they've got a raw deal." He patted the ground. "Thinks he knows several who'd jump at the chance. And a little extra money wouldn't go amiss either." Bontate paused, turned back to Salim and spoke briefly. Gambino saw the Arab shake his head vehemently. "They won't work at night though. Doesn't surprise me. It's not really their scene. And over here their bints have a big say in things. Like their boys to be back home when the sun goes down so they can keep an eye on them."

Eventually Salim rose and took his leave from Bontate who leant forward and clasped the man's hands. Gambino watched as the men kissed each other on the cheeks, Arab fashion.

***

"Tommy, listen. I need to talk and I want to be straight with you." Antonio wiped his mouth with the starched cotton napkin, pausing momentarily to appraise two young women stalking past their table. "There're a number of things going on up at La Trampa that don't fit." He sounded almost apologetic. "And there're some I don't like at all. Take those two characters shut away in the pigeonnier. I wasn't supposed to see them was I? But I did and it stinks."

Tommy Spadaro looked at the soft fleshy face of the man and saw immediately why he irritated Gambino. "The kid's dumb," Gambino had complained the previous evening. "Just wants to play around the whole goddam time. Thinks we've got nuthin better to do than get smashed and beat the town to hell. Sort him out. Take him to the city and get him fixed up with a coupla broads, for Chris' sake. Take him anywhere but get him away from under my shoes. OK?"

It had been the previous evening during dinner that Antonio had asked about the activities at La Trampa. Bontate and Tommy had seen Gambino's look, but Antonio had ploughed on, muttering about the hidden vehicles, the strangers in the pigeonnier and the peculiar, tense atmosphere. Later still, Bontate had had to calm Gambino, reminding him of Antonio's importance as cover, urging the Italian to be patient. "Well, keep the jerk moving," Gambino had hissed. "I'm bored with the schmuck, he's become a right pain in the ass. Fix him or I will."

Earlier today, Tommy had taken a table at La Carpaccio, a well-known Italian restaurant in Place Wilson near the centre of Toulouse. For an hour they sat with their aperitifs facing the boulevard taking in the scene as shoppers, students and beggars milled around the fountains in the middle of the tree-lined square. Tommy watched as Antonio ordered a second plate of hors d'oeuvres that had been brought with their drinks and listened, astonished, at the complaints about life at La Trampa. Bontate had been right. "The guy's either stupid or got the hide of an elephant," he concluded. "Mario wanted him out but we need him on side. The kid sucks but he's gotta stay, like it or not."

"And what's the great panic about keeping Mario's antiques hidden away and guarded like this?" Antonio asked sullenly, draining his glass. "What's *in* those goddam trucks for Chris' sake, Tommy? Something's going on up there, isn't it? Can you answer that for me?"

The Italian toyed with his glass, thinking hard. Twice he started to speak before eventually looking up. He put a hand on Antonio's arm. "Listen, my friend, and listen well. We both know Mario," he said slowly. "He's a careful man. Right? A very careful man. Has to be. That's the way he's made and that's why he's there. He's paid you well for the joint so let him do things his way. No questions. I dunno what he's got tucked away and I'm damned sure I'm not going to ask him," Tommy continued. "He's a business man. OK? Just leave well alone.

That's my advice. Seriously, man, keep your mind away from all that. The show's Mario's so don't go pushing your way in when the door's shut?"

But Antonio persisted. "But those two he's got in the pigeonnier? It can't be right. I mean, that's serious stuff, Tommy. They're Brits aren't they for crying out loud. Jeez, if Humphrey and Patricia ever got to hear about..."

"Well they won't will they, my friend?" Tommy cut in sharply, glancing at the diners on the next table. "Listen, sonny. We have a saying back home for them whose noses are getting a mite too long." He saw Antonio start. "When you've seen nuthin, you can't think nuthin. And when you can't think nuthin then you can't say nuthin." He pushed his dark glasses on to his forehead and peered across the table. "Antonio, my friend, you ain't seen *nuthin*. OK? If you know what's good for your health, you ain't seen nuthin – *nuthin!* Everyone's going to be just fine." The Italian paused: Antonio toyed with his glass.

Tommy could see the man was unsettled. He worked on him throughout the meal, reminding him of Gambino's generous payment, that the situation at La Trampa would soon be over. "Hey, c'mon, Antonio. Quit the agony. *Nu*-thin's going to happen up there. Right? Look on the bright side, my friend. Just look around," he waved his arm. "Life's not that bad, you know."

Antonio pulled a lugubrious face and shrugged but then laughed. "*Yes*, I suppose you're right. As you say, it's none of our business."

"Sure thing," Tommy answered cheerfully. "Just play it Mario's way and every-thing's gonna be fine."

***

They returned to La Trampa and met Gambino for drinks. Tommy, it seemed, had got the boy in hand. Tommy the diplomat, the fixer had worked his charm again. Later, the two men approached Gambino, Antonio as presumptuous as ever. "Mario," he blurted out. "I know what you're going to think but, listen. Tommy and I've been talking. We need to do something up here. Liven things up a bit." He saw the look on Gambino's face. "No, no. None of that, I promise, honestly, Mario. But the place's dead. Our friends around here know you're back and'll be wondering what the hell's going on. When you're here they look to La Trampa for fun. At the moment the place's like a morgue and people'll be wondering what's up."

Gambino stopped writing and was listening with his head inclined. "Honestly Mario, we can't tuck ourselves away here like a lot of bloody monks," Antonio opined. "People'll talk...they always do and then they'll come and take a look 'Just thought I'd drop in,' and all that. What then, eh?" he glanced at Tommy.

"Look, I owe a few folk around here something. They know I'm in town and I'd like to get something going."

"So, what are you thinking? One of your all-night marathons?"

"No, no, nothing like that. But we've got to do something. Tommy an' I reckon on a couple of dinners. Smart ones, black ties, something that'll keep them happy. Won't do us any harm either."

Gambino had to agree. "OK, a few to dinner over the weekend, then that's it. I don't seem able to get it into your skull that I've a lot coming up, and soon. So keep it low profile, and I mean that." He rounded on Antonio. "And I know you well enough, kiddo, so keep it there, right? Have a few good friends around, ones we know. Maybe get something up from Toulouse, some singer perhaps, or a bit of music. But just keep it down." He paused. "Just nice and quiet."

2

Paris
Sir Arthur Trant's flight got in late. The British Military Attaché met him and they drove straight to the Ambassador's residence where he was given an update. He and the Ambassador – the short, dapper Sir James Creasey – talked briefly about the situation and agreed to meet again the following morning before Trant went to Place Beauvau.

After rising early, Trant strolled along Rue du Faubourg St Honoré pausing to look at the exquisite clothes and jewellery in the shop windows. He walked past the United States and Colombian Embassies then came to the high wall and main gates of the Élysée Palais.

He stopped, mingling with the few other early risers, and looked on as the ceremonial guard of the 1er Regiment du Garde Republican marched out to change the night watch, watching closely as the Officer Commanding positioned the new sentries on either side of the high ornamental gates. His keen, guardsman's eye noticed the fine bearing of the guards, their bodies ramrod straight and motionless, their heads proudly erect under the gold embossed kepis with the tall, scarlet cockades. He nodded approvingly and moved on, crossing the empty Place Beauvau and walking past the well guarded Interior Ministry before turning down Rue Jean Mermoz. Here, he picked his way past the waiters in their black waistcoats and long white aprons, joking loudly with each other as they washed down the small patches of pavement outside their cafes.

At the junction with Rue Rabelais, the home of the Israeli Embassy, he crossed the street and skirted round an operational unit of the Garde Republican. Here, Trant found a very different scenario. A heavily armed, twenty-four hour guard was mounted at both ends of the short street to protect the exposed and vulnerable embassy. The combat dress, long batons and automatic weapons sent out a clear signal. He paused again at the Rond Point set around the vast, open expanse of the Champs Élysées. Even now, well before seven, the traffic was building up, heralding the start to another busy day.

Looking around he found what he wanted and walked across to a news kiosk where he bought a copy of Le Figaro before making his way across to a flower seller. The short, grey–haired woman, stooped low under her black shawl, saw him coming and emerged beaming from behind the colourful array outside her shop. They looked through the flowers together, the tiny figure in her flower-patterned cotton dress and the tall, elegant general chatting amicably as they made his selection, before she disappeared into the dark interior. As he waited for her to wrap the flowers, he breathed deeply, catching the wonderful melange of damp moss, wet leaves and the fragrance of countless blooms.

Fully refreshed and with his mission accomplished, he turned back towards the Ambassador's residence. Now he was frowning in concentration. His first priority would be to establish a good relationship with those in the Interior Ministry and win their confidence. Not always easy, he thought, and sometimes impossible. He needed to get to the heart of the problem quickly, identify the key issues and be clear in his mind of the options for his team. That would mean spending a considerable time in the Intelligence centre which, he hoped, would live up to its formidable reputation. And then there was the old, old business of command and control. Would they let him make the key decisions in time? Again, not easy. Those used to running such operations would be less than willing to hand over the reins to a complete stranger. But that's exactly what he would need if he was going to be of any use.

***

"Well, now you've slept on it, what d'you make of it all?" Trant detected a note of concern in the Ambassador's voice. Breakfast over, they were sitting with their coffee in the comfortable drawing room off the main hall. "Pretty bizarre, isn't it?" Creasey drummed the ends of his fingers together. "And damned awkward. I don't envy the poor French one jot."

"Could well be tricky," Trant replied. "On the other hand, if we can get a number of principles sorted out, command and that sort of thing, then it's not likely to be any more or less difficult than anything else in this line." He looked up. "Just *bloody* difficult," he said and they both laughed.

"Yes, I suppose so." Sir James Creasey brushed at some unseen speck on his trousers and cleared his throat. "You know more about that end of it than most," he commented. "I see it as my job to convince Lespère about our capabilities. He's the Interior Minister, incidentally. A sharp and very quick mind but perhaps

170

not the toughest of cookies. I've got to persuade him and the rest of the government that we've produced the best we possibly can and that they really are the tops. Incidentally, what do you know about this lot they're putting together in England?" The thin, intelligent face searched Trant's. "D'you reckon they'll be able to produce a good enough team...time's devilishly short."

"At this stage, I've simply no idea." Trant raised his hands and sighed. "I'm planning to get across there later today and have a damn good look but I've already had a word with the CDS. Graham Charteris and I've served together quite a bit over the years and we both agree that unless I'm a hundred percent happy then we scrub the whole thing."

"That's what I hoped you might say." Suddenly Creasey frowned. "But are they quite certain they can't get any of our Regular Special Forces across? I mean, surely they could get some away instead of having to rely on this hotchpotch collection. It'd be far easier, wouldn't it?"

Arthur Trant saw the look of concern. "I asked him that straightaway," he replied quietly. "And he seemed quite clear about it. It boils down to a combination of present commitments. They're stretched to the limit, and they need to keep the whole of our own standby team at home. Then there's this blackmail business over the use of Special Forces. Apparently the PM came to the conclusion that our guys could be vulnerable as well. And why not, if the opposition's as good as all that? But on the *quality* side of what we're putting together, I'm fairly optimistic." Trant paused and sipped his coffee. "They've pulled in Patrick Morton and he's good, one of the best. Did the Balcombe Street siege. And I know most of the Security Companies...they've got some very good people involved. Jock Sligo, for instance, and Billy Davis. Harry Llewellyn's a good hand as well. If they can cobble together a team of their best, then I'm game to give it a go."

A head appeared around the door. "Time we were leaving, Sir James."

"Thank you, Simon." Creasey glanced back over his shoulder. "All right, Arthur. I'll leave it in your capable hands. And we are...how shall we say, cautiously optimistic. Yup?" He slapped the arms of his chair and rose.

"Yes, but no more," Trant warned. "There's still a very long way to go yet."

✳✳✳

Before he was introduced to members of CILAT, Trant had a short meeting with the Interior Minister. Philippe Lespère had been given the task of controlling the operation by Prime Minister Jospin until such time as more positive information became available. As they went through the legal and constitutional implications, Lespère listened in amazement to Trant's near perfect French.

171

Sir Arthur Trant knew from past experience that operations like this were a legal nightmare. "And that's when we're operating on home territory," he emphasised. "When it's out here, like this, there're all sorts of additional complications." Lespère told him about Bigard's concern and they agreed it would be impossible for the operation to go ahead until the lawyers were happy.

"And he's quite right," Trant replied simply. "It all looks so neat and tidy until the shooting begins," he continued. "Once the world's press have got a body or two to show everyone, it gets remarkably complicated, and very quickly." Lespère looked at him and smiled weakly. Trant seized the opportunity to quiz him about the position of the French Special Forces. For several minutes he listened patiently as Philippe Lespère went through their deliberations, watching closely as the slim, rather fragile-looking Interior Minister talked.

"Was it *really* not possible to get enough of them out of the camps over a period of time?" Trant asked. "Even if just a few could be spirited out and organised into a team? Would not that be a better solution? Or what about preparing an assault force of Marines or Paras, holding them ready and pressing ahead with more aggressive intelligence gathering operations?" Lespère answered his questions factually and logically. Obviously he and the service chiefs had looked at every possible option. Everything he said made sense. The replies coming back across the desk were much the same as he would have given had the UK been in a similar predicament. But there was more.

As he listened to the replies, Trant recognised something he had found on previous occasions when the British had been caught up in similar international incidents. For all the rhetoric there had been a very slight hint of uncertainty, a lack of confidence. Nothing was ever said but he and others had often sensed an element of self-doubt. The Ambassador, although nervous enough himself, had been right. They had noticed this with the Germans at Mogadishu, and Trant had detected it many times when working with UN forces in the Balkans. Now he could sense it here. Over the years the success of the British SF had been such that they had become the perceived masters. The general public – indeed the whole world – had come to expect the impossible, award-winning performance every time. Flattering stuff, he mused, but a very dangerous double-edged weapon.

If only they knew, Trant thought to himself, what a tremendous element of luck was involved. They could rehearse and prepare for every possible contingency until they were blue in the face but, come the moment, they always needed that generous slice of luck. And if his highly trained professional soldiers back in Hereford needed that, his scratch team out here was going to need a whole lot more. He studied Lespère keenly and saw, behind the bland, confident façade, that touch of uncertainty. The Interior Minister, along with the rest of them, was glad of their company.

✳✳✳

Inside the Intelligence centre Trant studied the collated information. On the wall above the main desk was a large map of south-western France on which a big circle had been drawn around the countryside to the north of Toulouse. "Why here?" he asked the burly Gendarme Commandant on watch.

"Based on a number of facts, M'sieur," the officer coughed, got to his feet and smiled warmly. Trant waved him down and pulled up a chair. "First it was just the aircraft sightings. Initially we had three. One here, up near Grenoble." He stretched up to the map. That turned out to be nothing. Secondly down here near Bayonne." He looked at Lespère and grinned. "This happened to be a rogue aircraft and we picked them up at the airport. Smuggling smart cars, fast Italian jobs," he said, now shaking with laughter. "Quite spoiled their day, I'm afraid. Probably on their way to Spain. And lastly there was the one in and around the Black Mountains…here." He paused to choose his words.

"Following that we had a number of leads about other possible activities in the area. Mostly snippets of a low source and none too reliable. Until, that is, we got the debriefing of the woman they brought in from Alexandria. She's given some very good leads that point to an area in the Tarn to the west of Albi – up here. Just from the casual conversations she had with some of them over the days beforehand."

The Commandant looked at Trant. "And what she's told us ties in with the other bits and pieces. Obviously we are keeping our eyes and ears open everywhere else but this does seem to have the right look about it. So that's about it, so far, M'sieur."

"What else are you planning to do?" Trant asked pleasantly surprised at the clear, unruffled approach of the man.

"Well, obviously we've got the Conseil General of the Tarn on to it…house registers, car registrations and all that sort of thing. Those Department Headquarters hold a lot of background information, y'know," he said confidently, stroking at his clipped moustache. "He'll be keen to get his public services involved but we've decided to tread pretty carefully there. It's very difficult to get them underway without a hell of a lot of fuss." He looked at Trant, gesturing with both hands. "If the birds are there and we frighten them off, that's it."

"And what have you got up your sleeve once you reckon you are on to the right place?" Trant peered at the map.

"Well, that's up to next door, M'sieur. But we would want to get the place checked out - some form of close recce."

"Mmm, all right, but not at this stage." Trant replied turning to the Minister. "If they're half as good as we think they are, they'll be expecting us to do just that. Almost certainly they'll have some sort of early warning system in place. I would tend to stand off a bit longer. What about air recce? IR…Infra Red?" Trant looked around at those standing around the Minister.

"We're looking for a pretty sizeable group here," he went on. "There're only a certain number of places that could harbour such a crowd. What with their vehicles and everything. Good modern IR will tell you which places are occupied, pick up signs of vehicles and so forth. Can even suss out a couple having it away...more heat and all that sort of thing," he said grinning at their laughter. "No, seriously, they're hardly likely to have gone to ground in the forest – here or here," he pointed at the map. "Too easy to be picked up by IR, too few routes to play with and far too many people wandering around...foresters and so forth. They'll have thought about that, too. And what about telephone intercept?" he queried. "Perhaps cutting off the phones of a few likely starters then sending in France Telecom on a repair job?"

"Yes, we're on to that. And we're putting together a multi-language intercept team as well. But back to the recce, M'sieur. As we've been briefed, it's all a question of time. We've got just five days now and we're going to have to take chances sooner or later."

"Well now, hang on a moment." Trant turned to Lespère. "We don't want things rushed, not at this stage anyway. We've still got a bit of time left. Right now we work like hell at the intelligence but move very cautiously on the ground. No hasty decisions or over reaction. Everybody's *got* to keep their heads."

The group talked on for several minutes, exchanging ideas and debating the various options open to them once the group had been located. "And what have we got down there?" Trant waved a hand over the Tarn area. "Do we know anyone in the area, Brits, I mean? Has anyone checked out the British ex-pat community with the Consulates in Toulouse and Bordeaux? There must be a lot of folk down there, scattered about. In fact I know of one for a start. A very old friend, we served together. He has a big place down near Lavaur...here, no, wait...here look." Trant tapped the map. "There might be some useful contacts in the area and we should get a list made up. Some might even know the place when we identify it. We would want to pick their brains, use them as guides, that sort of thing." He turned to Lespère. "What d'you think, Philippe? We could get them all up on a map and, when the time comes, see who might be able to help."

Lespère took Trant through the remainder of the complex, introducing him to those on duty and explaining how each desk fitted in. Two hours later, after he had spoken to the UK MOD and the French Embassy in London he boarded his ministerial aircraft for the Sussex coast. There, at Lydd, he would meet the team he was to command.

3

MOD Range Complex, Lydd
As soon as he had finished with Bigard and the French Embassy, Morton drove hard for the coast where he had arranged to meet the Dover Brigade Commander. The three disagreeable telephone calls from troublesome senior

officers had not been lost on Brigadier Galworthy and, by the time Morton arrived, matters were in hand. Armourers, quartermasters, drivers and kitchen staff had been despatched to prepare the way. Galworthy had done his rounds and was satisfied. The two sat quietly together, Morton revealing as much as he could about the forthcoming training. Initially numbers would vary but would settle quickly to around twenty. When he apologised for being so vague, Galworthy waved his hand. "My dear General, I've seen it all before. As long as we don't resort to shouting, you're more than welcome."

Morton had already taken a guess at the most probable weapon mix and sent a signal to the Director of Special Forces at the Duke of York's HQ. Nobody had yet identified the nature of the opposition and he wanted the team to have every option of weapons available to them. Furthermore they would have to train with all the weapons until the final selection was made. He asked for a variety of weapons, two thousand rounds per barrel for training, a variety of pyrotechnics including stun and flash grenades, plastic explosive, det cord, detonators and initiation sets. Galworthy arranged for space in his armouries and helped Morton select the ranges he needed.

After the Brigadier had taken his leave, Morton settled down to wait.

✳✳✳

Shortly before their evening meal in Wales, King received his call.

"Jed, it's Peter...Peter Harrington. Look, I want you to put everything on hold. Something big's come up and it means a complete turn around." For a moment King was caught off guard. His team were now in their final few days of training and had Kenya on their minds. He turned this way and that for pencil and paper. "Who do you think your two best operators are?" Harrington went on. "Put it another way, if you had to mount a dodgy operation, who of those with you would you take?"

Jed thought quickly. His pulse was racing. "After Horse and Big Jim there's only one guy I'd feel a hundred percent with and that's Ned Kelly. Used to be in B Squadron. 1 Para before that. No problem there. Of the others...well, OK, the Marine, Sam Townsend's not a bad lad. Bit slow on the uptake but a good number nonetheless. Don't go much on the others though."

"We knew you'd ask for the Fijians," Harrington said with a chuckle. He remembered the astonishment of the selection board when King had demanded their inclusion for his last job. He had explained how the two had served with him throughout his tour with Special Forces and how he owed his life to Ligioni: the man they called 'Horse'. He heard how King's troop had been operating in the mountains near Bljelina close to the Bosnian-Croatian border. They had just withdrawn from their position overlooking the River Drina when the ambush had been sprung. King had fallen badly in the initial firefight breaking his left leg, and was lying exposed to enemy fire. He was helpless and was crawling to reach his rifle when Horse had come for him.

The big Fijian had swept him up and carried him through a hail of determined enemy fire to the cover of some nearby rocks. "Simple as that," King had told the Venture Risk panel. "I owe everything to the guy. I promised myself that wherever I went they would come too." And so they had. Venture Risk had seen the men two years ago, taken them on and they were now working with King.

"Right, that's fine. So, if we take you three, Kelly and Townsend and leave the others, who'd run the show? Blackman?"

"Yes, he's steady enough. But not much cop as a trainer."

"No problem. I'll probably borrow someone from one of the other companies."

"Hey, Peter, what the hell's going on?" Jed's voice rose.

"That'll have to wait 'til later. I want you five to pack your kit and get yourself down to Lydd..."

"Lydd?"

"Yes, Lydd, as fast as you can and meet up with General Pat Morton there. You know him don't you?"

"Yeah...ought to," Jed laughed. "He was my boss for nearly three years. King scratched his head in frustration. "Look, come on Peter. Give me a clue, for Christ's sake. What's the score, or is it one of those?"

"No dice. Sorry, not over this means anyway...later. Get yourself up and away as soon as you can. Hand the show over to Blackman. Tell him, from me, that I want them to stay put. I or one of the others will ring in the morning. We'll get another commander and four others down to them. Tell him not to worry, the job's still very much on but we're having to make a number of changes to the team. I'll warn Patrick you're on your way so don't hang around."

***

It was a long drive from the Welsh training camp. The five men reached Lydd shortly after midnight and made their way to where Morton was dealing with early arrivals. "Evening Patrick." King grinned widely. "What's the score then? My boss wouldn't say a damned thing."

"Hi, Jed. Good to see you. Yes, I know." Morton rose and the two men clasped each other's hands. "And quite right too. I heard they'd dragged you along…God, they must be pushed." He grinned back at Jed. "Dump you gear over in the block and give me a hand here. It's all happening."

The two men worked through most of the night. Bigard's handling of the meeting and the way his financial offer had come across had done the trick. By dawn, thirty-eight had reported in. Whenever there was time, Morton and King sat together and talked. As soon as he had seen Jed, Morton's mind was made up. He would be the team leader. Morton knew him as an outstanding SF officer and had tried hard to retain him. A strong, no nonsense disciplinarian, he called a spade a spade, had been a much respected troop commander and did a grand job with part of Morton's CRW team. He had seen combat, lead an anti-terrorist assault and, in Morton's opinion, was ideal.

He told King all he knew about the forthcoming operation explaining that, between them, they had just twenty-four hours to pick the team. They looked at the skills they would need and went through the list of names in front of them, but there was little they could do until the CVs arrived and they could see who was who.

***

Soon after dawn, Jed was up punishing himself on the steep shingle banks behind the ranges. Thighs pounding and lungs rasping, he drove himself for almost an hour, carrying thirty pounds on his operational belt and another thirty in his bergen. After the ranges he went into the gym where he worked out for a further fifteen minutes. He noticed three or four men doing the same and had spotted Morton earlier, way out on the marshes, with his bergen. Breakfast over, the two men divided up the responsibilities. Morton would run the shooting, Jed the fitness and team drills. They planned to get the team selected by mid-afternoon, keeping a few gaps for latecomers.

It was shortly before nine and the first of the candidates were already assembling. Some had found morning papers and were reading quietly, others chatted. Morton was in the well-furnished office to the right of the main entrance as King busied himself with the programme in the conference hall.

Out of the corner of one eye, Jed noticed the three men in a corner, one of whom he recognised. Two were smoking and the third had a can of beer in his hand. He saw King watching him, waved casually and raised his can of beer. King said nothing but noticed the man slip against the wall, spilling the beer. He heard them talking then laughing loudly. Suddenly and without warning, he threw back his chair and leapt across the room.

"I heard that," he shouted at the man with the can. "I bloody heard that. Get up and look at me. Up, damn you." Before the man had time to move King bent down, lifted him roughly and threw him against the wall. Taken by surprise the man made a half-hearted attempt to break King's hold but Jed had anticipated the move. He locked his wrists, half turned to cover his body and bent his arms, tightening his grip. Morton came to the door of the office, saw what was happening but said nothing.

"Right you little wanker. I heard that and I was meant to hear it wasn't I? Thought I'd duck it, yeah? Saw a big, yellow streak in me frightened of making a scene, did you? Well too bad, mate."

"Hey, hang on, boss," the man interrupted.

"And cut out all that 'Boss' crap. Just bloody listen." King banged the man against the wall. "Where I did my soldiering it was only the useless little fuckers that gave all that sort of shit. Or the ones with bloody great chips on their shoulders. And yes, I *am* an officer and I'm bloody proud of it. What's more I'm running this little party and you're going nowhere except out." King looked round at the other two men. "And that goes for you two, an' all. Go on. Pick up your kit and get out of here before I throw you out." He dropped the startled man and gave his pack a hard kick. "Go on," he shouted. "I said get out of here, *now*. Get your gear together and push off fast."

Morton hid behind the door, threw his head back and laughed silently.

"Right, Tak." King lowered his voice and spoke quietly to one of the Fijians. "Wipe that bloody stupid smirk off your face and get everyone in here," he growled. "Give him a hand, Horse. I want to have a word with this lot right now." As he passed, Ligioni gave a little jig.

✳✳✳

The thirty-five men and four women squeezed themselves awkwardly into the room. King closed the door. His lecture on leadership could have taken ten minutes or more but it was over in less than one. Some stared at him apprehensively but most avoided him. "Any questions?" King glared at the ranks of faces in front of him. Heads were shaken but there was no reply. There was nothing to discuss.

"OK, away you go. Get yourself ready for battle training. Ten minutes and we're off." He walked out of the room and into Morton's office. "Sorry about that, Patrick. A couple of blokes tried the usual crap. Pissed at nine in the morning, for Christ's sake."

Morton laughed. " I wondered when you were going to start winding yourself up."

Chapter Fourteen
Wednesday – Later

La Trampa

Said Salim returned that afternoon with two others. Bontate had asked them to come and walk the ground then discuss the security in more detail.

Time and again Bontate had walked to the edge of the grounds, turned and made his way slowly back to the house. He took careful note of the routes which offered the best cover and from which points the complex might be observed. He was now certain they needed a screen to cover the most likely approaches. During the day it should be out on the high ground, but after dark withdrawn to give close protection to the buildings.

✳✳✳

The four of them went over the ground again, first by vehicle then on foot. Salim knew it intimately and pointed out the routes taken by wild boar and the native chevreuil deer as they made their way towards the chestnut forests of Gresigne where they wintered. "And look over there, M'sieur, over there beyond the far hedge." He stopped and pointed. "That's always a problem, people picnic there the whole time," he grumbled. "It's public ground and it's a popular place because of the wonderful views to the Pyrenees. Mostly French and British."

"Anything we can do about that?" Bontate queried, walking up to the hedge. "We sure don't want a whole bunch of rubberneckers sitting around there all day." He turned and looked back. "Jeez, they can look right into the main garden and front courtyard."

"It's difficult to move them on," Salim complained. "If we upset them too much they go off and moan to the mayor so I get one of the men to do some work out here. Half an hour with a chainsaw or a big strimmer soon puts an end to

179

things." Bontate laughed then glanced in surprise at Salim's humourless stare. Something, he could see, was unsettling the man.

"What're you going to tell your men to say if the police or gendarmes come along?" Bontate asked looking up and down the road. "Isn't it a bit unusual having groups of Arabs sitting by the side of the road."

"Not really," Salim countered. "They all think we're a lazy lot anyway, so they won't be too surprised. And, in any case, they tend to leave us well alone," he added. "Language makes it too difficult and we don't help them with that." He spoke in Arabic to his two companions then turned back to Bontate. "It's quite usual for us menfolk to gather and chat, you know. But I'll get them to keep back. The bushes come right down to the road on that corner over there and at the crossroads near Mailhoc." On the way back to the house they discussed the security of the buildings and before he left Salim agreed to start work early the following morning.

An additional and more complicated problem for Bontate was holding and guarding Sir Alan Palmer and Amanda Gates. Palmer was not well. For the last twenty-four hours the archaeologist had alternated between lucidity and bouts of unconsciousness. Gambino wanted to keep them hostage but Bontate had protested, arguing that guarding them used up more of his precious manpower and landed them with an additional problem. He had argued for their disposal but Gambino overruled him. Bontate had shrugged it off but considered it would have been a tidier solution.

✳✳✳

An hour before dusk, Said Salem returned by himself. Tommy and Dino were sitting with Antonio on the front terrace when the gardener parked his van behind the house. He greeted Bontate politely then asked if they could speak together. Once alone Salim wasted no time and, immediately, Bontate detected a change in character. His ingratiating manner had disappeared and his voice now had an authoritative edge. Bontate was on the alert. "Monsieur," Salim looked him in the eye, "I've been thinking about our discussions and what you've asked me to do. I must tell you that I'm a member of the ISL. What does that mean to you?"

Bontate stopped and looked at the man. "You serious?" he asked peering closer. "You really mean that? *Libyan* Intelligence?"

"The ISL, M'sieur, The Intelligence Service of Libya is now the foremost Arab intelligence service in North Africa, more respected than the Egyptian Intelligence Service – the EIS." Salim looked at him haughtily. "You will remember that from your days in Oran, of course. I was recruited soon after we came to Graulhet and I have been working for them ever since." For some time Bontate was silent. He remembered them only too well. Their long arm stretched into every corner of North African life. No souk or bazaar was free from their presence. The ISL believed they had won the respect of the communities, not that they could care. In reality they were loathed and feared.

"Ye-es, all right. I think I know what you mean and who you're talking about." They had reached a low wall and stopped. Bontate was watching the Arab carefully. "But what the hell are you people doing? Nothing gives around here. The place is dead." Salim had struck hard and Bontate was worried. If the man was in the ISL then he would know a great deal.

"Well, M'sieur. You may know already that the Muslim population here, in this part of France, is very much a community within a community. Life's not always easy and we have to look after our own." Salim squatted by the wall. "Taffadal," he murmured to Bontate, gesturing towards the ground beside him. Bontate squatted down. "You see, although we tend to get on well with others, no violence or anything like that, we're not well liked by the French people in general or indeed by the British who have come and settled here. The French see us as an unwanted burden on their economy. This is the region of France where the National Front party is very strong and you know what they think. In order to protect ourselves from trouble we have a widespread network of informers. They're good, reliable men, M'sieur. Men whose loyalty has been tested time and again." Salim's eyes held Bontate's. "But, above that, some of us work directly to Libya. Tripoli wants to know what's going on in this part of the world. It's one of the centres of the French aircraft industry and home to many of their airborne units. Not exactly friends of the Arabs, you understand."

"Yes," Bontate murmured, nodding slowly. "Yes…go on."

"It's just maybe…well, now that you know we're here, perhaps you could use the services of the ISL, M'sieur? I have sensed that you wish to remain well clear of the authorities. That's why I agreed to help in the first place. I told you the story of my family and you can imagine how much I would like to help."

Bontate stared at the Arab. What did the man *really* know? Was this a trap? "How do I know you're telling me the truth, Salim?" He saw the man's face harden. "How can I ever guarantee this isn't some sort of a trick, that you're not in the pay of someone else? The authorities here? Just waiting for me to say something then point the finger at me?" He gestured towards Salim. "Remember I've lived and worked with Arabs for years. I'm half Arab for that matter. Remember?"

"Yes, I remember, M'sieur." Salim pulled a wry face. "And you speak the language as only an Arab can. But if I did what you're suggesting, neither of us would benefit." He paused, looking straight at Bontate. "That is why I've come to see you now. You see, the ISL knows about Alexandria. When something like that happens in a great seaport it's impossible for it to remain secret. I don't have to be a professor to understand the situation that's staring me in the face here. What is more, we know you have Renee and Blosch. Do you really believe that such an event could take place without us knowing, M'sieur? If so, you are badly mistaken."

"Go on." Bontate was wary. "I know what you're saying. What's this benefit you keep talking about? What's your price?"

"We want Renee and Blosch delivered safely to Libya...and soon."

"And if we refuse."

"You cannot refuse, M'sieur. We both know that. All we have to do, any of us, is to make just the one call to Paris. That's all."

"In the name of God," Bontate murmured to himself.

"Allah kharim," Salim replied quietly.

✳✳✳

They returned to the house where Salim spoke to Gambino. The Sicilian froze. He looked from one man to the other in silence, then back again. Bontate saw the muscles on his jaw twitch and watched as he rubbed his right shoulder. Mario Gambino was on the back foot. It was the first time in many years that Dino Bontate had seen his Mafia boss thrown. Gambino paced the room. His head was down and he was running his hands through his hair.

Suddenly he stopped and took Bontate aside. The ISL had moved fast. They had scented their quarry and were not going to let go. Gambino sounded out his 'caporegime.' "Why not let them have the two men and break cover now?" he asked. Bontate replied that, by doing so, they would be leaving themselves open to the full wrath of the French who would have nothing to lose. The buyers were not ready and, by coming out so early, they would have to find another staging point.

Gambino thought rapidly. Bontate was right, just as a good 'caporegime' should be. They should accede to Salim's request, but ask for more time before moving. "Then, as soon as we're ready, let them have the motherfuckers," he snarled. "And when we move we'll see to that Salim. He thinks he's smart but he's not that smart. Send him to me. Don't worry, I'll be nice n' easy. You do the talking."

When Salim heard Gambino's reaction, he appeared unmoved. He bowed deferentially when the Italian told him they could have the scientists just as soon as they were ready. He agreed to allow more time, but not much, and assured them they would be satisfied with the men he was providing for La Trampa.

182

"Go in safety," Bontate murmured, taking his hands and embracing the Arab as he left.

"And may the Merciful One be with you," came the reply.

2

Lydd Ranges
Slowly and methodically Morton and King worked their way through the list of names. In some cases rejection was easy. Others had allowed their physique to deteriorate and either collapsed or gave up on what Jed King had called a perfectly straightforward little march. Nobody knew what sort of operation they might be asked to mount but without doubt a certain degree of physical stamina would be required, perhaps a great deal. Before the action itself they might have to approach the target carrying everything with them. And when the shooting started, fitness was vital.

Once Morton had finished conducting the weapon tests he returned yet again to the men's record of military service and the work they had done with their parent security company. By early afternoon, several more had been eliminated. These were not necessarily men of poor quality, simply they had not had the necessary combat experience, thus a question mark remained.

New blood in the Special Forces was introduced piecemeal to such operations, and only after many months of careful grooming and preparation. Even then mistakes were sometimes made when a man would slip through the most stringent vetting and fail at the vital moment. Morton called the MOD again and asked for traces to be run on a number of men he wanted cross-checked. Each service had their own Records' Office where complete service records were kept and he needed to see these in order to satisfy himself.

✳✳✳

As soon as they were able, the two men set about identifying a second in command and patrol leaders from the list in front of them. "We need to go firm now," Morton told Jed. "There's a hell of a lot to do and we need to get them involved." Once the team had been put together, the training could begin in earnest. They decided to hold six in reserve, allowing them to run with the team, so the group could be fine-tuned while they remained at Lydd.

A number of the companies had telephoned Morton asking for the final selection to be delayed, allowing time for some of their best operators to reach the camp before the deadline. Alan Michael of Guard Watch had managed to catch his team in the Balkans as they were waiting to deploy. He reached them at Sarajevo, put the operation on hold and recalled two who were due in at Gatwick later that evening. Both were high-class operators and he called to warn Morton of their late arrival. Bill Davis of Electron asked for final selection to be delayed until one of his men got down from Scotland and Tom Cable had an excellent demolitions expert on leave from Angola.

Bigard had sent a shock wave through the world of Private Security. Undoubtedly there were some excellent men out there but the shutters had to come down soon and they would have to make do with whoever was available. More than forty-eight hours had now elapsed since the Egyptian ultimatum and Morton had to have the team in the flesh and on the ground rather than a list of names on paper. They decided to leave the door ajar until nine o'clock that evening. Trant was due in then and they wanted to present him with a properly organised team.

After a brief discussion they decided to appoint 'Ned' Kelly as Jed's number two. Jed had lobbied strongly for him. "He's got a great track record. Six years in G Squadron, 1 Para before that. I met him in Venture Risk and he was picked as my number two for the Kenya job." Kelly, thirty-one, small and wiry, came from London 'somewhere' in the Hackney and Bethnal Green area. "Well said, boss," he grinned when King told him. "Could always spot a good 'un, you could." As soon as Kelly had been selected, King put him to work. He required a comprehensive list of all the kit they might need to be made up which they would later check against what the team had brought in with them.

"Individual kit, patrol kit and team kit, Ned. We've got to think of the lot first time round," King warned. He knew enough about the little cockney to then forget the problem.

Next to be selected was Jock McCall. He too had been working with SF but his background had been 45 Commando RM. He had made his way into the SF via a tour of duty with Comacchio Company where he was involved in oil rig security off the Scottish coast. Jock came from the opposite end of the United Kingdom – Glasgow. Unlike most Glaswegians McCall was a big man, a very big man, but one who said little. "If Jock says 'What' then you've listened to a speech," they joked. Although short of words, his alarming facial scars bore testimony to a savage upbringing in the Govan, and as a warning to those tempted to push the man. "Aye," he muttered when Jed told him. "I can hack it, nay sweat."

They then picked Archie Small from 2 Para. He had never left the Paras but had served with their Pathfinders and had an excellent record of service in Northern Ireland, winning a Military Medal in South Armagh. A friend of his working for Crisis Trap had encouraged Small to leave the army and he had been working with Sir Jock Sligo for the last three years. King called the two men, broke the news then gave them tasks on the Close Quarter Battle range. "I'll give you a list of the most likely starters," King said. "Get 'em together and start working on their weapon handling. Pound to a pinch of shit it's manky."

"We'll soon see who's what," Small replied. He still limped slightly from where the two AK47 rounds had left their mark, blasting a lump of bone from his knee cap in the Ballymurphy contact five years previously. Two IRA gunmen had paid the price for over confidence as they sauntered up to check the body. Small, very much alive, had not welcomed such close attention, a point emphasised by his Browning 9mm semi-automatic. "But it took me three shots to finish the second bastard, for fuck's sake," he grumbled to the medics as the morphine began to take effect. Never again did he trust strangers with weapons and throughout the afternoon his eyes watched every move of those on the range.

***

The camp quartermaster opened his stores, changing or renewing whatever they needed. But Major Jim Ruddock was a Quartermaster of the old school, and a canny Scot who knew how soldiers behaved in his stores. "The Queen's nay in the bezziness for charity," he boomed at the assembled team. "Ye can hai whatever ye want, but you'll nay touch a thing until I say. An' what's more you're going to have to pay fer it right the noo. D'ye ken?" It was not a question. "And another thing, too. It's the cash or the cheque book, none of these fancy card things."

"Typical ruddy QM," 'Ginge' Harris muttered. "God didn't make that lot, they were dug up by someone who should've left them alone." Several had come with their own packs, clothing and sets of equipment. Those with SF experience had always been allowed to make up their own. As long as it could do the job, was well camouflaged and the owner was happy, they could choose whatever they wanted. The same with operational clothing. Those whose lives depended on each other could not give two hoots about where or how the neighbour's buttons were sewn on to his jacket or how many water bottles he chose to carry on his belt.

Weapons were a different matter and personal preference sometimes had to make way for the preferred weapon-mix for the team as a whole – it would be no good if everyone wanted to take 40mm grenade launchers or the latest Heckler Koch machine pistol. The all-important factor was the right combination of firepower based on the job to be done. The weapons and ammunition Morton had ordered were due to arrive later. Until they did, those under selection would continue to use the standard infantry weapons on loan from the camp including the universally distrusted SA 80 service rifle. Time and again rumours had spread about the unreliability of the weapon. Several well-documented case studies had sown the deep mistrust and, whenever it was allowed, hands would reach up to select something different from the armoury shelves.

Once the special weapons had arrived the five leaders would select the best combination, based on the skill of the men in the team and the type of operation they were most likely to undertake. Each man would then be allocated his own. Surprisingly enough, the names that came to make up the team at the end of the day were not all SF. As Morton had predicted, there were several excellent men out there, many of whom had proved themselves on operations since leaving the service. 'Col' Masters, 'Scouse' Wellings and the medic 'Len' Hutton all had long and well proven track records with SF. Sam Townsend and 'Ginge' Harris came from 40 Commando RM, 'Chopper' Edwards from 2 Para and Terry Fraser from the Royal Signals. Jim Machaver, one of Henry Llewellyn's best men from Centre Point, was ex-Intelligence Corps. The three Fijians – Tony Racatoni, Jim Tacamati and Horse Ligioni had all worked for years with SF. Before that two had been infantrymen and one, Tacamati, a signaller.

The final member of the team – Bill Sandeman – was also the oldest. He had served for over ten years with the Met where he had developed an unrivalled reputation as a locksmith. He then left the police and took his murky house breaking and safe cracking skills to the MI5 and M16 training school on the south coast. Sandeman, now 42, had been included solely for his peculiar and unique ability. He did not like guns. He steered well clear of the nasty things but agreed to come along on the off chance he might be able to help.

***

By seven o'clock Morton and King were satisfied with the team they had assembled. Reserves had been identified, two signallers selected to accompany Morton and two girls – Tracy Black and Marion Drew – picked to act as couriers and intelligence gatherers. Years of intelligence gathering in Ulster, undercover work by the Police and the experiences of MI5 had shown the value of girls in sensitive or dangerous passive operations. A few members of the team had voiced surprise at their inclusion but, as Jed King pointed out with a grin, it all boiled down to human nature. "When you're going down a dimly lit street late at night and you see a car full of blokes, you're right on your toes. You clock 'em like a hawk, ready for trouble. Come across a bloke and his bird snogging in the back seat and you look the other way...simple as that." But it was not quite as simple as that. Only King, Morton and two others knew that the older girl, Marion Drew, had pulled the trigger as viciously and effectively as the rest of the party in a ruthless and highly successful SF ambush. Quite literally the IRA active service unit never knew what had hit them.

The weapons arrived under police escort. Morton checked through the list as the team unloaded the cases. Every weapon was then checked individually. For personal protection he had ordered the Sig Sauer P226 and the Browning pistols. Both 9mm weapons had excellent reputations, but the Sauer held more rounds in the magazine and was often preferred. He had requested that they should be issued with Teflon-tipped rounds. At Mogadishu one of the terrorists, a woman, had survived a number of hits by 9mm bullets and should have been killed. Later, surgery revealed that the bullets had ricochet off the larger bones. The bullets tipped with Teflon were designed to smash their way through awkward obstructions, splintering bones and the like which, in turn, tore the flesh out in lumps thus completing the job more effectively. In addition to the 9mm pistols he had asked for a number of the smaller Sauer P230 to be sent. This particular 7.65mm weapon was sometimes preferred by those carrying heavier loads. Others chose it as a compact but highly effective second weapon.

For assault weapons he had selected the 9mm Heckler Koch MP5 and the older Ingram Mark10. Most would opt for the HK, widely regarded as the best assault weapon of the day, but the older die-hards still remained loyal to the Ingram. It had done them well in the past, they trusted it and wanted it now. The extremely high cyclic rate of fire was guaranteed to upset those at the receiving end. The most favoured standard rifle was still the Armalite M 16 A2. Very light, just 5.56mm, accurate and with single round or automatic options it was an old and well-tried favourite. With it came its first cousin the M203, capable of launching a 40mm grenade accurately up to four hundred metres. An excellent piece of kit for terminating irritating gunfire.

He had asked for two Accuracy International sniper rifles to be sent together with their Schmitt and Bender telescopic sights. This weapon had been designed by the SF in conjunction with Olympic marksmen and had proved itself time and again on recent operations. Jim Machaver, a member of the design team and reserve for the UK Full Bore rifle team, took one of the weapons off to zero it on the five hundred metre range. Included also were three Winchester pump action shot guns with solid shot. If Bill Sandeman was going to have trouble opening doors quietly the proper way, the Winchesters would do it noisily the improper way – hinges first. Finally, in case they were required, two trusty General Purpose Machine Guns, known affectionately by British soldiers as 'gimpies'. The devastating destructive power of the guns was regarded with awe, especially by their opponents – if any survived to talk about it.

Grenades had always been the subject of heated debate within the SF. While modern versions were designed to fragment into tiny pieces of wire to cover a wide area, it was the well proven 36 grenade that packed the punch. The last and largest piece of assault equipment was designed to blow holes through masonry large enough for men to move through at speed. Nicknamed the Harvey Wall Banger, the explosive charge had been designed by the SF and had already proved its worth. With no idea of what problems the target might present, Morton had requested several.

The personal equipment he had asked for was of the latest design and, here too, he was gratified to see that his requests had been answered. Individual Passive Night Goggles (PNG), Passive Image Intensified (II) weapon sights, Kevlar protective waistcoats and Protec head protectors. All had arrived safely in their packing along with several boxes of the S6 respirator. Finally, and to be used as personal and inter team communication, the brand new Marconi ST3 sets had been sent in by the Royal School of Signals, together with a number of Satphones for long range communications. The MOD had turned up trumps and it was now a question of deciding who should have what so that specialised weapon training could begin in the morning.

***

Sir Arthur Trant arrived at Lydd later than expected on account of his numerous meetings in London. After he had visited the Central Staffs he had spent half an hour with the Chief of Defence Staff. As the UK's senior serviceman, General Sir Graham Charteris had quizzed Trant closely about how he had found things in Paris and if he was happy that the operation could succeed militarily. He told Trant that they had received information that movements of their own SF had been monitored and, in his opinion, the risk of a UK deployment into France was out of the question. In reply Trant told him that, if the best possible team could be assembled and they managed to get enough time to sort themselves out, then the operation was feasible.

"I think it *can* be done," he went on. "There are the men around who could make up a very good team indeed. But it's not that which concerns me, rather it's the political rumpus if there's a nonsense. All I can do is to let you know that I'm happy with what we've got, then it's up to you to stiffen the backs of the politicians. Can't really see how we can do more than that."

"I know," the CDS sighed, opening the door. "Some are fine, others wilt like dying flowers at the mere thought of it. Don't take any nonsense at your next port of call."

After the MOD Trant went to the FCO where, much as he expected, the byword was caution. *Caution* to allow time for all other avenues to be explored thoroughly first, *caution* to minimise casualties and *caution* not to offend their hosts. Twenty minutes of this and Trant had had enough. He rounded on the Foreign Secretary telling him that, if his professional judgement was going to be held in doubt, he would cancel the operation there and then, return to New York and get on with his flag waving at the UN. He got up out of his chair, leaned over the desk and glowered at the diminutive, bearded Foreign Secretary now staring at him with his eyes bulging. "For goodness sake, man. Have a little faith in our ability. If the French, held to ransom as they are, can come to us like this, then why the hell has our own government got to start wriggling and squirming?" He stood back and straightened his tie. "And as for risk, of *course* there's a risk, just as there is every time a soldier puts a round up the spout. For God's sake stop thinking about your own wretched neck and put yourself behind us for once in your life."

Trant looked distastefully at the now silent figure behind the desk. The eyes said it all, there was no substance to the man. Happy to pontificate from the depths of the Whitehall pile carpets, he had never held a weapon in his life. Like Lespère and so many others, he had all the confidence in the world while the talking lasted but, as soon as the gloves came off, the ducking and weaving began.

***

Trant and Morton spoke for over an hour. Sir Arthur knew Jed King and a number of the men now in the camp, several having been in the Regiment when he was commanding. Morton's first problem was that he still had no idea of the target. He could equip the team for most options but needed time to regroup and train for whatever was finally identified. They agreed that as soon as Paris had an inkling, Trant would get the message across to him. Far better to have something positive to work towards rather than sitting around waiting.

A second and more pressing problem was that he had no idea how they were going to react once in France. The time between their arrival and the operation was critical. Trant told him that Bigard had demanded at least forty-eight hours from the French and this had been accepted. "We'll need to find a secure base somewhere within striking distance of the target," Morton continued. "There's a hell of a lot to do. We'll have to set up a recce programme and get our comms sorted out. An hour's drive has to be the maximum. And we're going to need covert vehicles, of course. We'll need the usual cross section of large cars and windowless vans plus a couple of good bikes. Someone's going to have to get them together for us. Bigard can't possibly do that sort of thing from Paris and whoever fixes the transport has got to think of an official but covert escort once we're on the road.

 "It's just like we have here at home," he continued. "We've got to cater for one of our vehicles getting caught up in an accident or running into a police check point. Imagine the local gendarmes' reaction if they opened the back of the van and found themselves staring down the barrels of a couple of gimpies." The two men roared with laughter but Trant was writing quickly in a dog-eared notebook. He promised to take these points back to CILAT. " I'll put all this to them," he said finally, catching his breath. "They're on the ball over there, pulling out all the stops and I can't see them letting anything get in their way."

3

Paris
Soon after Trant left CILAT, Philippe Lespère called together the other members of the team and briefed them on his meeting with the British General. In the short time he had been in the Intelligence Centre, Trant had put his finger on a

number of points they had not considered. Lespère urged them to reconsider every aspect of intelligence gathering and to consider the press very carefully.

Charles Tubon, the Prime Minister's Chief Press Officer, knew exactly how they worked and would react. Once they scented a coup it would be impossible to shake them off and almost impossible to control, but the government had now committed itself. "At the moment it seems to have gone well," he reported, "but if they get on to us, they're going to want to know what's happening." Tubon looked at Jospin. "But, in a strange way, this time limit we've got is to our advantage You see, we've got just over four days left to the deadline, m'sieur," he said, glancing at his watch. "Assuming we manage to run them to ground, it gives us a little over three days to do something about it. So we're looking at a seventy-two hour game with the press. Tight," he mused. "But possible."

"And if things break?" Jospin queried.

"Then it's a very different game, Monsieur. Once it's out in the open, it becomes a typical, high profile anti-terrorist operation and we deal with them all in the usual manner. As you know, our own media are tightly controlled and there're a number of legal restrictions on what they can say about us. It's the international press that's the problem. Once they get on to it, it's out but, hopefully, we can buy enough time."

"But not here in Place Beauvau…we're sitting like ducks on water."

"Funnily enough, it's probably been a good move to set up shop in here earlier rather than later," Seguin interjected. "At least we'll be in the best place to face such a scenario. Perish the thought of trying to reorganise ourselves if the crisis breaks and we're spread out all over Paris."

"All right, I can't say I like what we've done, but we need to have a watertight security plan," Jospin replied glumly getting to his feet. "Get one out and let me see it before you go any further." He nodded to Seguin and Tubon. "The press could make or break the whole damned show."

✳✳✳

Once they had left, those remaining poured over the security implications, attempting to coordinate the daily routine of government business with running the operational nerve centre at Place Beauvau. They decided to initiate a number of deception plans simultaneously. Ministers, their Deputies and Chiefs of Staff would enter and leave Place Beauvau via the underground tunnel which ran between the operation centre 'Jupiter' in the Élysée Palace and the Interior Ministry. They would gain access to the Palace via the security gate, tucked away unobtrusively down the sidewall in Avenue de Matigny, already cordoned off by the security guards.

The police and gendarmes were to cordon the area, using the forthcoming May anniversary of the founding of Israel as cover. Each year, security at Rue de Rabalais was increased dramatically as a routine precautionary measure for this occasion. Military, Police and Gendarme staff required to run the operation at Place Beauvau would enter and leave the building normally, under cover of the increased security for the Israelis. The Prime Minister had insisted that normal day-to-day business would continue.

CILAT had made the decision to maintain police and gendarme activities throughout France at the usual level. They decided not to invoke emergency powers such as the authority to enter and search buildings or to detain individuals on suspicion. Throughout the south-west suspicious activities were to be reported only, rather than investigated. The Civil Aviation Authorities across southern France were ordered to report any untoward activity or unusual flying activities while, in the south-west, customs officials and police were to mount covert surveillance on all border crossings.

**

Quietly and efficiently CILAT put into operation a huge intelligence gathering network and it was not long before the first snippets began to filter back. Much was irrelevant but gradually minute pieces of information appeared that caught the eye. From the Tarn came news that the Mayor of Mailhoc heard about the sudden and unusual staff dismissals at La Trampa. In a large community such information would not have been newsworthy but in a tiny rural hamlet it would be discussed in the boulangerie, on the steps of the church and inside the Mayor's waiting room. Earlier the postman on his morning round mentioned that he had seen a group of men in the grounds of La Trampa. Unusual, he thought, especially at that hour. A stranger had met him at the post box. He neither looked nor spoke like an Englishman. His accent had been foreign – Spanish or Italian perhaps. What, he asked the Mayor's secretary, was Monsieur Stamford-Barton doing up at the manor?

Soon afterwards Intelligence decided to initiate a telephone interception operation. Controlled from the France Telecom regional headquarters in Toulouse the operation was set up in Albi. All calls would be intercepted, recorded and then translated from Arabic, English and Italian by the Airbus Industrie translators the police used on such occasions. In Bordeaux and Toulouse, British Consular officials sent lists of British expatriates living throughout the region. The intelligence staff began to prepare a map overlay showing the residence of every name on the list beginning with those living closest to La Trampa and three other grand houses in the area that were attracting attention.

The overlay was placed over the principal map in the intelligence centre and the names and particulars of those nearest were highlighted. The Defence Ministry was asked to conduct high-resolution aerial photography flights over the four houses in question. These were later backed by satellite Infra Red photography in an attempt to confirm the numbers of inhabitants and the numbers and types of vehicles in and around the properties.

4

Paris, Chez Francoise

André Bigard should have been happy with the progress. The midday CILAT meeting had been an upbeat affair where he had heard about Trant's visit. Also the news from the UK was positive and the team was being assembled. The first part of his task had been completed and there was nothing more he could do. Yet, as the day wore on, he grew uneasier by the hour. By midday he knew why.

It was the two scientists. He realised immediately that this had been the worry at the back of his mind. Where the hell were they? More to the point who was working on that particular problem? Unless they could be traced and lifted successfully, the whole operation was doomed. When Cohen spoke about them earlier, he had considered them in isolation but they were, of course, vitally important and had to be found.

He returned to the CILAT conference and searched frantically for Lespère but he had left, leaving the Deputy Director of the National Police in charge. Bigard spoke to him in the Intelligence Centre, asking him for news of the missing men. "You tell us, my boy," he replied with an exaggerated shrug. "Right now we're turning the country upside down looking for the opposition. If those fellows aren't with them, then Heaven knows where they are. No one here's mentioned them. Suggest you get your address book out and start ringing your fancy chums," he added sarcastically.

✳✳✳

Now André saw the full extent of their problem and it was awesome. There were two entirely separate operations on the cards. The first was in hand and proceeding well. The second, and equally important, was not even being considered. Nobody had even thought about it, yet the two were inextricably linked. His only hope was Eddi Cohen. If anyone knew where they were it would be the Israelis. Of all the problems facing the tiny nation of Israel, by far the greatest was that sooner or later one of her more irrational neighbours was going to get its hands on nuclear weapons. Renee and Blosch could provide the knowledge for them and they had tried desperately to keep track of their movements. It was Eddi who had confirmed they had been taken first to Sicily. Bigard called him and they agreed to meet.

Half an hour later Bigard arrived at their rendezvous, Chez Francoise a little known, bourgeoise fish restaurant in Rue de Tolbiac just off Parc de Choisy. Cohen was there already. As usual he had selected the table carefully. Away from the gaze of passers by, he was sitting with his back to the wall but within easy reach of both the front door and the back exit past the kitchens. "Hi there." He rose to meet André but there was little of the usual banter. "Well, I was wondering when you were going to call. What's up?"

"Oh…so, so. What makes you ask?"

"Oh, come on, man. There's one hell of a buzz in the wind. Back at my embassy they're going potty. No one can put their finger on it but the smart money's on Egypt or Syria. So what's the score?"

André waited until their orders had been taken then turned to Eddi. "OK, my friend. You're dead right. It's all happening. Now look, I know full well that what I tell you goes back to your boss, that's all part of the game. But for God's sake, when they get hold of this they *mustn't* let on they know. One of the DGSE boys called me up the other night and got me involved and now I'm in it up to my armpits."

For the next ten minutes Bigard covered the situation. Eddi listened in silence, not moving except when they paused for the food and wine. When it was over he looked down, raised his eyebrows and blew slowly. "Holy Moses. That's big, all right," he said. "And under a week to crack it?" He took a deep breath. "You've got to get your skates on this time, Bigard, my boy."

"Don't I know it. We're almost a third of the way through the week and I don't even know which goddam continent those two guys are on…and that's only part it. And once we know where they are we've got to do something about them, like lift them before they make a home run. That's the other half of it, Eddi." Cohen said nothing, just looked at his friend. "This lot've got our masters by the knackers and we can't move. They reckon it's too dodgy to bring in the Brits – officially that is - so that just leaves you. And just imagine what the Arabs would think if you lot got involved. So where the hell do we go from here?"

Eddi Cohen sat back, put a restraining hand on André's arm and finished his mouthful. "Listen, first of all the good news. The other day we heard that they'd left Sicily and been moved on to Morocco, of all places."

"*Morocco!* Holy shit! Why've they been taken there? And why the bloody hell didn't you let me know?" André exploded. "For Christ's sake, man."

"Because, dear boy, we didn't have the slightest idea that this particular little lot had got your country over a barrel. *And*, what's more, if you'd told me about all *this* earlier, I would have given you the gen. Honestly, we hadn't a clue what's been happening. Seriously." He lifted his arms in a gesture of helplessness. "OK, so now we do and it's hardly the most cheerful piece of news to hear at the lunch table. The boys in the embassy are going to just love it. And the bad news is that we can't do anything about them while they're still there. The middle of Casablanca's hardly the sort of place for us to keep a bunch of heavies. It's all far too dodgy out there for my lot, and El Al gives the place a very wide berth into the bargain."

"But suppose they do get moved on," Bigard suggested. "If you *could* get a crack at them, d'you think you'd be prepared to have a go? I mean it's pretty much in your country's interest to have them back in the box, isn't it?"

"Yeah sure, but you know," Cohen paused, pulling a face. "It's not every day that our lads get given the go ahead to lift people just because we don't like the look of them. Tends to remind everyone what nasty people we Jews are," he added. "And also I'm damn sure my lot would put one hell of a high price on it."

"Like what?" André queried.

"How about downgrading the arms deal with Egypt, for instance? We're not exactly jumping for joy at the idea of several hundred brand new Leclerc Mark V tanks in Egyptian colours sitting just across the Sinai, you know. What the hell do they need them all for anyway?"

Bigard checked himself as the waiter led two couples past their table. "God's streuth, Eddi. That's one hell of a tough bargain," he continued. "The roof 'll come off Place Beauvau when they hear that."

"Well don't say a word about that or anything else just yet," Cohen replied. "That was just me, a very small fish, surmising on what the reaction could be if and when we can get our hands on these two jokers. At the moment, you and I are way ahead of the game.

"Some bloody game," Bigard muttered, licking his knife.

"All I can do at this stage is to take word back." Cohen paused. "Look, I'm going to have to come clean, you know, and start putting a lot of oil on embassy wheels. Even then at the end of the day they may well turn round and tell me to push off and mind my own business. But..." he thought again and shook his head. "I've a fair hunch they'll be keen to see this one through. And it's also my bet that the opposition *will* move the two scientists on. They're too far out on a limb there. Looks as though they've been trailing the coat a bit. They need to get them closer if they want to be certain of a home run to Libya.

"Yep." Bigard nodded.

"If it was me I'd bring them in to Cyprus, or even take them back to Sicily. Can't make out why they moved from there in the first place."

For some time the two men remained silent. Then Cohen looked up. "Mind you, they might try to get away with the whole damn lot," he continued. "Flog all this wonderful stuff they've dredged up in Alexandria for a huge fortune and keep hold of these two guys. Play cat and mouse with them later on. They're always going to be good bargaining chips."

"Yeah and if that happens, my head'll be off with a rusty knife." Bigard paused then groaned, stifling a yawn. "Shit, Eddi, I'm absolutely knackered. These two guys are beginning to get to me. OK, for the moment I'll say nothing at all. It'll be interesting to see if our intelligence crowd comes up with anything. Our Foreign Affairs lot have been sucking up to the North African Arabs for years now. See them as the back door to the whole Arab world where the real money is...and oil."

"Or what's left of it," Cohen parried. "And then what, eh?" he grinned ruefully. For the rest of the meal the two tried to second-guess the next move of the scientists and how their governments would react to the idea of Israel becoming involved. As they were getting up to leave, Cohen turned to Bigard.

"Oh by the way, I nearly forgot in the excitement of it all." He smiled at the look of despair on Bigard's face. "You ought to be aware that the press are starting to get nosey. I had a call this afternoon and was asked if I'd heard any rumours. I fobbed him off with some excuse and the cheeky bugger told me I was behind the curve on this one. The feelers are out, he told me, adding that I had a bit of catching up to do."

"Bloody hell," André grimaced and shook his head. "Jeez, that's all we need. As if we haven't got enough."

"That's right," Eddi replied, clapping André on the back. "It's not just raining out there now, my friend, it's fairly pissing down."

Chapter Fifteen
Thursday Morning

Paris

The French Government ministerial jet bringing Sir Arthur Trant from Lydd touched down at Le Bourget just after midnight. It had been a hard day but he decided to call at Place Beauvau before turning in. Entering the tall, grey building, he ran briskly up the two flights of stairs and went straight into the Intelligence centre. The midnight conference was still in progress.

As he entered the room Henri Gabron, the burly Chief of Staff to the DG of the National Police stood to greet him. Trant raised both hands signalling them to continue their deliberations and ignore his presence. He found a seat near the back and listened intently while Gabron called for the duty watch keepers to brief the assembly. As a result of the day's activities and the mass of information received, they had narrowed the field to three areas of interest.

First, the gendarmes had detected suspicious activities on an industrial estate near the busy town of Vizelle south of Grenoble. This information tallied with earlier reports that an unidentified aircraft had been spotted in the area and three warehouses on the estate were now under surveillance. The second was the area around Biarritz. It was Basque country, an area long regarded with deep suspicion by the French authorities. As soon as the gendarmes had empounded the smuggled cars they began a vigorous interrogation of those involved. It lasted for two days, yet they had little to show for their efforts other than a few names and addresses near Henday and St Jean-de-Luz, close to the border. The interrogators were exhausted. "Useless bastards," the intelligence coordinator had muttered, slamming the phone down. Those next to him had listened in silence as he had lambasted the head of the Henday gendarmerie for his lack of progress. "Get the sodding gloves off," he had shouted at the mouthpiece. "We need the answers, like now. Pull your bloody fingers out down there!" And lastly, there was the Tarn.

Trant watched those at work, noting carefully how the meeting sifted through and analysed every scrap of information. It was a refreshingly professional performance:

everyone in the room was aware that time was against them yet nothing was over-looked or discarded for being too problematical. He noted, too, how Gabron and the others scanned every available piece of intelligence that came in from the other regions. When finally the meeting was over he slipped next door and spoke to the intelligence coordinator, still smouldering over the lack of progress in Biarritz. He asked him to pass on to the morning watch the news that things had gone well in England but warned that much remained to be done at Lydd and here in France.

"Please thank everyone next door for allowing me to sit in," Trant called to him as he was leaving. "I found it all most interesting. Oh, and just one other thing. Could you try to arrange a meeting for me with the Interior Minister before the morning CILAT conference, if it's at all possible. And I'd very much like to have a word with the good Monsieur…er, Bigard too, if that's in order. Perhaps you would get word to him."

❋❋❋

The meeting between Trant and Philippe Lespère took place in the Minister's office at eight-thirty. Trant began by updating him on events at Lydd. "I'm much encouraged by the way things have gone," he said. "I've still reserved the right to cancel the operation if I'm not entirely satisfied with the team but it seems as though we might have been lucky." He went on to say that most of the best men happened to be in the UK. "Not all, mind you but it looks as though we're putting together a good bunch." Lespère could actually feel himself smiling. "I told them to get on with their training and preparations today but warned them to be ready for a move out here tonight. The sooner they're here the better."

 Apart from the aides, the two men sat alone discussing the points the British team had raised the previous night and their move to a holding area within strik-ing distance of the target. "I've already told General Morton that I need to see him here by lunch time," Trant continued. "I would like somebody to arrange for him and his party to be collected from Lydd, if that's all right. We've got one of the RAF Special Force crews standing by with a C130 cargo aircraft for the main team and all the equipment. It'll start loading at the end of today's training."

"We expected it to be a C130," Lespère replied. "The Air Force staff are getting a list of all the air strips that can take one, but hopefully we'll be able to use a mili-tary air base or a decent sized civilian airfield."

"My final point," Trant continued, "concerns the legal niceties. If this crowd are armed to the teeth and live by the gun, then a soft approach is hardly going to produce the goods. We certainly don't intend to go charging in with all guns blazing but if there's as much as a whiff of resistance then that's it. I don't intend to hang around waiting for some of my men to get taken out before we start getting tough."

197

"But of course."

"The rules of engagement have got to be crystal clear," Trant tapped a finger lightly. "And this must be tied up *before* they deploy," he stressed. "It's a difficult one for you and the lawyers to get right, but we can't afford to move if there're any grey areas." He described how the team had reacted to the news that they were likely to be facing a strong Mafia team. "The Foreign Office and Scotland Yard have pulled together a mass of information on them and the New York Police Department have been particularly helpful...as have your people here. The team's spent as much time as they possibly can studying them, their history, organisation, weapons, tactics, and God knows what. Everything...every goddamned thing."

Lespère nodded thoughtfully. "A lot of people have got some weird and wonderful ideas about the Mafia. I had the devil's own job to get our people on the committee to take them seriously."

Trant assured him that this was not the case with the British team. "It's the first time they've come across them and they'll be taking no chances at all." He gave a little laugh. "In fact I can't remember so much background work being done before."

Lespère tapped his note-pad and looked up. "Funnily enough, we've been doing quite a bit of thinking about most of these points of yours." He waved at the paperwork on his desk. "We're beginning to go firm on that place in the Tarn, y'know. It will be interesting to see if France Telecom come up with anything and we should have some of the aerial photography in by now. Mind you, there are three or four other places down there that Intelligence are finding interesting and we should have some news on them too." He got up and walked over to the window. "Anyway, look, we'll get a plane off to Lydd for your chaps and start work on the liaison teams." He paused, turned and spoke rapidly to one of the aides who left the room. "I was wondering about Bigard. He seems to have pulled a few rabbits out of the hat lately. Would he be any use to you?"

"Not out on the ground with the team but up here with me, yes, most certainly," replied Trant. "We need him here for who and what he knows. Anyway, he'd most probably be in the way down there. I've asked to see him here after your meeting."

As Trant was speaking Lespère glanced down the notes he had been making. "The cars shouldn't be a problem, but we ought to get your man, Morton, some money. What do you call that in the UK...a Fighting Fund or something? And he'll need cash, that's for sure." Trant smiled to himself. Lespère was thinking fast and along the right lines. "Well, let's go and see what the team's got for us. My guess, and my hope, is that things might be getting warm." He led the way across the corridor to the conference room.

2

La Trampa

The meeting with Said Salim had rattled Gambino. Up to that point he had felt in control of events and the plan was unfolding neatly. But now these Arabs were something else. What the hell were they up to? Bontate had often spoken of these tight-knit communities in and around the big cities. And here they were trying to put pressure on him. But, in the event it was immaterial to him if Renee and Blosch got to Libya or not. So *what* if the balance of power in the Middle East got upended as a result?

The important thing was that the two scientists were his trump cards. They would go to Libya only if and when he lost possession of the treasures and it would be in his time. He had played the cards once and the French had been forced to keep their Special Forces under lock and key. Were it not for Renee and Blosch, they would have been out of their camps and all over him like a ton of bricks. He had asked Salim for time and would continue to plead for more until he was ready. At that point he would order the two men back to Sicily and to hell with a bunch of blackmailing Arabs. The latest decision to move them on again had been the right one. If he *was* being watched, then those watching would believe their destination remained Libya. Either way they were perfectly placed.

✳✳✳

He heard footsteps and turned to see Antonio and Tommy standing at the entrance to the inner hall. There was still much on his mind but these two were not the ones to share his thoughts. "Looking for me?" he called, waving them in. "OK, come on up. If it's about the weekend, I hope you're plans are good. Time for a break, huh?"

"Hey, Mario." Tommy was smiling mischievously. "Listen to this will you. We've hit the jackpot. Antonio has been into Toulouse and, well, I'll let him tell you."

"I don't expect you've had time to find out, Mario, but it seems the Verdi festival's on in the city." As he reached into his pocket Antonio's face was wreathed in a huge grin. "I had a call from a chap called Malcolm Stewart; a good chum. He comes out here a lot. Leads the Liverpool Philharmonic but gets called over here to lead the International Orchestra in Toulouse when they've got something big. He's here now and they've got a free weekend coming up.

"Last night we had dinner after the concert and he brought along two of the principal singers. And absolutely magic they are too...a young couple: Amelia Philadorou, she's Greek and Ricardo Altagna the Hungarian tenor. They're two of the hottest properties around. *Fantastic.*" Gambino managed a smile as Antonio threw his arms into the air excitedly. 'The guy's a bum,' he thought to himself. 'But he bounces. I'll give him that.' "They've just come down from Berlin where they were performing Tosca. And you know what? We've got 'em." He clapped his hands together. "Yes, sir. All three of them coming up on Saturday evening. They've had a belly full of being cooped up in the city and want to escape for some fresh air. Happy to sing for their supper too, would you believe? Malcolm has promised to play as well. *Hey*," his knees jerked. "How about that, then?"

"You serious?" Gambino frowned, looking from one to the other. "No kidding now? Yeah, yeah, sure I've heard of those two, everyone has. Not having me on, huh?"

"No kidding, Mario," Tommy interjected. "Our man here had 'em all starry eyed with his tales of life and romance up in the vineyards. They're looking forward to it, really. And that's straight."

"What's more Malcolm suggested we rope in a pianist he knows who lives around here," Antonio continued. "I met her once, Humphrey and Patricia know her too. Rebecca Davidson's her name, lives just the other side of Gaillac. Apparently she's damn good. Malcolm reckons that she could do the accompaniment and the four of them would put together a programme. It'll be impromptu though…no time to practise. Hey, but look. With four like that it should be one hell of an evening."

"So what have they laid on for me?" Gambino asked. He loved opera; the music and singing stirred his Latin blood deeply and whenever he felt low he would retire to his study and put on something by one of his favourites – Puccini, Mozart or, best of all, Verdi. Invariably he would feel better. And now this. He smiled at the thought: life had not yet become too difficult.

"Well." For a moment Antonio looked serious. "I thought we'd organise an Italian evening for twenty or thirty of Humphrey's friends. It'll keep things sweet…let everyone see that life at La Trampa's normal after all. I can get some excellent wine and I thought we'd go for Saturday. Yes? That leaves time for a smaller do on Sunday, then that's it. They'll all live happily ever after," he said grinning widely.

"OK, OK, sounds fine. But listen," Gambino rounded on the two men. "No fooling around. Right? And nothing at all after the weekend. We could be moving on from here earlier than we thought. I want to keep next week free from all that kinda crap. Get a programme fixed and let me see it. Now, go tell Dino I need him.

✳✳✳

For several minutes Amanda had been hammering on the door and shouting for attention before one of the guards came to investigate. It took her some time to make him understand that she was worried about the condition of Palmer and was demanding to see Bontate. Twenty minutes later he came to the derelict room. "For Heaven's sake, just take a look at the poor soul," she cried, pointing at the figure on the mattress. "He's worse today...far, far worse."

Sir Alan Palmer seemed to have sunk into the mattress. He lay flat, quite still and his eyes were closed. Bontate, angered at being called to the commotion, did little to conceal his indifference. To him, the two foreigners were nothing less than a burden. He glanced casually at the recumbent figure and could see by the pale, drawn features that the man's strength had gone. He was unshaven, his hair was unkempt and, as Bontate detected, was beginning to stink. Leaning against the door he watched scornfully as the girl knelt and soothed his forehead. She lifted his head and motioned Bontate to look, nodding to the wound at the back of his head. The edges of the gash were red and swollen. Hair and dried blood lay matted together where the weight of his head had pressed down. She lowered him then smoothed his hair before looking up.

"You couldn't care one bit, could you?" she whispered in disbelief. "You just could not care. How can you just stand there like that? For pity's sake, man. Where's your soul?" She got to her feet and faced Bontate. "I want to speak to Mister Gambino about this, and I want to see him now." Her voice was raised.

"Not now, he's busy." Bontate shrugged and went to leave the room. "Maybe tomorrow."

"Don't you dare give me any more of that," Amanda shouted. "I want to see him now and that's where I'm going. There's nothing more to discuss." She got up and walked purposefully towards the door. "And I'll be pleased for you to let me pass." Now beside herself with rage, she glared at the figure in the doorway and tossed her head. "Accompany me if you wish but keep out of my way. Go on," she cried. "Get out of my bloody way."

✳✳✳

Gambino looked up in surprise at the commotion outside the study. The door swung open and Amanda strode across the room. "What the devil are you playing at," she blurted out as Gambino rose to greet her. Her hair was a mess and her face smudged with dust. Her hands were filthy and her dress torn but she remained the beautiful creature he remembered. Now there was something powerful, something earthy and erotic about her. "And I'll have none of your leering and shaking of hands until you've seen to Sir Alan Palmer." Her eyes were blazing. "He's in a dreadful state. He needs a doctor, Mario, and we've got to bathe and dress the wounds. The poor man needs to be cleaned up and moved out of that filthy hovel." Gambino cocked one eyebrow and Amanda glared. "You should be ashamed of all this...call yourself a Christian." At that Gambino laughed and raised his hand as if to calm the woman in front of him.

"How *dare* you laugh like that," she screamed, stepping forward and swinging her hand at Gambino's face.

She never saw the hand that caught her wrist in a vice like grip an inch from his cheek. The tall Italian looked down at her. The smile remained but any warmth or friendliness had vanished. Instead Amanda found herself looking into two penetrating eyes. "Madame," he said quietly, lowering his hand. "I admire your compassion but I'm now bored with this problem and you've become tiresome. If Palmer dies, it is of no consequence to me or my plans whatsoever." He caught hold of her by the shoulders and pushed her roughly towards the door. "Get back to your man and see to it that he does not die. I will make sure you get what medication you need. But that is it. Do not push me any further and kindly stay out of my sight. Am I clear?"

Amanda Gates was breathing heavily, her chest rising and falling. Suddenly she swung round. For a moment, the two stood looking at each other. Gambino's face was impassive yet, even now his eyes betrayed his desire for the woman in front of him. "My God, Mario Gambino. You're nothing more than an animal. May the good Lord forgive you," she said, shaking with anger. "You've no heart, no heart at all. If that wonderful, innocent man dies, his blood will be on your hands...for ever."

***

As the bolts slammed into place behind her Amanda collapsed against the door, her head bowed. She put her hands to her face and shook her head slowly. She was exhausted, drained and desperately tired yet she had to fight off the weariness. Nobody was going to help them, that was now obvious. Alan Palmer was a very sick man and it would be up to her to see that he was as comfortable as possible. Only later did the guards bring hot water, bandages and medication.

3

Paris
Bigard had started to clear his desk and was putting some papers into his case when the phone rang. It was Cohen. "Hey André, we need to talk. It's urgent, can we meet now, like right away? I can come over if you want?"

"Hardly now, Eddi, for Heaven's sake. I'm just off to Place Beauvau for the morning session. Then I've fixed a meeting with Sir Arthur Trant. I've just got to see him, and that's that." he added.

"Look, forget about all that," Eddi replied. "I need to speak to you *now*. Seriously." Bigard listened to the note of urgency in his friend's voice and felt his

202

pulse beginning to race. "Things have started to move and we need to get our heads together. Honestly, André, when you've heard what I've got for you you'll really get moving. Look, I'm not bluffing," Cohen pleaded. "So get on the phone, tell them you can't make it for an hour or so but, when you do get across, you've got to speak to the Minister. For God's sake get them to take that on board."

***

An hour later Eddi was sitting in the swivel chair across the office from André. "Now look, I told you that Renee and Blosch were on the move," Cohen began. "Less than a couple of hours ago we heard that they've arrived, guess where, in Malta of all places. As you can imagine once we knew that a move was afoot we had eyes and ears all over the Med."

"Bloody hell." Bigard held his face in his hands. "Now what?"

"At first we thought they might've gone into Nicosia or back to Palermo, but our boys in the customs at Luqa picked them straight off the passenger manifest. Quite a bonus actually." He paused. "I suppose it's the nearest to home for them." Cohen went on to say that their agents had followed them to the Sliema Hilton, less than three kilometres outside Valetta. "We thought they'd have covered their tracks far better than that. It doesn't ring true. Anyway, pal, that's where they are right now."

"Jeez," Bigard exhaled slowly. He folded his arms and pursed his lips. "That's bloody close to home. But you guys've got good tabs on life in Malta, haven't you? Is this good or bad?"

"A stroke of luck, really," Cohen replied. "We've got a strong team there, run by a girl what's more. She's good, sharp as a rattlesnake. For years now we've been watching the Arabs coming and going. They use that place the whole time, particularly the Libyans. Can't resist the best hotels…probably something to do with Arab pride and self-importance." He scratched the back of his head. "Anyway, as a result, we've got a number of good contacts there and at the Sheraton. They know exactly what to look for."

Bigard flipped a cigarette from the packet and tapped it on the table. He started to talk then checked himself before picking his words carefully. "Eddi, listen. If I go across to Place Beauvau and tell them this, they'll start flapping like mad. I mean, I've hardly got to spell out all the additional problems this little lot brings with it." He paused. "What d'you reckon the chances are of your lot doing a bit more than just watching them? D'you reckon you might be able to lift 'em?" Without waiting for an answer, Bigard got up and laughed, then shook his head. "Hell's teeth, Eddi. If I get over there and tell them their bargaining chips are a stone's throw from home, I'm hardly going to be the hero of the moment, am I?

203

But if I can suggest something like that...."

"Phew, that's way beyond me, pal," Cohen cut in. "Way beyond the Ambassador too. Even if we *could* do anything it would have to come from the top...right from the very top, back home. We all know the Maltese are in cahoots with the Libyans and one slip would screw it right up. All I can do at this stage is to quietly tip off our man here."

The two sat in silence. Cohen could sense that Bigard was desperate to take with him even a hint of an offer from Israel. "Listen, Eddi." Bigard swung round, smiling. "Why not float the idea? Then if he gets an official request from Place Beauvau, at least he won't be caught cold," he said hopefully. "Have a try. Nothing specific, just float it and get the idea across."

"Well, I can but give it a go," Cohen replied hesitantly. "But, in the meantime you're going to have to break the news and somehow let me know their reaction. My crowd'll want to know how the French are reacting. But watch it," he cautioned. "Remember a good number of your ministers don't actually like us Israelis around." He smiled ruefully. "We tend to get in the way when they want to start snuggling up to the Arabs over oil...and arms for that matter," he emphasised.

***

Philippe Lespère had had a good morning. The CILAT conference had gone well and they had received excellent news from Albi where the France Telecom monitoring team had recorded a number of calls from La Trampa. Four international calls had been of particular interest. The first had been to Punta Raisi airport near Palermo. Here the caller, who had remained unidentified, had ordered the aircraft to come into Albi on Sunday evening. The details of the aircraft – a Super Nor Lander turbo jet Number JA 306 – tallied with the flight details taken from the control tower recorder at Alexandria on the night of the theft. Another call had been to Baghdad and two to Moscow in which details of a meeting were discussed. The caller from La Trampa had specified that it would be held on Monday rather than Wednesday, as originally planned, and would take place in the early afternoon.

Evidence was now beginning to point towards the Tarn and Lespère sanctioned the formal request to be made through Trant for the assault team to be moved to France. The plan was for them to fly into the provincial airport at Carcassonne in the south-west and from there move to the Parachute Regiment barracks on the northern outskirts of Castres. The base was close enough to the suspected area for preliminary operations to begin and had excellent ranges and training facilities. Morale in the Intelligence Centre had risen noticeably. An air of expectancy pervaded.

Before he sanctioned the order, Trant poured over the intelligence. He wanted to be sure that they had not overreacted in their desire to press ahead. He quizzed the watchkeepers about the other possible locations that had been identified. Eventually he agreed to the request and passed the order back to Lydd. Morton and his advance party were already on their way. The French would expect them at Carcassonne at eleven that evening and would take them straight to Castres. Work would begin in earnest the following morning.

Earlier Trant had spoken with the British Consul in Bordeaux about releasing names and addresses of those expatriates living in the area who might be able to help. The Consulate had come up with three possibilities. The first – Andrew Robinson – had been a helicopter pilot in the Fleet Air Arm. After leaving the Navy he had worked in the city, before moving to France several years ago. He had continued to fly and worked with both fixed and rotary wing aircraft from Albi airfield and the smaller airstrip at Gaillac where he ran his own aerial photography business for a number of international house agents.

The second man, Todd Benson a retired Major, had served with the Parachute Regiment before his move to France. He knew the area and, so the Consulate believed, was well known amongst the local British community. The third contact, Doug Jourdan, had served with Trant years ago in the Radfan and later in Oman. Doug, recently widowed, lived in a large manor outside the picturesque market town of Lavaur where he ran an exclusive holiday business. Trant asked for the three men to be contacted, to have the situation explained as best as could be done and to rendezvous with Morton in Castres.

✳✳✳

By the time Trant came into the room for the midday conference it was crowded. He could feel a buzz of excitement and a sense of anticipation. Cautious by nature, Trant was alerted by the exuberant atmosphere yet he remained unmoved. As he stood just inside the door, listening to the animated chatter in the room, he felt a hand on his arm.

"Pardon Monsieur, but are you by any chance Sir Arthur Trant?" He turned and saw a nondescript middle-aged man of medium height standing in front of him. Scruffily attired in an old tweed jacket and baggy corduroy trousers, he looked as though he had dressed in a hurry then forgotten to brush his hair or straighten his tie. He appeared to be from a different world to the ranks of pinstriped suits and neatly pressed uniforms around them.

And yet, even as the heavily lined face stared back at him with an almost sad, melancholic look, Trant knew he had found his man. "Yes, how do you do. Arthur Trant, I don't think we've met, have we?" He held out his hand.

"No we haven't. My name's Bigard, André Bigard." The face in front of him crinkled into a friendly smile. Shuffling his briefcase from one hand to the other, the stranger took Trant's hand. "How do you do, General. It's very good to meet you at last. I'm afraid that I'm the one who spoiled your breakfast in New York the other morning." His eyes twinkled merrily and they both laughed. "I was wondering if we might have a quick chat after this?" Trant nodded and listened as Bigard continued. "Look, I'm terribly sorry, but just now, I must ask you to excuse me. Very rude, I know, having just said hullo, but we're about to start and I really must try to nab the Minister before he begins." He glanced around the crowded room, searching the faces. "The trouble is that he's just been in with the PM and I expect he'll be in overdrive. Would you possibly excuse me? I'll be back in a minute."

Trant was intrigued. Who on earth *was* this extraordinary, dishevelled character, ambling happily around the nation's top crisis meeting? He looked as though he had just come in from walking the dog. Neither a member of the government, the security services, the armed forces nor anything else, yet here he was, the one on whose shoulders the success or failure of the whole operation rested. He must have been the one to have got Sir Peter Oldfield dug out of bed in New York the other morning. It must have been through his efforts that Morton was now on the way to Carcassonne and Jed King was putting his act together at Lydd. What's more he didn't look the slightest bit concerned about it. What secrets, Trant wondered, were in that battered old briefcase and what message had he got with which he was going to ambush the chairman of CILAT?

He watched as Lespère and Bigard spoke in the hall. Lespère, just as Bigard had intimated, was now a man in a hurry. He saw him put both hands on Bigard's shoulders, nod vigorously and pat him on the shoulder before hurrying into the conference room. Obviously Bigard had not been able to get his message across. An expectant hush fell and the committee stood as Lespère went to his chair. Bigard made his way around the back of the table to the seat next to him.

Trant watched Lespère smile and rub his hands enthusiastically as he opened the meeting and listened as he called cheerfully for the head of the intelligence team to give an update on the situation in the Tarn and any other places that were still of interest. Looking around Trant detected, even as the conference was in session, the dangerous, heady atmosphere of overconfidence. He concentrated on the briefings and found himself once more intrigued by the thoroughness of the speakers who produced, for the first time, aerial photography of La Trampa and one of the three other houses in the area, the other two having been discarded. Lespère then called the Operations duty watch keepers to cover the deployment of the British team and the arrival of their advance party. When they finished, Lespère turned towards Trant asking him if he had anything to add. He rose briskly and spoke briefly on how he expected the team to react the following morning.

"We can expect them to get out on the ground as soon as they can. Obviously we are up against the clock so they'll start looking at this place in the Tarn right away. However, I would urge everyone to keep all other options open. I realise it looks like the Tarn but do remember we're still waiting for absolute hard and fast evidence that this is the place." He turned to the Director of Intelligence. "I'm sure your chaps are aware of all this," he said with a smile.

Trant glanced at his watch then looked over to Lespère. "Timings are very tight, Minister. They will need to get the decision to go sometime well before Monday morning. Once the assault has been ordered, it'll be too late to switch – so the decision's got to be the right one." Heads around the table nodded enthusiastically and everybody sat back. It was as though the last fence had been safely cleared. "I've given instructions for them to attempt it without having to resort to weapons." Trant studied the faces turned towards him. "However, you must all be quite clear that if live ammunition is used there are bound to be casualties, several probably. And finally I would urge you all not to be overconfident about the outcome. It is not going to be easy." A few moments after he had finished Bigard raised his hand. Trant noticed that everyone around the table immediately turned towards the man and were watching him closely. It was obvious that he had made his mark already and Trant felt a sudden air of foreboding in the room.

"Thank you, monsieur." Lespère raised his hand to Bigard, motioning him to speak. He stood, coughed and ran a hand through his hair.

"Messieurs, earlier today I learned from a very good source that our two scientists, Renee and Blosch, have been moved to Malta. They're being held there now and we can only assume that it's in preparation for the short journey to Tripoli." The room was now very still: earlier optimism was fast evaporating.

"Er, Monsieur Bigard." Lespère cleared his throat. "This is serious. Can you tell us more?"

Bigard went back over the ground such as he had been told by Eddi Cohen. Without divulging his source he traced the movements of the scientists first to Sicily where they had been held for some time, then their move to Casablanca which coincided with the events at Alexandria. He finished by explaining that what had worried him for some time was that the operation to prevent the scientists from reaching Libya had become divorced from the operation to secure the artefacts. "It's my opinion that we now have two operations which are entirely different but which are inextricably linked." Bigard cleared his throat huskily. "And they have to be coordinated with the greatest of care. If either went ahead without the other then there's going to be an almighty mess. For instance, if we recapture the scientists in Malta but fail to get hold of the treasures, we all know what Egypt's reaction is going to be. However, if we concentrate on this job in the Tarn or wherever at the exclusion of the two in Malta, and we miss them, they'll be lost to Libya." Trant sensed the tension mounting.

"Sadly, that's not all," Bigard continued. "There are other important points of coordination to consider as well. We have the problem of geography. The two targets are almost fifteen hundred kilometres apart and are in two different countries separated by a vast expanse of sea. I cannot speak for our relations with the Maltese government but I'm sure we will have to tread carefully over there." He looked at Lespère, sighed and smiled. "And finally Monsieur, as if I need to remind you, our own Special Forces are debarred from operations and the British team has already been committed. We need to find a way to identify the whereabouts of these two in Malta, then, above all, try to find a suitable strike force from somewhere to mount this second operation. And, what's more, it's got to be coordinated with what's going on here."

After a long silence Lespère spoke again. "And has this source of yours any idea how we might be able to get over this problem?"

Bigard, realising that he must now divulge his source replied. "Yes, Monsieur. He thinks it might be possible but it would be a very high level decision." He paused for a moment. "You see, and I will tell you now, my source, who believes this to be possible, is close to the Israeli embassy."

The room exploded.

- Were the Israelis to become involved and word of their participation ever to get out, the reputation of France would be destroyed throughout the Arab world.

- Not only would the forthcoming arms deal be cancelled, but several Arab nations would wish to see France brought to account for such behaviour.

- Everybody knew that the whole thrust of France's Middle East foreign policy was directed towards securing her oil supplies. Without oil from the Middle East, France would be brought to her knees before sufficient supplies could be brought in from elsewhere, the United States for instance.

Lespère banged hard on the table several times to bring the room to order. "Messieurs, Messieurs." He looked around angrily. "Messieurs, we have to look at the facts calmly and not allow ourselves to become swayed by either emotion or speculation. The principal issue is, so we are led to believe, that Renee and Blosch are now sitting on Gaddafi's front doorstep. Not only do we need to get our hands on them but we must pursue our other operation with the greatest of care; one false move there and our two friends in Malta will be on their way. I suggest we take a short break and then consider the problem in detail. We will reassemble in five minutes."

✳✳✳

Trant eased himself back in his chair. He might have guessed it. Once again Bigard was miles ahead of the field. He could imagine the huge web of contacts this extraordinary man must have established in order to operate like this. For a start he knew Patrick Morton, Decourcy, Jock Sligo and most of the top UK Security firms. He was a loner, operating entirely by himself out there in the murky world of arms deals, mercenaries and God knows what else. But he was also a character and Trant immediately warmed to the man. He leant across to Bigard. "Tell me, André. This source of yours, is he really reliable? I mean, this is very hot stuff."

"Oh yes. Absolutely, General. No problem there. I've known him for years. We were at Sandhurst together," he said with a boyish grin. "And I trust his judgement implicitly. You see, I have to live by my contacts and he's one of the best. He would never have mentioned this unless he was absolutely certain – one hundred and ten percent. Remember, no one has a greater interest in the whereabouts of these two guys than Israel."

"That's true enough," muttered Trant. "Well...it looks as though they've got one hell of a problem in here, and damn all time too. Did you say that the Israelis could see a way ahead?"

"Yes. Cohen, that's my source, reckons it could be done. They could get at them in Malta. Before, when they were held in Morocco they didn't have a chance." Bigard shook his head slowly. "But this will have to come from the top. We won't get any sort of an answer from their man here – I mean the Ambassador, Eli Schmuel. He's far too wily an old bird for that and, in any case, this is one for the Knesset - Jerusalem."

"Well let's see what they come up with," Trant replied. "As far as I can see, in the time available they've only got the one option."

Lespère came back into the room and the meeting reassembled. "Well, Monsieur Bigard," he said with a rueful smile. "I'm not sure whether to thank you or not for that delightful little piece of news but, whether we wanted to hear it or not, we most certainly needed to know where those two had got to. For that I do thank you most sincerely." He paused. "Now then, Messieurs, let's have another look and calmly too. You should be aware that I've just spoken to the Prime Minister. He's cleared his diary and will be with us in twenty minutes or so."

Chapter Sixteen
Thursday – Later

Paris

For the last half hour the Prime Minister and Lespère had been conferring alone. They left the Minister's office together, crossed the marble floor of the main hall and walked briskly into the conference room followed by their aides. Not wishing to become involved in what he saw would be a long and fraught conference, Trant slipped quietly out of the meeting but not before arranging to meet Bigard. The two men had formed an instant rapport.

After checking out with the security guards at the main gates, he made his way down Rue Faubourg St Honoré to the British Embassy where he made a number of calls from the Defence Attaché's office. First he rang Morton and caught him in the middle of the parade ground at Castres. They spoke briefly. Morton reported that he was making good progress and the young Secret Service officer with him – Jean-Pierre Rigal – had impressed the Commanding Officer of Le 8me Regiment de Parachutistes. "No complaints at all," Morton reported. "They've really fallen over themselves to help. Doors have opened everywhere. They've even let us have the use their classified Intelligence Centre and have produced large scale maps and some excellent air photos of the area we're looking at. Can you imagine us doing that?" he laughed. "I'm waiting to hear news of the flight into Carcassonne. Perhaps you would let the Army Chief of Staff know how grateful we are?"

Trant smiled as he crooked the telephone in his shoulder. "The advanced party's in at Castres," he glanced at the Defence Attaché. "And off to a good start by the sound of things."

His next call was to King who had just completed training. Jed was happy with the team although he had had to make a couple of late changes. Trant knew both the names he mentioned and nodded in approval when Jed assured him that they were excellent replacements. His final call was to the MOD where he gave a short update to the aide of the CDS. General Sir Graham Charteris was working late and took the call in his office. "Thank you, Arthur. Sounds grand.

Well, it's over to you now," he added with a chuckle. "I'll let the Defence Secretary and the PM know in the morning. Good luck!"

***

As soon as they heard the news of the scientists' move, Lespère and the Prime Minister had appreciated the full extent of the twin problems now facing them. Although they had been given a possible way out of the dilemma through the Israelis, they decided to consider it first. Perhaps there might still be a way ahead before they were forced to go cap in hand to Jerusalem. Prime Minister Jospin opened the meeting by calling for the latest information from the Intelligence Centre. As soon as Bigard had broken the news, the Foreign Minister, Jean-Paul Debroque, now back from the EC summit, had called their French Embassy in Valletta and left word for the Ambassador to call him. To date there had been no reply.

"Messieurs. You are fully aware of the facts surrounding this new problem." Jospin took off his glasses, blinked and faced the nine men around the table. "Our knowledge of the whereabouts of Renee and Blosch has added a whole new dimension to what was already confronting us. In simple terms, we now have to determine how to recapture them in a joint operation with the one here in France." He checked himself, held his glasses up to the light and replaced them. "So easy to identify, yet so difficult to resolve. I would like to hear your own views first." He held out his hand inviting comment.

One by one the men spoke and it soon became clear that the mood in the room was against any Israeli involvement. Bigard sat quietly, watching and listening, as the meeting debated the issues at stake. The spectres of Arab opinion and arms deals together with the wretched omnipresence of oil embargoes loomed large.

"Sadly, Monsieur, we have to consider the matter of our arms deals in the Middle East, not only the one with Egypt but the others as well," Pierre Rodin, the Defence Minister warned gloomily, fiddling with the empty glass in front of him. "We have got some very substantial ones coming up, in particular with Syria. The world is awash with arms and we've had to cut our profit margin to the bone in order to secure the Egyptian one. We can't afford to lose any of them."

"Were we to involve the Israelis, Egypt would feel slighted," Yves Saulot, deputising for Alain Déschampes the Culture Minister looked round the table as he spoke. The short, stockily-built man had taken off his jacket yet he was still perspiring and now scowled in concentration. "So much of the diplomacy in this part of the world depends upon *face*. If the Israelis were seen to be working on behalf of Egypt then she, Egypt, would lose face with her neighbours. And she could never accept that, especially after what has just happened." He paused, shaking is head despondently. "Regrettably, in order to protect her standing, she would simply cancel her arrangements for arms with us and look elsewhere.

That's how I see it. After that no Arab country would come near us for years."

Pierre Rodin cut in. "We cannot get away from the fact that we're tied to this part of the world by our umbilical cord – our dependence on their blasted oil. Of course we have substantial reserves here in France and we could always increase deliveries from the US and UK, but it would be a terrible blow." Jospin sat chewing on his lip. Occasionally he would look down and write, nodding slowly as he did so. "In the short term, France would suffer badly," Rodin went on. "Prices would be forced up sharply, at least until the inward flow had been reorganised and we know, only too well, what a complicated matter that is." He looked across at Lespère. "There would be all sorts of consequential problems throughout the country. My own view's that we should solve this without calling upon Israel."

"But suppose we are successful in what we are contemplating?" countered the Prime Minister. "No one's more keen to get these two back behind bars than Israel, for Heaven's sake. Can you imagine what a threat like this must mean to them? They're the acknowledged masters at this game, so why should they not pull it off? Why not? Mmm?" he queried those in front of him. "I wouldn't be at all surprised if they've got an operation underway already, without even telling us. As you know they're the ones this information came from, for goodness sake. If I was sitting in the Knesset, right now, and heard about this, I'd have my specialists crawling all over the various options and making a few decisions, I can tell you."

"Fine, Monsieur, if everything goes according to plan and the operations are coordinated." It was Yves Saulot again. "But the risks of failure are very high and we can't just let them have a go on their own."

"But that's exactly what they may well do. Why the hell *not*?" Jospin held out his arms. "If they consider that the very existence of their country's at stake, why should they worry about a rift between Egypt and France over some ancient treasures? Come on, think about it from their point of view." He paused and looked round the table. "Should we not be trying to involve them in the hope that we can operate together?" The Prime Minister gave a mournful shrug. "We should be trying to keep the reins on their natural desire for self-preservation. Not fighting shy of their involvement."

"Can we really trust them?" a voice from the back asked.

"I'd like to think so," Jospin replied. "But I'd be much happier if we were in this together."

"Monsieur, one moment if I may?" Jean Charbonne, the RPR junior minister from the Foreign Ministry held up his hand. Jospin waved him on. Heavily built and red-faced he rose, clasping the lapels of his jacket with both hands and shrugged his shoulders. He glanced down at the notes on front of him, then looked around disdainfully. "As I see it, Messieurs, we've allowed ourselves to become completely overawed by the situation. We're sitting here mesmerised like rabbits in front of the stoat. Renee and Blosch are just a pair of French criminals on the run, no more than that. And now they've been identified in Malta. Why, for Heaven's sake, don't we simply issue warrants for their arrest, just like we would with anyone else? At the very least we could apply for their extradition.

"No fuss, no gun waving," he continued. "Just a simple arrest after which we go across and pick them up. And then, when they're safely in the bag, we devote our attention to this other lot. There will then be no need for these British mercenaries whatsoever and, to be honest, I would like to see the back of them." He waved his arm dismissively. "Send them home," he growled. "Once these two are under lock and key we simply surround this place in the south and let our own chaps deal with it as they know best." He paused, satisfied that he was now winning support. "I think we're allowing ourselves to get carried away by all this. I mean, after all, we really should be able to deal with this sort of thing ourselves and not go begging for help all over the place." Charbonne, his eyebrows raised high in expectation and face now redder than ever, looked directly at the Prime Minister. "Monsieur, I think we're in grave danger of looking ridiculous and I believe we must consider the reputation of our country. Thank you, Monsieur."

The room was silent. It seemed so obvious, so easy. Heads began to nod in assent. Slowly André Bigard raised his hand. The Prime Minister looked across, and gave a weak smile. "All right, Bigard. I suppose that's all too easy. Yes?"

Bigard rose. "Messieurs, unfortunately the idea is flawed and it's all to do with this business of issuing arrest warrants and so forth. This will *have* to be done in conjunction with the Maltese. It will take time and will involve a considerable number of people. The Maltese judicial and political authorities will have to consider the implications in some detail. I think we are all aware of the complexities of extradition from anywhere. And that's where the problem lies." He sighed and put both hands on the back of the chair in front of him. "You see, the best Arab intelligence network throughout the Mediterranean belongs to the Libyans. The ISL has, for a long time now, been a thorn in our side. Occasionally they get it wrong, such as the Lockerbie affair in the UK, but that was misguided rather than a case of bad planning." He paused and grimaced. "In fact those involved achieved exactly what they set out to do. Libya, as we all know, deals very closely with the Maltese. Just look at their involvement in the recent Korean missile business. They have eyes and ears all over the island and in government departments. There's no doubt at all that whatever takes place in Malta, and which is of any concern to Libya, will be known in Tripoli, if not controlled by them."

"Oh, come on man," Charbonne blustered. "You can't say that. That's pure speculation, scaremongering."

"Not entirely, Monsieur. Allow me to refresh your memory. Think back to the mid-nineties. Remember those terrorist incidents we had in Marseille and here in Paris?" "Well, if that was your ISL, they weren't so damn professional, were they?" Charbonne said looking around the room triumphantly. "If I remember correctly we sorted out that little mess in no time at all."

"Indeed we did, Monsieur. After a few weeks of muddle – and a few deaths – it was cleared up very satisfactorily." Bigard paused. "You see it was the ISL that gave us the information. It was in their interests to do so and they gave us so much high-grade intelligence that we were able to wrap the whole thing up. Perhaps you were not aware of that, Monsieur?"

"*Stop.*" The Prime Minister interrupted hurriedly. "Not in here, Bigard. Monsieur Charbonne, I must ask you to accept that as fact but I'd like that particular matter left well alone."

"Pardon, Monsieur," Bigard nodded towards the Prime Minister then turned back to Charbonne. He had little time for the RPR man, regarding him as nothing more than an old-fashioned bullyboy. "Monsieur Charbonne," Bigard rounded on the man. "Monsieur, I could give you chapter and verse on the extreme professionalism of the ISL. However, let's look at the situation now. They will know for certain that Renee and Blosch are right on their doorstep, I mean those who sprung them from Frèsnes, the Mafia team, are in the process of doing a deal with their country whereby the Libyans stand to become a nuclear power. Do you seriously believe that the ISL are not running the negotiations? Come on, Monsieur, it requires little imagination. Right now they'll have a protective ring around them, all antennae up and waving, waiting for us to do something. I suggest that if we try walking in with arrest warrants, talking about extradition treaties and so forth and asking to have our scientists back we'll get nothing. The birds will have flown, a quick trip on Libyan Arab Airlines, before the ink's dry on the paper. Thank you, Monsieur." Bigard sat down to an awkward silence.

"So, Messieurs," the Prime Minister took over the floor, a hint of resignation now in his voice. "Let us address ourselves again to the problem…how do we do this, with whom and when?" Bigard listened as the meeting continued to wrestle with problems. Yet again they seemed to be going round in circles, getting nowhere. He looked at his watch. Two hours from now he had a dinner date. Didier Merle, the Middle East correspondent of Le Figaro had arranged for them to meet at the Café de Flore in Paris St Germain. As with Eddi Cohen, Bigard would arrange to meet Merle once in a while and together they would sift through the fallout from political affairs in and around the Mediterranean. Tonight the meal was on Merle and it would be interesting to see if he had got wind of events.

There appeared to be complete stalemate. Bigard sensed that Jospin had got himself trapped in a corner and it was no time for political manoeuvering. The problems were going to have to be grasped firmly and the Prime Minister was going to have to make some tough decisions. Again Bigard raised his hand. The Prime Minister looked across wearily but this time Bigard smiled, as if to signal that good news was in the offing. "Monsieur, I know that I've already done far more than my fair share of the talking and I do not wish to interrupt any more often than I must. However, from my distant viewpoint, it seems as though the best minds in the country have come up against a brick wall, for the moment anyway. I would like to take you back to the Israeli option. I know it's full of risk, indeed there's potential for disaster, but it appears to be the only way ahead." He looked around appealingly. "If you agree to approach them, Monsieur, there *are* advantages." Prime Minister Jospin turned towards Bigard, pushing himself into the back of his leather chair.

"Firstly we could coordinate the two operations from here, and I mean right here in this building. Secondly we could use some of our own personnel in conjunction with the Israelis. We could fly into Malta – on our way to Egypt so to speak. And thirdly, we know only too well that the Israelis will pull out every stop to get their hands on these two whatever we do. In fact, it's exactly as you suggested earlier, Monsieur. If we can work with them we might be able to restrain them from going it alone. So, there are certainly advantages.

"They'll simply kill them," a voice announced. "Far simpler that way."

"Not so," Bigard replied quickly. "Think about it. If they did that then the Libyans, and everybody else for that matter, would make a huge fuss. Anti-Israel feelings would be stirred up everywhere and they've got quite enough on their plate as it is. We'd find ourselves sharing the blame too. They were our prisoners, after all. No, Messieurs. That's not in their interest. They know we want them alive and, I suspect, they'll be keen to help if they can." Bigard paused, blew out his cheeks and glanced at the Prime Minister.

"What I'm trying to say, Monsieur, is that this is the only option we have. At the moment, there's a narrow window of opportunity but, unless we grab it immediately, the moment will have passed. There will be *no* second chance." He squared his shoulders and raised his voice. "Messieurs, there is no *point* in discussing things further because there are *no* alternatives and there is *no* time left. Thank you, Monsieur."

All eyes turned back to Prime Minister Jospin. He smiled ruefully. "I think that Monsieur Bigard has brought us to the critical moment. I fully appreciate your doubts and worries but has anyone got any alternative…I ask you for the last time. Let's go round the room." He pointed at each committee member in turn. Heads dropped, some were shaken slowly, otherwise nobody moved. "Very well," he said slowly. "I shall now make a formal request to the government of Israel. After that I will brief the President."

As the Prime Minister left so the room rose. Bigard slipped out behind him, raced down the stairs and hurried to his meeting with Le Figaro.

2

Lydd
Jed King walked briskly into the office and glanced up at the clock. It was now

just after four o'clock and he had arranged to meet the three patrol commanders in order to sort out the organisation of the team. They had agreed to be across at the airfield by seven to load the C 130. Take-off had been planned for eight and that, with a two-hour flight ahead of them, would get them into Carcassonne at eleven local time.

Yesterday, over lunch, he had told Morton that he was not happy with two members of the team. Morton agreed that they should try Joe Lark rather than going through the performance of trawling for fresh blood. Joe was something of a legend within SF circles. Years ago he had been badly injured in a horrendous road accident that had left him wheelchair bound. After years of medical treatment he had been allowed home and had set up his own employment agency. King rang him explaining what sort of men they were after and the reasons behind the last minute call. Joe had found them two. The first, 'Spider' Rider had been one of the best of the new generation of mountaineers in the Royal Marines. He had led several Alpine climbs and had taken part in two expeditions to the Himalayas, one to Everest. The second man, Kenny Armstrong, had just left the army, having done six years with SF, and was waiting to hear about his interview with Combat Power. They had arrived late last night and Jed had run them with the team throughout the day's training. They fitted in well and, just before midday, Jed made the necessary changes.

For forty-eight hours he had been rushed off his feet but was now happy that he had the best possible combination of skills and experience. Unless they were going in for major combat or had to do lengthy cross-country marches this lot, he felt, would get to the front door. And if they could get that far they would give a good account of themselves.

***

The three patrol commanders joined him in the office and they began to go through the options for grouping the team. As they still had little idea of what lay ahead they could only go as far as making a basic order of battle – orbat – which might change later. Assuming they would have to approach the target by stealth, a covert recce group was essential. They opted for two pairs, known as lead scouts, who would operate independently in front and on either side of the main body of the patrol.

Here they came across an immediate problem. If they were to make a silent approach what was to be done about any sentries or patrols they encountered on the way in? Normal practice in recognised operational theatres was for these to be dealt with silently. "Bit of a problem here, boss," said Kelly. "I mean, under normal conditions we'd just take 'em out. But we're going to be in France, for Christ's sake. Not the same, is it?"

216

"Not my decision," King remarked. "But I tell you what. As soon as you ask to do this sort of thing the politicians and lawyers start wetting themselves. It'll need a good shove from the top but I wouldn't want to do it any other way. All it needs is for one shot, or someone to start yelling his head off and that's it. Let's assume that Arthur Trant gets his way. OK, who shall we have out front?"

Two of the Fijians were obvious choices although Horse Ligioni always asked to operate by himself. "God knows what he gets up to out there all on his own," muttered Jock McCall. "But whenever he calls us forward there's never a sign of life anywhere." Eventually they settled for Horse and Toni Racatoni as one pair and Wellings and McCall as the second.

"The breach party shouldn't be too difficult," said King. "We've got to shove poor old Bill Sandeman in here somewhere." They all laughed at the thought. Sandeman had protested that he had come along to open a few doors and had not been enthusiastic about the idea of having to use a gun.

"I can't use them," he protested. "Ruddy things always go off in my hand." And indeed they had, twice. The first, narrowly missing his right foot, had blown a large chunk of hard packed earth over 'Ginger' Harris who had not been impressed. The second had disappeared through the tin roof, ricocheting noisily away into the distance. Uncle Bill, so they decided, should be escorted in and out, unarmed. The remainder of the four man team would be 'Ned' Kelly, Rider and Machaver, the first two carrying pump-action Winchesters with solid shot.

King would lead the assault party with Tacamati, Col Masters and Kenny Armstrong. They would go in immediately after the target had been breached and straight after their stun grenades. Three would be armed with the Heckler Koch but Masters would take his well-tried Ingram.

The last four would make up the reserve led by Archie Small. Townsend would take one of the sniper rifles, 'Ginge' Harris his armalite grenade launcher. He would double as number two to Terry Fraser on the gimpy. "I don't give a stuff where we are or who's the other end." It was Archie Small. "I like to know there's a gimpy around somewhere. If we're in the shite, we want it up and firing, no questions. And I don't give a fuck what that mob in Paris says about minimum force and all that crap." He looked round at the others. "I mean, we're here to sort out their problems for them and we've got to have the proper kit. For all we know about this lot, they're not exactly going to come out and shake us by the hand are they? They're going to fight like hell and we've got to be able to hack it."

***

Shortly afterwards King called the team together, went through the orbat then allowed each group to select their own breakdown of ammunition, grenades and pyrotechnics. He went from group to group discussing the details carefully and making minor changes wherever he thought adjustment was needed. The final hour and a half was spent on the short zeroing range where each man fine tuned the sights on his own weapon and adjusted the trigger pressure to suit himself. They changed into plain clothes for the flight, their camouflaged operational clothing packed away with their webbing and equipment.

After the light evening meal they loaded the transport and drove the short distance to the airfield. The C130 was waiting patiently by the control tower with its large rear ramp lowered. Leaving the team to help the aircrew load, King went across to the control tower and met the RAF SF crew who had come down from Lyneham earlier in the day. With just half an hour to go the engines were started and growled their way into life one by one until all four were running smoothly.

The team filed into the belly of the aircraft, moved down either side of the freight secured in the centre of the bay, and strapped themselves into the net parachute seats. Just before eight o'clock the pitch of the engines changed and the Hercules rolled forward on its way out to the main runway. As it reached the end of the apron it turned slowly, the engines increasing in volume as it stopped momentarily awaiting the all clear from the control tower.

Suddenly the pitch of the engines rose to a loud roar and the great plane lurched forward, gathering speed rapidly before lifting off. As it turned to the south and gained height, the undercarriage was retracted with a loud clatter. Jed, like several of the others, had ear defenders clamped over his head. The C 130 was a beast of burden with precious few creature comforts. Talking was impossible, occasionally a crew member would take off his ear defenders and yell incoherently into the ear of a passenger but that was all. He glanced round at his team. Several were already attempting to doze, others were reading quietly. They were on their way.

3

Paris
Bigard walked briskly down the wide Boulevard Paris St Germain. It was a warm spring evening and Paris was looking at its very best. Every step took him further away from the nightmare he had left in Place Beauvau. 'Wonderful,' he thought to himself. 'Just wonderful to get out for a few hours.'

Didier Merle, Bigard knew as an amusing cove, a bon viveur and very bright. He would have something up his sleeve for sure and, as he approached Café de Flore, André tried to second-guess the subtle, probing questions that were sure to come. It might not be easy but he would try to play hard to get. If Merle called his bluff he would have to stall for time.

✳✳✳

Merle was sitting at one of the little tables on the edge of the pavement near the junction with Rue St Benoit. He saw André approaching, waved and stood, smiling. "Well, well stranger. A long time, oui?" He held out his hand. "How's life?" He pulled out a chair. "Got anything lined up for an old hack? A nice little coup or something?"

"Oh, you know the score, Didier," André countered. "The whole bloody Kurdish nation's on the warpath again. But no, nothing apart from that. Zilch, quite boring, I'd say." The two men laughed and settled to watch the late shoppers and early evening revellers making their way. André was determined to let Didier lead the conversation and did not have to wait long.

He leant towards Bigard, "You know, of course, that there're whispers in the wind, mon brave." He tapped the side of his nose and stretched for the olives. "Something to do with Egypt, so I'm told."

"Oh aye? Tell me," André replied nonchalantly. "My mind's been on other things."

"Well, the drift from the souk is that our divers have made a right cock of it in Alexandria. As you know I'm following the arms deal out there and a chum of mine in the Panhard team was banging on about it. The Gypos are hell's up tight about something to do with this much-heralded archaeological dive that's going on in the harbour." Merle cocked an eyebrow, glancing theatrically at Bigard. "Apparently the other day, he and a couple of others went up to have a look, hoping to chat to some of our divers. Got no further than the main gate. A bloody great gorilla in a steel helmet stopped them in their tracks and told them to bugger off sharpish." He gave a quick laugh.

The waiter came and called them to their table. Didier had selected one where they could talk freely in the popular and crowded restaurant and they sat slightly apart from the other diners. Bigard was thinking fast. Merle knew, so there was only one thing for it. For the next ten minutes he went on to the attack, probing Merle ceaselessly about events in Syria. He had heard the new regime was looking for a number of subsidiary contracts to compliment the main arms negotiations that were taking place in Damascus.

As the meal wore on both men realised they had something of interest for each other, yet the cagey shadow boxing continued with little ground given by either side. Eventually Merle made his move. "Come on, André, you old sod. I've known you for years and can read you like a book. Even behind that sweet little choirboy face of yours." He chuckled at Bigard's scowl. "You're as twitchy as hell this evening. Something's up, and it's something big." He leant forward and stared at Bigard, eyebrows raised. "And I'm right, aren't I?"

"OK, OK, you've got it," André replied, with a resigned look. "Place Beauvau's gone mad but you know damn well I can't say a thing. But you know also that

219

whenever you get on to something of mine, we have a deal. So if you want any gen on this, let's keep it like that. OK? You keep off my back until the lid's about to come off, then I'll give you the full works ahead of the rat pack. But don't give me a hard time on this one - please."

"So, I was right, wasn't I? It's all gone to pot in Alex then?"

"Piss off, Didier. Do we have a deal or don't we?" Bigard put his knife and fork down and looked at Merle. "Seriously, matey, I'll let you know just as soon as I can. But don't push me on this one."

"Blimey, OK," he replied, sensing the sudden tetchiness. "All right, I'll back off. But for how long? There's quite a stir out there, you know."

"It'll be over in four days, one way or the other." Bigard moved his head from side to side. "Perhaps less, but no more."

"*Four days*," Merle exclaimed. "Hey, come on, man. You'll never keep the lid on it for that long. They can muzzle our own lot up to a point but not the international crowd. Think about it. Reuters will be going up the wall in forty-eight hours at the latest. You've got to let me have a line on it before then."

"No dice, Didier. You know how we've agreed to operate. All I can promise is that I'll make sure you get your line first. If it holds then I'll still get you your story but ahead of the press release. That's our deal, word for word, isn't it?"

"Right, you're on. But I'm going to have to fly a kite pretty soon or the others will know I'm on to something. Silence screams from the rooftops in this game you know. Where are we now?" he looked at his watch. "Thursday evening. OK, I'll start to get heavy on Saturday morning. Damn it, André, if half the French sales team in Cairo knows there's something up, why can't I have a line on it? Come on, fair's fair."

Merle stopped and listened as Bigard's phone rang then watched suspiciously as he left the table and talked briefly outside before returning. "And now you're going to bull shit me that that's Annie telling you that supper's ready," Didier mocked, laughing. "And your little carpet slippers are all nice and warm by the fire."

"Were it just that," Bigard countered. "Look pal. You're on to it. Right? Have faith in your old friend. I won't let you down, that's a promise. But for Christ's sake don't let this cat out of the bag. That call was from the Kremlin, and I've got to be on my way. I'll be in touch and, hey, thanks for the meal. We'll do it again in slow time once this's over. And enjoy it, too," he added. "See you." As he left the table, André took Didier's hand. This time, he had got away with it lightly. Merle had, as usual, pushed him hard, but not too hard.

✳✳✳

As he hurried up the main steps of the Interior Ministry, Bigard thought back to his meeting with the journalist. He had been given the gypsy's warning that the press were getting close. Furthermore the story, or part of it, was now common knowledge with the sales team in Cairo. They were not going to like the news upstairs but he would keep it until the Israeli Ambassador was there. It could just put a bit of pressure on them. He felt certain that Jerusalem would go for the idea of lifting Renee and Blosch and getting them back behind bars, but they would want a deal over it, that was for sure. At the moment, they would consider themselves to be on the high ground and in a strong bargaining position. If he could get the message across that the press were just a couple of steps behind them, it might put them off trying to go it alone.

At the top of the stairs he saw Lespère talking with two aides. Seeing him, Lespère smiled and walked across the hallway. "Well, Bigard. Thanks for coming. Monsieur Schmuel is on his way but we had to drag the poor chap out of the opera. Hope to goodness it doesn't put him in a bad frame of mind. He's bringing along his Defence Attaché and First Secretary. I think your man must have tipped him off."

"Yes, he would have done just that. He asked if he could pass the word back and I thought it might be a good idea." Using the back of his hand, Bigard wiped his brow. "Also, of course, I had to tell him quite a lot, to repay him in kind for letting us know about Renee and Blosch. And I know the Defence Attaché, by the way," Bigard continued. "Yitzac Levi...a tank man. Got badly wounded on the Golan Heights when he was just a kid and made a name for himself more recently in Gaza. He can be a tricky cuss but he's a good hard soldier and no friend of the Arabs. He, for one, will want to give it a damn good shot."

"Well, let's hope so," Lespère replied. "Look, hang around at the back and give me the nod if you get wind of anything. Try to make it good news for once." Lespère winked and put his hand on Bigard's shoulder as he led him into the room.

A few minutes later Prime Minister Jospin entered, leading the Israeli Ambassador and his team. The diminutive Eli Schmuel, his grey hair flowing like a mane and still in his white tie and tails, smiled and acknowledged the gathering courteously before taking the seat offered by Jospin. The Prime Minister began by explaining that he had discussed the matter with the Ambassador on the situation, then called for an Intelligence update. Nothing fresh had come in since the earlier meeting but they were told that the UK team had begun to arrive at Carcassonne. They would commence operations in the morning. But no, they had still heard nothing from the Ambassador in Malta.

"And so, there it is, Ambassador," the Prime Minister turned to Schmuel. "You know exactly where we stand and why I'm asking your country to help. We believe it's very much in Israel's own interest to have these two men accounted for." Jospin clasped his hands together and looked expectantly at Eli Schmuel.

"Thank you Prime Minister." The Ambassador inclined his head slightly. "Now, allow me to be absolutely clear in my mind about this," he said slowly, tapping the ends of his fingers together. "You are making a formal request to Israel in that you wish us to, how shall I put it, re-arrest these two men of yours in Malta and return them to you. What's more, you would like it done in conjunction with the British operation here, down in the south-west. And the coordination has to be timed perfectly – yes? *And* we have less than four days from now."

He paused again, pursing his lips, then turned to Jospin. "I have to tell you, Prime Minister, this is not exactly the easiest of requests and I do not know how my government will react." He spoke quietly, enunciating carefully, allowing for his poor French. "It is half past ten here, in Jerusalem it is half-past eleven, almost midnight. Not easy, you understand." He turned to his First Secretary. "If we get the go ahead, could we put enough of our people into Malta in time? They will need to prepare themselves carefully." He paused thinking. "Yes, it should be possible. We have a skeleton team out there now and we'll need more for certain. But yes, I don't see why not. And what about the coordination of the operations back here?" the Ambassador turned to Levi, the Defence Attaché. "We will have to have it tied up three ways between ourselves, the French and the British."

"Phew." Yitzac Levi blew hard and long. He put his face in his hands and thought carefully. "Hmm, this will be an interesting one." He looked up and smiled at the Ambassador. "It can be done but, as ever, command and control will be the key. Get this one out of step and there'll be an almighty mess." He looked at Schmuel and nodded. "Yes, it can be done."

Eli Schmuel studied the desk in front of him. Nobody moved, every eye was on him. Finally he looked up. Yet again the tension had mounted. Schmuel nodded at Jospin and smiled. "Yes of course," he said. "We can see you are in trouble, Prime Minister, and we appreciate that you have come to us. How can we refuse? But, I must say, time is not on our side. I'll now go and try to get things underway, not exactly the right time of day for that either."

"Merci." Jospin smiled. "And that's for sure, Ambassador. France is more than grateful."

Schmuel inclined his head. "What I suggest is that we should get on with things now, assuming that we *are* given the go-ahead. It's always dangerous to assume that but our military staffs can start putting a plan together right away. That will save valuable time later. However," he raised a hand in warning. "I must stress again that I can't guarantee you anything. The only other point, of course, is that not a word of this must get out. If the press get wind then our task will be that more difficult."

The Prime Minister looked around the room. Bigard took a deep breath and pulled himself wearily to his feet. "Monsieur, yet again I have some news that some present might find a bit disturbing. Earlier this evening I heard from one of my contacts that the press are already onto events in Alexandria. Not only that but they were given the word by some of the sales team in Cairo. Of course, I played it down but they are getting very interested and most of the broadsheets plus some of the tabloids are planning to fly a kite, that is run a vague story about the event, on Saturday."

As he spoke, Bigard watched the Ambassador closely. He could see at once that the news had caught him off guard. Quite literally his face fell, then the Israeli turned to face him. "Can you be sure?" he asked, with a concerned look. "I'm not altogether surprised but I'd certainly hoped for a little more time."

"Oui, M'sieur," Bigard replied. "My source was quite certain. I would not have bothered you if there was any doubt."

"That's bad…bad, but thank you for telling us. It's important we know that. Prime Minister, Messieurs, we have some work to do. Permit me to take your leave."

4

Carcassonne
Thirty minutes later, a giant RAF C130 banked in a wide arc over the Mediterranean, throttled back and began its long descent over the Beziers coastal plain. Deep in the belly of the aircraft , far beneath the passengers, the under carriage rumbled down into position.

***

Malta
A thousand kilometres to the south-east, on the outskirts of Valletta, a Colex crypto cipher machine began to chatter. On the top floor of the Israeli Embassy, a light came on and the duty cipher clerk bent over the screen.

***

Israel
Two thousand kilometres further to the south-east, on the ground floor of a nondescript and tired-looking apartment block on the Haifa road just north of Tel Aviv, the high pitched alarm on a secure telephone started to ring. Jonathan Bluett, head of the Mossad stand-by team, picked up the phone. "Jonni," the voice at the far end called urgently. "Jonni, we're on. Get your arse moving and get in here sharpish. I'll call the rest of the team."

Chapter Seventeen
Friday Morning

Paris

Trant studied his watch. It was just after one o'clock and he felt grey with exhaustion but, before returning to the Ambassador's house, he decided to go across to the Interior Ministry and catch up. The midnight conference should have finished and he wanted to make a careful study of the intelligence that had been coming in over the last two and a half days. He needed to get a better picture of this place in the Tarn and try to get into the minds of the people against whom he would be launching his team. Before leaving the embassy he put a call through to Bigard.

Bigard mentioned Didier Merle's tip off about the developing media interest then described the evening in Place Beauvau and how it had ended. "Can't say any more now, but how about coming over and joining me for breakfast. Not exactly five star, but it's all here," he quipped. "We'll give the morning conference a miss. I can let them know where we are and what we're up to, and it'll be a chance to bring you up to speed on all sorts of things." They agreed to meet at eight.

※※※

Trant let himself into the Intelligence Centre through a side door and found the place much as he expected. He recognised the layout at once. During the day such nerve centres were a veritable buzz of activity where telephones rang, faxes clattered incessantly and the constant presence of senior officers demanding information made life hellish for those working at the desks.

But late at night it was very different and now was the best time to visit. It was during these silent hours, that the analysts worked away uninterrupted, piecing together the tiny snippets of raw information that came across their desks from the multitude of various sources. Trant liked this late hour and recalled the many times in the past when he had sat with a plastic cup of coffee, quietly chatting to the young intelligence officers on whose work the senior commanders would later base their decisions. He walked across to the main desk and pulled up a chair beside the duty watch keeper. For a few minutes he said nothing, simply glanced through the logs, studied the maps and peered at some air photos. Eventually the officer looked up, caught Trant's eye and leant back. "So, what d'you reckon?" Trant asked.

"Well, it's very difficult to be certain, General, but…since you ask, I reckon we might have our first break through." The young DGSE officer nodded towards the intelligence map on the wall. "We've had our team down there working with France Telecom and they managed to get right inside that particular place. Pushed their luck a bit though." He frowned at the memory of the incident.

"Really?"

"Reckon so. We had a very good operator with them who made certain they didn't overstep the mark and upset the occupants yet they sure turned the place over." He checked back through one of the logs on the table. "Here we are…see here, look. The main fuse boxes're down in the big garage and when they got down there they had to clamber over a number of vehicles to get at the things. Couldn't see anything of interest though."

"Tell me." Trant was smiling. "Would I be right in thinking you've done some military service? I'll lay a bet on it."

"Oui, Mon General. Five years with the Legion Étrangère…Le Quatrième, the Fourth to you. How did you guess?"

"Oh, one can tell," he replied quietly. "There's always something. Let me see. The Fourth, ah yes, Le Regiment de Genie. Camp General Rollet. How about that?" Trant laughed and hummed the first few bars of the Regimental March 'C'est Le Quatrième.'

"Eh bien, well I'm damned." The desk officer beamed and held out his hand. "That's fantastic…Edouard Coudié, General. Only a humble sergeant, I'm afraid, but I wouldn't have missed it."

"That's for sure. I served with them down at Pau," Trant replied. "Had to sing the Regimental March all the way to church. Six hundred of us. Great stuff, I'll never forget it." He paused. "Right, back to the war. You were telling me about finding the vehicles. Do we know the type, number plates and colour?" he asked.

"They didn't have time for all of them," the officer replied, still smiling at what his visitor had just said. He reached forward to one of the trays on the desk. "But…oh yes. Here we are." He pushed the paper across to Trant who glanced down the list. "We're running a check on them now. Initial findings show they were hired last week and paid for in cash. Paris addresses. Might take a couple of days or so."

He put the paper to one side and turned back to Trant. "Then they did the accommodation where it seems as though we've got two areas of particular interest." He gave a little laugh. "At this point I really did reckon they were going too far but I was told to shut up."

"Mmm…all right. Go on."

"Anyway they found a couple of cottages which had been converted into one and the place was a virtual dormitory. They counted some fifteen bed spaces, would you believe?" He pointed out the buildings on a blown up architect's drawing of La Trampa. "All right in the summer, I s'pose, when you get school groups and that sort of thing. Fairly pack 'em in then. But now, here, in a private place like this? Doesn't seem to fit." He frowned. "Something odd there."

Trant eased back in his chair with his legs extended, his chin resting on his finger tips. "Then there was another smaller one under the old pigeonnier. Here look." The officer pointed again. "Seems like seven or eight more. We're getting them all put on to the house plan that France Telecom uses, and patched through to us. Sounds good to me." The young officer reached across and pulled a large air photo across the desk. "We got some good IR images in earlier as well which seem to confirm what the Telecom party found. You can see what appears to be the vehicles, here, tucked away under cover." He circled a number of areas on the photograph. "Compare this with the air photos and you can see exactly what's what." He placed the two photos side by side and the images became clear instantly. Trant pulled himself up in the chair then stood and bent over the photos. "Those old tiled roofs can't keep in the heat and it pours through all the chinks and cracks giving us excellent images. One of the few things the Roman builders didn't manage to overcome." He laughed and pressed an intercom asking for the most recent photos to be brought in.

"Before we got the gen from France Telecom, our photo interpreters had spotted that whoever it is, had a number of cars there and there, and two or three delivery vans, in this building here, look." He pointed at the photographs again. "They reckoned that the main sleeping accommodation is immediately next to them…here and perhaps over here. Nothing like getting a good cross-reference." He looked up at Trant, blinked and adjusted his glasses. "We've got all this down to your boys at Castres, General. "They'll be right up to date."

"And what about all these other places," Trant continued, back in his chair. "Grenoble, Biarritz and those other houses in the Tarn? I suppose you've lost interest in them now?"

"No, no. Not yet anyway. We can't tell you that these guys at La Trampa are the actual ones you're after. But we *can* say for certain that it's a hive of activity…at least fifteen or so people milling about, maybe as many as twenty-five. Then, once we add in all the telephone intercepts, it starts to look promising. They've picked up a good deal of local traffic and a number of international calls." He looked at the map and bit on his lip. "There's a long way to go yet, before we're certain...until then we're keeping everything on the boil." The desk officer shrugged and raised his eyebrows then reached across for a second log. "Talking of telephone intercepts, General, it looks as though there's some sort of get together or celebration's in the offing for the weekend." He paused and looked up.

"Cover, perhaps?" Trant muttered.

"Yes...maybe." The watch keeper paused. "Then these foreign calls indicate that a meeting or conference has been arranged for early next week. Then...over here," the DGSE officer stretched up to the map. "It seems as though they're planning to move quite a bit of freight. Most of the conversations are in quick fire Italian but, sadly, the Italian translating team's our weakest at the moment. They reckon they've called in an aircraft and, unless I'm wrong, the numbers tally with the one they had on the Alexandria air traffic log. Can't be bad."

"Would you put your money on this place?" Trant queried, lifting his chin and rubbing at the stubble.

"No doubt, General...but I've not got much to wager with." He laughed again.

"But you reckon there's enough to let us go in with authority to open fire...shoot to kill?" Trant asked again.

The watch keeper pursed his lips and looked at Trant for several seconds. "Phew...ye-es," he said slowly, moving his head from side to side. "Between you and me and if it were my decision, I would say you're going to *have* to go in prepared and if you have to open up then make sure you're first away." He paused. "If these guys are holed up anywhere in France with all this kit, the odds are it's here." He shook one of the photos. "Has to be, with all this lot."

"With one up the spout and the safety catch off?" Trant pressed. "Eh? And what about the sentries or guards on the way in? How would you deal with them?"

"Well, if you come across that sort of thing in the middle of the night down in the Tarn countryside, don't hang around asking questions."

"Yup, exactly," Trant replied. "I've had a query from the team asking just that. We'll try to get by without dropping anybody but I'm taking no chances." He stood up, stretched and yawned expansively. "Well, that's all great news and thanks very much. Look, I'm off now and in the morning I'm going to have breakfast with Bigard, over at his place. We'll be in later but that's where you can get us first thing."

***

Trant and Bigard sat facing each other over the pine table surrounded by the flakes and crumbs of several croissants. A percolator of freshly ground coffee bubbled away on the ledge through to the dining room.

They had spent the first hour in Bigard's office. Just as he anticipated, Trant found André Bigard to be an intelligence operator of the highest calibre. For nearly twenty minutes his host had led him through the whole story, from the moment the scientists had been arrested at Nantes. Slowly and deliberately Bigard worked his way through the tangled web of political corruption in Paris where bankers, business moguls, Prime Ministers, Presidents even, had had their names linked to sleaze and financial impropriety. Every newspaper editor, so André assured him, had a thick file on the corruption in and around the city and in government circles. Bigard had long suspected that the Mafia were behind many of the deals but information was hard to come by. "They've been here for years, feeling their way, biding their time," he told him. "D'you know that one of the reasons they get away with it, is that the rest of us either don't or can't believe the Mafia even exists," Bigard lifted his hands. "It's incredible, really. People either think they're a bunch of clowns from Hollywood or it's all made up somewhere. The other day I hard to work my balls off up in Place Beauvau to try to convince them. Even now, I'll bet some of them swear blind I'm barking at my own shadow."

Trant looked at the long, sad features and laughed. Bigard, he surmised, could bark – just like a very old bloodhound might. "But they're for real, OK. I've heard it said that they're after getting into Libya now. Sort of ties up with all this, doesn't it," he smiled and inclined his head. "Construction and engineering are the big fronts for their other activities. When you think of it, Libya's about thirty years behind everyone else. The potential for development there's mind-boggling."

He got up stiffly and refilled the two cups. Trant stood also. "Whatever *anyone* likes to say." Bigard turned and pointed. "These guys are in Paris and they're here to stay. Seems like nobody's got the inclination to dig around or look into dark corners. But now they've leapt right out of their box. *And* how...Jesus." The two men talked on, wrestling with the problems facing them. To complicate matters further, they now had the Israeli connection to contend with in addition to everything else. André explained how he worked with Eddi Cohen.

"The Israelis worry me," Trant confessed, remembering the way Schmuel had approached the problem. "They're only interested in the Maltese end of things. Their one aim in life is to get their hands on those two scientists." Bigard nodded. "As we agreed yesterday, they couldn't really give a damn about the Egyptian haul, the two Brits, or our little game here in the Tarn. And why should they? D'you think we can tie them in with us?"

"I think so." Trant didn't smoke but Bigard flipped a cigarette out of the packet on the table, lit it and drew deeply. "That's why I hit them with the business about the press, just before they left the room last night. They thought they had us where they wanted us but they don't like the press, no sir, and the press don't seem to like them, not in France anyway." He picked at a shred of tobacco on his lip.

"So how do we go about it?" asked Trant. "How do you reckon they'll want to play it?"

"They'll try to run their own show," Bigard replied. "Levi, the Defence Attaché, is a tough nut and will try to get his ambassador to let them do it from their embassy...security and all that sort of thing. Eli Schmuel is pretty good but keeps a wary eye on the Likud party back home. Jerusalem, and Likud in particular, see France as one of their problems.

"Really?" Trant leant back against the sideboard, cradling his cup in both hands.

"Sure. They know the French have to go cap in hand to the Arabs and they've put a strong team into Paris to keep tabs on what's going on. Schmuel and Levi will be watching like hawks. They won't want to get themselves sucked into any joint plan that they can't control. They hate having to comprimise." Bigard turned away to cough. "Sorry...yes, they'll feel they're being manipulated, hence their desire to do their own thing. But we mustn't forget the bait, now in Malta. Everyone wants them...Libya, France and now the Israelis. Suddenly these two crows've become mighty popular." Trant smiled.

"But the Mafia'll realise this," Bigard went on. "And they'll have fingers on them. They won't just leave them sitting there, waiting for somebody to come strolling along." He brushed his hand across the table to collect up the crumbs. "They'll have someone there all right. Could be our allies."

"Christ, what a ball of knitting." Trant shook his head and the two men were silent. "But look, back to the Israelis. What d'you reckon they'll want from all this? What's their price likely to be?"

"Well, if Cohen's anything to go by, they'll want something, that's for sure. Can you imagine what's going through their minds just now? I mean the country's in one hell of a mess. Right on their doorstep, Hizbollah and Fattah are going mad. Just across the Sinai, Egypt seems to be re-equipping like crazy and, beyond them, our friend Gaddafi's about to go nuclear." He shook his head gloomily. "And that's to say nothing about what's going on elsewhere...Syria or Iran for instance. If I was them I'd be playing every damned card I've got."

For several seconds, Trant said nothing. "I think we'll have to handle this one step at a time," he said eventually. "If I see them trying to divorce the Maltese operation, I'll have to put my foot down. Unless we all do it together there's a real chance of a cock up. Both ops *must* be coordinated from one and the same place. And that's *got* to be where the intelligence is. Trant stretched. "I can make a pretty good case for that side of things but I'm not over here to get involved in the Arab-Israeli conflict or anything like that."

The phone rang. Trant listened as Bigard spoke briefly, glancing at his watch. He put the phone down and picked up the empty coffee cups. "Well, General, looks as though the show's on the road" he said. "Apparently the Israelis have asked for a meeting and they want us back by midday. Should be interesting."

2

Castres, The Tarn
Morton and King led the three men into the airy, well-equipped briefing room. Half an hour earlier Jourdan, Robinson and Benson had arrived at the gates of Caserne d'Anjou, the home of the 8th Parachute Regiment, and were escorted across to the team accommodation. Doug Jourdan had not seen Morton for several years and King listened as they chatted about old times.

He had not served with Jourdan but had often heard his name mentioned. Doug Jourdan had commanded one of Morton's fighting squadrons in Oman at the height of the war. Before that, he had been involved in the early SF anti-terrorist planning and had been concerned with setting up a number of the early operations. Before that, again back in the sixties, he had served in Aden where he had commanded a troop in the Radfan mountains. Like so many others, Jourdan had left the army once it was clear that his days of active soldiering were numbered. He had come out to France several years ago to run a holiday business from his home in the Tarn some forty minutes to the west of Castres.

Jed had not met the others, but studied them closely as they introduced themselves to Morton. Andrew Robinson had left the Fleet Air Arm after serving in the Mediterranean and Far East where he had flown both fixed wing aircraft and helicopters during the Borneo campaign. A dapper, neat little man he spoke in the sharp, clipped manner of pilots as though he still had a mouthpiece strapped to his helmet.

"What d'you fly out here?" Morton looked closely at the intense, self-assured expression on Robinson's face.

"Just the two," Robinson replied. "The Tarrin Squirrel, that's the chopper, and the little four seater Regent DR 400, the fixed wing."

Jed listened as Morton quizzed him about the capabilities of the aircraft. "Let's take the chopper first. How many guys can you get on board? They won't have any heavy kit, just personal weapons and operational belts." Patrick Morton listened intently to what the man had to say and eventually he nodded: the man knew his stuff all right. "And what about night?" he asked.

"Again, no real problem. "Whenever I do night photography, I've got access to a huge arc light called Nitesun that we fix to the underside," Robinson continued.

"Does the job brilliantly. If I'm flying blind, I use Night Visibility Goggles or simply fly on my instruments. That's fine unless there's bad weather but we don't often get that. Comms are no problem either. I can get you a neat little ground-air set that we use for parachuting."

"And the Regent 400. How do you reckon that might fit in?"

"Not much cop once things get operational but it's a good little aircraft. Might do for a daylight recce but, once things start hotting up, it's the Squirrel you'll be after. It's your choice but I can only fly one at a time."

"Sounds fine," Morton said and was delighted when Robinson offered to put himself and the two aircraft at their disposal. He turned to Todd Benson and grinned. The two men, both very tall, stood looking at each other over the heads of the other three. "What have you got to offer?" he asked but then burst out laughing. "What a way to set up a team, for God's sake! Meet up with a bunch of complete strangers, find out what they can do, then tell 'em they're in the first fifteen."

Benson, aesthetic and studious, had left the Parachute Regiment and come out to France in order to escape. For years he had lived quietly by himself in the hills in the north of the Tarn. He had become friendly with the Stamford-Bartons and knew La Trampa well, often cycling out there for lunch when the family were in residence. He spoke about the forthcoming parties at the weekend, and suggested that he could go out again to La Trampa that afternoon to see Antonio. "I know them all well, he said. "It's unbelievable that we're mounting an op against this place. It's one hell of a pad. Seems bizarre," he muttered to himself. "Anyway, that's not my affair. If you want me to get out there and have a look, no problem either way. Antonio's a charmer but as daft as a brush. A great host and all that, but I keep him at arm's length."

"Well now, here's a point," Robinson interjected. "They're having this bash tomorrow night and another one on Sunday. Right, Todd? Apparently they've got some opera singers coming out from Toulouse. Antonio's Latin background again," he joked to laughter. "I know that because Rebecca Davidson's been asked to play and she's been over there practising. She's almost certain to be going out there again today. I wonder if we could use her somehow."

"Couldn't I go with her?" Jed King rose to his feet. The room fell silent. "Look, if she is going out there, couldn't I be a friend of hers out from England? Say that I've suddenly arrived for a visit and I'm someone who can't really be left on his own. Something like that?" King looked from one to the other.

"This sort of thing must go on the whole time out here," he went on. "If she could make out a case for getting me there, I could get a look at the place while she's practising. It's almost too good to be true. Hardly likely to get suspicious and shove me in the acid bath in front of Rebecca, are they?"

"D'you reckon this bird'll play ball?" Patrick Morton looked at Robinson and Benson. "I mean, we don't want her to start getting dramatic when the heat's on. Not likely to crack is she?"

"No, I reckon she'll go along with it," Benson replied. He had immediately seen the potential. "She's a pretty cool one, our Rebecca. Got her head screwed on. Anyone who can put on a solo concert for an hour in front of hundreds has got to have something there." He looked at Robinson. "Give her a call and sound her out. If she's on we could get Jed up to her this afternoon."

Slowly the five men began to plan the operation, pooling their ideas, their knowledge of La Trampa and its inhabitants. But there was precious little to go on. Nothing yet had come through from Paris about the identity of their opposition and, more worryingly for King and Morton, no clear descriptions or mug shots of the British hostages. Another disadvantage was the distance of Castres from the target. It was well over an hour's travelling time and they needed to find a base much closer in. After discussing the various options Doug Jourdan suggested they should move out to his place near Lavaur. The holiday season had not yet begun and the big house had ample accommodation, added to which the locals were used to a lot of coming and going. More than that it was almost half way there.

***

Jed's immediate problem was the programme for that afternoon. Earlier, Ned Kelly had taken him aside and asked about the plan. "Look, boss. Me and the blokes know we're against the clock. It's nothing to do with being impatient or anythin' but we've got to get out there and have a shufti. Just so we can get back into the swing of things an' we need every minute we can get. What chance this afternoon?" Jed had promised to get them away by midday and had already begun to work on the patrol programme. His problem was the old one – lack of women. If they were going to masquerade as tourists during the daylight recces then they were going to have to pass themselves off as tourists and that meant travelling around in family groups or, in this case, couples.

He explained what he wanted and why, then appealed to the three expatriates. "I want everyone to get a good look at the area and there's no way that several car loads of blokes touring about the place would get away with it. We need female company." Once the laughter had subsided, Robinson conferred with the other two and drew up a list of friends, several of whom they called, arranging for them to meet the team at Jourdan's house, Bosc Lebat. The plan was for the newcomers to split up and work individually with the vehicle parties creating more innocent looking groups.

However, before that, King wanted to get his close recce team of the two girls – Tracy Black and Marion Drew – and a couple of the men away on their mission.

Both girls had worked as undercover agents in Ulster and had been picked for their operational experience. They knew what to look for, how to go about it. "Just concentrate on the three critical points...security, routes in and out and the buildings," he ordered. "Obviously anything else you can bring back's a bonus. I suppose if there's one more thing I'd like to know is whether or not it's possible to get in really close by day. We need to try to get some positive identification, perhaps a camera team right in."

✻✻✻

Shortly before the meeting broke up there was a knock on the door and Mary Preston was shown into the room. She had been flown from Paris to Toulouse where she had been met by plain clothes police and driven out to Castres. She had with her the long-awaited package containing several photos and sets of identikit images of those she remembered at Alexandria. After she had been introduced to the group she handed over the identikit pictures and sat quietly at the back listening to the deliberations until the meeting was over.

Everyone had now gone on their way and the room seemed very quiet. King put his hands behind his head, leant back and gave a long sigh. "What a hell of a rush...always the same," he murmured, shaking his head. "Still, the money's good and it's better than waiting around for something to show up."

"Jed, I've heard a lot about you, y'know." Mary chose her words carefully.

"Oh aye." Jed cocked an eyebrow. " My masters've bin giving you the dope on their wild child, eh?"

"No, not them." She paused. "It was Amanda...Amanda Gates. We work together."

Jed King sat up and looked at her. "Oh yes," he exclaimed. "Yes, of course...the museum, the British Museum. Of course you know each other." He grinned, then stopped suddenly and leant forward. "But she's away...she's...hey, hang on. Hang on a minute."

"Yes," Mary nodded. "Yes exactly that. Hasn't anyone told you?" She saw his look. "Nobody, Jed? Oh goodness. No, they haven't, have they. I can see that. Nobody's told you that she and Sir Alan Palmer have been taken hostage...captured by whoever it is. It's them, you know...they're the ones you've been talking about."

Jed shook his head. "No, we haven't heard, that's true. But then we've hardly had a chance. We've been jumping up and down for info but it's all been stuck somewhere up there in the ether or whatever. And anyway, we're so far down

233

the line that it hasn't caught up with us. This must be it?" He tapped on the package. "Yes? And thank God for that." He paused and blew. "Crickey, well, well...Amanda. Yes, of course." He paused. "We'd heard that there were hostages but nobody said anything about *them*...oh shit."

"For Heaven's sake." Mary put a hand to her mouth. "D'you think you can do it now? I mean shouldn't somebody else be doing it if you know who's there...like at home with the police."

Jed shook his head. "No, no. We're not the police," he laughed cynically. "Christ no. They'd still be wandering around knocking on doors and things. No, we knew there were hostages there all right and that always makes it tough. You never know where they are or how they're going to react...they're in there somewhere, in the bloody way and you just have to be damned careful. Takes your eye off the ball a bit."

Mary Sutton sat back. "So you're quite happy then?"

"Yeah, yeah." Jed glanced at her. "Well, not sure about *happy* exactly but it makes no odds. It can't...they're all the same, hostages. You try your damnest to keep 'em out of it...the fire fight, I mean. Try like hell but if one gets in the way, then...." He looked at her and shrugged. "Well, that's it."

Jed King found his heart racing. Suddenly this was something new – and nasty. His girl, Amanda Gates, was going to be on the receiving end of a whole lot of lethal violence: she would be seeing and hearing things she'd never even dreamed about. And then, of course, it could be worse than that, far worse – it could be her. One slip of a machine pistol or a fragment of grenade could destroy her, ripping and tearing the flesh from that soft, gentle girl. But then it was always the same. The hostages were all like that: innocently caught up in the mad vicious firefight yet just one short step from freedom. They simply took their chance. There was nothing he could do about it but, for him and him alone, there was now something else. He wiped his mouth.

For the Secretary to The Keeper of Egyptian Antiquities at the British Museum this, too, was a completely new world, cruel, bewildering and sinister. Ever since being shown into the room, Mary had listened spellbound to what was being said and then with a mounting chill of fear she watched Jed King, the man she had heard so much about, take the news about Amanda and Sir Alan. That one of those who would be facing the guns of his team was a friend, and a very close friend at that, had hit him hard. For a moment she sat there trying to get it into her head that it was not some dreadful nightmare in which she had suddenly become some sort of bit player. She looked across at him, now glancing through the photographs he had taken from the buff coloured package. Jed caught her eye and smiled. "Sorry, Mary. Just checking the post. Listen, time's against us I'm afraid and I've got to get on."

"My God, Jed. This really *is* going to happen. It's for real, isn't it?" She spoke quietly. "I mean, there really is going to be shooting, and...killing. People are going to die."

"Yup, reckon so," he replied looking at her. "Now look. You've got a car haven't you?"

"Yes," Mary nodded. "They've given me a car and driver."

"Great. Then I'll beg a lift if I may. The blokes have gone on to Jourdan's place and I need to get after them." He rose and collected the photos together. "But I've got to check my weapon first. They sometimes go off line a bit when they've been bounced around on a journey. It won't take long so why don't you come over with me."

✳✳✳

Mary watched as he knelt and checked the weapon carefully. Having fed the rounds into two magazines he lay on the ground, held the pistol in front of him with both hands and fired. The sudden explosion made her jump and, as he fired the remaining shots slowly and deliberately at the life size target, she stood with her hands over her ears and her face screwed in discomfort. After he unloaded the weapon, they went forward to check the target and she stared horrified at the neat, tight group of shots just below the centre point, right under the heart.

She looked at King and shivered as she realised that, sometime during the next couple of days, the tall strongly built man studying the plywood target would be doing this against flesh and blood. The next target would be alive: a soft human body like hers, moving, talking and thinking. And one of them was going to die. Would it be this man standing in front of her or would it be one of the others – Bontate perhaps, or even Mario Gambino? Or Amanda and Sir Alan Palmer? Might it be them? For a moment she closed her eyes. Oh, dear God, please no, not any of them.

After firing ten more shots, King dismantled the weapon, wiped the pieces clean and oiled the mechanism before reassembling it. "Right, that's it, I'm happy. Next time...well, we'll see." He grinned and shrugged his shoulders. "It's up to the big ref, up there." He pointed to the sky. "Nothing I can do about that. Ready?" He saw the look on her face. "Hey...steady on. Look, we'll be OK." He walked across and put an arm around her.

"Oh for mercy's sake...if only I could wave a wand and make it all go away."

"'Fraid not," he chuckled. "They're out there all right and they're real enough, too."

3

La Trampa

Mario sat with Antonio and Tommy in the oak panelled study just off the main hall. For the last half hour they had been going through the details of the party. Gambino admitted to having been impressed by Antonio's efforts. Somehow he had unearthed a little known Italian wine merchant just off Rue des Lois in Toulouse. How he had done this or what been said, Gambino had no idea, but he had done well. They had decided to begin the evening with champagne but for the meal itself they would drink only the finest Italian wines. To begin the meal they would have Gaja Chardonnay '96, a beautiful light white. Then, for the main course, Antonio had found three cases of Barbi's '85 Brunello di Montalcino and the famous Tuscan Sassacia '90.

"Hey." Gambino looked up smiling. "Well done, Antonio. You've done well. That's superb, real smart. I won't ask how you managed to get your hands on it, or how much it's going to cost me. Never mind. Now, what about the music?"

"Rebecca suggested we keep it all until after the meal...probably around eleven. The singers have got to get back to Toulouse so we can't be too late. She reckons it'll last about an hour." He brought out a piece of paper. "Now...let's see. This's what she's put together. She'll start with one of Liszt's Sonatas, the B Minor, I think. Then she's going to do a number of Chopin's Nocturnes. She knows you like them. Right aren't I?" Antonio smiled and nodded towards Gambino. "Found your soft spot, has she?"

"Then we've got Malcolm Stewart. He's keeping it pretty close to his chest but Rebecca's been practising the slow movement from Beethoven's Violin Concerto. We played the CD last night when she'd finished practising. Remember? Then, after the break we hand over to Amelia and Ricardo. They are planning to do three arias. Well, here's the list. See for yourself." He handed the paper to Gambino.

Gambino scanned the list, nodding approvingly. "My God, this is going to be good. *'Oh belle'* from 'I Lombardi', 'Rigoletto's' *'Il sol dell'anima'* and my favourite – *"Qual mare, qual terra"* from 'I Masnadieri'. Marvellous," he mused. "Marvellous."

The phone on the desk rang. Gambino picked it up and listened. He smiled broadly. "Rebecca, *good* to hear you...yes, this afternoon...and who's this lucky man? *So*, that's why you always hide away from me. Yes, yes, of course. Around three...we shall look forward to it. See you then." He turned to the others. "That was the girl herself. She's got an old friend with her," he winked. "A very good friend, you understand, out from England. Can't speak a word of French or Italian. Can he come along while I practise or he'll get lonely at home waiting for me?" Gambino shrugged expansively. "What could I say, but of course."

4

Valletta, Malta
The two men got out of the white Nissan Patrol, walked purposefully across the car park and into the foyer of the Sliema Hilton. Ismail Mehmet, a burly, well-dressed Arab led the way, pushing roughly through the glass revolving doors. At reception he held out his hand and snapped his fingers. The receptionist spoke quickly into the phone, jumped to her feet and ran to the keyboard where she selected number 2374 from the rack. The hand snatched and the two men made for the lifts at the far side of the lobby.

Barely ten minutes earlier, Mehmet had left the busy, overcrowded offices of the main LAA - Libyan Arab Airlines - building in George Street. The short swarthy man accompanying him, Francesco Tradonia, an Italian émigré from New Jersey, had arrived from Tripoli earlier that week. The two had known each other for more than three years. Tradonia, whose family originated from Palermo, had been working for the Gambino family since leaving school. Now in his early fifties, he had been appointed head of the Libyan Offices of Zagossi International, set up in Tripoli in 1998. It was there, a day Francesco was unlikely to forget, that he and a number of prominent men of the Gambino Family had met Ismail Mehmet, then a senior ISL officer. A year later, the Libyan had been posted to Malta to command ISL operations and, less than two weeks ago he had been ordered to control the movements of the two nuclear scientists. The meeting in the LAA offices had been tough and uncompromising.

Ismail Mehmet was not used to having his word challenged. He had been ordered to secure the prisoners before the Mafia Capo changed his mind, and had been determined to do just that. Unfortunately for him, Tradonia had been ordered to keep his hands firmly on the two scientists until he received orders for them to be handed over.

"Don't you let those goddam ayrabs get their hands anywhere near them." Gambino's orders to his man five days ago had been explicit. "*We* keep our hands on them. Right? I need to keep hold of them and you just make sure it stays that way." The Don had lowered his voice. "If they get out of our sight, we'll never see them again. And that would be too bad for you, Francesco". The message had been clear.

In the end a deal had been struck in that both parties would watch over the two men. Difficult and clumsy but for Malta where the Arab and Latin worlds met, it was not unusual. The meeting in Room 2374 with Renee and Blosch was brief. Neither Francesco Tradonia nor the burly Libyan wasted time over the social niceties. They spelt out exactly what was expected of their captives and how they were to behave. The terrified scientists were only too happy to do anything required of them and there had been no questions.

5

Paris

Trant and Bigard walked into the CILAT main conference room at Place Beauvau together. Lespère saw them, smiled and came over to meet them. "Something's up," he said. "The Prime Minister's tried to catch Schmuel but he keeps getting held up by calls from Israel." He got no further for an aide took his arm and pointed. "Ah, good," Lespère nodded his thanks. "Look, they're here...better take your seats."

The Ambassador sat to the right of Jospin and looked around the room, nodding to those he recognised. "Messieurs," Jospin began. "I have asked the Ambassador to let us know the result of his discussions." He turned to Schmuel and extended a hand. "Ambassador...please."

"Monsieur Prime Minister, Messieurs. I apologise, most sincerely, for the lengthy delay but, as you can imagine, such a request as this requires very careful consideration. It is perhaps not always easy to understand the situation from just one side...to appreciate fully the position of the other party.

"However," he cried triumphantly. "I am delighted to report that we are prepared to give what help we can in this matter and that we are able to agree to your particular request concerning Renee and Blosch. But time is very much against us and I must tell you that we have felt it necessary to impose two conditions." He looked around gravely.

"The first condition is that we command and control the operation in Malta...concerning the two scientists. We feel that it has a far greater chance of success if there is one simple chain of command. Furthermore we consider that our team in Malta are best placed to decide where, when and how these two men are apprehended."

"And your second condition, Ambassador?" Jospin asked.

"That your arms deal with Egypt is cancelled forthwith," Schmuel replied quietly.

Chapter Eighteen
Friday Afternoon

Nobody moved. Everyone, it appeared, was transfixed. Some looked at the Israeli Ambassador in disbelief, some stared at Prime Minister Jospin. Others gazed nervously into space. Eli Schmuel looked down at his hands, folded as if in supplication while, next to him Levi, arms crossed tightly across his uniform, stared at the papers on the table. From the far side of the room Charbonne glared at the Israeli delegation.

When he finally spoke, Prime Minister Jospin looked across the table at the Ambassador. "Thank you for that, Monsieur. You know, I had a very good idea you would come back with precisely that message. It tells me much about your country." Trant glanced up sharply. He had detected a hardness in the voice and Jospin's first few words had been spelt out slowly and deliberately. He was going to fight his corner and the gloves were off.

"We French are currently in a very difficult position," the Prime Minister announced. "You are fully aware of our predicament, of course, and have no doubt informed your people. However, just as you said earlier, there are two different points of view to every situation and I thought you might have considered with some care how we would react in these particular circumstances. You have put us in a tight corner and what you ask is simply unacceptable." The Ambassador remained impassive. Jospin shuffled the papers in front of him, looked up at Schmuel and smiled thinly. "Allow me to explain." By now, everyone was looking at the Prime Minister except Charbonne who glanced around the table grinning widely.

***

The Prime Minister began by reminding the Ambassador of France's need to trade with the Arab world and, in particular, in military hardware. Any threat to that trade would, he stressed, be detrimental to France and she would feel disad-

239

vantaged. The Israeli demand was just such a threat and, if France complied, she would lose the trading initiative throughout the region. They were thus forced to consider the two military operations confronting them – recapturing the scientists and recovering the Egyptian artefacts - then decide which of the two would be of the greater consequence to France's position in the Middle East.

Trant leant forward, one hand on his chin. He could see the Prime Minister was rising to the challenge and Schmuel knew it. Twice he had attempted to interrupt and Jospin had blocked him. It was fascinating stuff and he listened intently as Jospin explained why the loss of the scientists to Libya, although embarrassing, was not a body blow. France, he pointed out, unlike others in the region, had no particular quarrel with Gaddafi. Relations were harmonious and, he added cynically, he doubted if France would feature on the Libyan Dictator's target list if and when he developed his own nuclear arsenal. "On the other hand our operation in the Tarn to recover the Egyptian treasures is of far greater significance. Egypt has been patient. She, for one, knows what we stand to gain or lose here." Alain Déschampes, the Culture Minister, nodded in agreement.

"For us, the success of this operation means much more than just the recapture of Renee and Blosch, even if we took all the attendant problems into consideration. So, if I am forced to forgo one or the other in order to reassert our position, I would abort the Maltese operation. It is of less consequence to us." He waved his hand dismissively, explaining that time was now of the essence and there was precious little anyone could do about the scientists should their captors decide to move them. But, here, in the Tarn it was different.

"It would take very little to disturb the birds in either nest but, in the case of the Tarn, we are ready to move, even as I speak. We have the intelligence and the British team is in position down there. We would have to fight, that's for sure, but it is in our own country and, after a couple of days or so, the world would regard it as an internal affair." Charbonne looked across expectantly to Rodin, the Defence Minister.

"But Malta?" Jospin took off his glasses and shrugged. "I would suspect that you are not yet ready. It's a complicated operation and one that requires careful planning...which takes time." Jospin glanced across to where Rodin and Trant were sitting together. "If it's rushed then it will be a very messy and public affair. The world will wonder what on earth is going on and who is doing such a thing. Can you imagine that?" The Gallic shrug emphasised his point.

"So, unless you are ready, Ambassador, your government might care to reflect on the wisdom of forcing me to act right now. Let me assure you that if I consider a gun is being held to my head then I *will* act, without hesitation and you know where." Jospin wrapped his knuckles on the table. Trant saw the look on Schmuel's face. The Ambassador was glaring at the papers in front of him and writing furiously. "And, if what I've just said is not enough, I would ask your government to consider what would be Egypt's reaction if we cancelled the arms agreement."

He paused, allowing Schmuel to finish writing. "Let *me* tell *you*. Within hours she would be calling London or Washington – or Moscow even - and asking them to submit tenders. If we were forced to pull out, Egypt would not just sit there wondering what to do. The problems on your western front will hardly be solved if France does not proceed with this deal. In fact the situation there might well deteriorate. What you have proposed makes no sense whatsoever."

The tension was palpable. The usually polite, mild mannered Jospin had turned the Israeli demands to his own advantage. Now Israel was on the back foot.

✳✳✳

"Prime Minister, I appreciate your point of view entirely," Schmuel replied, moving in his chair. "But you must understand our position. While the rest of the world sits by and watches, nation after nation builds an ever stronger ring of steel around us. At the same time the Palestinians are clamouring at the gates of Jerusalem. We have to monitor each country and every situation and ask ourselves why are they doing this. *Why?*"

The Ambassador went on to query Egypt's need such for re-armament. Israel would feel her western border to be under very considerable threat. He spoke about the new regimes in Syria and Jordan, countries with whom they had gone to war in the past and with whom they were now making strenuous efforts to foster better relations. In spite of this they, too, were in the process of re-equipping their armed forces. "And then there's always Hizbollah in the Lebanon and Hamas in Gaza. As you said yourself just a few minutes ago, Prime Minister, all of this is of little consequence to you." He swept his hand as if to ape Jospin's gesture. "But while that may be so, to us it is the very stuff of our existence. Life's not easy for us, Prime Minister, and I believe it is quite reasonable for us to ask you to forgo this treaty."

Jean-Paul Debroque, the Minister for Foreign Affairs, raised his hand. "Monsieur Ambassador. You and I have talked on many occasions about these matters. The Prime Minister is well aware that your country has asked us to assist you with Syria. You know that we are in close dialogue with Damascus, not only over future arms negotiations but with regards to their position along the border." There was a conciliatory note in the Minister's deep, slow voice. "We are very much aware of your feelings about their recent involvement in Bierut and have already brought the matter up with them."

The Minister stood and pointed to emphasise what he was saying. "Right now discussions are at an early stage but there is room for improvement. I believe that we might be able to do more here. You know they have asked us to increase our sales and the situation in Syria is the exactly the same as it is with Egypt. Syria will always remain well armed, if not by us then by the Russians.

Debroque looked across at Jospin confirming that just last week he had urged a greater effort to be made with the fledgling Syrian regime. In his view relations throughout the area should be considered together and to take any one situation in isolation, such as the problem in Malta, could be dangerously destabilising. There were many separate issues at stake in and around the Middle East. "A demand such as you have made is bound to bring other factors into focus," he concluded.

Eli Schmuel looked at the Minister suspiciously then turned to Jospin. "So," he said with a note of exasperation, "As I see it you are prepared to go ahead with your operation here in France and are indifferent to the recapture of Renee and Blosch."

"No, not at all. That's not so." Jospin replied, wagging his finger. "Nothing like that. We would very much like to get our hands on those two men. That's why we asked for your help in the first place. However if you insist on imposing such a demand on us then something, somewhere has to give. I have to look at the options and make hard decisions. What we have now is a very difficult situation and we can't just sit here watching the hands on the clock turning. But neither can we tear up an arms deal that is worth so much to us." Jospin paused, took in a deep breath and looked at Debroque. "If you can get this decision reversed then we are prepared to put as much pressure on Syria as we dare, and indeed Jordan. And that'll be solely for your benefit." He pointed at Eli Schmuel. "Furthermore we will be able to proceed as planned in Malta and take care of these two men…a situation from which you will gain most, Ambassador."

"Well, I can but try," Schmuel replied, shrugging his shoulders. "When I spoke last there did not seem much room for negotiation." He looked down. "But you are right, we would indeed be grateful for assistance with Amman and Damascus. As for others taking your place in Cairo, we have considered this too, of course. But such a move would create many other problems in the region and it would all take a great deal of time to implement." He stopped, slowly turning a page of his notes. "As far as our other request is concerned, can I take it that you are happy for us to look after the problem in Malta ourselves?" Schmuel shot a glance at Jospin. "It seems to make a great deal of sense, does it not?" Jospin looked across to his Defence Minister then towards Trant. He raised his hands with a shrug and looked at them inquiringly.

Trant whispered a few words to Rodin and rose to his feet. "Monsieur Ambassador, I have listened to what you have suggested very carefully. It would indeed make for a great deal of military sense if we took Malta in isolation; *if* we were able to, that is. However, we can all see that the two operations have got to be handled together and synchronised very carefully indeed. To do this I believe we will have to work together. If one or the other fails then, at the moment of failure, the other operation becomes dangerously exposed. What I propose, and I've discussed this already with the Defence Minister, here, is that we work from a joint operations centre and it should be situated here where we can all benefit from access to real time information. That said, I believe your operation in Malta should act as the trigger for ours in the Tarn."

Schmuel glanced at his Defence Attaché whose head was shaking.

"In order to do that we would give your team as wide a time frame as we can for them to execute their plan. As soon as both teams are ready we should stake out our target in the Tarn...perhaps for several hours and your team will have the freedom to act within that window whenever they consider the moment's right." Trant stopped suddenly. "I'm sorry, Prime Minister. Would you like me to continue?"

"Yes, yes, go on. Let's hear it now." Jospin waved his hand. Trant saw Levi writing.

Trant, now addressing the whole room, proposed that, rather than waiting until the last moment namely Monday morning, the deadline set by the Egyptians, the operations should be brought forward by twenty-four hours. Co-ordinating these two operations, he explained, would require complicated and finely balanced decision making, and leaving things until the last moment would allow just the one chance with no fall back position. Conditions for the two operations had to be right and everyone would be glad for the chance of a second attempt if conditions did not prevail on the Saturday. He reminded them that an additional factor to be considered was the close proximity of the two men to Libya and he advised that the sooner the operation to secure them was mounted the better it would be. "So, this is exactly why Brigadier Levi and I should be here. Right here, in each others pockets, throughout the countdown to both operations, where we have access to all the vital, last minute intelligence. We're going to have to be reactive to the situations in two entirely different operational areas. Furthermore if we limit ourselves to that single, last minute shot we're actually increasing the risk factor."

By now every head had turned towards him; one or two were nodding slowly. "Therefore, I propose we put these points to the two operational commanders on the ground and ask them if they think it's on. Whatever we do we musn't try to *run* the show from here. We haven't a clue how they might interpret what we want in relation to how they see things out there. I wouldn't dream of getting any further involved than that." He looked at Jospin. "Prime Minister, may I suggest we put it to them now and see what they come up with?"

As Trant sat he could see Levi smiling at his last remark. The attaché nodded and turned towards Schmuel, speaking quickly and referring to the notes he had been making while Trant had been talking. Prime Minister Jospin looked across to Trant appreciatively. He and the others felt that the Israelis had been given convincing arguments yet had not been forced into a corner.

"Eh bien, Prime Minister, Messieurs. I think we have a clear understanding of your position. I'll get back to Jerusalem and see what can be arranged. In the meantime I propose that our military staffs here continue to plan ahead. I appreciate that time is of the essence and I'll report back to you just as soon as I've any news. Brigadier Levi agrees entirely with General Trant's views on the timings, so perhaps we should plan on that. If, as you say, the men on the ground can handle it then it could be a very wise move." With that the Ambassador and his Defence Attaché hurried from the room.

2

Valletta, Malta

The hot, windowless conference room on the third floor of the Israeli embassy was crowded. Jonni Bluett wrinkled his nose. With chairs enough for less than half the occupants, several were forced to perch on lockers, the drinks table or simply sit on the floor or lean against the walls. The place stank of cigarette smoke and stale sweat.

 He and the five others had touched down at Luqa just before seven o'clock in the morning local time. The flight had taken almost four hours. Before that there had been a mad scramble as they collected their equipment together and attended two briefings at the Ministry of External Affairs and the Headquarters of Mossad, known simply as 'the Office'. As soon as they had arrived on the island, they started to work on the operation, beginning with a short report from Lyla Bett, Head of the Malta Detachment.

***

Bett, now in her early forties, looked more like a comfortable middle-aged housewife than one of the finest Israeli agents of her generation. Behind the sallow, attractive face, lay a razor sharp, analytical mind. She was also a ruthless field operator, as the two Iraqi secret police had found seconds before they died. Those soft, well-manicured hands could load and fire an Uzi machine pistol with the best of them. If those in the room did not know Bett personally they had heard of her, and heard enough to be impressed.

After she had gone over the background she gave the team her ideas for future plans, stressing that she would confirm or amend her ideas once they had studied the target in detail. Jonni and the others had snatched a quick meal before going out on the various assignments Bett had given them. They had returned less than half an hour ago and were now crammed into the confined room - hot, sweaty and dusty.

He looked around at the sixteen others. The Mossad permanent Detachment consisted of Bett, one other girl and four men. Their charter on the island was wide ranging but included the initial planning and preparation of tasks identified by their masters in Tel Aviv. This included reconnaissance, research and advice on how future operations might be conducted. Later, if orders came to proceed, they would be instructed either to carry out the operation themselves, or wait for support from Israel and to assist wherever it was practical. That was the case today. Three days earlier Bett and her team had been alerted to the arrival of the two scientists. Since then they had built up a comprehensive dossier on the men including their movements and surroundings. Thirty-six hours ago they had been directed to begin work on the detailed plans on lifting the men who were to be exfiltrated by air from Luqa airport.

Bett had asked for reinforcements and late yesterday evening they were told that extra manpower had been allocated. The team would be found from the national standby squad and would travel out overnight. She had been instructed to finalise plans and was told that, once the team in Valletta was complete, operational control would be exercised through the Defence Attaché in Paris. The affair was being co-ordinated in conjunction with others elsewhere and Brigadier Levi, the Defence Attaché, would be responsible for issuing their final co-ordinating instructions. Once completed, command of the Malta Detachment would revert to the Office. Finally, she was warned that she must be prepared to execute the plan at short notice, probably at some point over the weekend. Earlier in the day she had driven out to the airport herself and collected the team.

※※※

Apart from Bluett, whom she had known for several years, the party of newcomers included three other men and two girls. The remaining five people in the room, although Israeli agents, were all Maltese nationals who had been recruited locally – two from the airport and three from the staff at the Sliema Hilton Hotel. Mossad had long since appreciated that most foreign visitors of diplomatic status stayed either there or at the nearby Sheraton. Agents of other nationalities, in particular the Libyans, Egyptians and Iraqis, were also aware of this diplomatic penchant for the most opulent hotels; a situation that often resulted in deadly games of cat and mouse played out around the plush corridors and extensive gardens of the two luxury hotels.

Over the years Israel had managed to penetrate security at both Luqa and the Hilton. By now a number of agents were in place. Ruth, the tall, dark girl, worked at hotel reception. Danny was a member of the main dining room staff, doubling as a bell hop, and Sarah, a hotel chamber maid, made up the numbers. Bett opened the meeting by asking everyone to confirm their agreement that the preferred option in this case would be to lift the two men straight from the hotel rather than attempting to pick them up on their way to the airport. "We looked at the outside option but, to be frank, it's a non-starter," she said to Jonni. "We wouldn't be in control of events and that's fatal. Furthermore we'd have no idea when or how they would come out or which route they'd take. And if all that wasn't enough, we've no idea who would be with them." She paused momentarily.

"We've been told that this has to be a covert op, and if we ended up in a running fight for them in the open or we got into a chase, that would be the end of that. Anyone disagree?" Bett moved from side to side, catching the eye of everyone in the room but nobody moved. "Right, so inside we go. Now, we know where they are living, and when and where they eat. What do we know about their security? I mean who's looking after them? Danny, got anything on that?"

Danny the waiter, older than the others, peered round the edge of the clothes locker from his position on the floor. "To be honest, Lyla, it's been worrying us a bit. They seem to be left very much on their own. Normally when we're on to something like this the targets are well covered. Remember those three Lebanese guys last year?" He craned his neck and looked across the table to Sarah. "We know most of the Libyan security operators and some of those in the other organisations but we haven't seen anyone around these two for most of the time. Mehmet's shown his face now and then, but not much more than that. It's odd."

"That's right," Ruth chipped in, emphasising her point by waving her pencil. Willowy, neat and with the sexiest mouth Jonni could remember, Ruth was a popular member of the team. Early last year she had been withdrawn hurriedly from the Istanbul Detachment. Her cover had been blown in an operation when she had been cornered outside the Covered Bazaar and narrowly escaped arrest. It had taken Bett and Danny three months to arrange a job for her in the hotel reception. "It looks as though there might be somebody in one of the rooms a bit further along the corridor from them," Ruth continued. "But we don't know who they are. After that several are still empty. They're not ISL, at least not as far as we can tell. It's almost as if these two guys have been told to go upstairs and wait like good boys until they're called forward," she added. "All rather strange and I don't know what to make of it. Sorry Lyla."

She caught her breath. "Mind you, that arrogant fuck-pig, Mehmet, came pushing his fat gut around this morning. Went charging off up to see them about something or other. He's an asshole, that one." Bett saw two members of the Tel Aviv party look up in surprise.

"OK," Bett cut in. "We'll have to cater for that room you've identified and work it so we have a standby team around in case we get jumped from somewhere. Now for the difficult bit…how to get at them and how to get them down the stairs and outside. What about the room keys, Ruth?"

"Done yesterday and we tried them this morning. We've had two spare sets made, and incidentally they're the new plastic card variety not the old fashioned metal jobs. I'm keeping a close watch on bookings, by the way." She paused, lifting her arm and pulling at her tee shirt. "We've got a number of fresh bookings coming in for the weekend's festivities, but nothing unusual for the moment. I've kept back a couple of rooms near Renee and Blosch. We might need them later. The people in that room may be the ones from an Italian delegation that's booked in for several days." Ruth sat back and smiled coyly at Bluett who she knew had been watching her as she spoke.

"Good, but keep watching the bookings. These two can't just be left there on their own." She tapped her pencil on her pad. "Doesn't ring true. But *now*, when we eventually get our hands on them, and unless we can get them to walk out of the front door with us, I believe we should put them out in the usual way." She indicated a jab in the thigh. "But after that…we've got to be very careful how we handle them. Some of you may remember that Romanian job when we lost those two blokes." Jonni grimaced and nodded. He had been part of the team that had incapacitated the two men and remembered the panic when they had had to cram them together into the boot of the Mercedes behind the bus depot in Athens' Sepolia district. One had died within the hour, the second four hours later. It had not been one of Mossad's more auspicious moments and heads had rolled.

"Yeah sure." Jonni Bluett looked round at his audience. "Once they're down and out, they're in a pretty delicate state. We can't just roll them up in a laundry bag or shove them into a box or they'll simply stop breathing. It's fine if you're conscious…you fight like hell for air. But if you're out, the body won't put up much of a fight. So we've got to be damned careful."

"OK. Now, let's get down to business," Bett continued. "At this stage it's only a rough draft but it does give us something to work from." The Mossad team poured over the plan, discussing and arguing every twist and turn and attempting to second guess the scenario if anything should go wrong. After a short break Lyla Bett gave them their operating instructions for the next twenty-four hours. Each member of the team was given part of the plan to confirm, in some cases she directed two or three to work independently on the same task.

✱✱✱

Shortly before she brought the meeting to a close she turned to Joe Berak, one of the two customs men at Luqa. "Look Joe, I'm none too happy about the airport security. There seem to be just two alternatives. Either we can go straight for the front gate quite openly and bluff our way through or we select some point out on the perimeter fence, cut our way in and pass them through." Berak sat up and swatted at something on his neck. "Frankly, in my opinion, the fence's all but a non-starter," Bett said firmly. "Too many things can go wrong let alone guards, dogs and God knows what else. What do you reckon?"

"Well, let's take positioning the aircraft first." Joe Berak scowled as he shifted his ample frame in the cane chair. He was hot, uncomfortable and the nails in the seat had penetrated his trousers. "That's no problem. You reckon it'll be a French military job? Yes?" He coughed and pulled on his large Kaiser Wilhelm moustache. "Fine. If anything like that comes in and goes on the blink they direct it to park up on the apron over by the engineering hangars. They're quite well lit up but you don't get many people around there at night, mind. Occasionally there's a late job so we can fix things with the control tower and security, make out that the French have got to get on with things there and then." He grinned at the idea of putting one across the universally detested security detachment. "If it's a military aircraft, security won't come near them and the control tower couldn't give a damn who it is as long as they do what they're told. But the gate. That *could* be difficult," he announced. "*However* tomorrow's the big Pentecost festival, don't forget," he continued, looking round the room. "Everyone who can get there'll be down in Valletta enjoying themselves. An' those left behind'll be right pissed-off and not exactly chuffed with their lot. Shouldn't be too much of a problem."

Lyla Bett looked at Jonni and smiled. "Great, Joe...and thanks."

"But listen," he continued. "Might be worth seeing if we can get a couple of the French air crew to leave the aircraft, come into town with us then return with us when we we've got the blokes." Berak wiped his face with a large spotted handkerchief. "If not them, then someone from the French Embassy perhaps. You know, bods from the Services or Embassy people on their way out to a military aircraft are hardly going to be stopped at the front gate." He chuckled at the thought of it. "Leave it with me, I'll think."

A radio operator knocked on the door calling for Bett. "You're wanted, Lyla. Secure phone, better take it up in the shack." As soon as she picked up the phone she recognised Levi's voice. They spoke briefly, Levi explaining how both operations were to be coordinated from Paris and that her own operation had been given a short time window from which they could chose their optimum moment.

"We aren't yet sure what time the Brits are going in," the voice crackled. "We're waiting for them to give us their earliest and latest time but it's likely to be between midnight and first light. "Incidentally," he went on. "They've come up with the idea of trying to go for it tomorrow night thus giving us a second shot on Sunday if we have to abort the first attempt. Can you have a look at that? Seems to make sense, that's if we can get our act together in time." The voice paused. "The actual time of their H-hour will depend on what's going on around their target. Can you give me some idea of yours?"

Bett thought fast. They would have to get the two men away from Luqa by first light. That meant they must pick them up no later than an hour before that. The earliest they could lift them with any safety would be midnight bearing in mind that the whole place would be out celebrating. One o'clock might be safer. "It's off the top of my head but it looks as though we might go for them between one and three-thirty, how does that sound?"

"Fine," Levi crackled, "Gives us something to work from. And the Saturday night option?"

"Bloody hell." Bett was silent for a few moments. "OK. It's one heck of a scramble but it might work for us. They've got this huge festival here over the weekend and Saturday night could well be the *better* time." She nodded to herself. "Furthermore, once we've got our act together and can see a way ahead, I'm all in favour of going in as soon as we possibly can. So yes, unless we come across some drama, let's go for it."

"OK, we'll work on that. Now, the only other thing is that the French military aircraft, a Nord Atlas, will be on its way soon. We're planning for it to go off the road when it's on the ground out there and then wait for parts to be flown out from here. They're going to put a complete medical team on board. The French seem desperate to get them back alive." He laughed drily. "If it were me I'd knock the bastards off and dump 'em in the Med…from thirty thousand."

Bett smiled. "Thanks, Yitzak. Yeah…agree. Keep in touch through the shack here. Speak to you soon. Kisses. Bye," she whispered. The line went dead. As she reached the door there was another knock. It was Danny. "Lyla, sorry to disturb you but thought you ought to know. Just heard that we've spotted a couple of the ISL chaps in the Hilton. They were up on the same floor as Renee and Blosch."

"Oh Gawd. Thanks, Danny. OK, I'll be right with you."

3

The Tarn
Tracy Black pulled in to the side of the road on the outskirts of Gaillac and stopped. Usually a team on such a mission would be briefed carefully before departure but, as time was so short, she had decided to stop on the way to the target and discuss their plan. They had opted to work in pairs. Marion Drew and Terry Fraser, in the back of the car, would make up one pair and she would work with Jim Machaver. They had bought lunch and planned to picnic somewhere where they could see La Trampa. She turned to look at the others.

"The boss wants us back by five. That'll give us time to prepare a decent run down on what we've seen." She glanced at her watch. "It's just gone one now, so we'll be lucky to get much more than a couple of hours for the recce itself. I reckon we should each take one side of the target and try to answer all three questions from there. We haven't got time to start moving around from point to point and, in any case, they might well have a screen out. Just like the Dicks in Ulster.

"Yeah, that Major bloke…Benson. He was on about that," Fraser said. "That means we'll have to drive straight into some point from where we can see the place, have our grub there rather than go swanning around. Now there's a point just here on the map." He pointed with the tip of his pencil. "See here. Shown as a viewpoint. Seems to look down on the place from the north. Why don't we just go straight to it from here, by going up this road past the end of the drive and set ourselves up. Brass necked as that. We're simple Brit tourists remember? Grockles out for a few days in the sun."

***

They turned north off the main D600 and headed up through an area of scrub and woodland. Tracy started to speak into her throat mike and Fraser began filming the countryside on the camcorder he had concealed under the back seat. As they crested the hill Machaver saw the group of three Arabs. "Down," he hissed then leant out of the window, smiled and waved. "Just as I thought, there's a screen out. Look, another pair coming up, and that's the main drive down to the place. Turn left at the crossroads, Trace, then make for the high ground over there. Look at this, another two on that corner. Got 'emselves well staked out, that's for sure."

They drove along the crest road before turning left at the Mailhoc crossroads. The road, now little more than a track, wound up through a line of oaks, at the end of which they found the layby they had identified on the map. "I'll pull in here," Tracy called, easing the car off the road. Without thinking, the short, dark-eyed girl from Swansea glanced at her make up in the driver's mirror and saw Marion's face looking at her. "Ready?" She nodded at the mirror. "You and Terry go round to the right first, then Jim and I'll take the other side. Give you ninety minutes, OK?" She could feel the adrenalin flowing already. Once out and on the move she was fine, just the waiting hurt.

La Trampa lay in a shallow depression in the ground some five hundred metres in front of them. Tracey compared the countryside with the air photos she had brought and could see it would be a difficult daylight approach. Her trained eyes took in the cover and dead ground as she scanned the routes for obstacles. She had done this more times than she could remember yet the heart always began pumping. The four members of the party sat taking in the countryside. They were looking down on to the back of the complex and studied the layout against the photos.

Machaver walked forward slowly, moving casually into a patch of scrub then, using his powerful zoom binoculars, began to study the complex in detail searching first for signs of security then quartered the ground, sweeping slowly from left to right. As he searched he spoke into his throat mike noting every piece of cover and fold in the ground. After a few minutes he detected movement and picked out what he took to be two guards. Both men were well concealed and appeared to be alert. Marion and Terry would be unable to approach the complex over the open countryside which meant an overt approach as they had discussed.

His eyes returned to the building and he studied the structure. It was a classic old French 'manoir' with massive walls and a high, tiled roof. The walls must be almost a metre thick, he thought, and the windows at least three feet off the ground, but it was the shutters that caught his attention. "Shut them and you'll need a bloody chain saw to get through," he muttered. "They'll test old Bill Sandeman." Tracy had asked him to look for a route by which Drew and Fraser could work their way round to the south side of the complex. It was going to be tough but the land fell away to his right into a well covered re-entrant. That's the way he would go. The choice would be theirs but he would prefer to go quite openly rather than creeping around in the bushes. For a start it was too far and the cover too thick, added to which if they were seen behaving like that the game would be up.

***

He returned to the others and they talked briefly before splitting. Tracy gave the second pair an hour and a half, while she and Machaver remained with the car and attempted to add to the information already gathered. The couple set off as Jim Machaver had suggested and the land soon fell away steeply into the narrow valley which covered their movements.

After they had been moving for ten minutes the buildings came back into view and the couple saw the front of the complex. They made their way onto some higher ground behind a small copse and found they were able to see the pigeon-nier and other buildings beyond the main house. Terry Fraser began to talk into his mike and Marion studied the corners of the house and gardens, picking out the two men Fraser had seen. Lying motionless, she watched them for ten minutes taking careful note of their positions in relation to the buildings and esti-mating their likely arcs of observation. After a time one moved off and she turned her attention to the routes into the complex. As she was studying the edges of the gardens she heard a noise in the field below the wood. "Down," she whispered, pointing towards the sound of the noise and putting a finger to her lips. Fraser disconnected the mike and waited while Marion looked through the cover in the hedge. Almost immediately she crouched, turned and hurried back.

"Two men coming up the field towards us. I'm pretty sure they've seen us. No chance of running for it. Come on boyo, don't be shy. We'll go for the tit and bum bit. Get your kegs off." She stripped off her tee shirt, unhooked her bra and lay back on the grass. Fraser slipped out of his shirt, unbuckled his belt and eased his trousers over his hips before lying across Marion. He smirked at the feel of her soft flesh against his. "Made your day, this has," she whispered in his ear, giggling quietly.

"Well, come on then, let's be realistic," he replied, forcing his hands between her legs.

"Hey, on yer bike, mate," she chortled, gripping his hand between her thighs. "Shhh, listen. Sounds like we're on. Stop breathing in my ear. Can't hear like that." They could hear the men coming through the undergrowth calling to one

251

another. "I'll do the shouting," she whispered. "When I get going, you hop to your feet and start sorting your trousers out. Come here though."

She pulled Fraser towards her, put both arms around his neck and kissed him fully on the mouth, her eyes searching the area of the bushes behind them. The two men came into view less than five metres from the couple. They stopped and as they looked at one another Marion sat up, endeavoured to cover her body and started to shout. Fraser struggled to his feet, hopping from foot to foot, and attempted to pull up his trousers, adding to Marion's cries.

The two men backed away towards the bushes holding their hands in front of them and apologising. Marion shouted after them then, feigning tears, and reached for her clothes as Fraser moved in front of her shielding her from the two intruders. The ruse had worked but they had been compromised.

4

Bosc Lebat
Soon after five o'clock the team began to reassemble at Bosc Lebat. Knowing that the debriefing would take some time, King had given them an hour to prepare. He planned to leave again for the night's close reconnaissance soon after nine, aiming to get on the ground at ten-thirty, soon after last light.

Tracy and her team were preparing a large sand model on the concrete floor of the barn next to the house. They used small blocks of wood and pieces of shaped cardboard to represent the house and buildings, cut out strips of green cloth for the undergrowth and placed large pieces of felt on the model to represent the trees and hedgerows. Behind the model they arranged a series of photographs from the camcorder together with the air photos.

King asked Tracy to begin and listened as the young woman covered the ground in detail pointing out the few areas they had not been able study. He realised at once that the girl was highly professional, covering each point in detail and answering the questions comprehensively. Without a flicker of embarrassment, she described how they had handled their detection, only when the laughter had subsided did she turn to Fraser. "Never mind, Terry. You gave me the hots, I'll say that for you."

When she had finished, King asked the others to describe their own activities. The last one to speak was Todd Benson who described how he had cycled to La Trampa, and confirmed the positions of the screen Tracy had pointed out earlier adding two others he had seen. "D'you reckon this is a twenty four hour job," King asked. "Or would they pull these guys in at night?"

"Only out by day, I reckon. First they would have to have one hell of a lot of blokes to keep all that going around the clock. Secondly...well you know as well as I do, the Arabs are none too keen on that sort of stuff in the middle of the night, not this sort of Arab anyway. Might be different on the jebel but it's the soft life around here. It's my guess that, come last light, they'll be off home to join their bints. But one can never be too sure and one of the patrols had better take a look up there tonight."

Jed King then spoke about his own experience. Everyone in the barn fell silent and listened intently as he described the recce. "I told her how I wanted to play it on the way in, and she didn't seem to turn a hair. We were met by a couple of blokes and went straight into the music room where she started to play. I sat near the door trying to get the layout of the place when a couple more guys came and listened. Italians for sure. One spoke English and offered to show me round. It's a big place, several rooms opening on to the main hall. I've done a sketch." He turned and pointed.

"Anyway, this bloke, somebody called him Nino or Tonio took me outside. I wobbled a bit at first and sized him up in case he was going to have a go. He took me out to the front garden and I got a good shot of the house. Then got him to take me to the side, the west side, and I got a glimpse of the back of the place." He went on to describe the layout of the buildings, what was in the garden between and the approaches.

But he was not to know that his movements had been studied from the upper floor, or that on his return to the main house he was being scrutinised closely.

5

La Trampa
When Antonio had taken King outside, Gambino came down the stairs. He crossed the hall quietly to the music room where he stopped and leant against the doorway listening to the music. He looked across the room watching Rebecca as she played, noticing the concentration on her face as the notes of Chopin's second nocturne floated gently from the depths of the great Bechstein.

As the last notes faded, Rebecca leant forward holding the keys, sitting quite still with her eyes closed until there was silence. She jumped, startled as Gambino clapped slowly and walked across to join her. "Wonderful, Rebecca. Quite beautiful." He looked past her towards the garden doors. "And here comes Antonio with your friend. Right on cue...but don't bother with introductions now, you've got to be on your way."

As they left for their car with Antonio, he studied them from the study window. As soon as they had gone, he called for Bontate and closed the door. "What did you make of all that?" he asked curtly. "Sense anything strange? Anything unusual?"

Bontate thought fast. Gambino was on edge. He had been alerted by something. "No. Nothing I can think of," he replied slowly. "It all seemed perfectly normal to me. I mean, we had Rebecca and that boy of hers here…no problem there." He paused. "And only that strange Brit on his bicycle, Todd somebody or other." Bontate smiled. "Antonio knows him well. Always coming around like that apparently. Odd sort but quite harmless. Antonio says he's crazy about Patricia."

"Yes, but listen," Gambino rounded on Bontate. "If the weirdo was that damn crazy about her he'd know she's not here. Wouldn't he just?"

"Well hardly, Mario. And even if he is only half with it, he'd hardly chase after the beautiful Patricia on an old bike dressed like that, would he now?" Bontate replied laughing.

"Then what about those other two? The couple, Enrico his team picked up on the side of the hill over there, eh? What about them?"

"Mario, Mario, for Heaven's sake," Bontate cried out raising his hands. "Listen, this is France, it's Springtime and a lovely sunny day. What d'you expect people to do? Do I have to spell that one out to a full blooded Sicilian? Half the goddam country's at it right now." He paused. "Jesus…put an ear to the ground and you can hear the whole place trembling"

"Yeah, OK, I hear all that but I'm still not so sure," Gambino replied. "Something out there's making me nervous. Can't put my finger on it. As soon as these guys have left on Monday we pack up and move out early on Tuesday. Right? Maybe somebody out there's getting a little close. I don't know…just don't know."

Bontate bowed and left but Gambino sat on alone.

254

Chapter Nineteen
Friday Night

Paris

Bigard arrived at Place Beauvau and ran up the main steps two at a time. He had to see the Interior Minister before the Israelis returned with their answers and he was late.

Two hours earlier he had been called by Didier Merle who asked to see him urgently. Bigard had invited his old friend back to Avenue Michel Bizot and listened quietly as Merle told him his news. "You've *got* to get them to take note of what's going on," he urged. "Honestly, the *whole* of the press corps is about to storm the barricades." Bigard studied him closely and could see the man was rattled. "It's starting to get big, André. Not just our crowd here in France but the whole bloody lot - News International, Washington Post, Die Welt and all the others, not to mention the drama merchants and gutter press. No kidding, unless you can somehow put the lid back, it's going to break before the job's over. Then what? This one's for Maurice Carnet – the head of the PM's Press Office."

Bigard grunted and reached for his packet of Gitanes.

"The Government's got to be cunning and start stalling for time…and fast, too. It's no good just sending a young sprog out on to the steps to read some drivel from a script and then run for his life." Merle took out a large handkerchief and mopped his brow. "It's way past that now and unless they're damn careful, it's going to be all over the front pages, warts and all."

"You're dead certain are you?" Bigard asked, realising immediately the importance of Merle's information. As far as anyone knew, the Mafia were unaware that they were closing in. But one small leak and they would be alerted. Bigard could imagine the reaction – exactly as they had spelt out in their ultimatum.

"Look," Merle leant forward. "You've got the ears of Place Beauvau and if you can manage to get them to do something, they're going to have to understand how much the media knows already. Right now, thank Heavens, it's not too much 'cos the Gypos have slammed the door with a bang. Anyone caught snooping around out there now gets chucked in the pokey and forgotten about, so no one's going near the place." He dabbed at his brow again. "But good for them, the Gypos…at least they've bought us a little time."

"Well, you're the expert," André replied gloomily. "Trying to get you lot to cooperate's like pushing on a rope. What can *I* do about it, for crying out loud?" He got up, sighed loudly and fumbled for the cigarettes.

"Right, look." Merle's eyes, already wide now opened wider. "As I said, it's no good fobbing them off with some cock and bull story. I reckon that the P.M.'s got to order Carnet to call in the editors and put it on the line. Once they know they're being taken into his confidence they'll play along…like when a kid's gone missing. If you can manage that, you might get another forty-eight hours out of them and that should do you, shouldn't it?"

"Yes, that should fix it." Bigard raised his chin and exhaled slowly, brooding over what Merle had said. The man was right. If they played it wrong, the press would know they were bluffing and crucify them. "But how the hell do we find out exactly who knows what?"

"Perhaps this is where I can help," Merle answered. "Look. You and I are doing a deal, right? You're giving me a head start on the full story for my silence. OK, if you're still on for that, I can do a bit of homework and see who knows what. It'll take a bit of time to analyse but, for the moment anyway, the story's not moving."

Bigard stared at him. He might look like the old hack he was but he was still pretty nimble on his feet, still able to twist things to his own advantage. "You're not trying to steamroller me are you, you old rogue?"

"No," Didier laughed. "This is absolutely dead straight. If I tried a fast one here, you'd never speak to me again. Would you?"

"Too damned right. OK, it's a deal but for God's sake keep me up to speed with what's going on out there so I can pass it all on. They'll be bloody rioting in the corridors if we start drip feeding them stuff and they find themselves behind the action. Best to get Carnet's team to handle it in toto." Bigard got up, stubbed out the cigarette and took up his jacket. "Just you keep it coming, straight to me on my mobile, then I can take it all in while I'm on the move. Forget trying to get me here; I'll be out there somewhere and that's where I'll need the gen."

✳✳✳

Bigard went straight to Lespère's suite and spoke to a young aide in the outer office. He had not seen the youngster before and listened patiently as he was told why Lespère would not be able to see him. The Minister, so he was informed, was in conference and was likely to be detained until the Israeli delegation returned. After that he was due to see the Prime Minister. "It was simply not possible," the young man said, closing the Minister's diary and turning back to the papers on his desk. "I'm afraid everyone's very busy."

Bigard scribbled a short note on a piece of paper, handed it to the aide and nodded towards the door. "Go and slip that on his desk, nobody else's."

"But I cannot do that, m'sieur."

Bigard leant over the desk, grabbed the aide by the lapels and dragged him out of his chair. The astonished youth found himself examining an untidy pattern of scars running above and between two bushy eyebrows. Two unpleasantly bloodshot eyes were staring at him. "That's right, laddie," Bigard growled. "Look closely and listen carefully." The eyes were now uncomfortably close. "I'm the one who started this whole miserable, goddamned business the other night. It was the Prime Minister himself who got me turfed out of my little pit. If it wasn't for me kicking up this almighty fuss ever since then, everyone would be away enjoying a long weekend by now." The aide was trying to nod. "So, get your chubby little arse into overdrive. Open that door and get in there sharpish." Bigard released his hold and stood back. "If you don't, I will." For a moment the young man stood there adjusting his jacket and tie. "Go on, move it," Bigard said raising his voice and pointing towards the door. "I'll give you three."

Less than a minute later the aide returned. "Monsieur Lespère will see you shortly. My apologies, Monsieur." The door opened and Lespère ushered Bigard into his office where he listened in silence to the news about the media. He saw the problem immediately. He, too, realised that one slip by a rogue editor and the story would be out. Within hours the radio and TV networks would be full of it and the story would be beamed right into La Trampa and fifty million other homes across Europe. He spoke rapidly on the intercom to a senior aide telling him to liaise with Bigard and go with him to Maurice Carnet. It was Friday evening and getting late. If the editors of the main newspapers were going to respond to anyone it would have to be a call from the top. Bigard met his guide in the hall and followed him down the stairs just as the Prime Minister and Israeli Ambassador came into the building for the CILAT meeting.

✳✳✳

As soon as Schmuel reported that Israel agreed to go ahead the atmosphere in the room changed. After he had thanked Israel, the Prime Minister asked the three military commanders to address the assembly on their particular areas of responsibility thus bringing the CILAT committee up to date.

The Prime Minister spoke last. "Messieurs, that is most satisfactory and I for one am beginning to feel a little happier. Once again I would like to thank Ambassador Schmuel for working so hard on our behalf...one way or the other, in a little over twenty-four hours the problem will be resolved." He smiled wrily. "We must, of course, always be prepared for the unexpected but it appears that, at national level anyway, there is little more than can be done. No doubt the situation on the ground is a very different affair and our thoughts are with those who are at work right now."

As Jospin left the room, Levi gestured to Trant and pointed at his watch. The two men moved across to the Intelligence Centre where they discussed the co-ordination of the operations. "Our problem," Levi explained, "Is that the team cannot forecast when they will go for the snatch. It's the big Pentacost weekend in Malta and there'll be thousands milling around all over the place until the early hours. All I can ask of them at this stage is to work within the bracket they've given us."

"That's fine," Trant replied. "Unless we come up against something unexpected, I'll get our team to be in position around the target at the beginning of your time frame. Obviously they'll have to lie up a little way out, but if I give them the go ahead as soon as you let me know your team's on the move, our assault should be no longer than thirty minutes or so behind yours.

He glanced at the ex-Tank man and watched him trying to put himself in the position of the team leader. It was the eyes, Trant thought. Levi was miles away, staring hawk-like at some distant point. As he raised his chin, Trant caught a glimpse of the deep, livid burn mark on his throat and wondered to himself how much further it went under the neat uniform, and of the story behind it. There was a short silence. "Look," Trant continued. "If we keep things that tight, there's no way that word can get back to Malta about what's happened. Even if it does, by then the whole scenario will have changed. Once we know your team's done the lift, we can simply contain our lot and tell them to come out quietly with their hands up." Trant was grinning. "You know...games' up and all that. As soon as I hear that your team's gone in I'll give ours the nod. Let's leave it like that. We'll stand back and let them get on with it." He paused and looked at Levi and grinned once more. "Let the boys have their bit of fun!"

Brigadier Levi nodded soberly then looked up and smiled broadly. "You bet," he growled. "That's fine by me."

"However, let's look at the other end of the time frame." Trant continued. "Let's suppose that your team gets held up and time marches on. You'll have to let me know if they're going to go for it or abort it. If that's the case we won't be able to go ahead with our op here...or your two birds will get wind of what's happened this end." Trant pointed out that if the Israelis had not gone in by three-thirty, the mission would have to be aborted, the teams withdrawn and a fresh attempt made the following night...Sunday. "And that'll bring all sorts of problems, not the least of which is the press who've smelt blood already, apparently. So we're really looking for things to move tomorrow night. Have you got a good commander out there?"

"Yes," Levi replied. "Bett. Lyla Bett's one of our best and we've brought in a very good second-in-command from Tel Aviv. If they can't pull it off then nobody will. But, there's always a first..." he said ruefully. "The last thing we want is for the story to break before we've done our damnest to nail the bastards."

"Too right," Trant replied. "And there's not much more we can do from here...nothing at all. C'mon." He put a hand on the Israeli's shoulder. "Coffee?"

2

Valletta, Malta
Lyla Bett moved cautiously along Albert Street before turning into the narrow alley by the newspaper kiosk. After checking carefully behind her, she made her way briskly up the cobbled street and stopped in front of an old and carved doorway. Pausing to search her shoulder bag, she knocked twice gently on the heavy knocker then, without waiting, let herself into the cool interior. Adjusting her eyes to the gloom of the hallway, she climbed the two flights of marble stairs until she came to a badly chipped door where she stopped and knocked again. Jonni Bluett opened the door and Bett slipped into the dimly lit shuttered room where she greeted the three others.

No 197 Maelotti Street was one of Mossad's safe houses in Valletta where Bett and others met their agents. She had called the meeting to consider the news that the Libyans had been seen in the vicinity of Renee and Blosch.

"So, Sarah...what've you got? Let's hear you."

"Well, I've seen them both before and I swear the older one was one of those involved in that Korean business last year. Remember when they were trying to get parts of the Long Eye missiles through?" As the tall, slim young woman gave her reply, Bett listened intently, trying to work out in her own mind how such events might effect her plan. "And the younger guy's quite often sniffing around. Works up at their Consulate, I'm sure. Can't say exactly what they were up to but I had nearly finished the rooms when I saw them for the first time so I ducked into the linen room and watched for a while." Sarah paused, biting her thumb nail, now worried that what she had to report was of little importance. "They didn't seem to bat an eyelid as they went past the scientists' rooms. My hunch is that they're probably planning something in slow time and were just casing the place. If they'd been in a hurry or there was some sort of a flap it would have shown."

Jonni Bluett studied the girl. Bett had told him that Sarah was a meticulously careful operator, often identifying minute characteristics in those she had been assigned to watch. "What made you think that?" he quizzed.

"Body language," she replied without hesitation. "Just looked as though they were thinking about something rather than wanting to go into the rooms. I got the gut feeling they were simply talking about them...or whoever was inside." She smiled unassumingly.

"So, if they're planning something then it has to be the onward move," Bluett chipped in. "Can't be anything else to plan on that floor." Sarah shook her head.

"Joe." Bett turned to Joe Berak. "Do the ISL always use the routine Libyan Airways flights in and out of Tripoli, or do they slide in using something smaller?"

"Nearly always the routine flight...and the next one's due back out tomorrow evening, just after ten."

"Just after *ten*," Bett exclaimed. "Shit. That's earlier than we expected...far earlier. That throws things a bit." She chewed on her lip, thinking quickly. "But I'm damn sure I know what they're up to. They're planning to get them out of there sometime tomorrow and put them on that flight. No point in them looking over the place today if they're not going to do anything for the next week or so."

Despondently, the five sat debating their options. Every time the plan seemed firm, another problem arose. The first option was for them to take a chance on it and simply sit back, leaving the two men alone in the hope that this was a false alarm. The second was to keep the place under observation but have a team deployed outside ready to pick them up on the way to the airport.

The only other alternative, and it was a high-risk option, was to assume the worst and lift them from the hotel before the ISL team moved in for them. The main danger here was that, once the ISL got word back to France, the British operation in the Tarn would be compromised. After a brief discussion they eliminated the first option, arguing that to sit back, do nothing and then have the two men snatched from under their noses would be a dreadful failure. They wanted the scientists badly and, if necessary, were prepared to stick their necks some way out. The ambush option that they had discounted earlier was simply too complicated and it would be a mammoth undertaking to cater for all contingencies. Furthermore, it would still be daylight. Should anything go wrong and the Maltese police get involved it would be a disaster.

The early lift seemed to be the only solution, but *how* early could they do it without upsetting the operation in France?

✳✳✳

Gradually the team worked their way towards a plan based on how they believed the Libyans would operate using the Libyan Arab Airlines shuttle to Tripoli the following night. They assumed the two men would be taken from the hotel at the last possible moment and driven straight out to the parked aircraft. The most likely time for this would be around nine-thirty, allowing half an hour to get to the airport and another half hour to get them on board unobtrusively. The Israelis decided to go for their snatch an hour before that – at eight-thirty. "We can hold them in one of the safe houses until the original handover time," Bett suggested.

"And another thing," Jonni chipped in. "If there's a problem, we could always get them straight out to the aircraft and hold them there. Or get the French to lift off right away." Whichever option they chose they would have to assume that the absence of the two men would be detected almost immediately, approximately two and a half hours before the British assault was planned to go in. As soon as those in La Trampa got word of the snatch in Malta, the Mafia would be forced to break cover.

"We've got to be careful there," Jonni warned. "We don't want to stir things just as the Brits are putting in their assault. They'll find the place heaving and wouldn't thank us for that." Once more the room fell silent. The Mossad team knew exactly what was at stake and could well imagine the final preparations going on in France. As fellow professionals they realised the potential dangers to the British plan once surprise had been lost.

Finally Bett spoke. "Right, I've made my decision. We *will* plan on an early lift and I'll tell you for why. First, we need to get our hands on these two guys and right there in the hotel. That's important. But secondly, if the other end was tipped off about it and were in the process of getting away, it might actually be quite a good time for the Brits to attack." She fingered the amber pendant around her neck and looked at the others. "Think about it. Everyone inside the place would be packing up and concentrating on looking after themselves. If they realised they were pulling out, the guards would hardly be doing their stuff properly out there while all that was going on. Added to which there'll probably be a whole lot of shouting and rushing about. Lights will be going on, engines starting up and all that sort of thing. We know they've got an aircraft pre-positioned nearby and if they've heard that the game in Malta's up they'll be moving out...fast."

She paused, before continuing slowly, "It would certainly give the advantage to the assault team...and that would be no bad thing. If I was in their shoes I wouldn't mind that too much." She paused again. "I'll put Paris in the picture and warn them that we're having to bring our plans forward by a couple of hours. The Brits can then get themselves into position immediately after last light. That cuts the time scale right down. Yes," she said firmly. Then she thought for a moment. "If I was down there, I could live with that. We'll go for that."

3

Bosc Lebat
Once Jed King had started to concentrate the team on their tasks at La Trampa, Morton kept himself in the background. He remembered only too well the irritation junior commanders felt when they were being constantly tapped on the shoulder and offered advice or ordered to change this or that at the last minute.

King had proved himself time and again and everything that Morton had seen here bore witness to that. He had discussed Trant's request for the plan to go ahead twenty-four hours earlier with King and his patrol commanders. Jed had taken the idea calmly and had immediately seen the advantages. Morton listened as he sold the idea to the team. He then reported back to Paris that they would work towards an H-hour the following night. The team was now looking to Jed King as their leader and there was no room for anyone else. Morton decided to devote himself to testing the communications and preparing his own team for their role tomorrow. Tonight was his only chance.

✳✳✳

He studied the map with Paddy Merrow, the communications expert. They needed to get as close as possible to the target in order to pick up the faintest signals if the team were in a difficult position. La Trampa, being in a shallow depression, was badly positioned for these kind of transmissions. They needed to select a piece of high ground where their principal radios and the mobile phone back up would have the best chance of getting through. They picked the village of Villeneuve-sur-Vere off the map. It was set on a high rocky outcrop just three and a half kilometres from La Trampa and immediately south of the main D600 road. If they could find a point on the northern edge of the village they would have almost direct line of sight to the target – every signaller's dream.

Shortly after eight the patrols assembled in the big barn. Every man knew what was required of him and King's briefing was aimed at co-ordinating the activities of the patrols rather than giving out specific orders for set tasks. Tracy Black began by covering the ground around the target area once more. King then called out the patrol commanders, one at a time and got them to describe how they planned to use the ground and where they had decided to lie up. They marked their routes with strips of ribbon and placed coloured markers on the model to indicate where they intended to position themselves before moving in. Always fearful of a clash between his own patrols, the dreaded 'blue on blue,' King made everyone study the positions meticulously, taking precise note of each other's routes and the timings.

Andrew Robinson spoke briefly about the weather. The moon was at half strength and on the wane but would be at its peak late in the night, giving considerable light before dawn on both nights. "I'm afraid to say the weather prospects aren't all that brilliant. This last week's been too bloody hot and they reckon there'll be storms, either later tonight or tomorrow."

"That's a bore," Doug Jourdan pulled a face. "They're usually pretty heavy and can last for hours," he drawled. "Usual form's a slow build up during the day then it chucks it at us early in the evening."

Inevitably the rain would be heavy, he advised. Sometimes there would be violent hailstorms and they would often be accompanied by high winds. "Known for it here, I'm afraid," Robinson added looking around at the glum faces. "And it can be bloody awful getting caught out in the open. Hailstones can be the size of marbles, yes, honestly…and give you one hell of a smack. And the rain's bloody freezing." The faces were glaring at him. "Sorry, fellas. Should've picked a better place for your holidays. So get your prayer mats out," he added with a grin.

"What about flying?" Jed asked anxiously. "Presumably it's a non-starter if something like that's in the offing?"

Robinson sighed. "We-ll, I have to admit I would rather not be up there. The stuff fairly lashes down and the wind knocks you all over the place. But let's be positive…if there's any way I can get airborne then I'll be there. Incidentally, I'll be up for half an hour or so tonight to give every one a chance to check comms. But back to the weather." Robinson bent over the cloth model. "The only possible problem if we're right in the middle of it…apart from a complete engine shut down, is that I might not be able to put you down exactly where you want. I'll do my best but with these winds you have to be careful, especially if we've got a full load up."

Jed then took each team through its specific tasks for the evening . He forbade the use of weapons. Stealth was the byword and they were unlikely to come across anything more than a lone sentry. "Work your way around them. Remember, this is rural France not a declared operational zone. And you, Horse…you Fijians keep your fingers to yourself. Tomorrow night'll be different."

✳✳✳

The teams sat quietly waiting for the moment of departure. It was always a tense time. Each man knew what was expected of him and, as the patrols waited, everyone had his own thoughts. Some ran through their orders or fiddled with pieces of equipment, others sat reading or playing cards. Were they honest, most would have admitted to a quickening of the pulse as the moment of departure drew near. It was an eerie, tense atmosphere and time always dragged. All three vans were going to be used independently of each other, dropping the parties off some two or three kilometres from the target. The transport would then return to Bosc Lebat before going back out to collect the patrols shortly before dawn.

King kept Tracy and Marion back. He planned to send the girls out again early the following day to collect any further intelligence that was necessary. He told them they would get their instructions after he had spoken to the patrol commanders in the morning.

He went outside and sat quietly by himself, leaning against the ornamental bird table with his knees pulled up under his chin. It was Amanda. She was up there right now, just she and Sir Alan Palmer. If it came to a shoot out they would have to take their chance. He'd told himself this a thousand times and the team, he knew, would do all they could but there was always that chance shot or a deflection or a richochet perhaps. But they would lie low – wouldn't they? Surely they wouldn't try to make a run for it and get in the way. Pray God, they would not do anything daft and end up getting caught in the crossfire. But what, he wondered, would the opposition do to them…abandon them, take them on as hostages or keep hold of them and use them as human shields. He'd been through this time and again as well.

At ten o'clock, Patrick Morton and Paddy Merrow moved out. Shortly afterwards the others followed.

4

La Trampa
Just as the last van dropped its patrol and headed for home, the heavy storm clouds over the Pyrenees far to the south moved across the face of the moon. For ten minutes, while the very last of the light faded from the western sky, the men lay silently in the ditch by the side of the road accustoming themselves to the darkness. Gradually their ears began to pick up the night sounds around them. In front the land rose gently towards the outlying homesteads of Mailhoc, highlighted on the crestline. King had asked them to approach the target by way of the village in order to check out the whereabouts of the Arab screen they had seen earlier in the day.

Sam Townsend adjusted his night goggles and searched the countryside in front of him. Across the road he could make out the endless rows of vines, the young leaves a pale ghostly green in the viewfinder. Beyond the vineyard he spotted the tall broken hedgerow Tracy had described on the model, and beyond that again the high pastures next to the village. The goggles picked up the images of the grazing cattle, the heat of their bodies showing clearly against the dull grey of the surrounding countryside. For several minutes they lay doggo to double check, watching the area for signs of life. Satisfied that the area was deserted they moved on, crossed over the high ground and began the gentle descent towards their target.

They made their way cautiously through a patch of dense scrub until they identified the shape of the pigeonnier, now less than two hundred metres away. A door or window at the bottom of the building was opened, illuminating the area between the high walls brightly before it closed again. They could hear the sounds of muffled voices and laughter coming from the room underneath. A few minutes later and slightly to the left, they saw a faint light followed by the glow of a cigarette. Now crawling forward using the cover of the hedgerow, they moved to within fifty metres. They watched as the sentry left the safety of the building and walked slowly towards them, stopping only a few metres short. They could see his outline against the light of the window and waited patiently for him to move on.

Townsend and Fraser crept forward again. From the shadow of the walls, they inched their way towards the door and stopped near some old farm equipment. For a full hour they lay observing every movement and listening. They watched the sentries change, noting that the new man stayed close to the door, preferring to remain in the shadows behind the light of the open window. They noticed also that the guards were well organised in that they remained out of sight and made little noise.

Gradually they eased themselves away from the front of the building and back into the cover of some undergrowth before moving slowly round to the far side. Once in position, Townsend crept forward to the building and glanced through a chink in the shutters. He counted eight camp beds or mattresses amongst the usual mess of clothes and personal belongings scattered around the room. He noted, too, the narrow stairs leading to the first floor and, once back with the others, saw the dull glow of light shining through the shutters above the main downstairs room. The hostages perhaps, or a lookout tower? Either way it was a place to note.

On the other side of La Trampa, Racatoni and Horse reached the edge of the formal gardens. They lay still in the deep shadow watching the front of the house. From time to time the front door would open when people came out to talk or smoke. Eventually they spotted the two sentries and inched their way towards the one at the corner of the house. Blissfully unaware of the two big Fijians in the grass less than five metres away from him, the man fiddled with his rifle and hummed quietly. They waited for him to move away then eased themselves across to the far corner of the house where they watched the other sentry.

***

Luigi Barzini checked the blanket tacked across the window then picked his way past the recumbent forms on the mattresses and camp beds. Dino Bontate had given him the responsibility of organising the guards around the main accommodation. He knew that beneath their room, in the garages, Bontate and his boss had stored something of importance. They had been told to keep out. He did not know what was there and was not about to try and find out. Barzini was just twenty-three and for the last two years had been working as a sicario, a killer, in his native Sicily. He was a big, powerfully built man and would have been even bigger had not his Creator dispensed with his neck. Instead, the muscles at the top of his shoulders simply rose in great slabs towards his ears. His eyes, mean and hostile, stared out from the centre of his pock-marked face, giving their owner a look of permanent malevolence.

He had first killed at the age of fourteen after his sister had complained to him about the unwanted attentions of a young hopeful in the next village. Twice Barzini had warned him off; on the third occasion his lupara had blasted the hapless youth through the window of a baker's shop. The magistrate later dismissed the charges on a technicality. A year later he had become a picciotti for the Gambino family. Very early in his newfound career, Barzini had learned not to question orders and never, under any circumstances, to disobey them. Whatever was down there in the garages was not his problem.

The two men at the corner table – Frank Rolli and Geraldo Alberti – had, like himself, been brought across to France from Monreale, a southern suburb of Palermo, their hometown. When Bontate told them they were to work for the mighty Don himself they had been thrilled – and afraid. Thrilled because of the honour, afraid because failure to do their job satisfactorily would be seen as having failed the family, and for a sicario to fail in such a manner the penalty was always the same. Sometimes death came quickly, sometimes more slowly...but it always came.

"OK, get your gear." Barzini looked at his watch. "You're on in a couple of minutes," he said quietly. The two men left the table obediently and picked their way carefully across the floor to the locker near the back of the room. As he checked the six shells into the breach of his pump action shot gun, Rolli, a short swarthy man of the hills, raised his head, flicked back his lank hair and squinted through the haze of tobacco smoke. Next to him Alberti turned his Colt semi-automatic on to its side, pulled back the working parts, then tested the mechanism several times before placing a full magazine of 9mm copper headed bullets into the butt.

Rolli waited while his companion checked his pistol then watched as the tall Alberti lifted his lupara from the rack. The twelve-gauge double-barrelled shotgun had both barrels sawn to half their original length. Again he watched as Alberti broke the weapon and placed two Large Game cartridges into the breach, before gently clicking it shut. "OK," he whispered. "Ready."

"Right, listen. You're out for two hours, OK?" Barzini motioned the two men to move close to the door, glowering at the two faces. "No talking or smoking. If you hear *anything* let me know. Don't go blasting off...folks round here don't like it. Right? I'll get Gallo and Cassara out to you when it's time." He removed the blanket from behind the door. "No noise now." He motioned to the forms on the floor. "Ready?" Barzini, switched off the light, opened the door and the two sicarios moved out into the night.

***

By now Jed was convinced that the artefacts were held away from the manoir, probably somewhere close to where the guards were housed. He had given himself and Ned Kelly the task of identifying the exact location and finding the best entry points. Kelly moved first, manoeuvering his team to a point from where he and Bill Sandeman could make their way to one of the shuttered windows. Bill had spent the day at Bosc Lebat with Doug Jourdan studying French shutters and their mechanisms.

He had been shown how both the new and old varieties worked and now he pulled gently at the base of the one nearest. Many of the older shutters were warped and would not close easily. The one he pulled moved just enough for him to reach up with a thin metal rod and gently lift the inner catch. He moved to the next but it would not move, neither did the two he tried after that. The windows, if shuttered, were going to present a problem.

An hour later Jed's patrol passed through Kelly's and moved to the front of the accommodation building. If he was honest, his mind had been concentrating on where the hostages might be. The nearer he got, the more pressing the question became. But he had to forget about them. His task was the main accommodation. He *had* to get a look inside the building and his patrol lay hidden studying the options. The sentries were alert but Jed detected they had left a blind spot in the area of the front door. Eventually he decided to go for a bold approach, trusting that the late hour would momentarily confuse anyone who saw him.

Earlier, he and the others had watched the comings and goings at the main entrance. Those inside were used to such activity and rarely checked the new arrivals at this point. He moved forward alone, then lay still at the edge of the shrubbery for a further ten minutes, watching the two sentries. He knew what had to be done yet he could feel his heart pounding and the trickles of sweat running down his face.

He checked the guards for a final time before suddenly and quietly rising to his feet. Forcing himself to move casually, he walked up the steps through the main door and into the spacious hallway. He stopped, listening for sounds, then quietly opened and shut the doors on either side of the hall. A few seconds later he retraced his steps, turning away from the sentries and moving away behind the block. Keeping to the deep shadows, he skirted round the well tended lawn to the corner of a low hedge and rejoined his patrol. It had been a risk, albeit a slight one, but he now knew for certain that the doors to the accommodation block and the two apartments inside were left unlocked. His mind was made up. Unless anyone could come up with a better idea they would assault the building by going straight for the front entrance.

His final task was to locate the exact whereabouts of the garages. Remembering what he had been shown earlier and Tracy's description, he decided to check again. The two patrols met and Jed explained his plan, taking Bill Sandeman and Ned Kelly forward to the large new double doors beyond and below the sleeping accommodation.

Using the night goggles Bill checked the locks carefully before opening up his pack of tools from which he selected a thin plastic strip and a long thin screwdriver. Delicately and patiently he worked at the lock, stopping now and again to choose a different tool. All of a sudden the doors swung open. King rose silently and moved into the building, Sandeman and Kelly following him. Once inside, they pulled the door close and for several minutes lay still. There, through the lens of their goggles they saw three delivery vans and a Mercedes saloon.

The can Jed struck with his foot rattled noisily across the floor. All three froze, listening for sounds of voices or running feet. Eventually he moved quietly back across the floor towards the door motioning the others to follow. Silently and carefully they let themselves out, pausing only for Sandeman to secure the locks behind them. Outside the night was dark and airless. The moon, now low in the sky, had been hidden by banks of cloud. Far away on the horizon they could see flash after flash of lightning rippling against the clouds followed by distant growls of thunder.

✳✳✳

One by one the four patrols came into the deep layby near Villeneuve-sur-Vere which they had selected for Morton's base. Jed moved across to where he was working with his signallers. They talked quietly, each concerned about the communications. "Not too bad," Morton replied. "But not good either. And on a few occasions they were bloody awful. Might be these electrical storms but I could only just hear Andrew Robinson in the chopper. Mind you he was several miles away. What d'you reckon, Paddy?"

"Just like the jebel, boss." The Irishman had been listening and now stepped forward. "Given a fair shot these are damn good comms but the Almighty was kicking up rough out there tonight. You know...one hell of a lot of electricity flying around his patch. Better luck tomorrow, eh?"

"And the target, Jed? Any problems?"

"Not that we could see." He shook his head slowly. "But they're on the ball up there...and it's bloody hot too," he muttered. "We clocked the sentries for long enough to see they know their stuff. Armed as well...two weapons each. Reckon that puts the place beyond any doubt." He paused, blowing at the drip of sweat on the end of his nose. "But the walls and windows are a non starter," he shook his head and looked at Morton. "Like the Tower of London...our kit wouldn't touch them. They're several feet thick and there's too much soft stone and mortar. I reckon we'll go straight for the front door. The sentries have left a number of blind spots and I managed to walk right into the place just after one." Patrick Morton chuckled quietly. "Reckon that's the best way, so we've got to hit the accommodation first and take out their team. Once they're out of the way, the rest's easy."

"And the hostages? Any ideas…*if* they're still alive?"

Jed hesitated. Morton was right in that they might have been killed already. The very mention of it suddenly brought it all into focus again; her death was the one thing he had not considered. "Difficult to tell," he replied." Sam Townsend reckons he might have found a place…but they could be anywhere."

Morton nodded. It was bad enough knowing exactly where any hostages were but far more difficult if you had to play it blind and look for them as you went along. "Get rid of the opposition first…that's my advice," he urged. "Once they're out of it you can take your time, but don't try to do everything at once or it'll turn to rats."

"Yep, that's the plan," King replied. "And given a fair chance we'll take the place OK. Whether or not we can do it without a fight's another matter. I'll get the two girls up there again in the morning to check out a couple of things and I want to run through a few patrol drills after lunch. That's it really." He wiped his face again. "Anything from the other end?"

"Nope, nothing at all. Arthur Trant wants a chat in the morning." Morton glanced at his watch. "Hey, three o'clock would you believe…tomorrow already."

"Aye, that's for sure." Jed turned away. Just one squeak from the opposition and that would be that. No second chance.

Chapter Twenty
Saturday – Early

Valletta, Malta

Lyla Bett eased her way slowly through Valletta and on to the city's outer road. Her final destination was the International Airport at Luqa, but first she headed south-west, driving fast through the light morning traffic. Eventually she slowed and turned right, on to the narrow Medina road where she began to filter her way through the twisting country lanes towards the ancient hill top town of Mosta. Everywhere the streets were decked out in flags and bunting for the weekend's festivities.

Today was one of the island's great annual holidays. Already those involved in the preparations had begun to gather around the busy cafes and market stalls set up in the village squares. Realising that the same drive later in the day might involve a number of detours, Bett had asked Jonni to accompany her and check the route they would be taking the two scientists.

***

"You know, we could never have organised an ambush out here," Jonni said, looking in amazement at the countryside between the villages. "Even if we were desperate. Look at it…the place's just a maze of tiny lanes and tracks. We wouldn't know where to begin. And most of them've got these high stonewalls on either side. And look at this…hardly room to pass, let alone park up under cover."

"Yes, I agree," Bett answered. "At least we got that one right. And in any case, the whole thing's dominated by timings. Yitzac Levi's got us tied in with the Brits and we can't budge from the sched." She slowed as they passed a young girl, little more than a child, tending the family herd of goats. "At least we've got a bit of control doing it the way we are. Just pray we've second guessed the ISL accurately, eh?" She looked across at Jonni and raised her eyebrows. "What in

God's name do we do if the Libyans come for them early? In the middle of the afternoon, say?"

Bluett had been thinking about the same problem and they talked it through as they drove. If they were concerned that the ISL was going to lift the scientists early, they too were going to have to bring their plan forward and either take the two men to a safe house or make straight for Luqa and hand them over to the French. It was a tough decision but the alternatives were far worse. If they were not early enough and got to the scientists at the same time as the ISL then they would either have to fight for them or sit and watch as the Libyans lifted them from under their noses. Worse still would be to arrive after the Libyans and find the cupboard bare. Bluett raised his hands in a gesture of despair. "Whatever gives, Bett, as long as we get tipped off in advance, I'd sure like to have a damn good go at them. Nail the bastards if we have to."

"Now now…that's fighting talk," she chuckled. "No way, I'm afraid. Orders are orders and the Office wants them back where they belong and in one piece. And, in any case, this is a tiny place with virtually no cover and we'd never last five minutes if we tried anything like that." She slowed at a narrow crossroads. "No, I've decided that if it all comes down to an early move and we *have* to react quickly then we go in and then, grab 'em and hand them over. It's risky, but I reckon it's worth it. And, to be honest, I bet the French'd buy that. All they've got to do is to turn their aircraft round and head for home. Anyway, we'll think about that later.

"Right, so much for tonight's route. Happy?" She slowed and turned sharp left. "We're now off to the house in Mosta…to meet Joe and Barce from the airport. They're bringing in a couple of the French aircrew and there're a number of points yet to sort. Having a few of them around in their uniforms a bit later might be a good ploy." She paused, looking for traffic coming in from the right. "Once we've got this end tied up we can get back to town and concentrate on our two friends. I've asked everyone to meet us back at the embassy at six this evening for a final get together, by the way."

✳✳✳

They pulled in through the wrought iron gates of a tall, ivy-clad house, well hidden from the road by high hedges and a line of cypress trees. The door opened but was held by a chain as an elderly man in a grey short-sleeved pullover peered at them before slipping the catch and allowing them in. He shuffled down the hall and waved towards the main salon where the party from Luqa was waiting. Bett nodded at the assembled company and introduced herself. She then began explaining how she and those working in the hotel had decided to carry out the snatch. "As far as the hotel part of the operation goes, we've planned it in three phases," she announced. "First we have to get into their rooms and incapacitate them. We looked at the possibility of walking them out but it's too risky. If one of them called out or made a run for it that would be that. Anyway we are planning on giving them a jab…Midazolam valium, just enough for half an hour or so." The newly arrived French aircrew glanced at one another.

"We're then going to put them in to a couple of those large laundry trolleys and get them out via the service lifts." Bett looked across at Ruth and raised her eyebrows. "Got them? Fine." She turned back to the others. "There's enough room to lay them out properly and we can then cover them with a few sheets, that should be OK. That's the second phase." She paused, and looked round. "OK? Right. Once down the lift and outside we've got to get them across the service area at the back of the hotel, where all the garbage crap is…and into the van that'll be parked in front of the garages next to the refuse collection area.

Bett reached across and took the file Jonni passed to her. "All so dead simple isn't it, but I'm afraid nothing's quite like that," she said taking out some notes and a number of annotated photographs. "What I'd like to do now is to go through each stage slowly and build on the rough outline I've just given you." She turned towards the Lieutenant and two Sergeants from the French Air Force. Marie-Christine Dumas, the attractive, petite Lieutenant had introduced herself and her two crew members earlier. Roland Christian, the tall medic and Jean-Paul Pleyrol, one of the cabin staff, nodded and leant forward

"Good to see you," she smiled. "There are a number of things we've got to tie up carefully. First of all, we've got to have a doctor with us. If not a doctor then a top-rate paramedic. Danny can give them the shot but once they're down and out I want to make sure they're handled properly and stay alive."

Dumas spoke rapidly to Christian then turned to Bett. "Sergeant Christian here, he's your man," she said. "He'll be in the van to see that the two are all right on their journey out to us."

"Sure, but I want him in the hotel before that. We don't want to end up handing over a couple of stiffs. Whoever's going to do that had better come back in with us and we'll show him the trolleys and the route out of the place." She re-pinned her hair and reached forward for a glass of chilled grapefruit juice then turned back to the French officer. "Also, I'd like you and Sergeant Pleyrol to be in your air crew uniform to help us through the main gate. It's a big van, rather like a larger version of a minibus. You see 'em all over the airports, doing crew shuttles and that sort of thing. If we use one of them, it'll be far less suspicious. They hardly get a second glance at the gate, but a closed van is an invitation for nosey security guards to start poking around in the back. We can get them both comfortably on the floor and cover them with some linen and empty boxes. One of Joe's men will be driving and if you two are up there near the front in all your kit we should be able to bluff our way through."

Joe Barak lay slumped deep in his chair, gently grooming his moustache. He was hot, hotter in fact than the last time they met. As his name was mentioned so he raised his hand and let it fall limply back on to the arm of the chair before returning to the business of Lieutenant Dumas' legs and all that he might do with them. They were, he decided, legs that knew how to work properly and, exposed to him like they were, offered endless possibilities. Lieutenant Dumas was, Joe believed, just the sort of officer any sane man would gladly follow.

"From then on it should be just the short run out to the aircraft and we've checked that route. Once on board it's over to the team from France. Our job's done and that's that," she said wiping her hands and smiling.

Jonni Bluett shook his head slowly and Bett looked at him. "What's up, Jonni? Something bugging you?"

"Yes, but nothing to do with that." Bluett was leaning forward, frowning. "All being well that's a plan that should get us through with no problems. If it *does*, then we're laughing." He looked up. "My concern's how we're going to play it if we get the tip off that the Libyans are going in earlier. And I mean a *long* while before our new time of eight-thirty."

"Oh, for Pete's sake. We talked about that in the car didn't we?" Bett frowned.

"Yeah, to be sure, and it's been bugging me ever since," he replied. "Yesterday, Joe told us that it was usual for them to use the shuttle aircraft, but we don't know that for certain. He couldn't guarantee it." Jonni looked from Bett to Joe and shrugged. "What I'd like to see is some fall back plan, up and ready to run from the time we finish our preparations tomorrow morning until we're due to go in for them at eight-thirty in the evening. I *know* it's a long time to lie up and I *know* I'm probably going way over the top. But," he tapped the table with his fingers, "I would like something in place. I don't want to miss these two."

"Well, go on then," Bett prompted. "What's on your mind?"

"I think we should have the van and driver ready by the service entrance at the back of the hotel. We could leave Joe and one of the French team in the back of the vehicle...Sergeant Christian perhaps. Ruth's told us that she's kept the two rooms next to the scientists free. In that case, I reckon we should move in there and hole up for the afternoon. Hell's teeth, it won't be that bad. Our team working inside the hotel will be able to keep in touch with us. And we've got our comms." Bluett glanced round before continuing. "Obviously we're going to have to tie up how we're going to be warned about anything. If you get the buzz, we can lift them there and then, as soon as you give us the nod. That would cut out all the hassle of running around getting things into place at the last minute."

Bett nodded and looked at him. Jonni shrugged in reply. "What happens after that or what we do with them for the next few hours is not my business, but at least we'll have got hold of them."

Bett inclined her head. "Yes," she replied slowly. "I'll go for that. That's good...good thinking, Jonni. Then, if we hear nothing, we just flesh the whole thing out until we're back on to the original plan. Let's have a closer look."

***

For several hours the Israeli team worked on the plan. Again and again Lyla Bett made them talk their way through the sequence of events, pausing only to think through the variety of contingency plans catering for the unexpected. By the end of the afternoon she had developed her own group and three members of French Air Force Flight Number Alfa Foxtrot 876 into a well prepared team. As soon as she had returned to the embassy she called Paris on the secure link, warning the Defence Attaché that they had been forced to bring their operation forward by several hours. As they spoke she detected concern in Levi's voice.

"Why so, Bett? That's one hell of a change and it'll throw the Brits badly. I mean, for Pete's sake, we've already moved everything forward by twenty-four hours and this could force them into a daylight op and I'm damn sure they won't go for that."

"There's no way round it, Yitzac. You and I want these guys, right? And the ISL are after them as well *and* there's a shuttle leaving for Tripoli later tonight. We can't take the risk of letting them slip through our fingers. In fact we're planning to stake the place out even earlier to get them if we hear they're going to be moved sooner."

"OK, OK." Levi whistled slowly. "You'd better hang on there for a bit while I get over and see General Trant, the Brit commander. There's no way we can do this without them being with us. I'll be back in an hour or so."

***

Trant took the news calmly. From the start he had appreciated that the Mossad team would do what they could to lift the two men and had anticipated they might well ask to advance their plan in order to be certain. "That's all right, Brigadier," he replied. "As I said before, if you have to go for an early lift, then so be it. Once you've done your bit we just contain our target and call in the heavy mob. However, I've got to think of the safety of my men down there. From what you tell me, your lift might go in at any time and will almost certainly be in daylight...remember we're on the same time zone as Malta. I can order my team to deploy before last light but *not* to close in on the target." Levi watched him closely. "If they deploy early they'll have to lie up and then move in after last light," Trant continued. "And that's after ten. I'll have to give them another

274

hour or so to get themselves into position, so we're talking of an H-hour at not before eleven. If that's the case there might well be a difficult time gap but I can't get them to go in any earlier than that."

"So, what do you think?" Levi asked. "D'you reckon we leave things as they are and take a chance?" He looked at Trant anxiously, scratching at his tightly cut hair. "If we go to the French, I'm afraid they'll start to unscramble the whole thing and will want to start laying down priorities and options then we'll all get into a devil of a muddle."

Trant blew and thought for a minute. "Grief, it's a nightmare all right," he said, chuckling. "Just think about it…a team of Brits in southern France trying to take out a whole bunch of Italian hoods while a team of Israelis in Malta try to lift a couple of French scientists. All jacked up in five minutes flat and controlled from Paris. Not bad, eh?" Levi shook his head and laughed with him.

Trant sensed the plans were on the verge of getting out of hand, as was so often the case when over-zealous commanders starting worrying about every conceivable solution to every possible problem. There came a time when a line had to be drawn or those on the ground would become hopelessly confused. "Look, let's leave things exactly as they are." He held up his hand. "It's too damn complicated as it is and there're far too many imponderables. Get your team to stake the place out in preparation for an early lift but tell them to hang fire for as long as they possibly can…the later they can leave it, the better for our chaps. We'll stick to the original plan but get ourselves ready for an earlier move. I'll warn my lot to get out on the ground and lie up but not to move in until they hear from me that your chaps have had to move quickly. That's *it* as far as I'm concerned…no more chopping and changing. The boys down there have got enough to be going on with without us lot back here flapping around. Tell your lot that we agree and to keep us up to speed."

2

The Tarn
Jed had asked the patrol commanders to meet him at nine but he was up soon after seven. After a short run along the old Roman road he had a swim in Jourdan's pool, then breakfasted by himself before going into the barn.

They had learned a great deal last night and he was having to amend the plan in a number of areas, in particular the assault. Most importantly, by executing a bold move like this, they should be able to get right on top of them before they knew what was happening. Whenever an assault began with an enforced entry there were always those few moments of chaos when anything could happen and either side could take the initiative.

Before the meeting, Morton came into the barn looking for him. "Jed, I've just had Arthur Trant on the mobile. The Israelis have got a problem their end and are having to go in earlier. They asked us if we could do the same, but Arthur's compromised with them. He's asked us to get out there well before last light, lie up and be prepared to go in as soon as we can. However he wants us to hold back until he gives the word because the Israelis are hoping to fall back on to the original timings. What do you make of that?"

"Not much frankly," said King bitterly. "Doesn't surprise me. It's a bloody marvel they're not asking us to go in yesterday. You know…'Certainly old bean. After you, my dear good chap.' What the hell will they want next, for fuck's sake?" King looked at Morton and shrugged. "No," he went on, slowly. "That should be OK, as long as we can get into some decent cover up there. "But you can tell 'em back there that I refuse to move out of cover in broad daylight. We're not doing a bloody battalion attack on the place. There's not many of us and I don't intend to lose anyone because some joker in Paris has got his knickers in a twist." He looked at Morton. "That's it, Patrick, no more changes."

Morton sensed the tension was getting to King and could see why. For the last five nights, none of them had much sleep. But as commander, King had to think and plan ahead as well as look after himself. The lot of a junior commander on operations was a hectic, bewildering mass of information, planning, teamwork, receiving orders, writing out their own and then passing them on. And always against the clock. Most difficult of all, he had to prepare for the time when things went badly wrong and the casualties began to mount. But King, Morton knew, had been there before. When he blew his top momentarily like this he was merely warming to the theme. He simply nodded.

✳✳✳

The five men talked through the changes to the plan. It seemed simple enough but they needed to find good positions to lie up. Known as LUPs, the lying up positions had to be reasonably close to the target yet far enough away to be out of immediate trouble. They had to have good cover and a number of entry and exit points. King called the two girls and briefed them from the model.

"You can see the routes the patrols want to take. Well, go back a couple of kilometres from our planned drop-off points and look for four good LUPs. You know what to look for but remember we'll have to get into them in broad daylight…and that's with weapons, so we don't want to be anywhere near local beauty spots. So, off you go…and, hey, I need you back here by lunch time with the gen 'cos we're gonna have to run through all the drills time and again."

Paddy Merrow called the two young women over to where he had stored his signals equipment. "You're off now, girls? Right, well don't forget your comms.

And what about leaving your route with someone?" the Irish brogue queried. "Suggest you stay on the mobile and remember to call in every half hour, OK? You're on your own out there this morning and there's some nasty folk about, y'know." He nodded knowingly. "There's a map in my office so mark up your route and let me know before you leave. Keep your heads down, now."

***

Morton, King and the patrol commanders discussed the change in timings and its effect on the patrol. "It's not quite so bloody easy as that, you know," Jed said angrily. "Tonight we're going in bombed up to the eyebrows with weapons and ammo and if we're seen de-bussing ready to go with that lot, the locals are going to shit themselves. I mean what would be your reaction, for Christ's sake, if you were out walking the dog and round the corner came Jim Tacamati with a gimpy? Work that one out. I mean, you'd bloody die of fright." He shook his head angrily. "Anyway, no sweat, it's the same as ever it was – last minute fuck-ups everywhere. Right, let's have a look."

"How about just a couple of LUPs?" Archie Small asked. "Or just the one even? There's all that cover to the south of the place, plus that re-entrant where Terry and Marion bared all?"

"Little point really," Jock McCall chipped in. "Might save us a bit of time initially but it'll take longer to get right around the buildings if we come in from just one or two points and then have to split. Reckon we wait and see what the girls have found. Trace knows her stuff."

"OK, agreed." Jed nodded. "Now, about the main tasks. I've decided to go straight in through the door, no messing. They seem pretty much on the ball but the main block appears to be open the whole time. Too hot and too many blokes in and out, I suppose. It's the same at the other place isn't it, Sam?"

"That's right, boss. The guards there are on the ball, an' all." He thought for a moment. "Yes, damn certain that's the best way to crack it here too. Their door's unlocked as well, Looks like there's about eight blokes kipping downstairs and maybe one or two more up top. If it were me, that's the way I would do it." He paused. "Talking of that pigeon-house place and what's up top…reckon the hostages could be up there, y'know. Someone is, that's for sure."

King looked across and they held each other's gaze. "Well, you're on, mate," he said quietly. "It's got to be you. You've seen it up close and that's what counts. I've decided to switch things round a bit. Jock, you and Horse will still lead with the recce pairs. Right? I'll go for the main block with my team and Sam, you take on the pigeon loft with your team. That leaves you, Ned and your lot. I'll tell you what I want and we can then kick it around."

He explained that once the recce group had dealt with the guards he wanted them to become his immediate reserve on the ground. However, he required a second reserve standing back from the initial action and in vehicles. He gave that task to Kelly pointing out where he needed a blocking position on the road should the opposition make a run for it. Their second task would be to come to La Trampa if he called for them. He wanted the helicopter to illuminate the area of the target initially, then to stand off and await further instructions such as moving patrols or evacuating casualties.

"Don't like to tell you," Morton said, "But the forecast's really shitty for tonight. The fireworks we saw to the south last night are due here this evening."

"S'pose that came from the wankers in Paris, an' all," said Archie Small. Everybody laughed and for a moment the room relaxed.

3

La Trampa
The two girls drove past the front drive of La Trampa before turning left down an overgrown track. The recce had gone well and this was the last of the LUPs. Yesterday Marion had seen a patch of tall scrub in front of the wood beyond where they had their lunch. They parked the car in a gateway then walked as far as the hedge where they found a narrow gap and lay looking at the land to the west of La Trampa. They had been there for about five minutes and were starting to take notes when they heard the slam of a car door and dogs barking. They turned but it was too late.

There, in the field and moving quickly towards them, were three men with two powerful guard dogs. As they watched the men split. One moved swiftly to the high ground with his dog, another ran across the field and on to the track beneath them. There was no escape. "Listen, we're Brits, we're tourists, we're bird watching and we want to see the police," Tracy whispered to Marion, cleaning off the map on her jeans.

"*Hey…you*. Stop. *Stand still*. Don't move." The leading man came up to the girls, panting hard and with one of the dogs. He caught hold of Tracy roughly by the arm and spun her round.

"What are you doing?" she shouted, shaking herself free. "Leave me alone. I'm English and we're on holiday."

"Francesco, Francesco," the man shouted. "They speak English." The other two hurried over.

"So, you are English, yes? What are you doing here? This land is private. Why are you here?"

"Mind your own business. And keep your hands *off* me." Tracy tried to tug herself free "There's nothing to say we can't be here. If you don't like it then call the police. Go on," she challenged. "Call them now."

"Oh yes, I see," the man replied. Then raising his voice he shouted in broken English. "*Nobody* talks to me like that. You hear that. Nobody." He moved closer and raised his hand. Tracy shielded her head but the heavy blow knocked her to the ground. One of the others grabbed Marion, pinning her arms behind her back.

"What the *hell* are you doing?" Marion cried, struggling. "We're just out for the day bird watching. We're on holiday, staying in Lavaur. You've no right to do this." The three men talked rapidly in Italian amongst themselves. One of them sniggered and pointed at the two girls, gesturing crudely.

The other two laughed and one of them shrugged. The third, Francesco, spoke again. "You do not have rights on this land. This is private and you were not watching birds that's for sure. You were watching the big house over there. Why were you watching the big house? Eh? Speak to Francesco now or I make it unpleasant for you."

"I wasn't watching any house," Tracy cried defiantly. "I was doing what I told you. This is France and we're on holiday. You can't do this to us."

"One last time, I tell you nobody speaks to Francesco like that. I can do just what I like with you. Now I take you both to the big house. Any trouble, my little friends, and we give you big stick. Yes? OK, come on, now."

There was a short silence. The man holding Marion looked across to the last and most menacing of the three. "Hey, Nene," he called, pulling Marion's pinioned arms tighter behind her back. He nodded towards the girl and grinned. The guard needed no further invitation; lunging forward he caught the girl roughly by her breasts and tore open her blouse.

Marion screamed loudly, lashed out and caught her assailant on his leg. He grunted, bent down and rubbed his shin then stood and faced the helpless girl. Slowly and deliberately he raised his hand and struck downwards time and again, hitting the girl hard on the sides of her face, first one side and then the other. He paused, scowling, then lifted his hand and brought it back viciously, standing on his toes to put more force into the blow. Marion's head snapped round with the force and she slumped forward. Blood began to drip down her chest from where his rings had cut into her face.

The three guards manhandled the girls roughly, calling out to those at La Trampa as they made their way over the stream bed and into the orchard beneath the house.

***

"They've done *what*?" Gambino hissed, rising from his chair. "Picked up two girls, beaten one of them and brought them back here, *here* to La Trampa? For Christ's sake man, tell me you are joking." Gambino swept his hand through his hair, glared at Bontate then stared out of the window. "Has the man gone *crazy*?" He paused, fuming. "OK, OK so they were on the hill over there but to rough them up and then to bring them back here...the man is out of his mind, Dino.

"What the hell are we going to do with them? Say sorry? I'm so sorry for you," Bontate recoiled at the look of fury on Gambino's face. "And then we give them a pat on the back and show them the way to the front gate?" He laughed sarcastically. "And what do you think they will do then? Huh? What then?" He thought for a moment. "Lock them up with Palmer and the other woman," he ordered. "But we cannot hold them long. These girls haven't dropped in from the heavens, you know. They belong to someone. Somebody will miss them and go crazy? Can you imagine? Then the police will be called. Then what?"

As he paced up and down so his mind was racing. He realised that his hand was now going to be forced. Sooner or later people would start looking for their young women. So he would have to move, but where? Buxtrada had yet to reply to his call and he could not contemplate running back to Sicily. Just too many problems. But to remain here was now a dangerous option. How much time would he have? Two days perhaps, three at the most? "Jesus man, it was crazy to bring them here. *Crazy*, d'you hear." He turned and crashed his fist down onto the table. "That Francesco," he pointed a finger at Bontate. "He may as well have gone straight to the police and saved everybody a bit of time. And as for that Nene..." Gambino shook his head. "Tell Barzini to see me...I have a job for him."

Alfredo Bontate stood meekly while Gambino paced up and down the hall. From time to time he turned towards him as though about to speak before throwing his hands in the air and continuing his walk. "So, where are they now?" Gambino asked.

"They are where you suggested, Mario." Bontate replied quietly. "They put them up in the loft with the other two."

"And how many more people are we going to collect?" Gambino continued, rounding on Bontate and opening his arms. "God dammit, if we go on like this we'll be needing a hotel. And what about tonight, this great party of yours? Does that go ahead with a whole loft full of people next door? And what about tomorrow, and Monday? Do you think we can just sit here like this? Send me Antonio. I will tell him. Those two girls...let me tell you something." He came up to Bontate and waved a finger under his nose. "When two young girls like that go missing the whole world goes mad. Everyone becomes a hero and rushes around looking for them and that motherfucker, Francesco, has brought them here and dumped them on us. *Jesus!* Does the fool realise what he's done? OK, OK leave me for the moment," he muttered. "I have to think. Give me time and we'll try to find a way through. I'll call you and we'll see if we can arrange things. But get over there fast and make damned sure that those girls are treated well, really well. If anyone one of those bums lays a finger on them I'll rip his heart out. Tell them that. Go on. Get out."

4

Bosc Lebat
Jed and Patrick were sitting together beside the pool. Jed looked at his watch and saw that it had just gone two. He had asked for the team to meet him in the barn at three when they would discuss the final plans, rehearse a number of drills and make a final selection of weapons and ammunition. They heard footsteps coming down the long flight of steps from the top lawn. It was Paddy Merrow.

"Excuse me, boss. Mind if I have a word…think we might have a problem. Might just be a nasty one, at that." The two sat up. "The girls are overdue…they should've been back an hour ago and they've just missed their second call in to base."

"Oh, shit," Jed muttered rolling off his sun lounger. "Sure, are you? I mean, comms up there aren't very good you know."

"Aye…sure as I can be, boss. The radio was off a bit last night but not the phones and that's what they were using today. Even if they *were* on the blink they'd have rung in from a call box. But seeing they're overdue as well. Don't much like the look of it myself"

"Come on, Patrick," said Jed walking towards the steps. "I think I'm going to need you here. Where the hell do we start? Did they give you their route Paddy?"

"Aye boss. On the map in the office and it looks as though they were planning to go in pretty damn close. You know Tracy."

5

Valletta
Lyla Bett and Jonni were in the cramped Embassy conference room when there was a knock on the door. It was Danny. "Lyla, sorry to butt in like this but we've had a bit of a jolt at the hotel. Two blokes came to reception and have tried to book into the two rooms those guys are in. Ruth was on duty and told them that they were already taken. One of the men said they thought the rooms were due to be free at around seven and they wanted to take them over."

"Bloody hell. That's all we need. If that's the case then it looks as though we've got our early lift. Jonni, get on to the airport and see if Joe Berak's got anything on a new aircraft coming in." She motioned to the phone. "Tell him we want to know, sharpish. Now then Danny…before we all start going mad, what did Ruth have to say about it? And, several of our lads are deployed for the early lift are out there already, aren't they? Has anyone seen anything?"

"Not that I can tell for sure. Ruth and Sarah are checking that out now."

Jonni came across the room. "Joe on the line, Bett," he said passing her the phone.

"Hi, Joe. What's the news?"

"Nothing so far, Bett. Trouble is that when the ISL are using one of their own aircraft, Air Traffic sometimes doesn't get to know about it until an hour or so beforehand. Right now though we've only got the shuttle and that seems to be on sched." Bett put the phone down and held her head in her hands. It was now going to have to be a daylight lift followed by a holding operation in one of their safe houses. She was only too aware of all the additional problems this would bring and now they began to tumble through her mind: the movements of the ISL, the people in the hotel, extracting the two unconscious men in broad daylight and the question of which of their houses to use, and for how long?

For sometime she was still, then she looked up at Jonni, her fingers pulling down at her cheeks. "OK," she said quietly. "We stay calm. Nothing's definite yet. Jonni, get around fast and check everything. Make sure everyone's in position. Tell them the score and remind them that we're still on for eight-thirty, *but*, and listen, they're to stay in touch and be ready for a quick move. Got all that? Any change and we'll let them know. I'll warn Paris then I'll stay here by the phone."

Chapter Twenty One
Saturday – Later

Paris

Trant was standing next to Prime Minister Jospin. The heady atmosphere which had prevailed at the start of the CILAT meeting had evaporated as soon as he and Brigadier Levi had broken the news about developments in Valletta and the Tarn. He had sensed it before he had spoken, but the looks of concern on the faces of the committee members around the table and the sight of so many bowed heads confirmed how much the reports had shocked.

As Trant told the gathering how the commanders of both operations had been forced to alter their plans, the room had been silent. Co-ordination had now become critical and there was no room for further adjustment.

"So tell me, General Trant, what is your considered opinion?" The Prime Minister asked. "Are you still confident?" Trant's head moved slowly from side to side as he weighed the odds. "All I can say, Monsieur, is that we have two very high grade commanders out there doing all they possibly can. They know what's at stake and I have every confidence in their ability. However, that said, we can not afford any more last minute twists."

"Obviously you have considered all this very carefully with Brigadier Levi," Jospin continued. He, too, was acutely aware of the delicate position and had been wrestling with the problem for some time. "I would not wish to interfere in any way with the tactical situation, but is it really so critical to have the two operations synchronised like this? Would it not be possible to separate them a little and give ourselves at least some room for manoeuvre?"

"We've been looking at that," replied Trant. "However, if we did I would be confident of success with one of the operations but not the two." He knew that, if the worst came to the worst, Jospin would abandon the Maltese operation in favour of securing the treasures. "We have assumed that you remain anxious for both to succeed."

"For sure. And which area looks more positive at the moment?" Jospin asked.

"We are further down the line in Valletta, Monsieur." Trant watched the Prime Minister, gauging his reaction. "The Israeli team have staked out the hotel and could lift the men now. It would not be a covert operation, however, and would undoubtedly create an enormous stir." Trant looked around the table. "In fact, Messieurs, it could be a disaster. But in the Tarn things are different again," he continued. "I think we've accepted that this could develop into something of a fire fight. But to force the pace and go in now would be suicidal. There would be a great many unnecessary casualties and I could never permit that."

"Monsieur Prime Minister," Charbonne rose clumsily and raised his hand. Jospin waved him on. "Some time ago you stated, quite clearly, that if you had to decide one way or the other, your preferred choice would be the Tarn. If that is still the case, Monsieur, then why do we not get the British to move on to their objective now and simply contain the opposition...hold them there." Charbonne glanced around the table expectantly. "At the same time we ask the Israelis to lift these two men in Malta. Once we have done that we can use whatever force we consider necessary back here. I am still of the opinion, Monsieur, that we're going about this far too cautiously." He stuck out his chin and glared defiantly at his Prime Minister. "Really, Monsieur. We must seize this opportunity. We should act...right now."

For a moment, Jospin appeared non-plussed and hesitant. Bigard was about to raise his hand but Trant spoke again, his voice measured and calm. He sensed that Charbonne was agitating dangerously and needed to be disarmed. If the committee lost its nerve and pressed for a quick fix it would spell chaos. "Monsieur Charbonne. I am well aware of your political attributes but I'm afraid I know nothing of your experiences as a soldier. However, I would suggest that to go in now like you say would *not* be a good idea...not a good idea at all." Trant walked to the centre of the room where he could see everyone clearly. "Let's take Valletta first. *Your* country has asked Israel to help them with a very difficult operation. *You* have asked them because you considered them to be the best people for the job, because they are well placed geographically and because it is in their own interests. They are not going to move until they are ready." Charbonne smirked and shook his head. "For a start, you would be forcing them to conduct their operation in broad daylight, at a time of your choosing and from this distance. It would be seen by the world as nothing less than an illegal kidnapping. The Maltese would be outraged and there would be a monumental outcry." Trant noted Jean-Paul Debroque, the Foreign Minister, nodding in agreement.

"But..." Charbonne began to rise again.

"No, no. Hang on a minute," Trant interjected. "The other point is the media. It would be a sensation of global proportions and I'm sure none of us here want that. Of course, all these dangers remain whenever and however Mossad decides to go in, but we owe it to them to allow them to choose the moment. If they can see a way of achieving this silently, without being compromised, then they must be allowed to do it. It is quite wrong for us to put pressure on them from here." Trant looked at the Defence Minister. "And then we have the operation in the Tarn. Reports coming back suggest that our opponents are well organised, that they're well armed and we know they are utterly ruthless...and now they're cornered."

He turned back to Charbonne. "If you ordered my team to contain them, there would be a blood bath. I simply have not got the numbers to establish any sort of cordon. They'd try to battle their way out. At the first sign of a cordon going in they would get the scientists on the move and that would force the Israelis' hand in broad daylight." He shrugged and looked back at Jospin. "So, Messieurs, that brings us back to square one again."

Trant paused momentarily and pursed his lips. Morton had called him about the loss of the two female operators, who they believed had been picked up at La Trampa. "At the moment it seems likely that they have picked up two of my young female operators. They may have killed them already but, hopefully, they are being held alive." He could see the point had struck home. "Then there's the safety of the other two British nationals we know they're holding. If anyone tried to rush their position in broad daylight without the necessary overwhelming force it would become very ugly."

"But surely that is possible now, is it not?" Charbonne, his face red with anger, persisted to challenge Trant. "If we have the people in Valletta surrounded, then why don't we use our own forces here in the Tarn? If you're not prepared to use your own team, I can assure you we have plenty of excellent troops and gendarmes in the Toulouse area."

"You can, Monsieur Charbonne. Indeed you can. You can go in with as many of your own forces as you like, but don't expect us to go with you. Your government has flown me over from New York to command this operation, however I am very happy to stand aside if something like you have suggested is put into operation."

"Thank you, General," Jospin cut in. "You have my full support but...that is as far as we need go in this vein."

"I beg your pardon, Monsieur." Trant was aware that this was his one chance of calming the situation. "However, I believe it's imperative that everyone under-stands exactly what's really at stake. Even if this were a hostage scenario here in Paris, it would be difficult enough to control. But now we have something far, far more complicated, both politically and militarily. The two operations are at a critical stage and poised delicately. It's too late to make last minute changes or to try to force the pace." He took a deep breath and turned back to the table. "If you want Brigadier Levi and I to continue, then I would ask all of you to appreciate the problems and to back the two teams. Thank you, Monsieur."

"Thank you, General." The Prime Minister turned in his chair. "And that's quite right. Now then, who's giving us the intelligence update?"

2

The Tarn
When King broke the news about the loss of the two girls the team took it calmly. Their immediate reaction was to resort to the well-tried drills for such an occasion. Jean-Pierre Rigal had telephoned the local gendarmeries, police stations and hospitals but without success. They had studied the map, estimated the position of the two women at the last call then, knowing how they both chose to operate, had worked out their most likely position.

Morton was certain they had been picked up. Even allowing for a total failure of all communications, they should have been back by now. "However you care to look at it, they were very close in," he said, peering at the map on the wall. "I suppose they might just have gone off the road somewhere but it looks as though they've been compromised."

"OK," King replied. "Suppose they have." He, too, had accepted the situation and wanted to assess the possible damage to the main operation. "Let's have a look at the position up there. The opposition's going to pull out in a couple of days. They've got a 'do' on tonight and they've still got those other two hostages...Amanda...Amanda Gates and Sir Alan Palmer." He cleared his throat. "And mind you we haven't seen a thing of them," he added hastily. "The girls haven't got any criminal tag to invite this Mafia justice we hear about, so my guess is, and this assumes they're still alive, my guess is that they'll be held but no more than that."

"I dunno, boss," said Col Masters, one of the oldest men in the team. The big, dark haired ex-SF sergeant could recall numerous occasions when those taken alive on covert missions had been badly tortured. He had seen it in Ulster when working with RUC Special Branch and again in the Balkans. "This lot aren't playing games. They're hard bastards and if they reckon the girls know anything they could be in for a rough time, and I mean a bloody rough time."

Suddenly the group was uneasy. Caught up in this uncomfortable feeling of helplessness, each one was imagining the scene at La Trampa knowing well how any terrorist or criminal organisation would react to such an intrusion. "Don't like to say it, boss, but I agree," Sam Townsend's deep voice broke in. Not prone to over-reaction, the thickset West Countryman shook his head. "This crowd must've been prepared for summat like this. And if they twig the girls were on a recce, they'd want to know all about it. What's more, they'd know how get it out of them, too. I mean...we all know what I'm talking about."

King sensed emotion creeping into the discussion. "OK, we've all got the message but there's nothing more we can do at the moment is there?" He turned and looked up at the tall figure behind him. "What do you reckon, Patrick?"

"I think you've just about got it." Morton replied, forcing himself to sound unconcerned. "They're hardly going to skin 'em alive with everything else going on. My guess is that they're holding them and may or may not have given them a bit of third degree. But, and I'm sticking my neck out here, I'd say their lives are not in danger, not for the moment anyway."

Morton looked at Jed. "As soon as this's finished, I'll get Jean-Pierre Rigal to organise a sweep and try to pick up their vehicle. And you're right, there's nothing further we can do at this stage." He sensed that King, in one fleeting and uncharacteristic moment of doubt, had looked to him for reassurance. The patrol leaders, tough professionals to a man, had been in danger of allowing the situation to get on top of them. It was the female element in it, Morton thought to himself. A classic case of men losing the focus when the women with them were hurt or in danger. He looked at his watch. "Look, time's moving on. We all know what's got to be done and we've got to get on with it. We've got to sweat this one out. Remember, we move out at seven-thirty and there's a still a lot to do."

***

King turned back to the operation and took the patrols through their various tasks. He had decided to carry out the assault in three phases. In the first instance he wanted as many of the opposition as possible held or neutralised in the accommodation blocks, telling Sam Townsend that his patrol would assault the pigeonnier. When he heard confirmation of his task, the ex-Marine simply looked up and nodded. "That's fine," he muttered.

"Once we've got those two buildings, I want Jock and his patrol to go through the main house. Don't move before I give the word, Jock. I may need you to give me a hand on phase one." King picked up the piece of stick they had been using as a pointer and went over the ground on the model. "We can't do all three buildings at once so that means by the time you get amongst the chiefs in the big pad, here look, they'll all be bright eyed and bushy tailed. They'll be waiting for you, so you'll have to clear each room one at a time. I'll let you lead on that one, but we'll move in right behind and can take over if you're stuck."

Jock McCall glanced up from his notebook. "Aye, boss…..nay problem."

"That'll be phase two and then, lastly, we'll have to work our way through the other buildings and get the four hostages out…that's if they're not where Sam reckons they might be. I'm assuming they won't be in with the main group or in the main house. They'll be tucked away somewhere and they're bound to be under guard. We're gonna have to keep our eyes peeled…OK?"

"Won't they get the chop?" someone asked. "If they're being held, like you say, and all this is going on, they'd be the first to go, surely?"

King paused. "I'm afraid that's a risk we've got to take. Priority one's the stolen kit, and to guarantee *that* we've got to get rid of the oppo first. It's tough but that's the way it is." He paused, detecting a feeling of unease at his last remark. "Look, there's no argument about it," he said flatly. Earlier, when he heard about Amanda, he had been sorely tempted to switch his priorities – to search for the hostages first but that was not what he had been tasked to do. However, the presence of four captives now made the elimination of the opposition his number one priority and that suited him fine. The bastards deserved it and they had it coming. Added to which, as long as he retrieved their stolen goodies for them, the French were unlikely to start asking difficult questions about how he did it. "We're here to do a job, those are the priorities and that's the end of it."

Patrick Morton watched closely. As far as he was concerned Jed had got his priorities right. He was never to know how he arrived there but that was not his affair and he sat back. The atmosphere in the room had changed again. The clinical professionalism had returned and any squeamishness about prisoners or hostages had been pushed to one side. King took them through his plan slowly, allowing plenty of time for each man to absorb what he had been told.

For the next hour they discussed the various options for using the helicopter and tasks for the mobile reserve which, they agreed, was to be used as a roadblock initially. They decided to position it on the minor road leading to La Trampa from the main Albi road junction. "If anyone does manage to break out, they're going to head straight for the airfield at Albi, where their plane's parked and ready," Archie Small announced, pointing at the map. "And they're not going to hang around either. They'll be away like shit off a shovel. My bet's that they'll go straight down the main drag and if we put Ned in just the other side of the wood, on those bends, there look," he pointed at the model. "If you put the car across the road, Ned, you'll have 'em cold. And it's less than two clicks from the house."

"Sounds good," Jed looked from one to the other. "But if they batter into the car, that's our famous mobile reserve stuffed. We've gotta have a second car up our sleeve and out there on the deck. Perhaps you could fix that Patrick, eh? With Todd or Doug? I'm sure they'd love a night out." He looked at the two men and grinned.

"Now, the chopper. What about it, Andrew? We've got these little sets plus the main link which will be through to Patrick at the village. But what the hell happens if the weather clags in and we lose comms?"

Robinson remembered the Borneo days. Hour after hour they would go back and forth over the jungle canopy listening for signs of life on the radio and searching for coloured smoke drifting up through the trees as those out of communication attempted to make contact. "Well look," he replied. "If comms fail then I'll keep overhead while you're still sorting it out. The first thing after that would be to come down or hang around to see if anyone tries to break out. If they do then I follow them until they hit Ned. Yep?" Robinson nodded. "Let's go for that. Now, the nasty one...casualties."

"OK, I'm clear on this one," Jed nodded. "First instance we look after them ourselves. Usual stuff. Every patrol's got a medic and everyone's got his own morphine and shell dressings. Each medic's got two litres of plasma. We've got to be able to sort ourselves out until it's safe to bring you in. We'll plan on getting a landing spot fixed. Failing that I'll give you a white flare. Where's the best place to take casualties?" he asked.

"Albi's got an excellent hospital with a landing site...all the motorway stuff goes in there. They'll be able to deal with most things and, if necessary, they can air-med them to Toulouse. Down there, they can deal with anything you want...change your heart if necessary. I suggest that when Patrick gives him the nod, Jean-Pierre gives Albi a call and gets something put on standby."

"Right, assuming there are no more horrors to come out of the woodwork, how're we going to wrap the whole thing up?" Jed asked, looking at Morton. "To whom do I present this lovely little lot at about three-thirty on Sunday morning? It's going to spoil somebody's weekend, that's for sure."

"I reckon that's where I come in," said Morton. "You guys will have done your bit by then and we want you out of the way. I suggest that as soon as you give me the all clear, my initial rendezvous is at the road block...here with Ned." Morton pointed to the model. "If he's had a contact we can sort that out, then get up the hill to you at La Trampa. *Jeez.*" Patrick Morton raised his eyebrows and pulled a face. "Someone's going to love signing for this little lot."

Paddy Merrow came out of the office. "Captain King. General Trant on the secure means from Paris. Take it in the office, boss, it's quiet in there."

Jed listened as he heard Trant's voice. "Jed, a bit of good news at last. We've heard from Valletta that they're not going for the early lift. That means they're looking at eight-thirty, possibly nine o'clock, which means you should get a clear run at them before they get the wind up. No news of the girls I s'pose?"

"'Fraid not, General. But thanks for the news. That's great."

3

La Trampa
The door of the pigeonnier burst open. As she stumbled into the room, Tracy tripped and fell heavily. Behind her two men half carried, half dragged Marion up the stairs. At the doorway one of them let her go but the second man, Nene, the one she had kicked in self defence, threw her on to the floor where she lay face down. The door then slammed.

"*God!*" Amanda leapt to her feet. "What on earth...what...who are you, for

Heaven's sake?" Tracy levered herself into a sitting position and pulled the matted hair from her face revealing a long, red welt down one cheek and her badly swollen lips. "Oh, for God's sake." Amanda sank to her knees.

Tracy sighed and smiled weakly. She realised at once who Amanda was from the identikits and photographs and glanced at the figure of Sir Alan Palmer lying under the window. But she knew also that their operation had been compromised and that they would be coming for her again. They would now be worried, wild with rage and determined to find out all she knew – everything.

For three years she had worked alongside the RUC Special Branch and knew what the penalty for capture was. Now, suddenly, it was her. Sometimes they heard first hand from those who had survived - more often they heard reports of the brutally disfigured bodies, and were left to imagine the agonies suffered by the victims before life had been torn from them. All of a sudden she felt the first, cold chill of fear. Without doubt, they would be coming for her and she knew exactly what they would be going to do.

"Shush," she whispered, crawling across the mattress and taking Amanda's hand "It's OK. I'm fine but Marion's in a bad way. D'you have any water or dressings?" Working together they turned Marion gently, Tracy slipping her arm behind the girl's head. Amanda gasped at the sight of the blood-soaked face, the deep gashes on the cheek and the half-closed eye.

The two women pulled the semi-conscious girl on to the mattress, washed the blood from her face and neck then tore one of the sheets into a series of bandages. After they had done what they could for the young intelligence officer, they tried to make her comfortable. Tracy looked round. The room was unlikely to be bugged but she could take no chances. Motioning to Amanda, she pressed her down and put her mouth to her ear. "Listen," she breathed. "I can't tell you who or when, but we're going to be all right. Help's on its way but we're going to have to be patient. We're going to be OK, though. Honestly…believe me." She squeezed Amanda's hand and smiled.

Amanda shook her head. "God, I hope so. No more of this…please. They can't go on," she muttered. "Look at him," she pointed at Sir Alan Palmer. "He's in a terrible state, poor soul." Then she turned to Marion. "And now this girl here…and then there's *you*. But who *are* you, for Heaven's sake. Who are you and where're you from?"

Tracy looked at her. She could see she was exhausted to the point of breaking. Saying nothing was not going to help. If there was no more than a stony silence in the room for hours on end, the girl might well collapse completely. She needed reassurance. "Here, get down. Right down, by the mattress." Tracy pulled her down. "Now then, shush." She put a finger to her lips. "We're Brits. OK? We know you're here and there's help on the way." She put a hand on her arm. "Look, I can't say anything…not that I don't want to but it's best if you don't know anything at all. Just trust me, OK...*trust* me."

Amanda grimaced tearfully, shook her head slowly then propped herself up on one elbow. Tracy saw the strain on her face. "Honestly, love...believe me. Marion'll be OK in a while and it's just a case of waiting...of hanging on in. So stop worrying...that's enough." It was only when both were silent that Tracy felt the cold fear returning. How would they start their dreadful work, she wondered. What would that first violent shock of searing pain be like? How loud would she scream?

4

Valletta, Malta
It had just gone four. Bett sat alone in the drab staff lounge of the Israeli embassy, the details of her visit to the hotel running through her mind over and over again. Half an hour earlier she had returned from checking that everything in the Hilton was ready and in position. The hotel had been crowded and there was a party atmosphere about the place as guests and staff prepared for the evening's events. The management had planned a fancy dress swimming gala that was going to be held at the two large pools in the main gardens. After that, and once dinner had been cleared, there was to be a firework display on the front lawn.

She lay back on the sofa and closed her eyes, turning over in her mind again and again the contingency plans she might have to implement. She jumped but it was only her mobile and she half sat, levering herself on to one arm. "Yes...oh, hi there, Joe."

"Hi...just to let you know, there's been a delay with the Tripoli shuttle. It's been put back at least ninety minutes. Take off now scheduled for around midnight."

"Thanks...certain?"

"Absolutely. It's not due in until ten at the earliest and then there's always a couple of hours for the turn round. Oh, and by the way, no sign of anything else due in. I've checked with Air Traffic."

"Great. Keep it like that. Bye for now." Bett thought quickly. The Libyan team who were after the two men were already on the island and could operate independently of the aircraft. If departure was now around midnight they would be unlikely to come for the scientists before eleven, but there was always that slim chance. Working backwards, she calculated how long she would be able to delay her lift and what the problems might be. Eventually she settled for nine. That, so she reasoned, would give the Brits a bit more time and, if the Libyans came for the men at eleven and found the cupboard bare, well – by then the op in France would be well underway.

She went up to the cipher room on the top floor, identified herself at the grill then waited while the two operators unlocked the heavy metal door. As soon as they had patched her through to Paris she heard Levi's voice. "Hey, good news at last, eh?" he replied. "That's great and I'll pass it on to Trant. Now, don't go away just yet. We can work out from that, what time you'll be delivering them to the French aircraft. I'll double-check that they can accept them straight away. I'm sure they will…so they can get the hell out of the place. Hang on…"

A few minutes later he called back and confirmed that the British team had been warned about the revised timings and that the French were happy to get on the move right away. She looked at her watch and decided to call in at the hotel where she told Ruth news of the change.

At last it was time to move. Bett put one final call through to Luqa where Joe confirmed with Flight Arrivals that there had been no further changes. Everything, he assured her, was as he had explained. Using the heavily secured side gate, she slipped unobtrusively from the embassy grounds and into the densely packed streets. The entire population of the island appeared to be on the move parading up and down in the warm spring evening. Traffic had been either been banned from the streets or brought to a standstill. She pushed and twisted her way through the crowds along the Sliema waterfront. No car would have made it tonight. The operation was underway and, as she approached the hotel, Bett felt that familiar irresistible surge of excitement.

When she had given command of the snatch to Jonni they had agreed that she would wait outside in the service area close to the rendezvous with the van and see them safely away. Once that phase had been completed she would collect her car and drive to the house in Mosta where she would wait until she heard word from the airport.

Inside the hotel Jonni glanced at his watch. The last few hours had dragged. Unable to smoke or talk in anything above a low whisper, the tension in the hopelessly overcrowded bedroom suite had been almost unbearable. He had left them to their own devices until ten minutes before H-hour. Aware of the inter-minable wait ahead of them, most had brought books or cards. Yacob Nester, the big, jovial émigré from Belgium who was part of his own team had simply taken a rug from the clothes cupboard, curled up on the floor and slept. At first Jonni had attempted to read, then he watched the card games and, finally, he had tried to doze. It had not been easy but now, at long last, it was time to go.

After going through the drills one last time, they opened both doors simultane-ously. Sarah, followed by Danny and the four men, crept silently into the main corridor where they stopped and listened. Far away, down in the main foyer, they could here the sound of laughter and music but, high on the second floor, it remained eerily quiet. As soon as Danny gave the word, Sarah unlocked the first door of the large suite, held it open then ran to the second which she unlocked and stood with her back to the open door allowing the team into the room. They were well rehearsed. Two ran into the first room while Danny lead the others into the second. The moment they were inside Sarah closed both doors behind them to eliminate any noise. The first one she locked, but stood ready by the second.

The struggles were brief and the men, taken completely by surprise, offered little resistance. Danny took their hands and, one after the other, injected a small ampoule of Midazolam valium into the intern vein. Seconds later and before the two men had been sedated, the laundry trolleys were brought in, this time both doors closing behind them. Sarah remained by the lock with her hand on the key.

Almost immediately, the drug took its effect and the two men lost consciousness in the arms of their captors. Their collars and belts were loosened before they were lifted gently into the trolleys and laid limply in the recovery position. As Sergeant Christian placed artificial airways into their mouths and checked their pulses, the bundles of dirty linen Sarah had left in the trolleys were placed over the recumbent figures. Jonni, who had stood back from the events, motioned to Danny who moved cautiously back into the corridor. He stopped and listened then signalled to Sarah who raced to the service lifts she had kept on hold. Those still in the rooms waited patiently while Danny checked again before allowing the teams to move out.

It was over in seconds. Once they were in the lifts, Danny, Sarah and a second man ran back to the rooms and collected the personal effects of the two scientists. Having bundled the clothes and belongings into two large laundry bags they gave the rooms one final quick check then closed and relocked them before running down the service stairs.

The driver had already started the engine and left it idling as the two men were transferred to the back of the van. It began to move as soon as Danny gave the word. The vehicle immediately changed gear and swept out of the complex before turning onto the main Sliema concourse.

***

By the time Bett reached Mosta, the van had cleared the gates at Luqa and pulled alongside the aircraft parked near the engineering hangers. The powerful engines were already turning quietly and several members of the crew stood waiting by the ramp underneath the freight door. The two bundles were lifted from the van and passed into the freight bay where the French medical team had prepared an air-ambulance complete with stretcher beds.

At exactly nine twenty-five, local time, French Air Force Flight AF 876, en route for Alexandria, was called forward by the Luqa control tower. As he gave final clearance for take off, the air traffic controller watched idly as the huge aircraft lumbered towards the end of the runway. There it paused and turned slowly before rolling forward and gathering speed until it lifted off. It climbed steeply to twelve thousand feet then levelled. Ten minutes later and clear of Maltese air space the Nord Atlas banked sharply to the north-west, lost height rapidly and set course for France. The sudden, loud crackle of the intercom made those waiting tensely in the Intelligence Centre jump. "Hello Zero, Hello Zero. This is Alfa Foxtrot 876. *'Vitesse'*, I say again *'Vitesse'*. Over."

"Hello, Alfa Foxtrot 876. This is Zero. *'Vitesse'*, I say again *'Vitesse'*. Our congratulations…have a good trip. Over and Out"

"Well, Messieurs," said Prime Minister Jospin, beaming widely. "That's an excellent beginning. Neither operation was ever going to be easy and who could have said how things were going to work out. But this is most satisfactory. Now then…let us concentrate our efforts on the Tarn and I will pass this piece of good news to the President. Incidentally, you would wish to know that he is taking a close interest in both operations and has asked to be here with us tonight from midnight. General Trant, the good wishes of all France are now with you and your men. Please let them know that."

Chapter Twenty Two
Saturday Night and Sunday Morning

The Tarn...inside La Trampa

The tall grandfather clock had just struck seven when the first cars pulled up at the front door. Mario Gambino heard voices in the hall and walked across his bedroom to the antique mirror by the door, pausing long enough to hear Antonio greet the arrivals. He leaned forward, patted his hair then adjusted his black tie and the yellow rose bud in his buttonhole. Pulling himself up to his full height he smoothed the front of his white jacket and tugged at his cuffs before turning as far as he could to check the back. Satisfied at last, he walked slowly down the wide staircase to meet his visitors.

The last three hours had been busy. As soon as he had recovered his composure, Gambino had forced himself to sit quietly and think. Yet again, his uncanny sixth sense had been nagging him. He smiled grimly and shook his head. Over the years his intuition had saved him time and again, but now the sharp cutting edge appeared to have gone. He was getting slow.

Somewhere out there, somebody was closing down on him. He should have seen it days ago for the signs had been screaming at him. Throughout the long afternoon he had put his plan together and now he was almost ready to move. Almost but not quite. One final question remained and he would find the answer this evening. Earlier, he had called his aircrew in their room at the La Mayenne Hotel on the outskirts of Albi. He told them the departure date had been brought forward to tomorrow. One of the pilots, he instructed, should come out to La Trampa this evening. The second should join them tomorrow morning when they would discuss the flight plan to Medellin in detail.

They would be taking his preferred route. As usual they would fly first to Las Palmas in the Canary Islands and from there to Port au Prince where they would stop for the night. The next day he had an evening engagement in Bogota. That would be their last port of call before flying on to their destination. He then made several international calls. When he had finished he called for Antonio and told him to cancel the engagements for the following evening. There was no option and he asked him to ring those involved personally and break the news – conveying his most sincere apologies.

***

Every call made from La Trampa that afternoon was intercepted. From the reception satellite stationed permanently over France, the traffic was beamed to a monitor unit orbiting at a constant height, seven thousand kilometres above Cayenne in French Guiana and from there down to the France Telecom Data Collection Centre at Clermont- Ferrand. Here the short calls made at La Trampa were identified, tagged and extracted from the millions of other calls made that day then fired in a single burst transmission to the Aerospatiale research station in Toulouse before finishing their journey at Albi.

The simultaneous translators working in the Albi Police Headquarters made transcripts of the conversations which were passed immediately to the Intelligence Centre. Trant read the signals and selected two pieces of information to be passed to the team. The first was that tonight was their one and only chance for the operation. The second was a warning that some of those at La Trampa had been alerted. The place, Trant told Morton, was becoming restless.

Gambino eased himself through the noisy gathering, a glass of chilled George Goulet, his favourite champagne, in his hand. Pausing here and there to chat with the guests, he made his way gradually across the hall to where Rebecca Davidson was standing apart with the other musicians. For a while they talked and joked, Gambino congratulating her on the music she had rehearsed earlier.

Outwardly calm, his mind was racing. Two hours earlier he had summoned Antonio and Tommy to the study, where he told them to bring the programme as far forward as they dared. "Get that crowd in here at seven sharp, fill them with food and drink then get 'em the hell out of here straight after the show," he had ordered. "And get those music people to do their business straight after the meal. When they've finished the show, get 'em away. No hanging around, right? Then we move. I want to be clear of the joint before that damned Francesco finds anyone else screwing around out there."

Promptly at eight-thirty Tommy and Antonio ushered the guests into the magnificently panelled and beamed dining room where he gave the signal for dinner to begin.

Outside
Three kilometres away the four patrols lay patiently in their hides. The infiltration of the team had passed without incident and the vehicles had long since turned for home. Further away still, Andrew Robinson sauntered over to the

Gaillac Air Club office alongside the airstrip and called Toulouse. He heard what he feared most: that storms were now a certainty and were moving north-east from the Gers. They should be expected in the Gaillac area around eleven and the forecast was that they would be heavy, with severe electrical disturbances. With time to spare he wandered out to the helicopter and carried out his preliminary checks. He knew he should cancel the trip there and then. Night flying on one's own in a small helicopter, and in such weather, was crazy, tantamount to walking blindfold across a busy motorway. Only a madman would go out on such a night, yet he could not let them down. He had made the decision and given his word. As long as he could lift off he would do what he could.

***

Once again the moon was hidden behind high banks of towering cumulonimbus cloud. Soon after ten the light began to fade but the evening was hot and airless. Lying in the ditch at the edge of the thicket, Jed turned to the over-sized pair of boots in front of his face. "Hey, Jock. Look at those bloody great clouds. We'll be lucky to escape that little lot."

"Aye, that's a fact," replied McCall. "When the weather's like this, I wanna be up and on my way. Nay good hanging around waiting for the Old Man to lift his kilt."

Jed looked at his watch. "Give it to quarter past," he said. "That's twenty minutes." The earpiece of his mobile buzzed. It was Morton. "Just heard from Paris, Jed. The Israelis have pulled it off and they're on their way back. Oh by the way," Jed heard him laughing, "tell the lads that the French Prime Minister would like them to know that whole of France wishes them well. Bye."

Jed buried his face in his arms. His whole body shook with laughter causing the others to look across at him. "Oh, for Christ's sake. Hey Bill, one for you," he called quietly to Bill Sandeman.

"I bet they bloody do," Sandeman grumbled. "Must be rough back there. Screw 'em."

At ten fifteen the patrols rose silently from their cover and spread themselves into a loose formation on the open ground. Weapons were cocked quietly, night goggles adjusted and they began to move forward. Jed had arranged to meet them two thousand metres short of the target. The night was now dark enough for them to see the flashes of lightning over the countryside far to their south. Once they had closed on to the target, they would lie up again, listening and watching. H-hour had been set for twelve-thirty.

***

Inside
Dinner was cleared from the table soon after ten-thirty. Tommy, the 'bon viveur', had enjoyed himself throughout and now, heady with the finest of his native wine, he left the room noisily with a lady guest on each arm. The remainder followed soon afterwards, leaving their menfolk to sit chatting over Gambino's vintage Napoleon. Antonio, well aware of how he had promised Gambino so much, fussed breathlessly in the music room as the four musicians made their last minute preparations.

As Mario and Antonio led the guests towards the music room the large curtains by the hall windows billowed, filled suddenly by a strong gust of wind. Outside a bright flash of lightning, followed seconds later by the distant crack and deep rumble of thunder, signalled the approaching storm.

The music lasted for almost an hour. The audience was enchanted, rising together time and again, applauding rapturously and calling for more. Mario remained alone at the back of the room near the doorway leading into the hall. Watching the flicker of distant lightning through the French windows, he could feel himself moved deeply as the evocative notes of Verdi's duets filled the room. For a time he had returned to the little town of Castelvetrano where he had first heard the music with his mother. He sat quietly, spellbound with one arm across the back of the chair. Like the others, he was captivated by the young couple. As the aria reached its majestic climax, he shook his head and wiped a tear from his eye. Once the applause had died away he came forward to thank the four musicians.

Holding up his hands for silence he said, "Ladies and Gentlemen. It has been a most wonderful, wonderful evening and so lovely to see you here but now, if you look outside, the Almighty is telling us that we should return to our homes and our beds." He looked around at the guests, raised his arms and shrugged. "I fear that the storm will soon be with us and you must be on your way. But before you go, Amelia and Ricardo, I beg you." He turned to the opera singers with his hands clasped together in appeal. "Perhaps we might have *'Qual mare, qual terra'* just one more time? No? That would make a little boy from Sicily sleep well tonight and dream of home."

✳✳✳

Outside
The patrols had reached their positions and the scout teams were now lying up a few metres from the buildings. As they lay hidden the lightning increased, sometimes flashing and rippling for several seconds before the following crack and deep rumble.

Jed, concealed in the undergrowth behind the thick shrubbery, watched the sentries change. Fifteen minutes later he saw the scouts inch their way forward and begin stalking their prey. To his left the Fijians started to move towards the figure he could make out in the faint light at the edge of the building, while across the lawn to his right, Jock McCall and Scouse Wellings were closing in also. The windows of the music room were open and, from the far side of the lawn, he could hear the final haunting notes of the great aria hanging on the night air. Gradually the music fell softly away, drowned by the applause.

***

Shortly before the scouts struck, several car headlights lit the far side of the house and the high trees behind La Trampa as the first guests departed. Jed looked over to the left and saw the shapes of the two Fijians rise and stand momentarily. Seconds later they pounced.

He heard nothing more than the sound of bodies colliding and the rustle of clothing. Instinctively he knew from the silence that they had begun their work. After a few minutes he saw, rather than heard, the figure of Horse emerge from the blackness in front of him. The big Fijian pulled Jed's head down and whispered quietly in his ear. Jed could feel the tickle of the man's hot breath as he spoke. "We reckon there's another one out there beyond the end building, boss. Maybe they've put more out tonight…we'll go and find him."

"OK," Jed replied. "But hey…" he hung on to his sleeve. "Take care mind. Look out for the other two around this side, they won't know you're there."

"No problem," he replied. "We know where they are." Jed frowned and studied the dark shape of his friend in front of him. He had seen the two men at work before and stared into the inky blackness after them. Shortly after midnight the warm breeze increased and began to ruffle the leaves and vines in the gardens. A few minutes later the first drops of rain began to fall.

***

And inside
As the last car drew away from the drive Antonio closed the front door. Turning, he saw Tommy beckoning him from the library just as Gambino called out. He ran up the steps and followed Tommy into the dimly lit panelled room where he found Bontate and Hans, the Nor Lander pilot. "Close the door and take a seat," Gambino ordered brusquely as he moved to the far side of the desk, pulled across the black, high-backed leather chair and spun round to face the four men.

"OK," he said quietly, looking from one to the other, "I'm getting old, probably too old and I'm slowing up." The four looked at him quizzically. "But I must tell you that we are not alone here at La Trampa. For some time now I've been getting that nervous, uneasy feeling where little things keep needling away down here," he patted his stomach. "A few years back I would have been there, on to it in a flash...but now, I'm not so quick. However this evening it all came to me."

"You see a problem, Mario?" Bontate queried, his voice rising in surprise. "But," he shrugged. "What is it?"

Gambino eased back in the chair, elbows on the leather arms, the tips of his fingers drumming together. "My friends, I have to tell you that we have been entertaining a number of uninvited guests. I am now quite certain about that. First, the other day when France Telecom came to check the phones. Did any of you see where they went and what they did? Do you remember they insisted on checking everything to do with electricity in the house...remember? Why did they do this? Was it not strange, and why had no one picked this up?

He went on to talk about his suspicions of the young couples seen near the house, on their own land."Well then, how about the fact that one of those bits of stuff was here on both days? Enrico swears blind to it. Up here one day, getting her arse humped then back again, the very next day, with a girl friend. Either the bitch's gone plumb crazy or she and her friends find us very interesting people. So interesting they keep coming back for more. And why do you think that might be?"

By now he had become angry. "Was the man on the bicycle a coincidence as well?" he queried. "And the man who had come as a friend of Rebecca Davidson?" He told them how he had watched this stranger in the garden, how he had seen him studying the buildings when Antonio was showing him around. By the time he described how he had duped Rebecca into revealing that she knew nothing about the man, Gambino was white with rage, shivering as he spoke. Those in the room stood nervously.

"And this evening, before dinner, I asked Rebecca how poor Jean had hurt his hand, the left one that was bandaged the other day. 'Oh,' she said hurriedly. 'Oh, that. He fell and cut himself. Poor Jean,' she said. 'He's so accident prone.' Accident be *damned*." Gambino's hand hit the table. "Our Rebecca knows nothing about the guy nor cares a stuff. Our poor little English boy had no cuts or bandages anywhere. And he's not called Jean either, he's called Jed...or that's what she called him the other day. And the bum's built like a prize fighter. So much for that little love match...she didn't even know his goddam name."

No one in the room moved. "So," Gambino continued, "These last two or three days we've been under surveillance...right? But now it's time to get out and get out fast. I've told Enrico to put the Mercedes and Volvos behind the chapel, on the parking lot." He ordered them to prepare for a quick move. They would leave before dawn and drive to his aircraft parked ready at Albi. With the exception of his drivers, he did not want any of the team forewarned about the plans.

✳✳✳

As the door closed, Gambino turned to Alfredo Bontate. "Did you get the boxes sorted?" he asked quietly.

"Sure...the ones you wanted, six in all," Bontate replied. "Mainly body jewellery...rings, bracelets, necklaces and belts. But I was able to get some of the smaller table ornaments in as well, those cats and sphinxes you like. I've left the original boxes in the vans just as they were. These Volvo estates can take a lot so I've managed to leave one of the back seats for Hans."

"Uh-huh...OK, good. Come the time and we'll get the vans away first. Use them up front in case the highway's blocked...we'll go after them, sneaky like. Take the back route as soon as we hit the top road." He nodded to himself as if to confirm what he said but then suddenly rounded on Bontate. His voice had hardened. "Now see here, Dino...get back out there and be sure those people we brought in here to look after us are doing their stuff." He pointed in emphasis. "I don't want anybody getting near the place. You hear that...nobody. We've had too much attention. See to it, Dino."

Bontate did not hesitate but went straight to the accommodation block. Barzini listened anxiously as he heard about Gambino's concern. Three men were outside and they were good men. "They are our best men," Barzini assured him, gesticulating. "Geraldo Alberti, he is to the left of the main door, in the bushes. And he is armed with his shooter and his lupara. Nobody will pass him, Dino, nobody."

Bontate watched the dark, scowling face looking at him. The man was a brute and would they were all like that, he thought. "OK. Who else?" he asked.

"Ninni Cassara and Sammy Gallo, both good men. Trust me, Dino," the Sicilian pleaded.

"OK, OK. But keep it that way. The Don's mad about something. Make sure your people get his message." He waved at the several figures in the room, and made for the door. "Keep them sharp. D'ya hear?" The door shut behind him.

✳✳✳

Outside
Ninni Cassara and Sammy Gallo were dead. They were lying together where they had been carried with their heads flopping lifelessly under their bodies. They had been covered by leaves and grass, as had the tracks of Horse and Big Jim Tacamati who had carried them. Whoever found them would say that some mighty force had snapped their necks, killing them instantly.

Jed had seen the movement around the main building and lay watching until he was certain the activity had died down. Easing himself slowly back into the undergrowth, he rose and moved around to the rendezvous with his patrol. From here they would move to their final assault positions and lie up until H-hour. Three sentries had been taken out and both parties assured him that the route to the buildings was clear.

"OK, I'll believe you," he whispered. "But I'm taking no chances. Five minutes and we're on. Back here after phase one. Good luck."

Near the other side of the house, barely a hundred metres away Geraldo Alberti backed into the shadows. He had heard something and he quietly slipped his lupara from his shoulder. Seconds later he saw a shadow. As it drew near he made out the figure of Barzini. He whistled softly and watched as the figure crouched. He whistled again and Barzini joined him.

✳✳✳

Three kilometres to the south, Patrick Morton walked across the layby as Archie Small and his team climbed into the big Renault. "OK, lads. Not a dickey from up top. Let's assume all's well. The car for the road block'll be along with you shortly. Make sure you park yours up on the target side of the block."

On the edge of the deserted airfield, Andrew Robinson strapped himself into his seat and carried out the final instrument checks. A couple of minutes later he listened to the high whine as the engine fired and the large rotor began to turn. At first the slow rotation rocked the machine but then, as the engine increased power and the blades picked up speed, so the airframe steadied. Before lifting off Robinson called the Albi control tower who asked for his mission. "Usual air reconnaissance and night photography," he answered. "Ten kilometres north and west of Albi."

"Roger. You are clear for lift off," came the reply. "Be advised of heavy storms in the area. Have a good trip. Over and out." As the aircraft gained height, Robinson saw the huge clouds to the west. It was going to be rough, he thought, tightening his harness and checking around the cockpit again for loose objects.

Just before H-hour the storm struck. The earlier shower had stopped and, in the stillness, they could hear the wind in the valley. At first the hailstones were light but suddenly they increased as the wind began to buffet the house. Leaves and dust were swept into the air and several loose shutters flapped noisily. As the men lay in the open so the hail began to drum down. After the hail came the rain. Sheet upon sheet of ice-cold water from thousands of feet above lashed down, soaking them, their clothing and equipment. Within seconds the men were sodden, cold to the bone and shivering, their breath rasping as the icy trickles worked their way into every corner of their bodies.

Col Masters winced as the hailstones struck him, stinging like stones from a catapult. He could hear them stripping leaves from the nearby shrubs and watched in amazement as thousands struck the ground around him and bounced high. He gasped as the icy deluge enveloped him, blinking and spitting as it ran down his face. Nothing was spared and he gave up the hopeless business of protecting his weapon from the water. The path next to him was awash and he looked on grimly as the wind blew the rivulets into spray.

Jed wiped the water from his eyes and looked at his watch. Turning to the others he had to call loudly against the roar of wind and rain. "OK, lets go."

✱✱✱

They walked the last few yards, climbed quietly into the hall and paused by the doors. All four eased the pins from their stun grenades and waited. "Go," Jed barked. Both he and Armstrong opened the doors and tossed the grenades inside then slammed the doors and flattened themselves against the walls. Out of the corner of his eye, Jed saw light coming from underneath a door further down the hallway.

For seconds there was nothing, then the silence was shattered. After the heavy, sharp explosions, the doors flew open and smoke billowed out. Behind and around them they could hear the sound of breaking glass. Inside the room it was chaos. Two men were screaming, others shouted for help and some curtains had caught fire. Jed leapt into the room. *"Stop. Police. Stop...Stop or I shoot."* He could hear Armstrong in the room behind him. As he shouted two men dived from their beds; a third man on the floor swivelled towards them, gun in hand. Tacamati had seen them also and both he and Jed opened fire, the explosive crash of the Hekler Kochs filling the room. As they stopped they heard firing from the next room.

Hearing the high pitch whine of the helicopter, Jed glanced outside. Through the sheets of rain sweeping horizontally across the sky, he saw the brilliant arc light of the nitesun appear above the house. Armstrong was still shouting above the firing in the room behind him. Seconds later came the heavy crump of a grenade followed by a further burst of fire. Jed ran back to the main door.

"Jock," he yelled to McCall. *"Jock,"* he screamed again. "A hand over here, quick... get Scouse and Horse. There's another room further down on the right. Forget the main house for now." The two men dashed across the open space weaving from side to side. Jed grabbed Horse by the shoulder. "In there," he shouted. "Look out for Jim. There's another room and they'll need a hand. I'm going over to Sam."

✱✱✱

The Pigeonnier

Earlier and soon after they had been given some food, Tracy had beckoned Amanda over to where she and Marion were sitting against the wall. Marion lifted her head, looking down her nose to see her from under the bandages on her face. Palmer was still lying by the window. Occasionally he muttered to one or other of the women but, most of the time, he slept.

Tracy put an arm round Amanda's shoulder. "Now, listen," she whispered. "They're coming for us tonight...soon. Do exactly as we say, and you'll be fine. We'd better talk about it now in case this lot put somebody in here with us. Get down."

"Feeling OK?" Tracy, lying beside Amanda, looked at her. "Don't worry, love. They're good...the best, now listen." There would be a lot of gunfire and loud explosions, she explained. If it went according to plan the rescuers would come for them, searching the rooms, one at a time and calling their names. Amanda should make certain she was flat on the floor and should not move. If possible she should put their heads under pillows, mattresses or rugs in case stun grenades were thrown. Once in the room the rescuers would not shoot as long as there was no movement. They were to lie absolutely still until they were called. They should answer but remain where they were until they were told to move.

Amanda stared from one young woman to the other, a look of sheer horror on her face. "Dear mother of God," she whispered. "It's all like some terrible film...but it's really happening, isn't it?"

"Yes, it's for real," Tracy replied, putting a finger to her lips. "But don't worry, honestly. If I'm not here, Marion will help you and Sir Alan."

"What d'you mean you won't be here?"

"Well," Tracy checked herself. "It's like this. You see they caught us out there but we didn't tell them nothing. But they'll want to know and are bound to come for us, like. I'm telling you now just in case."

"But you won't tell them anything...you can't." Amanda's frown returned.

"Christ no. Not if I can possibly help it...but it may not come to that...you never know. It may not come to that at all." She paused. "And look, there's Sir Alan as well. Best get him right down then leave him where he is," she continued. "If I'm here, I'll try to get across to him when it all starts happening. But the lads'll be looking for him." She paused, craning her neck to look at Palmer's face. "Yes, he's best there, out of the way."

***

"*Down everybody. Get down*," Tracy screamed as the first grenades went off. "*Amanda…over here*. Get into the corner, pull the mattress over yourself and put this over your head." She threw a pillow across to Amanda as two large explosions under the loft rocked the room, sending several chunks of plaster crashing down from the ceiling creating a thick cloud of swirling dust.

Tracy leapt across the room, pushing Marion down next to Palmer just as Amanda turned to grab another pillow. Windowpanes shattered and pieces of broken glass cascaded down onto the group huddled in the corner. Suddenly and without any warning, Sir Alan Palmer scrambled to his feet and lurched towards the window. Before anyone could stop him he had wrenched open the shutters. "*Jack*," he called loudly. "*Jack*, are you all right? It's dad here." He leaned further out of the window, now shouting desperately. "*Jack, Jack*. Take care, dear boy. Take *care*. It's dad." But he stopped, spun round and crashed to the floor. Even as they looked on, gouts of dark blood spurted from the wound in his head.

Just as the door burst open, Marion threw herself on top of Amanda. "*Police*. Stay where you are," a voice roared. "*Stay where you are*. It's the police. *Don't move* or I shoot." The silence seemed eternal but it lasted no more than a second as whoever it was scanned the room for signs of life.

"Marion? Tracy?" the voice called out. "Are you there? Answer now." Marion glanced up: it was Ginge Harris.

"Yes it's us. We're here, all of us," Tracy's muffled voice replied.

"OK, love. You're safe. Come on quick, there's a fire downstairs. Come on. On your feet. Let's go."

Marion and Tracy got up slowly and stood looking at the two men in the door. "Ginge…Scouse," Marion called. Tracy threw her arms in the air. "Jeez, am I glad to see you two," she shouted. Then suddenly she stopped and turned. "Hang on a minute…we've got a problem."

Tracy lifted Amanda to her feet. Her head was still in her hands. "It's Sir Alan," she gasped. "He's dead…they killed him. They've killed him."

"Oh Christ," Marion shouted from the corner. "The bastards've done him." She crouched over the figure on the floor. "He's gone." Ginge Harris joined her but it took no more than a cursory glance. Later, the pathologists report stated that the bullet had entered the left temporal bone slightly behind the ear. It followed an oblique trajectory and exited through the right temporo-parietal. He had been shot through the head and death, so the report ran, would have been instantaneous.

"Come on, love," Ginge called out to Marion. "Get yourself down with the others. I'm afraid he's a gonner. No hope there. We'll get him out later…come on, move yourself, quickly now."

✳✳✳

As soon as he heard Jed's command, Horse sprinted towards the main building, dodging and weaving to avoid the gunfire. Catching sight of Jim Tacamati standing at the far side of the hall, he dashed up the steps and started across the open space. The burst that hit him came from behind the half-closed door.

 Horse buckled, took two more steps then slithered to his knees before falling forwards on to his face. Tacamati threw himself down, reached out and pulled his fellow countryman out of the line of fire. But it was too late. The mighty Horse, the great clown prince from Viti Levu in the South Pacific, had been mortally wounded and lay dying in his arms. As Tacamati turned him over, his head lolled sending a mass of frothy blood spewing out of his mouth. The body heaved and coughed twice then lay still. Ligioni was dead.

For a second Tacamati froze, his hand still on the dead Fijian. He then looked up at the door to his left and, moving slowly like a big cat, rose silently and stood by the oak panelled door. The door did not actually open. It flew apart. For a second, the three Italians inside saw nothing. Then, to the left of the door and partly in shadow, they made out a figure. Standing quite still, his wet clothes gleaming in the light of the flames from the other room, Jim Tacamati was ready.

It is said that only three things raise the blood of a pure bred Fijian warrior to boiling point: beautiful, promiscuous women, 'kava,' the fiery, locally brewed dynamite, and the thrill of physical combat. To casual observers, Jim Tacamati might have been smiling. Had anyone dared to look closer, they would have seen that his upper lip was drawn tightly back over his teeth. But there was no smile. Nothing moved save his eyes, now just two small red coals set deep the ebony face.

His guide, mentor and lifelong friend lay dead on the floor behind him, Big Jim Tacamati's great body was primed and ready for physical combat. The last move made by Carmelo Rappa was a small one. In fact it was a very small one. His right hand had started to flex in preparation for an innocent move when the first six shots from the Heckler Koch blew the top of his head into the air. The next ten converted what was left into a pinky-grey porridge that decorated his clothes, the bed linen around him and the ceiling above. The remains of his lower mandible helped distribute copious quantities of blood over the wall behind him. .

The two men at the far end of the room were transfixed, mesmerised by the spectacle. In all probability they would have seen Tacamati's next move, but no more than that. Jed King only got to hear about it long after the operation was over. Sam Townsend, himself no newcomer to combat, told the story back at Bosc Lebat. "I reckon 'e must've used that little jeep shovel we found in there, boss." Morton came over and joined them. "The shaft was broken clean off. Brand new t'was, an' all. The force to do that must have been terrifying." He paused to catch his breath. "Anyways, there weren't much left of they blokes. At first we thought there were three of 'em, until we put the bits together, that is. Aye, I reckon Jim must've done it with the shovel." He thought for a moment. "*Cuh*...fuck that," he muttered, shaking his head.

***

Luigi Barzini did not like rain. As the first drops started to fall he motioned to Alberti and the two took shelter in the doorway of the stone shed between the pigeonnier and the main house. When the full fury of the storm broke he pushed back into the doorway, then hit the door with his shoulder. The lock snapped and they stumbled into the derelict building. Feeling their way cautiously and straining their eyes to see what was in front of them, neither man saw the dark shadows flitting past.

As the roar of the explosions rocked the building, the two dropped to the ground. In an instant Barzini had cocked his pistol, replaced it in his waistband and held the lupara ready in front of him. He waited, deathly still, his mean little eyes flickering, searching for movement. They did not have to wait long.

***

As he ran towards the pigeonnier, Jed heard the gimpy coming into action. The deep, harsh clatter of the big gun was unmistakeable. He glanced back, then ran on, looking up through the heavy rain for Robinson. Then, as he slipped and half fell he heard the roar of a gun to his left. '*Horse*', the thought flashed through his mind as he ran on. He could see that Robinson was having trouble holding the machine steady in the wild squall and, as he reached the pigeonnier, the glare of the nitesun was veering away. What he had not seen from his position were two sets of vehicle lights moving away from the garages on the far side of the house.

When he was close to the building, Jed ran on to Kenny Armstrong crouched over a figure on the ground. "It's Spider, boss," he shouted. "Got it pretty bad in the face. Jaw's shot away, I could see right in to his throat. Left femur's smashed, too, and he's losing a hell of a lot of blood." He shook his head and grimaced. "Must have taken it full on. I've given him a couple of shots of morphine and got the plasma going but I have my doubts. I've got him for the moment anyhow. Over there look," he nodded towards the pigeonnier. "Sam could do with a hand."

Jed ran towards the door and stopped as he felt a hard slap on his shoulder. He turned, saw nothing and ran on. "Over here, boss," he heard Sam call. "A couple of 'em have holed up in the back room. I'm going in. *Down!*"

As soon as the grenades had exploded, Jed and Sam charged. Once inside they dived to the ground, rolled away from the door and took up firing positions to see their opponents cowering in a corner, stunned and helpless.

***

Jock McCall heard the explosions at the pigeonnier and shouted to Wellings. The two men began to work their way towards the flames, then stopped at the edge of the accommodation block to check. As McCall knelt in the shadow of the wall, Wellings hissed, touched his arm and dropped to the ground. Twice the lupara crashed as Barzini fired from the shed they had left earlier and twice splinters of masonry showered on to them as the shots ricocheted away. Beside Barzini, Alberti was firing from the window, the muzzle flashes lighting up the frame and wall around him.

"Seen," McCall snapped, raising the M203. "Try this, mate." As the 40mm grenade exploded against the back wall sending showers of debris crashing through the undergrowth, so the tiled roof of the shed disintegrated. "OK, Scouse, got you covered." Wellings scrambled to his feet and zigzagged his way towards the smouldering building. Just short of the door he checked himself, lobbed the grenade then dived and rolled away. When Jock McCall later examined the sawn-off shotgun, he counted twelve notches carved crudely into the underside of the butt. "Aye," he said. "A right evil bastard, that big fella."

***

Three more sets of vehicle lights illuminated the buildings and avenues of trees as they made their exit. Just over half way, where the road cambered by the stump of an old acacia tree, the leading Volvo swerved suddenly to the left then sharply back across the road. The driver, scowling hard in concentration, knew nothing about the stray burst of machine gun fire that shattered the rear window before half severing his neck. For a moment the tail lights seemed to pause before the vehicle plunged steeply into the deep waterlogged drainage ditch where it rolled onto its back.

"*Shit.*" Gambino glanced briefly at the upturned chassis. "OK…foot down," he hissed. "Keep her moving and keep the gas coming." He put out a hand to steady himself. "Left at the road…steady…*slow*…slow down…Jeez." The heavy estate slewed on the gravel at the junction. "OK, left here. Now go for it, Dino…let's get the hell out of here." He half turned in his seat. "Over to you, Hans…wha' d'ya know?"

"Easy, man…no problem." The blond-haired Nor Lander pilot cleared his throat and leant forward. "I'll be taking her down…right down below the tree tops.

First west-sou'west down the Tarn valley then straight across Toulouse city. And there we'll be real low, so goddamned low you'll be looking up skirts…then right on up the Garonne valley."

"Ya reckon?" Gambino twisted further round.

"Sure thing. Stick to the rivers all the way then up over the border just south of Cauterets. Weather's clear there now…none of this crap."

"And how long?" Both men lurched as Bontate swung the vehicle hard at the corner.

"Hour…sixty-five minutes, maybe. Your man's got the Orreaga airstrip ready."

Gambino nodded and glanced at his watch. The Basque, he knew, would be there. When they spoke earlier about meeting up, Philippe Buxtrada had promised he would be and when The Wolf gave his word he kept it. The Don turned back and settled into his leather his seat frowning darkly.

❋❋❋

Jed backed away from the pigeonnier and fumbled for his radio. Seconds later he saw the nitesun approaching low and fast over the rooftops. They watched as Robinson turned slowly into the wind and began to claw his way towards the ground. Before they could reach him, he had left the aircraft. Dropping to the ground, the pilot crouched by the skids then ran forward waving the team towards him. They gathered in a tight huddle and listened as Robinson shouted above the noise of the engine. "The road block's been sprung by two vehicles," he yelled. "There's been quite a punch up and there're a number of casualties. Come on, get in. Let's go."

Two of the patrol scrambled into the empty space behind Robinson while the remainder sat in the open door space with their feet on the skids. Robinson lifted off, turned and flew low over the trees until he reached the road, which he followed until they picked up the vehicle lights and a fire below. As they descended, the nitesun illuminated the area around the roadblock. One of the vans had rammed the Renault, slewing it across the road. Behind the wrecked vehicle, the other van had stopped side on.

They descended further and hovered until they picked out the wet figure of Archie Small, arms raised, marshalling them down. Robinson lifted the aircraft, turned then brought it down. Jed leapt out and ran.

"How's it going, boss?" Archie shouted above the noise of the rotor blades."

"Bloody hard, mate," Jed replied. "We've lost one for sure, Horse. Perhaps Spider as well. Kenny's caught a packet too. What's the score here?"

"Shit," Small paused. "Not so bad here…bloody daft, really," he commented. "We had 'em cold but they tried to smash their way through. One of them started firing…an AKMS it was. Nasty little Soviet job. They got Jim Machaver, not bad though, and that was that. We let 'em 'ave it. Nailed two and the rest jacked it in."

Ginge Harris came over and joined them, smiling and rubbing his hands. "Aye…a couple more, Archie. Terry's patching 'em up now. One's quite bad and we've given 'im plasma. The buggers made a break for it. Legged it up the road. They're up there on the road behind the last van."

***

Satisfied that Small was happy and that Machaver was comfortable, King returned to La Trampa where the contact was still in progress. Ligioni was dead but if Spider Martin was still alive his main concern was to get him away, then Kenny, Jim Machaver and any other casualties. After that they would start clearing the buildings and search for the artefacts. Col Masters grabbed hold of him. "Hang on a minute, boss." He turned Jed around. "You've been hit. Know that? Here…up on your shoulder." Col looked at him. "OK, are you? Not feeling funny or nuthin?"

"No, I'm fine. Throbs and stings a bit though."

"Stand still then, I'll put a dressing on it." He tore the shirt from the wound. "I'm afraid it didn't like that tattoo of yours up there. Chewed it right up…good job it wasn't on your arse."

Jed bent down. "Christ, Col, look. I've taken another one. Just a nick but it's bleeding a bit and stinging like hell." Machaver looked at King's thigh.

"Oh aye. Not as bad as your shoulder though." He looked up at Jed. "Tell you what, y'know…if you were a Yank they'd have all sorts of crap pinned on you for this. Hang on a mo." He held his leg. "Let's get this one covered as well."

***

An hour later, Morton called Paris. It was just after four in the morning and dawn was beginning to break over the city. Again the conference room fell silent as the speakers crackled briefly before those listening heard the thin, distant voice above the static. "Hello Zero, hello Zero, this is One Alfa. Success. I say again, success. 'La Grande Vitesse, Over'." Immediately loud cheering and clapping broke out. The President and Prime Minister jumped from their chairs and hurried across the room towards Trant. He had the ear phones clasped to his head but held up a hand, shaking it vigorously for silence

"Zero, roger, Sunray speaking. Well done. Can you let me have an initial sitrep. Over" He turned towards the room frowning, still holding one hand in the air. Everyone stood, listening intently.

"One Alfa. Yes. We have found the hostages but, sadly, one of them has been killed in what appears to have been crossfire. The other three are safe and well. We have also secured what we believe to be the bulk of the artefacts but these will have to be checked out.

"Casualties. To the enemy, eight killed and six prisoners. We are continuing to clear the area but have not come across the three leaders who we believe may have escaped. Our police liaison officer has warned all civil authorities. Albi airport has been surrounded. Own casualties. I'm afraid we have lost two killed and four wounded, including Sunray, but only one seriously. As soon as we have the area secured I shall hand the whole thing over to the gendarmes who are with me now. That's all for the moment. Over."

"Zero. Thank you and well done again. Out"

Chapter Twenty Three
After the Storm

Lavaur, The Tarn

Thirty-six hours later Jed King was sitting up in bed. He had been taken to the town hospital in Lavaur with the other casualties, where the surgeons had cleaned and packed their wounds. He lay propped against a pile of pillows. Underneath his bedclothes the nursing staff had placed a wooden and metal frame to keep the weight of the bedclothes off his thigh wound. A drip had been inserted into his left arm.

He had come round some time before dawn and for the first few hours had lain there trying to focus his mind. Initially it had been difficult. Later, as his head began to clear, his feelings had been confused. They had managed to take the place, he remembered, but it had been tough. Spider, the new man, had gone and so had Horse. It seemed unbelievable that the great Fijian was no more. They had lived together for years; drank together, partied together and fought together.

But then, it was all part of the great game. Horse had loved the life. He knew the risks and had taken his chances. In the end he had gone the only way he wanted to go. As for himself, Jed knew that he had been lucky – again. He'd be out in a few days, back home again, doing the rounds and looking for the next job. "Anyway, Jed King, you're a jammy sod," he muttered aloud. "And the money's not so bad either."

✳✳✳

An hour earlier Ned Kelly and Jock McCall had called to see him, to check him out as they put it. "Lying bastards," Jed had joked. "You're after seeing what the nurses've got under their tight white uniforms, aren't you?"

McCall was uneasy in the confined space of the ward and paced up and down restlessly. "Sit down, for God's sake, Jock," Jed complained. "You're making me nervous. What's up?"

"Och, I dunno." He peered out of the window, checking this way and that. "Difficult to trust anyone after the other night. Just summat aboot the place. Canna put my finger on it, mun. No one's said nuthin', mind you." He turned back to Jed. "Anyway, boss. Take good care o' youself wi' yer wee friend, here. Can't be too careful in this business." He nodded towards Jed, winked and stood back.

Shortly after they had gone, a knock on the door woke him. A young nursing orderly ushered Amanda into the room. For a few moments she stood there self-consciously. "Hi, there," Jed smiled bashfully and held out his left hand. "Long time no see, an' all that. How're things?"

As the door closed behind her, she moved to his bedside, took his hand then crouched down by his side. "Oh, Jed," she whispered and shook her head slowly. "I never knew a thing until they told me afterwards."

He smiled again and reached out for her. "I know," he said quietly. "But *I* did...I knew you were there...ever since Mary Preston told me the other day." He saw the look in her eyes and twisted his fingers gently in hers. "Safe as the Bank of England so you were. Come on," he said, squeezing her hand gently. "That's it...finished, all over. You're safe."

2

Bosc Lebat

Morton strode urgently into the garden, the mobile phone to his ear. As he spoke, he paced about the lawn before stopping suddenly. "You're *serious* are you. I mean you've had it confirmed as such?" He paused, listening to the voice the other end. "Christ alive," he muttered. "*Streuth.*" He listened again. "How much time have we got. Bloody hell. OK, we'll do our level best. Let me get off the air and I'll get some of the guys on the move." Morton turned and sprinted towards the main house, shouting for the team as he ran.

"I need four of you," he panted. "Four guys right now. Any four of you...get hold of your weapons and grab some ammo." He reached the main hall, cupped his hands together and shouted again. "Come on, come on. Down here...any four of you now. *Paddy*," he yelled towards Merrow's room. "Get one of the cars ready. Any one, doesn't matter which. But get on with it...come on," he shouted. "Come on, get with it...move yourselves." It took only a minute or so but, to the usually imperturbable Morton, it seemed like an age. The four men ran to him, some adjusting clothing, others carrying their equipment.

"OK, Listen in. I want you to get down to the hospital as fast as you can. Take sidearms and get to Jed King. No messing. Don't let *anything* get in your way or stop you. Once you're there sit on him like he's a big, comfy armchair. Don't let anyone get near him. *Nobody*...doctors, nurses, brain surgeons, nobody. Keep them all at bay until either we get down there or the gendarmes turn up.

"I've just had General Trant on the line. Intelligence is telling us that there's a contract out on him. Apparently a guy called Buxtrada's on the loose...Philippe Buxtrada, the top Basque ETA man. He killed a couple of gendarmes outside Toulouse early this morning and is heading this way. I've never heard Trant so uptight before. The guy's a mean bastard...and he's out to avenge the blokes we nailed the night before last. OK. On your way and I'll get four more guys down to you as soon as I can."

3

Paris
The two men looked at one another. "Well, I've done what I can," Trant said with a shrug. "I just hope we're in time."

"So do I, General...so do I. If there's one guy that gives me the creeps it's that Buxtrada," Bigard replied. "They call him Le Loup, the wolf...and with good reason. He's the most vicious killing machine I've ever come across...and I've known a few. If they've got him going, he'll shoot, knife and God knows what, all the way in to the target if he has to. And he's made a pretty good start with those two gendarmes near Toulouse." Bigard looked at Trant. "Right now, General, that boy of yours in Lavaur hospital's an endangered species." He pulled a gloomy face. "Seriously endangered."

4

Lavaur Hospital
Amanda smoothed the edge of the bed and was about to sit. "Not there, honey," Jed advised. "It's still a bit dodgy down there at the moment. Sorry about that." He grinned, self-consciously and nodded towards the wall. "How about the chair? Over there...pull it up to the bed."

She sniffed loudly and laughed with embarrassment at her tears. "Heavens...I didn't mean to behave like this...sorry. It must've been...oh, everything."

"Don't worry," Jed murmured, rubbing his thumb across the back of her hand. "It's fine by me."

"I'd better tidy myself up." Amanda nodded towards the door in the far corner. "I feel an absolute mess…won't be a minute."

***

Jed lay back, half closed his eyes then opened them again. The main door had opened slightly and he watched. Suddenly it was thrown wide open and three men were standing there. The first, a swarthy, heavily built man and larger than the other two, moved quickly into the room. The second and shortest of the trio was dressed in a surgeon's green coat, a facemask and a white surgical skullcap. The third remained outside in the corridor.

For a second nobody moved. The figure in the mask looked across to the man already in the room and nodded. The heavily built figure crossed to the window, drew the curtains then picked up a pillow. As he did so, the man in the surgeon's mask stepped further into the room and drew a pistol from the waistband behind him. At that moment, Amanda opened the door of the bathroom and stepped back into the room.

Even a year later, she was able to recall exactly what occurred next. "I don't know why or how, but everything seemed to happen in slow motion. It must have all happened at once, or nearly, but I saw it all, blow by blow…literally." She shook her head in disbelief as she recounted the events.

"As the masked man raised his gun, so the one already in the room moved towards Jed with the pillow. Suddenly there were these three or four deafening shots. The little one appeared to jump and was thrown back against the wall. His gun went off and there was blood everywhere. At first I thought he'd killed somebody and had been covered in their blood. But it doesn't work like that, does it? It was his own blood. He'd been shot.

" I looked at Jed and he was just lying there. The frame thing they'd put under-neath his bedclothes had mostly collapsed. Before I could do anything, there were two or three more loud shots. The big man, standing by Jed just took off and crashed into the corner. Again there was even more blood, all over the place. It was horrible. I think that's what made me sick. The third man had run off and I was left there just staring at Jed. There was a lot more smoke and some black holes in his bedclothes. 'Oh, my God,' I thought to myself. 'They've shot him. They must have done. But then, where was his blood? Jed looked up at me and smiled. I couldn't believe it.

"'Sorry about all that,' he said. 'I warned you the bed was a bit dodgy, didn't I? A couple of the lads came in earlier. Jock McCall, the canny old sod reckoned things might still be tricky, so he left me this. Here look.' I stared in amazement as he lifted his bedclothes. 'It's my little friend, and still smoking, at that,' he announced, grinning. 'See here.' And with that he'd produced his automatic pistol from under the sheets. He'd had it there all the time since the others gave it to him. I just could *not* believe my eyes. Really I couldn't...and I still can't."

THE END

GLOSSARY

Many of the terms used are explained in the text but where this has not been the case or there is some ambiguity, I have covered them here. Some might be well known, others confusing and others quite inexplicable military mumbo-jumbo.

AK. The standard magazine-fed Russian army rifle. It comes in several variants and most fire either single shots or automatic.

Armalite M16 A2. A light, versatile infantry rifle produced by the USA during the Vietnam war. Popular with SF because of its weight, ease of maintenance and because it fires either single rounds or automatic.

Belt order. On operations a man carries most of his kit in his bergen, however he has to survive without this encumbrance and live off his belt which contains just ammo, water, medical and survival kit.

Bints. Arabic for wives or women (I never knew which).

Casevac. An abbreviation for Casualty Evacuation. Always a key subject when preparing for ops.

CILAT. French Interministerial Liaison Committee Against Terrorism.

CDS. Chief of Defence Staff. UK's top serviceman. Head of the Army, Navy and Air Force, the CDS answers directly to the politicians, in this case the Secretary of State for Defence.

Comms. An abbreviation for all manner of Communications be they the simple telephones, or radios – hand held or vehicle mounted.

CRS. Companie Republicane de Securité. A para-military force trained and equipped to deal with civil disorders, student riots, British football hooligans etc. Very effective

CQB. Close Quarter Battle. Fighting at close quarters, often one to one, either hand to hand or with weapons.

CRW. Counter Revolutionary Warfare – quite literally the opposite or counter to Revolutionary Warfare (Terrorism) thus counter terrorism.

DGSE. French Direction Generale de la Securite Exterieure. Similar to MI6 or SIS.

'Double tap'. In a CQB situation a semi automatic pistol is always fired twice in rapid succession – 'one to stop him, one to drop him'.

DST. French Direction de la Surveillence du Territoire. An organisation dealing with international terrorism which has been supported by foreign states or groups. Similar to MI5.

EIS. The Egyptian Intelligence Service. Once reigned supreme throughout the Middle East often responsible for terror and subversion such as in Aden (Southern Yemen) in the early '60s.

GIGN. French Groupe d'Intervention de la Gendarmerie National. (Gendarme counter terrorist unit.)

GPMG 'Gimpy'. General Purpose Machine Gun. The standard British Infantry light machine gun. 7.62mm, belt fed and accurate out to over 600 metres. The Gimpy packs a tremendous punch and is a much revered companion of all those at 'the sharp end'.

G 60 stun grenade. A grenade specially designed for assault teams giving a very large but harmless explosion and several million candle power of bright light. At the moment of attack the assault group surrenders the element of surprise but the G 60 stuns the opposition for those few vital seconds, without killing them, thus allowing the initiative to be regained.

II 'Image Intensification'. A night viewing device that illuminates the field of view by multiplying the ambient light.

IR. Infra Red. Many variants but in this case the term refers to a weapon night sight or detector that picks up natural heat emanating from a source – human bodies, vehicle engines etc.

ISL. The Intelligence Service of Libya. Efficient and ruthless.

Jebel. Arabic for mountains. The mountain Arabs, or Jebalis, are fiercely proud and independent, often, but not always, brilliant guerrilla soldiers like the Pathans.

LUP. Lying Up Point. Where soldiers go to ground and hide.

M203. An armalite rifle with a 40mm grenade launcher under the barrel. Very popular weapon with SF.

M60. The American equivalent of the GPMG. Used by the IRA to good effect.

Orbat. Order of Battle. Literally a list of the players, be it an Armoured Division or small infantry patrol.

PWD. Public Works Department. The important but unglamorous body of souls who carry out all routine maintenance in places such as harbours, dock yards and airports.

RAID. French Research, Assistance, Intervention et Deterrence. (Counter-terrorist unit).

Recce. Short for reconnaissance in either verb, adjective or noun form. ie a recce patrol or to go on a recce.

RG. The French Intelligence Service Directorate – Renseignement Generaux – which deals with domestic terrorist cases that have possible international connections.

RV. Abbreviation for Rendezvous in either verb or noun form.

S6. The standard British service respirator, widely regarded as one of the best.

'Screw the nut'. Soldiers' slang meaning literally "Shut up and get on with it."

SF. Special Forces, a generic term encompasing a number of organisations including the SAS, SBS, special police units, intelligence gathering agencies and others.

Sitrep. An abbreviation of 'Situation Report.' It is literally that – a short report on an event. Used at all levels throughout the Armed Services.

Souk. Arabic for market or bazaar.

Sunray. Military term for a Commander at any level ie a Corporal, Captain or Colonel.

UCLAT. French Unité de Coordination de la Lutte Anti-Terroriste. (Counter Terrorism Intelligence).